LOVE AMONG THE RUINS

LOVE AMONG THE RUINS

LILY ZANTE

of chicken to fall out of his pita and land on his lap. He picked it up, dusted it off, and took another big bite.

"Is that the one we're partying on tonight?" she asked.

Stefanos slanted a hand to his forehead and squinted. "Could be. Cassia says tonight's party is *very* important and there are some seriously rich—"

"Disgustingly rich, shouldn't-be-allowed-to-be-that-rich people," Eleni interjected. Her stomach roiled at the thought.

"She says we have to be on our best behaviour tonight."

"Your aunt always says that."

"And you have to watch your temper." Stefanos waggled his finger at her. "Cassia is hoping to get a lot of business after this."

Eleni gritted her teeth, before popping a piece of chicken into her mouth. Spetses, the glittering little jewel of an island —a playground for the global elite, celebrities and Greek tycoons—was littered with yachts. The wealthy rubbed shoulders with locals in the cafes and tavernas, the hotels and restaurants, as well as in the island's many nightclubs.

Cassia jumped with joy each time a new yacht moored here. She welcomed the wealthy like bees to honey. Her business provided catering to the insanely rich and Eleni worked for her on the side, during evenings, weekends, and whenever she could. The only problem with working these events was that she didn't get any tips. But Cassia paid well, and it helped.

Everything helped.

Eleni rubbed her hands together. "I only need another five thousand euros, then I'm gone."

Stefanos' face hardened. "You're not going forever, Leni. You will return. You're climbing Kilimanjaro, not K2."

It was a big, bold thing to do, and no one thought she was capable of it. Not even her mother. But then, her mother was

CHAPTER ONE

ELENI

The pristine white yacht jutted out of the aquamarine sea like a killer shark's fin.

"That's new!" Eleni wrinkled her nose at the sight of it as she tightened her ponytail. "It wasn't there yesterday."

"Your yacht watching worries me, Leni. When is this going to stop?" Her friend Stefanos took a big bite from his souvlaki pita and looked at her with a dash of tzatziki on his lips.

They sat on a wall, overlooking the Mediterranean Sea and the port, not far from the taverna owned by Adamos, Stefanos' uncle, where Eleni and Stefanos both worked.

"It must have arrived overnight," she mused, ignoring his comment. "It's so *big*. How can you *not* notice it?"

Stefanos gave her a wicked grin, wiping his mouth. "I usually would, especially since it's *upright* and *hard*."

She swatted him playfully across his back, causing a piec

always waiting for her to fail—that's what it seemed like to Eleni.

She often stared at the picture of Mount Kilimanjaro she'd pinned to the corkboard in her bedroom.

It was a dream. It had been *their* dream. Something she and Jonas had been planning for.

"At least now I have a reason for getting out of bed in the morning." She didn't have to cry herself to sleep every night now that she had a purpose.

Stefanos put an arm around her shoulder, hugging her to him and kissed her head. "I wish you wouldn't go, but I understand why you have to."

The last fifteen months had plunged her into the depths of grief because of the tragic death of her boyfriend, Jonas. He'd been killed in a horrific jet ski accident caused by reckless, drunk party goers off a yacht like the ones she now found herself waitressing on. They'd entered the water near where Jonas was swimming. A fitness fanatic with a love for adventure, Jonas had planned to one day set up a water sports business on one of the larger islands in the hopes of attracting tourists. He and Eleni had often talked about this, but her mother had scoffed at their plans.

"Stupid young love," she'd called it. But, like with most things, Eleni ignored her.

Jonas had been Eleni's first love and her best friend, and his passing had been a cruel blow. He'd been taken unexpectedly, way too soon and now he was never coming back. All their young dreams and plans had vanished forever, leaving Eleni devastated and rudderless.

Engulfed in her misery, she'd spent the first few weeks numbed by his death from such a tragic, senseless accident. A revulsion grew deep in her soul over people who hadn't known their limits or cared about the dangers of their frivolousness.

Bad memories had forever stained this island for her. She had nothing to stay for here. No Jonas to plan a future with. Her mother didn't seem too bothered about her. It was a miracle that they managed to live under one roof—a small roof nonetheless—but what they shared wasn't a home. She'd never known her father and she felt more at home in the taverna alongside Stefanos who was like the family she'd never had.

But now her heart was starting to heal.

Between her two jobs she stood a good chance of earning the money she needed. At the taverna it was easy being friendly and cheery towards most tourists. It was the ones with their Rolexes, pearls and diamonds the size of ice cubes, who made her stomach turn. Yet she forced herself to be nice around these people because they sometimes gave the best tips.

Not all of them. It had surprised her how stingy many of them could be, how many of them looked down at her as a waitress and others like her.

Tourists flocked to Spetses during the summer months. They loved the island's little alleys, the cobbled streets and charming black and white pebble mosaics decorating the courtyards. They gushed over the sparkling white walls of the houses, set ablaze by bougainvillea, jasmine and hibiscus in splashes of red, baby blue, pink, mauve and orange. Pretty houses stood proudly along the seafront, between the Old Harbor and the Dapia. But these places held no allure for her anymore, and her desire to leave the island grew stronger. Though she couldn't leave yet; the summer months were her best chance to make extra money.

She nudged Stefanos with her arm before leaning against

him as she stared at the sea. He'd seen her in her most heart-wrenching moments. He'd been there for her when her eyes felt as if they'd been sandpapered because she'd cried so much.

"Eleni." Stefanos's arm went around her shoulder, warm and protective. She tilted her head, laid it against his shoulder. "Don't ..." he cautioned. But she couldn't drag her attention away from the water, or the yacht. Her eyes misted up. It came and went, just like that, out of the blue, when she least expected it.

Even now, all these months later, flashes of that fateful day returned, flooding her mind with painful memories. Her grief had turned to anger, and rage stewed inside her. She hated the wealthy tourists with their super yachts, their riches, their condescending gazes.

"Jonas wouldn't want you to still be sad."

"I'm okay." She inhaled a big breath. Making the decision to climb the mountain, something Jonas had desperately wanted to do, had given her a new purpose. He'd said it was fine for beginners, and that they could do it together. He believed it would make them stand out when they started their water sports business.

Who wouldn't want to know the business owners who'd climbed Kilimanjaro? Jonas saw it as a way of standing out. Only, his dream had died with him, but now Eleni sought to revive it. Instead of wallowing in sadness and grief, imagining a life of 'what might have been,' she was focused on this one goal.

It made her jump out of bed every morning and fly out of the door, past the mother who was too wrapped up in her own drama to care about Eleni. It enabled her to fake-smile and make trivial conversation with people she cared nothing for, in an attempt to earn good tips.

Stefanos jumped off the wall. "We should get back before my uncle comes looking for us."

They returned to the bustling taverna to find tables filled with people. Laughter and chatter floated across the air along with the aroma of fresh coffee, the smoky, juicy scent of cooked meat and fresh bread.

"That was fast," Eleni muttered, surveying the scene with trepidation. Lunchtimes this busy indicated a long, hard day would follow.

"He looks cute. Table in the corner." Stefanos gripped her hand, the way he often did when he insta-crushed on someone.

Eleni cast a glance in that direction to find a man sitting alone surrounded by a paperwork and a briefcase lying on the chair next to him. He wore aviators with attitude, dark slacks, expensive looking loafers, and a watch.

There was always a watch. Big, bold and brash.

Eleni's gaze traveled over his slim fit, short sleeved, cotton polo shirt. It was white with a thin blue stripe running across his shoulders; not that he needed to draw any more attention to them. Wide and thick, they hinted at more than his masculinity. They promised protection. Comfort. Strength.

She shook her head; certain she was coming down with something. But her gaze went back to the man whose short shirt sleeves strained slightly under biceps that teased her attention. Her eyes dropped lower, and she was in danger of drooling over his forearms: lean, veined, muscular and, for as long as he didn't notice her, hers to ogle freely.

One quick laser glance and she'd figured him out. Not because she was a fashionista. She wasn't, didn't care much for such things, but because Stefanos was a fashion whore who admired a well-dressed man as much as any hot-blooded woman.

The man's attire alone probably cost more than she earned in a year.

"I don't think anyone's seen to him yet." Stefanos' voice turned squeaky high with uncontained excitement.

"He's all yours." Eleni rushed to the kitchen and whipped on her half-apron, as did Stefanos. She tied the apron around her waist, before pulling out a notepad and pencil from one of the deep pockets. Then she got ready to tackle the customers.

Stefanos turned to her. "You can have him. You need the money more than I do." He veered off in the opposite direction before she had a chance to tell him that she didn't want this particular customer, but he'd left her with no choice.

She approached the man's table and saw him looking through notes and scribbling things down.

"Hello," she attempted a breezy greeting. Aviator sunglasses hid his expression, not that he was looking at her. She cleared her throat hoping to get his attention. "What can I get you?"

He looked up slowly. "You are open, then?"

An American.

She gave a small laugh, not understanding his comment. She even forced a smile. "Yes, sir. We open from—"

"I've been waiting for hours for someone to serve me." His voice was crisp and sharp, and he looked at his watch as if confirming how long he had waited.

She forced another small laugh. "It can't have been hours." He raised an eyebrow which, given that she found herself reflected in two shiny black lenses, didn't help her to gauge his expression. "Lunchtime is a busy time for us."

"Then get more staff."

She blinked. "I'll be sure to pass your advice on to our manager. What can I get you?"

"An espresso."

"Will that be all or would—"

"That's all." His attention returned to his cell phone again.

Rude.

And no 'please' or 'thank you', either. Another one of those rich, ill-mannered, arrogant ones. Eleni walked away, sliding her pencil into the front pocket of her apron, and gave the order to the barista.

Stefanos stopped to share his observations. "Have you seen the size of his hands?" he whispered. "He must be hung like –"

"Don't," she hissed.

"I wish I hadn't given him to you."

"It's not too late. You take his espresso," she offered. But Stefanos had already rushed off.

"Espresso." The barista slid the small cup across the counter to her. She placed it on a small tray with a napkin and walked back to the rude American. "Your espresso." She placed the cup on the table.

The man grunted. At least, she thought he did. He didn't look up but seemed vexed by something on his cell phone and jabbed his finger, texting away.

She was about to walk away when he asked, "Do you have freshly squeezed orange juice?"

"Yes, would you like some?"

Still not looking at her, he nodded, making a noise in his throat. Something on this phone had grabbed his attention.

"Was that a 'Yes?'" she queried with a smile—hoping for a good tip—it was always for the tips.

He put the cell phone to his ear. "A large glass," he said, absentmindedly.

She had visions of throwing it at him. "Only the one glass,

then?" She was about to turn away when his tone stopped her. "The Acropolis? Linus, are you fucking kidding me?" he barked. "It's a wasteland of ruins. What is wrong with the man?"

She frowned as she listened, unable to move.

"Tell him to go to hell," he snapped. Then, "Don't. Wait for me to get back." He slammed the phone on the table, before sitting back and resting his arms on the armrest. "Jesus." He raked his hand through his sandy brown hair. Eleni fought the urge to give it a good yank.

She couldn't help herself. "It's not a wasteland, and they are not ruins."

Dark shades stared back at her. "Were you listening to my conversation?"

"Does an elephant have ears?" It wasn't quite what she intended to say, but her anger had reached boiling point and rage simmered under her skin.

"You refer to yourself as an elephant. Interesting."

She was about to shoot back a response about his sunglasses, about him being visually impaired, but didn't want to stoop so low. Grounding down on her molars, she lifted her chin. "The Acropolis has ancient buildings which bear great historical and architectural significance."

She walked away, her heart in her chest, knowing she'd done it again. Being rude wasn't a part of who she was, but some people, like Mr. Arrogant and Rude, brought out the worst in her. She could not hear this man talking trash about the Acropolis and say nothing.

"Are you walking away?" He raised his voice, and she was sure people heard him two tables away. Customers turned to stare. She raced to the kitchen and poured out a glass of orange juice.

Maybe she had taken it too far this time.

"What's going on?" Stefanos hissed, glaring at her as he reached for a tray of food to deliver.

Eleni shook her head. She didn't know how he did it; took care of his customers and kept an eye on her at the same time. "The man is a nightmare. You should have served him."

"It's too late. Adamos is watching you, Leni. Don't mess it up."

"I'm going to fix it."

She would. Mr. Arrogant was just this side of being too grumpy and too rude. He grated on her like the sound of metal scraping across a squeaky-clean plate. She walked back to his table, a glass of ice-cold orange juice in her hands, mentally preparing to be submissive, to put on an apologetic demeanor without verbally begging for forgiveness. Bracing herself to be nice and friendly when she felt anything but that. These types of men responded well to women like that.

As she reached the table, something wrapped itself around her ankle and she went flying. The glass of orange juice slipped from her hand at the point of impact. Thankfully, it didn't break but slammed to the ground with a thwack.

Meanwhile, her hands and face smacked against the American's chest. In her dazed state of shock, as another pair of hands helped her off him, her brain registered a body that had been hard. A wall of steel. There had been no give.

"I'm so sorry," she gushed, as Stefanos helped her to standing. The American also jumped up, picking at his wet shirt.

She looked down to find her foot trapped in the long strap of a handbag.

"I am so sorry. It was my bag you tripped over. Are you hurt?" A timid looking young woman holding a toddler stared at her. A stroller stood nearby, and another slightly older child sat at the next table.

"I'm fine," she replied. Eleni glanced behind her to see Stefanos helping the American. Wiping him down with napkins. A wet dream unfolding in real time.

The mother, face red and eyes popping, rained apologies on Eleni. Was she okay? Had she hurt herself? She looked so upset that Eleni forgave her on the spot, needing to hush her. She reassured the mother that she was okay, then untangled her foot from the bag and handed it back.

She and Stefanos had one goal; to make sure Adamos wouldn't hear the commotion.

Although, this really hadn't been her fault.

She hovered around and listened as Stefanos fretted and fussed over the American. "I'll get you another glass of juice, sir. Don't you worry. Is there anything else I can get you? On the house? No? Are you sure?"

"This place is a joke." The American gathered his papers together. "Get me your manager."

Stefanos smiled widely, quickly standing between Eleni and the American. "Please, sir. There's no need."

"Your manager." The American growled.

"Don't do that, sir. Please. She needs this job."

Eleni couldn't take this anymore. She couldn't let Stefanos beg on her behalf. It was time to plead, and to appeal to the American's better side, if he had one. She waded in. "I'm so sorry. I tripped, but it really wasn't my fault." That didn't help, but also, it was the truth.

"Jesus Christ. I'm soaked and I smell like an orange." The man pinched his shirt which now clung to his chest.

"At least it now has some color," Eleni countered, nodding at his shirt and trying to make light of the situation. The American removed his shades and this time when he glared at her, she felt his wrath. "Imagine if it had been the espresso, you might have suffered burns."

Stop talking.

It wasn't like her to ramble. She usually knew when to shut up. The American lifted his head, immediately drawing her attention to his angular jaw. Emerald green eyes—just like the water a stone's throw away—filled with fury and stared back at her. Her heart jolted.

In a panic, she stepped away, confounded by her reaction, by her noticing these very things. Something odd was happening to her. Her heart was racing in a way it had not for a long time.

The man squinted. His brow furrowed, his lips parted.

She waited for his tirade.

When he didn't speak, she rushed to fill the prickly silence, confusion mixing with trepidation and causing her brain to short circuit. "Not that there's anything wrong with your shirt but ..."

"But?" The word shot out like a bullet.

"It could have been much worse. You could be wearing Giouvetsi."

"What?" He gave her a look that could have harpooned a whale.

It didn't stop her from explaining. "Greek beef stew ... with orzo pasta. We have it on our Specials menu today."

CHAPTER TWO

DOMINIC

The waitress wittered on about Greek beef stew and pasta and the specials menu.

"How exactly do you think this could be any worse?" Dominic inspected her and tried to work out her IQ.

He hated company, and he hated being interrupted. But more than that he hated incompetent people. Like this wide-eyed waitress who assessed him with a cool, unfettered gaze. The smell of orange juice, the dampness of his shirt soaked in said liquid and sticking to his skin, made him want to retch.

He'd only ventured out to have a cup of goddamn coffee.

All he had wanted, before the party tonight that he couldn't get out of—something his father wanted him to attend—was to go through his paperwork, enjoy one, small, fucking cup of coffee and return to his hotel suite.

He clenched his jaw while dabbing at his shirt with the

pile of about one hundred napkins the other server had brought over.

"I would say you've had a lucky escape," the waitress countered, standing by and doing nothing while her co-worker fussed over him like a mother hen.

"Enough," Dominic growled through gritted teeth. The man stopped immediately and shrugged at the waitress.

This was Dominic's idea of hell, and it had been made worse now that an incompetent waitress was uttering such nonsense to his face.

The sparkling, azure blue water in front of him and the cloudless, vibrant blue sky above would have made for a gorgeous day for most people. He was not most people. He did not enjoy pretty islands, he did not thirst for parties, he had no desire for company.

The waitress shoved her hands into the wide front pocket of her apron and pulled out her notebook and pencil before surveying the tables around her and getting ready to take more orders. Someone like her was a health hazard to customers.

She caught him looking at her. "I can't apologize enough. I am sorry this happened to you, but it wasn't my fault." There was something harder, more serious in her tone now, as if she was making her final apology and he needed to accept it. As if she was done with being nice and couldn't care less. She straightened up, standing taller, her shoulders back, her chin lifted.

He remembered her co-worker pleading on her behalf and he felt like an ass. It wasn't her fault that he was in a bad mood. It wasn't her fault that Hector Galatis—the Greek shipping tycoon and one of Greece's richest men—had Dominic running around him like a playful puppy eager to please, but Dominic's short fuse was starting to ignite.

The eccentric old man was testing Dominic's mettle. Hector Galatis was the biggest player in Greek shipping, and had one of the biggest fleets in the world. Steele Shipping, one branch of Dominic's father's vast empire, was eager to form an alliance with Galatis' company in a move that would prove highly beneficial to them both. It was a bold proposition. Steele Shipping wasn't a giant in the industry, and his father had almost sold that part of the business off, but this deal could fast track them to the forefront. This deal, if Dominic could pull it off, had the potential to be worth billions.

It wasn't the family's core business, which was why his father had tasked him with it, but if he could do it, he'd more than prove himself.

He would also be turning thirty this year, and he needed to prove himself just like his older brother Alexander had when he'd reached this milestone. It meant that Dominic's share of the company increased from ten per cent to twenty-five.

He had much to prove, and his family had thrown him in at the deep end. It wasn't only that he was concerned about Galatis, he was also in charge of the Athens office for the summer, not an easy feat with Nikolaos, the managing director, away for a few months taking care of his sick wife. Dominic's father and brother were waiting patiently on the sidelines for Dominic to fail. Alexander no doubt was waiting in the wings to swoop in and seal the deal himself.

But Dominic had no intention of failing, much less giving his older brother the satisfaction.

If Hector Galatis needed Dominic to be at the Acropolis, or the museum, or the Odeon of Herodes Atticus, Dominic had every intention of being there.

Hell, he would keep the Olympic torch burning like they

used to throughout the celebration of the ancient Olympics on the altar of the sanctuary of Hestia— a fact that Galatis had casually mentioned to him at their first meeting—if that's what Galatis wanted him to.

Dominic would court favor with the man if this was what it took.

He and the waitress eyed one another like boxers in a ring when someone approached them.

"I am Adamos, the owner." The man's voice was deep, his belly was big and round. "What is the problem here?"

The waitress folded her arms. The man looked at Dominic's shirt, his face turning apologetic. He snapped at the waitress. "How did this happen?"

Dominic flexed his jaw muscle. "It wasn't her fault. It was an accident."

Please, sir. Don't do that. She needs this job.

He understood that stress. He needed this deal with Galatis just like this waitress needed her job.

Everyone needed something, no matter their status or position in life.

"I can get you anything you want on the house, sir." The manager beamed a smile at him and looked ready to launch into a full-blown conversation.

"I'm fine. Please leave." Like a Jedi mind trick, those words delivered curtly had the effect of making the man nod and disappear as quickly as he'd arrived.

"Thank you." The waitress unfolded her arms.

"It was an accident, I suppose," Dominic ground out, reluctantly.

"It took you a long time to realize that." The words seemed to have tumbled out before she could stop herself. Her eyes widened, indicating her shock at what she'd said. She slowly started to back away.

"Stop." Curiosity sparked his interest. "Do you do this often?"

"Do what, often?"

"Piss off the customers." He could think of no other reason why her friend would plead for her job on her behalf.

"It depends."

It depends? She couldn't be a waitress. No way. Not with *that* attitude. "You accept that you do actually piss people off?"

"As I said, it depends."

He couldn't believe his ears. "On?"

She eyed his watch, deepening his confusion; he had rarely met a waitress who was rude and unfriendly. He was used to these people—waitresses, and women in general, tripping over themselves to get to him. This woman had literally fallen over and landed on his chest, and now she was looking at him as if it were his fault.

Whatever her problem, whatever pissed her off, he no longer cared. "You know what? Leave it. I don't want to know." He stormed off. He had a goddamn party to attend later.

More drinks, more canapes, more banal conversations with imbeciles. He didn't need to waste his time making small talk with someone like her.

He bumped into the waitress's friend in his haste to leave. The man flashed him a too-wide smile and rushed after him. "Is everything okay, sir?"

"I'm as happy as can be," he snarled. Then, recalling how this man had begged on behalf of the waitress, "We're all after something, pal. We're all hustling to make money. She needs the job, and I just wanted a cup of coffee."

"Her boyfriend was killed not so long ago. It was a tragic

accident in the sea. People on jet skis crashed into him and he was killed instantly. Eleni is heartbroken."

Dominic's jaw dropped. "That poor girl," he managed to say, feeling as if he'd been punched in the stomach.

The server gave a slow nod. "She's heartbroken and has taken it badly. She is still not over it."

CHAPTER THREE

DOMINIC

The aroma of something warm and fishy wafted through the air over the bubbling chatter and laughter of the party goers.

Dominic declined the offer of artistically created and artfully arranged canapes when the server stopped by. However, the man he had been talking to could not resist and reached for an oyster before slurping it down. Then he reached for a prawn canape and shoveled that into his mouth.

Dominic pressed a finger to his temple and tried to unsee the man talking and chewing at the same time. He tried to ignore the little speck of prawn hanging at the corner of the man's mouth as he boasted about the new multi-million-euro mansion he'd bought off the coast of Croatia.

With irritation creeping over him like an army of ants, Dominic couldn't do it; he couldn't stand and listen to it any longer. The sticky prawn only heightened everything he hated about these parties.

He wasn't the partying type. These events were like pulling his teeth out with a pair of pliers. He wanted to return to his suite and deal with urgent matters, because ever since he'd arrived in Athens a month ago, everything in the Greek office seemed urgent.

But unfortunately, his father had insisted that he keep his head in the game, and it was at extravagant parties like this that the movers and shakers, the men with money, mingled and made deals. Deals could be made anywhere, his father often reminded him, but they were easier to clinch at social events where the lure of alcohol and pretty women lowered men's guards.

He excused himself politely from Prawn Face and was about to head out for some fresh air, and to get away from people.

"Dominic." Someone slapped him on the back and, before he knew it, a man he vaguely recognized was shaking his hand and grinning at him as if they were best friends. He reeked of alcohol, making Dominic flinch.

"You no remember me?"

Dominic tilted his head, the man's face registered but he drew a blank at the name.

"Ioannis," the buffoon said. "Written I-O-A-N-N-I-S but you say 'YANNIS', eh?"

The spelling bee specialist. Dominic remembered him now because he'd had the exact same conversation with this bore before. "How could I forget?" he commented, dryly.

"You Americans have a problem with Greek names."

The man had been drunk the last time as well—at a dinner Hector Galatis was supposed to have attended, but instead he'd sent this guy who was a close associate. It meant

Dominic couldn't easily excuse himself and had to ingratiate himself instead. "What brings you here?" he asked, mentally reaching for his 101 social skills handbook. "Spetses isn't your playground."

Ioannis jabbed a finger in Dominic's chest. "My playground." He laughed. "I like to play, it is true." He raised his glass tumbler and swirled something the color of bourbon. "I go where the parties are, and ... the entertainment." He jerked his head over his shoulder where a group of women were dancing out on the deck. Long tanned legs, short tight dresses, big hair, big lips and big breasts.

Dominic lowered his head and fixated on the floor for a few seconds, trying to keep his fists clenched by his sides.

"You want one?" Ioannis asked, prompting Dominic's brow to crease more than it had the entire day.

"Want what?"

A drink?

Someone to stab him and take him out of his misery?

The Greek winked at him and nodded in the direction of the women. "I make an introduction. A good-looking man like you should have some fun tonight, eh?"

Dominic grimaced, the pain of the conversation eating him from the inside out. He wasn't sure of the man's words; whether the women were paid escorts or guests, but either way he wasn't interested. He detested the way this man alluded to those women as property he could have, as if the ownership of them was dependant on Dominic's desire, rather than on the women's interest.

He eyed the deck but no longer wanted to head in that direction for fear of the pimp following him. Casting a quick glance around, he looked for an emergency exit.

And found it.

Or rather, he found *her*.

He peered for a second, unsure as the young woman server breezed past him. Her hair was tied up in a bun this time instead of a ponytail, but a glance at her side profile confirmed that it was her—the waitress from the taverna.

"I need a drink, excuse me."

He cut through the crowd, expensive cologne and sickly-sweet perfume mingling into one heady scent as he brushed past people, keeping his eyes on the waitress. She moved fast, rushing down a long hallway which appeared to lead to a kitchen area.

He sped up his footsteps in his haste to follow her, and to put a distance between him and the idiot Ioannis. He walked in and saw other servers busy refilling their trays, but the waitress was taking food from a half empty serving tray and putting it into a container which she then quickly slipped into a drawer.

He watched, puzzled and fascinated. The young woman glanced at the others in the kitchen as if she were in danger of being caught. He observed her as she calmly repeated the exercise with another half empty serving tray. Scooping up the few remaining canapes, she put them into a napkin and then into another plastic container. When she glanced around, she caught him watching her.

He moved out of the way to let the servers pass and walked towards her. Caught in the act, she threw her hands palms up, dismissively. "They throw the food away, and I hate seeing it go to waste."

She was honest, if nothing else.

"I'm not judging you."

"Are you lost?" she asked, without a shred of guilt.

"No." He walked closer, saw another tray that was a quarter full of canapes. "Don't let me stop you." He nodded his chin indicating for her to resume her activity.

Her hands moved to the countertop, but she didn't touch the tray. "You're not supposed to be in here."

"Clearly."

"It's not stealing if they don't want it."

He didn't care what she took, and she was right about it being wasted. "It's still stealing if it's not yours."

Asshole. Shut up. Let her take it.

"If *you* took it, then it wouldn't be stealing?" There was a quiet challenge in her eyes, and he was momentarily thrown by her question.

"I'm a guest, I'm invited. Those canapes have my name on it."

"You really believe that?"

He snorted. "It's true."

"When companies take land because they need to make hotels and they force the locals off, is that not stealing?"

He jerked his head back in surprise, assessing her as if a mask had been lifted. "Activist?" Because she sure sounded like one. Uppity little smart ass.

"Human."

He tried to suppress the amusement that caused the corners of his mouth to lift. "Human. Yes, I can see that."

"Not too different from you." She wiped her hands on a napkin and moved to the other end of the kitchen where she started to fill a clean serving tray with canapes. "Why are you here?" she asked when he followed her over.

"I'm bored."

Her face registered alarm at the comment and she stopped plating the canapes.

"Not for any reason," he said quickly, remembering the way Ioannis had spoken of the other female party guests. He had a feeling someone looking like she did would attract a lot of attention. "I don't really *want* to be here. I don't like parties, or people, or mingling, so I followed you to get away from the guests."

This time her brown eyes grew larger. "Why would you do something you don't want to do?"

He opened his mouth then hesitated. It wasn't usually a problem talking about business, or the company. In the US people knew the Steele name, knew who he was, but here, someone like this waitress wouldn't, and it didn't matter. He sensed this woman didn't have much time for people with money. "I had to show my face. Make an appearance." He shrugged. "I was killing time, waiting for a while before I left."

"Hmmm." She folded her arms and leaned back against the countertop, assessing him as if he were a curious specimen. "That's peculiar."

"Why?"

"Do you want me to tell the truth?"

"It hasn't stopped you so far."

"You look like a man of importance ..." She bobbed her head as if she couldn't believe herself that she'd made such a comment. She gestured at his wrist. "Your watch, your sense of self-importance—"

Indignation spiked inside him. "My sense of—"

She held up a finger. "You said you wanted the truth. Can you handle it?"

Nobody had ever spoken to him in this manner before. "Hit me with it."

"Your sense of self-importance. You think you're better than me, the way you spoke to me at the taverna, the way you looked at me, the little things you let slip, everything about you screams it, from your clothes right down to your shoes."

"You must be a designer label junkie to know these things."

"I'm good at reading people. It's something you learn to do in my profession. I know about clothes and accessories even if I do not buy these things. Let me guess, you also have a yacht?"

He laughed. "A yacht? No, I don't."

"No plans to go to space?"

He marveled at her directness. "Only Athens for this summer. No other plans." Unless he changed his mind and accepted the invite to Demi's wedding. They'd had a short summer fling many years ago, and he'd been surprised to receive an invite to her wedding.

"Your point?" he asked, "regarding my so called 'self-importance'?"

"For such an important man, I find it hard to believe that you would rather hide in a kitchen than go home."

He wasn't hiding. He had been bored at the party and upon seeing her had been intrigued enough to follow her. Always surrounded by 'yes' men and women, this woman was different enough to make him curious. "I can see why you might think that."

"Are you going to tell about the food?" Her eyes filled with worry.

"No." Why would he? "You're not hurting anyone." But he wondered how bad things were at home that she had to steal leftovers from a party. "You should take these." He jerked his chin at the tray. It was bugging him that she refused to.

"Can I get you anything?" she asked, ignoring him and smoothing down her dress. Black and clingy, it hugged her figure like a second skin drawing his attention to her slim, svelte body for the first time. She was striking, now that he'd had a chance to examine her face closely. Brown eyes, and her hair, dark like ink against her olive skin. Her face long and sculpted, was arresting, and when his gaze fell to her lips he had to look away.

"No." He moved to the countertop and did something so unlike him, he wondered if he was about to have a seizure. "You work two jobs?" he asked, grabbing a napkin to lift the canapes and move them into an empty container. Not only was he talking to a complete stranger, a server, no less, he was helping her to steal food. The Mediterranean air had obviously messed with his head.

"What are you doing?" She stared at him in horror.

"Putting these away for you."

She frowned. "They're not leftovers. They're for the guests. I can't take those."

"*I'm* a guest, and this is my share. Take them."

She looked at him but refused. He walked over to where she'd stored the other containers and put it in the drawer.

"You work two jobs?" he asked again.

"Some of us have to." Her words and tone implied an us-and-them.

"I work long hours, too."

"Are you working now?" Her slender fingers gestured at the surroundings. "Is this a party for you all to network and make deals?"

"All?" What did she think he was a part of?

"These people. Are they friends or business acquaintances?"

"A bit of both."

"And tonight, is it business or pleasure?"

It had been purely business, but this was the longest conversation he'd had all evening, and it wasn't so bad. "Pleasure, maybe."

"This is what you do isn't it? Make deals over your champagne glasses. Network."

He assessed her with interest. She wasn't being rude, but her tone and her words weren't exactly what he expected from someone like her. Servers were meant to be deferential and polite.

Deferential and polite? He was beginning to sound as bad as Ioannis. "You ask a lot of questions."

"You were bored, and you came looking for company. I'm keeping you company." Her ability to read his mind startled him.

"I appreciate that." His answer startled him further. For a man who hated company, he seemed to have done a complete U-turn.

"Only because you didn't get me in trouble at the taverna."

"Your friend stood up for you."

"Stefanos." The waitress smiled. "He's always looking out for me. I say things I sometimes shouldn't."

"You speak your mind, and that's refreshing. I didn't expect that."

"You expect me to smile and pour you another drink and say nothing."

"I prefer to *drink* my drinks rather than wear them."

"I'll try to remember that next time."

CHAPTER FOUR

ELENI

"You should leave," she said, glancing nervously over her shoulder, wary and watching that Cassia might see them. "The party can't be that bad."

The American stared at her as if it killed him to make a move. "It is. Believe me."

Guests were not supposed to be in here, and she was not supposed to fraternize with them. This man had walked in like he owned the place, so him being here wasn't of her doing, but her boss wouldn't see it like that.

"Then go home," she begged, wishing he would vanish instantly. "You'll get me in trouble."

Stefanos walked in then and did a double take when he saw the American. "Oh, helloooo." He sashayed over, the smile on his face widening. "We must stop meeting like this."

The American looked at him suspiciously. Eleni hated the way her friend was insta-crushing on the American.

"This gentleman was leaving." She still didn't know his name.

"I was?" asked the American.

"Let him stay," cooed Stefanos, giving him a careful head-to-toe appraisal. "If he wants to hang out with us—"

"You should go." Eleni urged her unwanted guest before moving to the other side of the kitchen. She busied herself in prepping another tray ready to serve to the guests. If Cassia saw them now, she would be furious, and Eleni had no desire to anger her boss. Stefanos joined her.

"Are you drunk?" she hissed at Stefanos who was prepping his own tray. "Stop flirting with that man."

"He's a dreamboat. Did he come with a partner? Did you see? I can't get a vibe off him. He might just be—"

She shook her head, annoyed. "Your aunt would go ballistic if she heard you. Get a grip on yourself."

"I'd like to get a grip on him."

"Put your tongue back in your mouth and shut up." She walked out, her tray at the ready, leaving the American and Stefanos in the kitchen.

"Hey! Over here." A middle-aged man, also with an American accent, a heavily Botox'd face, and teeth that were so white they looked odd against his tanned skin, waved his hand at her. "Let me see what you got." His eyes were glazed, and she was immediately on her guard, careful as ever around people who were drunk or high on drugs.

The man looked at her as if she were edible and an internal knowing—a small siren—sounded in her head as she slowly walked towards him. She'd dealt with drunken men before and was no stranger when it came to dealing with leeches like him who made disgusting advances and suggestions as easily as breathing.

She'd never encountered this when she'd been with Jonas.

Her boyfriend had fended off unwanted interest by virtue of being by her side. It was a moral pity that this is what it took to deflect lewd attention away—the presence of another man. She noticed it more now, the sleaziness that some men directed at her. Wherever she went, men looked at her, appraised her, raked their lusty, greedy eyes up and down the length of her body. Maybe her guard was down more, and she was more introverted, the weight of her grief putting her at risk of imploding.

It was worse in this job which she sometimes regretted taking, but the opportunity had been hard to resist when Cassia had branched out in an attempt to diversify and run a small business of her own, leaving her husband to take care of the taverna. Stefanos had begged her to come on board. "It will keep you busy," he'd said, hating the way she would often lock herself in her room for hours drowning in sadness.

But once she'd made the decision to climb the mountain, she needed a second source of income, and though the money was good, there were parts of the job she didn't like. It wasn't only the inappropriate advances, but the outfit she had to wear. Cassia was clever and shrewd. She wanted the female servers to wear figure hugging dresses. What they didn't reveal in skin, they made up for in leaving little to the imagination. This dress fit Eleni like a second skin and now this man was staring at her as if she were naked.

Standing as far away from him as was feasible, she offered him the tray. He gave her a greedy grin.

He took a step back, forcing her to take another step towards him but she moved the tray as far towards him as she could without moving—something she could do because she was long limbed, tall and slender.

He took another step away, forcing her to advance towards him again.

She was about to swivel on her heels and get the hell away, but she needed this job, and so she had to force herself to be nice. "Would you like these or not, *sir?*" She spat the last word out like venom. He nodded, his eyes moving from the canapes and falling to her chest. "I *do* like something. I like something very much."

With a surprising agility she didn't expect him to have, he was in her space, an inch or two in front of her, his hand sliding around her waist. Like an expert, she moved to the side, managing to escape. She had perfected the art of dodging eager hands and fingers as surely as if they were bullets.

The Botox'd man pouted, flashing her an ultra-white smile that momentarily dazzled her. "I'm only trying to be nice, sweetheart."

Eleni's muscles clenched. She glanced over her shoulder to check her exits. But this corner of the room had emptied, and people were gravitating towards the deck. Alarmed, she stepped back, hitting something soft and warm behind her. A man's body. Big and fleshy.

"You losing your touch, eh, Evan?"

Goosebumps broke out on her skin at the sound of the mocking Greek voice behind her. Her body froze, paralysis setting in. Sandwiched between these two predatory men made her feel like a fly caught in a web.

A rough hand cupped her breast, the shock of the violation causing her to drop her tray. It landed with a resounding crash on the floor. "Get off me!" Panic made her lash out wildly. She elbowed behind her as hard as she could.

The man yelped, making a feral noise, a mixture of a grunt and a growl. "You little b—"

"Leave her, Ioannis." The man in front of her moved away, waving his hand as if to say he'd given up, but the second man, the one behind her, spun her around, his hands hard and rough on her shoulders.

"Who do you think you are, eh?" He reached down and gripped her wrist even harder. She tried desperately to free herself, but he was too strong for her. Then he grabbed her other wrist.

"Get off me!" she screamed, fighting to free her wrists and failing.

"Hey! Ioannis, get the fuck off her." Another voice, American again, but this time somehow familiar bellowed behind her. Confusion rioted with fear, a mental coup seeding chaos in her mind.

"What the fuck are you doing?" The American yelled.

It was too much. Three men. Uncertainty. Panic. Adrenaline rushed through her veins, and she kicked out, hitting the man between his legs. He doubled over in pain, clutching his body as he squealed like a pig.

Eleni staggered back and turned to find herself staring into the eyes of the man who'd caught her stealing the food.

He knew the guy who'd assaulted her? The taste of bile in her throat made her retch. They were all the same, rich, sick and disgusting.

She managed to rush away; her body charged with a sudden burst of energy.

DOMINIC

Ioannis. The man was a fucking idiot.

Dominic hadn't intended to follow Eleni. He'd sensed she was uneasy, and he figured he'd killed enough time that he could now leave and get back to his hotel room, but he'd heard

a scream. It was only when he'd walked in that he'd seen
Ioannis with his back to him, and then the waitress had
kicked him.

"What the fuck were you doing?" he asked Ioannis,
calmly watching as the man writhed in pain. He'd deserved it.

"She looked as good as those appetizers," Ioannis replied,
between pants. Dominic held his tongue. He would have
gladly punched this man in the face, but he had to be careful
because this man was a good friend of Galatis' and Dominic
couldn't afford to make enemies.

It sucked.

His fists steeled by his sides. He hated that he had to
restrain himself as he talked to this motherfucker. Some men
should never be allowed near women.

Ioannis straightened up slowly. "She's full of fire, that
one." His eyes shone wildly, something dangerous shimmering
in them. "Wait till I get my hands on her."

Dominic flexed his fingers, practicing a restraint he didn't
feel. "You can't do that." He jabbed the man in the chest,
hard. "Always think of your reputation. Hector Galatis
wouldn't want any blowback, would he?"

That seemed to catch Ioannis attention, but before the
man could reply, Dominic walked away, feeling compelled to
go into the kitchen to check in on the waitress. This wasn't
like him, and he couldn't explain why. He should have walked
away, gone back to his room. Dealt with paperwork.

But he did not.

The waitress was coming out of another door and when
she saw him, she rushed back in from where she had come.
Dominic reached the door just in time to push it open; his
concern for this woman overriding how this might look. He
walked in and shut the door behind him, and only then did he
realize that he was in a washroom with her.

She slunk back, her eyes large with fear, afraid of him. The idea made him sick to the stomach. "Are you okay?"

"What are you doing in here?"

"I wanted to see if you were okay."

"I am. Why do you keep following me?" She hadn't cried, which made him feel some sense of relief.

"To see that you're okay."

Mistrustful eyes stared at him. "Why? What do you care? Did he beg you to make sure I didn't say anything?"

Dominic frowned. He hadn't seen what had happened. He'd only seen the waitress kick out, and Ioannis double over with pain. He'd walked in on something, but exactly what, he was too scared to ask. "No, nothing like that, and he's not my friend. That guy is an asshole."

"You party with these guys. You're worried about him."

"That's not true."

There was a knock on the door, then "Eleni?"

Was *that* her name? Eleni?

"Did you have to come in here?" she hissed. "Now I'm really in trouble."

Shit.

"I'll explain." He moved towards the door.

"How?"

He opened the door and a woman charged in. She looked at him, then at Eleni, her mouth hanging open. "What's going on?" Her voice was deathly quiet. "What are you doing in here with a *guest?*"

"I can explain," Dominic replied, with the confidence of a man of his station.

Asshole.

The woman ignored him and glared at the waitress. "You are in so much trouble. Did you kick one of the guests?"

"I can explain," the waitress said. "He grabbed my breast —and then he—"

"It wasn't her fault." He couldn't stand by and listen to this. That fucking Ioannis. Dominic was tempted to go up to him and punch him.

The older woman spun around, her blazing eyes softening as she surveyed him. "You're not supposed to be in here."

"I was making sure she was okay." He gestured to the waitress. "I saw what happened. I heard her scream. It wasn't her fault."

The woman studied his face and didn't appear to believe him. "You really should leave, sir." She turned to the waitress. "You kicked a guest, and not just *any* guest. That's Ioannis Baros. Do you know how important he is?"

The waitress threw her hands up in dismay. "I don't care who he is."

The older woman took a deep inhale. "Eleni. I have tried, I really have, and only because my nephew told me to give you a chance. I'm sorry for what happened to you before, but you are a liability to my business. Go home and take some time off. Take a month off."

"A month? But Cassia it wasn't my fault. The man was a pig. He touched me inappropriately. What do you want me to do? Let him?"

"What I can't do is let you kick my guests."

"But what about him?" the waitress shouted, shaking with anger.

"It wasn't her fault," Dominic didn't like the way the woman was blaming the poor girl. His temper sparked. "Are you not listening to what she's telling you?"

"Go home, Eleni. Go home before I fire you. I have a party full of people I need to impress. Important people,

people who I need. I can't afford for your behavior to mess things up for me."

The waitress threw her boss a contemptuous look and stormed past him.

"Get to work," her boss yelled at the tall thin guy he'd seen earlier.

Dominic left the washroom quickly, feeling useless and uneasy; a new and unfamiliar emotion sweeping over him—he felt sorry for the waitress and the situation she was now in.

On his way out he saw Ioannis flirting with one of the women who had been dancing on the deck. The sight made him shiver in disgust.

ELENI

Eleni arrived back home desperate to crash onto her bed and decide on her next course of action, but as she put her key into the lock, she heard the noises. Eleni squirmed, not wanting to take another step.

Her mother's new boyfriend was over.

"Oh, yes ... yes! Yes! Like that. Deeper ..."

Bile trickled down her throat and a heavy weight settled in her gut. She couldn't stay here during this. She turned around and tiptoed away.

Her forty-two-year-old mother having sex was drama she didn't need.

CHAPTER FIVE

DOMINIC

Dominic couldn't sleep. He'd left the party soon after, disgusted by what he'd seen and heard, by what he'd discovered.

The next day mid-morning, he returned to the taverna, uneasiness eating away at him. The injustice of what had happened to the waitress, both the assault and the unfair reaction of her boss, stirred something in him.

The tall thin guy he'd met at the yacht yesterday, saw him and at once rushed over to him. Dominic wasted no time. "Is your waitress friend coming in today?"

The guy gave him a once-over. "Why?"

"I would like to talk to her."

"Why?"

"That's between me and her." It made him wonder if this guy, Stefanos, was interested in the waitress for his own reasons. It was perfectly understandable. Now that he'd seen her a few times he couldn't help but notice her looks. Her hair was long, falling over her shoulders, shimmering inky black, her eyes medium brown and shiny, like satin. She was tall and slim, as graceful as a gazelle, as arresting as a goddess.

"But *why?*"

"What are you, her bodyguard?" Dominic asked. He had no time for explanations. He wasn't used to explaining. People listened and did as he ordered them to.

"You like her?"

The man's directness surprised him. Come to think of it, everything about this guy's overfamiliarity was beginning to grate on him. "I don't like what happened to her."

"You don't need to worry. Eleni is okay." Her friend dismissed Dominic's concerns with a flamboyant wave of his hand. "Can I help you?" The server flashed him a smile, hand on hip, which only angered Dominic further. He didn't have much time. He needed to get back to Athens, and because of last night, he hadn't been able to focus and go through the paperwork he'd hoped to tend to.

"No. I need to speak to Eleni."

"What about?"

"Jesus. This is Groundhog Day," he muttered to himself.

The server looked confused. "What day?"

Dominic's frayed patience wore thinner and before he could open his mouth to say something, the man asked, "You want her number?"

"No." The sheer thought of it made him uncomfortable. "It's nothing like that." He didn't want her number. He had no intention of anything like *that*. But the server's eyes narrowed some more, as if he didn't believe Dominic. "I didn't like the way she was treated last night."

"There are a lot of dirty old men around."

The verbal spear hit hard, especially with its emphasis on

the 'dirty men.' Dominic's lips twisted. "Do not mistake me for one of those men."

"What's going on?" Eleni stood between them, looking from Dominic to her friend. Her hair cascaded along her back; his eyes riveted. It looked as if she was on her way to start work. She still had a handbag on her shoulder, and no work apron.

"This gentleman wanted to see you." Stefanos stepped aside. Eleni's eyes fell on him. "*You,* again. Why do you keep following me everywhere?" She didn't sound happy to see him.

"I was worried about you."

The waitress gestured to herself. "I am okay, as you can see. You can go now."

He didn't want her to be just okay. "I didn't like the way your boss spoke to you."

"It's not your problem."

"It isn't, but I'd like a word in private."

She folded her arms. "Why?"

"I'd like to offer you a job."

She laughed. "Why?"

Because he felt sorry for her. "Because I can."

"Because you can," she snorted. "What are you, a billionaire?"

"As it happens, yes. Or rather, my father is, but it's all the same."

"It's all the same," she mused, looking at him as if he was crazy. She seemed to be making her mind up about him, but judging from the look on her face, he wasn't hopeful of her assessment being in his favor.

"You told me you were working two jobs. You've been laid off for a month. I'm offering you a job for the summer, and maybe longer, if you want." He hadn't given it much thought, but he was Dominic Steele and he could do anything he wanted.

"That's kind of you." She gesticulated with her hands, as if searching for a word, "that's ... how do you say it? Very noble, but I don't need your charity."

"It's not charity."

"What would you call it?"

"An opportunity. A break. Why is this so difficult for you?" He was giving her a golden ticket to a better job, more money. He was handing it to her.

She seemed flabbergasted. He stood up. He'd done his bit. "I'll leave it up to you. Here's my business card." He placed it on the table. She stared at it but said nothing. "It's my father's company."

"Lucky you." She picked it up and examined it. "The Steele Corporation."

He detected disapproval in her tone. "I'm not like that guy on the yacht. I would never treat a woman like that."

"I don't need you to feel sorry for me."

"I don't. I've offered you a job, something that might help you."

"What would I do, at this job?"

"You would ..." He struggled to think. He would find something. "You would work in an office. There is plenty of administrative work available."

"What sort of money are you offering?"

He looked up as he shoved the last of his papers into his satchel. "Better than what you're currently on." He glanced at her, gauging her level of interest. "It seems all of a sudden that money is important to you."

"Money is important."

"And yet you seem to have some disdain for it."

"Not for money, but for men like you who have too much."

"Men like me can help. Are you interested?"

She lifted her chin, eyeing him with even more suspicion. "I might be."

"If your interest spurs you into action, come for an interview, and we can discuss numbers."

He left. If she wanted to take up his offer, she could call him. He was only here for the summer, so she'd have to make her mind up soon if she wanted to make good money and fast.

ELENI

"What did he want?" Stefanos asked when the American had left. He followed Eleni to the back of the kitchen.

Eleni surveyed the business card he'd left behind, but Stefanos snatched it out of her hand. "He offered me a job." One she didn't want, or had any interest in. "He said he felt bad about what happened last night." She wasn't sure why. She didn't need the rich man's pity or his concern.

"These men." Stefanos examined the business card. "They fall for your exotic Greek beauty. Dominic Steele. The Steele Corporation."

"It's not going to be a hotel or catering company. That's all I know." She put her handbag away and put on her apron.

Stefanos grinned. "After your roundhouse kick last night, I think it's best that you lay off any customer facing jobs."

"It was not a roundhouse kick."

"The man was still holding his balls when I walked past with the crab appetizers." Stefanos held the business card in front of her. "You should consider this." And when she folded her arms refusing to take it, he slipped it into the pocket of her apron. "Of course, he might be hitting on you. It wouldn't be the first time."

"He's not hitting on me." She didn't get those vibes from this man.

"Not that it would be a bad thing."

"Stop it."

"Jonas wouldn't want you to become a nun for the rest of your life. He'd want you to live your life, Leni."

"I will, once I've climbed the mountain." Though she had no interest in meeting anyone.

"At least consider it. This man is offering you a job and he's been good enough to come and see you this morning."

"I'm not working for him."

"Because he's rich, or because you have better options?"

Because she had never worked in an office before. She had done menial jobs all her life—like cleaning and waitressing— which were in high demand for the seasonal nature of the island. Jobs she was comfortable with. But there was another issue which made her uneasy. She had never yet met a man with money who also had a heart.

"Think it over, Leni. It could be a good opportunity."

"You're only saying that because you want me to work for him so that you can see him again."

Stefanos placed his index finger across his chin, contemplating. "He's as straight as a ruler. This could be fated. It's your birthday, a billionaire offers you a job ..."

She groaned. She was turning twenty-one next week and she wasn't remotely excited about it. "My mother says that age ruined her life."

Stefanos face turned apologetic. "Your mother says a lot of things."

Her mom. Eleni had crept home again last night after two hours of sitting by the sea. It was safe in Spetses, and she could do that, and it was quiet when she'd returned. She hadn't seen her mother this morning when she'd left for work either, or the new boyfriend. Her mother's love life was rocky, like one of the soap operas she liked to watch so much.

Eleni was tempted to go to Athens, to take this man up on his offer, but she needed time to think about it some more. She didn't feel comfortable turning up at the office of a man she barely knew because of an offer he'd hastily given her.

Why would he do that? People weren't that nice. They didn't do nice things for no reason.

Not unless they wanted something.

The rest of her day passed relatively quietly, and she returned home in the evening, none the wiser about her decision. Her mother was painting her toes and watching one of her favorite soap operas when Eleni walked in.

"I spoke to Cassia." Her mother announced as she dropped the bombshell.

She knew.

Eleni tried for deflection. "I came back early last night. I heard you and ..."

Her mother's eyes grew large. "You heard?"

"Can you try to keep the noise down?"

"I didn't expect you to back so soon."

"You should be more respectful of the neighbors."

Her mother closed the top of the nail polish bottle. "Why were you back so early?"

"Cassia told me to take some time off."

"Just like that?"

Her mother knew but was enjoying squeezing the truth out of her. "I kicked a guy who made a move on me."

A low noise sounded in her mother's throat. "Good for you."

"I tried to pull away, but he grabbed both of my wrists, so I kicked him."

Her mother sipped from her wine glass. "I hope it was hard."

"He bent over in pain. You were right, Mama. The people on those yachts are assholes."

"A rich man?" Her I-told-you-so voice grated on Eleni's nerves like fingers scraping along a blackboard. She was going to start again, her rage against the elite, the people with the yachts, the rich ones. "They're all the same."

"Be careful of these men. They are pigs."

"I know, Mama. You always say."

Eleni went to her room where she slid off her shoes and collapsed on the bed. Life was so unfair. She'd been groped, and now she'd been fired. It didn't matter that Cassia had told her to take a month off. As far as Eleni was concerned, she had been fired, and it wasn't right.

Now her second source of income was gone. Unfortunately, the summer months were the time to make good money on the island. The rich threw parties on their fancy yachts and in their mansions. She'd been relying on the extra money to help her reach her goal, and she was still a few thousand euros short of the amount she needed.

She had no other option. She pulled out the card the American had given her, but her fingers hesitated over her cell phone. After a few seconds, she made the call, but hung up after a few rings.

The guy was rich. He was the epitome of all that she detested.

She couldn't do this. Not after what had happened to Jonas.

She ripped the card into two.

But then her phone rang.

Her heart jolted.

The number on the caller ID was the same one she'd dialled.

The American was calling her back.

————

DOMINIC

His phone rang and he stared at a number he didn't recognize. It stopped ringing after a few rings, but his curiosity got the better of him and he called back. "Hello?"

There was no sound from the other end.

"Hello," he barked, losing patience, and hating pranksters. He was about to cut the call when someone said, "Hello. Is that ... Dominic Steele?"

The voice sounded familiar. "Who's this?"

"Eleni ... the waitress from the—"

"I know who you are." He moved his paperwork away and placed it on the seat beside him.

She wanted the job.

"Yes?" He wasn't going to make it easy for her. She had to tell him she wanted it.

"I was calling about the ... job. You said you had something." She didn't sound anything like the haughty woman he'd spoken to earlier.

"The job?" He wanted to enjoy this.

"You said I could ... you said ... you said if I needed to work I should call you."

"What made you change your mind?"

"I've had time to think about it."

"And?"

"I think I might be interested in working for you ... your company, if you ... have a job for me."

"Hmmmm." He let that dangle in the air for a few silent moments. "There are things you can do to help me."

His phone buzzed and when he glanced at it and saw Galatis' name, his gut turned hard. "I have to go. I need to take this. How about you call me tomorrow? Maybe we can do an interview on the phone and take it from there?"

He hung up, and just as he answered the call from Galatis it occurred to him that he really hadn't thought this through. Eleni was a waitress and she worked on an island that was a few hours away from Athens. She'd need to get to the port and then take a ferry. It wasn't an easy daily commute. He'd have to put her up somewhere.

He really hadn't thought this through properly at all.

CHAPTER SIX

ELENI

Her mother had already left for work by the time Eleni was ready to leave.

It was a good thing, too. She didn't want her mother jinxing her, taking a look at her smartly dressed up outfit and asking too many questions.

She had called in sick at the café—it was too late to call Adamos and ask him for the day off. Then she'd called Stefanos when she was on the ferry. Athens was two hours away, and Dominic hadn't told her when to come, but she figured that today was a good a day as any.

"You tell me now when you're on the ferry, when I can't come with you?" Stefanos hissed.

"We can't both be off work. Adamos will get suspicious."

"When did you change your mind? You said you weren't interested."

"You said it was an opportunity and to go for it," she cried, feeling defensive.

"But I could have come with you!" Stefanos insisted.

"He offered *me* a job, not you."

"Twist the knife more, why don't you?"

"Stop being so dramatic. I'll call you later once I've finished."

"I can hardly wait."

"I told Adamos that I was sick, so stick to that story." She hung up, a gnawing itch pinching in her belly. She had no skills; no office training and she was going for an interview she was ill prepared for. She felt sick in her stomach thinking about it, but she'd done her best to look business-y. Wearing a smart pencil skirt and heels. She prayed that she would make it to Athens and back tottering in these. Then she had a lightbulb moment. She'd wear sneakers on the ferry trip and change into her heels once she neared the office building. She tied her long hair up into a neat bun. It made her look years beyond her twenty-one years, but she couldn't turn up for an interview in smart clothing with her hair wildly falling down her back.

The thought of the trip to Athens and back had her doubting what she'd gone and done. She tried to put a positive spin on things. Nothing was going to land in her lap here in Spetses. She could grow old here, waitressing and waiting for the summer and the tourists to dictate her income levels.

Or she could leave. This was what Jonas had planned to do, to go to a bigger island, but now there would be no future with Jonas, no shop to open, no small business to help grow. Now she was left saving up for a trip that she felt compelled to make.

But something good had happened after a long time of

suffering; the offer of a summer job in Athens filled her with hope. Maybe this could be a steppingstone not only to earn enough money for the climb, but for other things?

This could be a way for her to leave the island.

Inspired by these thoughts, she strode into the lobby of the building and informed the receptionist that she had a meeting with Dominic Steele. The woman looked at her sharply before typing on her keyboard. She peered at her computer screen then at Eleni. "There's nothing here."

"I spoke to him yesterday. He asked me to come here for an interview."

The receptionist's eyes filled with suspicion.

"He won't be happy with you if you turn me away," Eleni insisted, pulling out her cell phone and getting ready to type his number.

The secretary begrudgingly relented. "Go to the third floor. You'll see Mr. Steele's PA at the reception desk. I'll let her know you're on your way."

Eleni followed the instructions and went up to the third floor. The receptionist here had a softer look. She was plump with a soft face and freckles. "Did you say you had a meeting with Mr. Steele?" The receptionist ran her chubby finger down her paper diary and shook her head. "There's nothing here."

This didn't bode well. Eleni folded her arms. The heat made her neck damp, and she could feel clammy patches under her arms. "I spoke to him yesterday. He knows I'm coming."

The receptionist typed away, then glanced at Eleni. "There's nothing in any of his diaries. What did you say your name was?"

"Eleni Trakas."

The woman shook her head again. "I'm sorry but there's nothing here." She gave Eleni a half-smile. "What time was your 'meeting?'"

"He didn't give me a time. He told me to come."

The woman blinked at her. Disbelief spreading over her face like a mask. "He told you that?"

"Can I go in? I spoke to him last night."

"Last night?"

"He called me."

"*He* called *you?*"

"I've come a long way. I know you don't believe me, but can you please tell him I'm here?" Eleni tipped her chin up in defiance and inhaled a long, deep breath.

"But he's not expecting you."

He was obviously important given that she couldn't get past two women to see him, but she'd had enough. She moved away and eyed the few doors that she saw. Then she caught sight of an office slightly around the corner and behind the PA. She started to move in that direction when the secretary came tottering after her in her heels making a clacking sound on the wooden floor. "Y-you can't do that."

"Oh, but I can."

"He's... he's not here. Please go." The PA was flustered, her cheeks red, and clearly looking uncomfortable. "Please don't get me in trouble," she cried, when Eleni ignored her and wrestled with the doorknob. She opened the door to find a large dark wooden table and a big empty leather chair. There was no one there.

Had he played her? Was this some kind of sick joke with him and his rich friends aboard the yacht? It had taken a huge leap of faith, and desperation for her to come all the way here.

The poor PA looked as if her day had suddenly gotten

worse. Eleni decided to put her out of her misery. "I'm going. You can pretend this never happened." She got into the elevator, her heated cheeks an indication of her anger. It had been a waste coming here, and she'd lost out on a day's wages from the taverna.

But as the elevator reached the ground floor, the thought of getting back on the ferry and returning to the island, the taverna and Stefanos, didn't appeal. Something steely and resilient hardened inside her. She couldn't face the further humiliation of going home a failure, of not having even tried.

She would wait. She took a seat in the lobby to try again, but this time, the other receptionist, the one in the main lobby area, stared at her as if she didn't belong. As if she were a fake.

Eleni braced herself. She hadn't come all this way for nothing, and now she was more determined than ever to wait it out even though the receptionist periodically looked at her and gave her the death stare.

But as the minutes ticked by, it was becoming slowly and painfully obvious to her that Dominic Steele was having a joke at her expense. He was exactly who she had pegged him out to be: a self-assured, smarmy, businessman who had slipped her his business card. She'd come here on a whim believing the words and promises of a man she barely knew.

She didn't belong here.

But she didn't belong on the island either, or at home where she was an extra in the romantic soap opera drama that was her mother's life.

She called the American's number again, to tell him she was sorry, but she had changed her mind, but it went straight to his voicemail. A few seconds later, her cell phone rang, and when she saw Stefanos' name, something warm and comforting swept over her, settling her nerves.

"Leni," he shrieked. "He's a billionaire!" Stefanos sounded excited, as if this news might somehow impact his life for the better.

She looked around, checking to see if anyone else had heard Stefanos' high squeak, and turned the sound down on her phone. "I know."

"You know?"

"He told me."

"And you're still okay about working for him? I thought you hated—"

"I need the money."

"Good. I'm glad you changed your mind because that's going to be your best shot."

"That's why I'm here."

"It's a shipping company."

"What is?"

"That address where you're at."

"A shipping company," repeated Eleni, wondering what sort of work she would do here.

"But his family has a lot of businesses all over the world. Didn't you check any of this before you left?"

"No." No, she hadn't. Her nerves had been so fried creeping back home at three in the morning, then tossing and turning, that she hadn't had time to do anything but wake up and come here.

"Have you seen him yet?"

Stefanos and his million questions. "Not yet. I have to go. I'll call you later."

Doubts had started to seep in. She knew nothing about shipping. She didn't have any qualifications. She'd show herself up and look like a fool. She could not do this.

She got up, smoothed a hand over her shirt and skirt, then collected her dignity as well as her jacket and handbag.

Determined to not look at the receptionist, or the security guard, she marched towards the exit. She walked through the main doors and immediately inhaled a gulp of fresh air.

It hadn't felt right.

This did.

Leaving here did.

Just at that moment the heel of her shoe impaled itself into a crack in the pavement. She couldn't move.

It was at that very moment that she saw him.

It was the aviators she noticed first. They were perfect for that angular face of his, that sharp jaw, bones chiseled in a way that could make people stop and stare and wonder what lay behind those shades. He looked so cool, so sexy, so full of confidence as he came towards her. Her breath caught and held like a fist in her throat, and when her gaze trailed down the rest of him, she had to suck in a breath.

Had he always been so strikingly handsome? Had she forgotten? Or had she been in denial about it? He seemed so much *more* now. Time slowed down as he strode towards her in a midnight blue suit. Wide shoulders, slim hips. His watch glinting. She squinted in the scorching summer sun. He was so hot, her eyes were burning.

"Eleni?" He lifted his hand to remove his shades. She didn't know where to lay her gaze first; to his bicep that strained his jacket sleeve, or his eyes, now that they were revealed. His gaze raked down her length and back up again to her face. "What are you—"

She tried to take a step forward, hoping valiantly to pull her stiletto heel out, but she couldn't.

Not one to advertise her faux pas, she stood still and smiled at him. He moved towards her, and someone tall and scary looking, stood a few inches behind him, like a shadow.

"You asked me to come." Her smile held, but it felt

unfamiliar, wrong. Not like her to smile at someone like *him*, or for so long.

"I said for you to call me, and we could have an interview over the phone."

He had? She wished the crack in the pavement could swallow her whole.

"You're here now. We can do it face to face."

"That would be good." She tried to be discreet as she wriggled her shoe in vain.

"When did you get here?" he asked.

"About an hour ago."

"An hour ago? You've been waiting that long?"

"I called you," she said, ignoring the wave of his arm as he motioned for her to turn and lead the way back into his office.

He stared at her when she didn't move, a line forming on his brow when she didn't immediately do as he asked.

Because she couldn't.

"I've been in meetings all morning. I had my phone on silent. Shall we?" He beckoned again for her to go in.

She couldn't, so she did the next best thing. She gazed at the sea in the distance up ahead of her.

Dominic shoved a hand into his trouser pocket, his Rolex watch glinting in the sun. "What are you doing?"

"Admiring the view." She wriggled her heel. "Isn't it beautiful?"

Dominic half-turned to see what she was looking at. Then, "Is your heel stuck?"

"Huh? N—" But before she could finish her denial, he'd crouched down, his hand on the heel of her shoe, trying to loosen it.

She gasped at the skin contact.

"There. You can walk now. Shall we?"

Her foot was free. She looked up at the sky, thanked God, and followed Dominic into the building.

The only consolation, and it was a big one, *monumental,* was to see the look on the uptight receptionist's face as she walked in with Dominic.

CHAPTER SEVEN

DOMINIC

He'd had back-to-back meetings all morning, but thankfully nothing with Galatis.

That would have darkened his already black mood. Eleni followed him dutifully. In a smart business suit, her hair up in a knot, wearing heels, she looked different and behaved differently too.

It had amused him the way she'd tried to hide getting her heel stuck and pretended instead to admire the view.

Slim ankles.

Long legs.

He tried to dislodge these thoughts from his brain. He got on his knees for one thing only and helping out a damsel in distress was not one of them.

No sooner had he gotten out of the elevator than Linus accosted him. He'd been hovering by Miranda's desk but as soon as Dominic appeared, he pounced.

"I need to talk to you about—"

Dominic loosened his tie. "Not now."

"But it's important. The report you wanted."

Dominic growled quietly. Linus' problem was that he mistakenly believed he was important. "Five minutes." He turned to his side, barely managing to glance at Eleni who was patiently waiting. "Take a seat. I'll call you." He hadn't meant to be so brusque, but something about Linus always brought out the worst in him. "Keep the door ajar," he growled, when Linus went to close it behind him.

He stripped off his tie and a few seconds later his shirt was off. This goddamn searing heat was unbearable, and the air-conditioning left much to be desired. He went to his cupboard where a few crisply clean shirts were hanging and grabbed one. Sliding his arms in brought instant relief. The cool freshness of unworn shirts chilled by the AC calmed him down.

He eyed Linus as he did up his buttons.

"The figures that Galatis wanted." Linus slid a binder across the desk. "I typed up a report."

This wasn't urgent. "Is that all?"

"Don't you want to discuss it?"

"I'm busy. Later."

Linus looked displeased. "Who is the girl?"

"A new hire."

"A new hire?" Displeasure hardened Linus' thick voice. "I don't know anything about—"

"You don't need to know."

"But who is she? Where is she from? You've already hired her? For what position?"

Because he didn't have all the answers, and because he sensed Linus' disapproval, Dominic shut him down. "Trust my judgment." He opened the door and gestured for the man to leave. "If you'll excuse me. I have an appointment."

Linus' left the office, his head turning towards Eleni who was sitting there looking nervous. Dominic could only imagine the dirty look Linus must have thrown her.

"Come in," he told her. Then tried not to stare at her as she moved past him and towards his desk.

She sat down, crossed her legs and looked the picture of poised calmness. Were it not for her constantly playing with the strap of her handbag which rested on her lap, he would have believed it.

His irritation from dealing with Linus soon melted away.

"What position am I interviewing for?" she asked, putting her hands together on her lap.

Dominic still hadn't given it much thought, but then he hadn't expected her to turn up unexpectedly at his office. He was impressed that she'd been here this early, and that, if nothing else, indicated that she was desperate for work.

"I have a number of positions." He tried frantically to think. Linus already hated her on sight, because Dominic had left him completely out of the loop. One thing was certain, it would be better to have here her, on this floor, where he could keep an eye on her and make sure the ambitious and paranoid deputy manager didn't make her feel unwelcome. This poor woman had already suffered enough and had had her share of dealing with douchebags.

"Like what?" Large brown eyes stared back at him, wide with anticipation, as if her entire life hinged on his answer. He was reminded of her stealing the food from the serving trays. His gaze raked over her once more, she was slim, but not skeletal. His eyes landed on hers and found them full of disapproval. He'd been caught out. Clearing his throat, he looked away, praying she wouldn't lump him in with the other wretched men she'd been unlucky to meet. "You speak Greek, I expect?"

"Yes."

"That's a start. I struggle to make sense of some notes and emails sometimes."

"Then, I would be a ...?"

He frowned, trying to follow her line of thought. "A ...?"

"My job title. What would it be?"

Another fine question. "Something in admin."

"But *what* in admin?"

"I'm sensing that titles are important to you."

"I don't care so much for titles, but I do want to know what type of work you expect me to do."

"What are your skills?" Just by asking that question he realized how wrong he was in going about this. He hadn't even asked for her resume, had no idea about her education, or skillset. Didn't even know her age.

"I can cook, and clean, and I'm good with customers. I have a—" She stopped talking, eyeing him with guilt. "I promise not to kick anyone."

"If you're ever in that unfortunate situation again, I hope you will." He looked away. She seemed so fragile, so vulnerable, so young. This wasn't the waitress from the taverna or the yacht, now she was altogether something else. Desperate, suffering consequences for which she wasn't to blame, and he wanted to help her.

He didn't usually give a flying fuck about other people, and yet he couldn't look at this woman and not feel sorry. "I don't need you to cook or clean or do any of that."

"I can ... I'm not stupid. I can use a computer."

"You never thought to look for other work?" She was smart, savvy and unafraid. She should have wanted more.

"What's wrong with what I do?"

"Nothing, but have you never considered other alternatives to what you do?"

She gazed down at her lap and fiddled around with her handbag. "Like what?"

"I don't doubt that you're smart, Eleni, and we both know that you have opinions."

"I do want more. People mostly do. They want a better life than the one they have. Unless ..." her eyes blazed at him. "Unless you are a billionaire, and then you have everything."

"It's not as blissful as you think."

"I'm sorry for your hard life." She did it again, blinked, then sat up, maybe regretting the words that shot out before she'd had a chance to filter them. Not that he could blame her, knowing what had happened to her.

He watched her silently, waiting for her to dig herself out of the gargantuan hole she'd landed herself in.

"I mean ...I don't mean to be rude," she said slowly.

"But you couldn't help it," he offered. She stared at him for the longest time, and he could only guess at the thoughts going through her mind. It was clear, she did not like him. Or people like him. Moneyed people.

"I would be happy to do anything here. It's a great opportunity for someone like me." She sounded almost grateful.

"What happened?" he asked softly. Yesterday she had been so against working for him. "You didn't want to work for me when we last spoke. What changed your mind?" People who said money wasn't important, were full of shit. It wasn't important until they had none left.

"I don't have a lot of opportunity in Spetses. I came because ... I need the money for something important."

"But you were on your way out when I saw you."

She looked uneasy. "My friend Stefanos called me and

told me that you had a shipping business, as well as other businesses." Her chest rose and she pressed her lips together.

"Why would that bother you?"

"I don't know anything about shipping or working in an office."

She was unsure of herself and scared about messing up. He hadn't expected her to crumble so easily, and her vulnerability unnerved him. "There's not much to it. The work you did before was much harder, I imagine. You're busy, on your feet, dealing with some terrible customers. *Rude* customers, I imagine."

She tried to hide her smile.

"This will be much easier, I promise."

"Why are you hiring me?" she asked, the question he'd been fearing. Partly because he'd felt helpless, walking in on Ioannis assaulting her, then standing by like a useless bystander unable to help her. There were other reasons, too.

This had been his way of making it up to her, although there was a worry that his actions might be misconstrued wrongly, by Linus, by others, by Eleni.

"I feel guilty for not doing anything that night on the yacht. I hated that your boss laid you off for a month. It was unjust. You'd suffered enough and it wasn't your fault."

"You feel sorry for me, that's why you're hiring me?"

"I felt hopeless and inadequate to help." Thank goodness his father and brother could not see him now. Or the other employees. He'd turned to mush around this woman, and he owed her nothing.

Give her a job and be done with it.

She was silent and he hoped his words would soak in, that she would believe them. "You were the one who called me," he reminded her.

She scratched her cheek. "I'm here now."

"We have a lot of administrative work to do here. Shipping comes with a lot of risk and there is a lot of insurance paperwork as well." He gave her a brief overview of what his company did, and the different roles, and told her that he'd put her in an office on this floor, under the watchful gaze of two older women who had been here a long time. Agnes and Isidora would show her around the online computer system which was at the heart of everything they did. This would work. He'd feel as if he'd done his bit. "Does that sound like something you could do?"

Her smile brightened. "Yes. I've had to order supplies for the cafe and take care of deliveries."

"I promise you this will be a breeze compared to working at the taverna or dealing with assholes."

"A breeze?"

"Easy, simple." Linguistic nuances notwithstanding. "Think about it some more and get back to me." He needed time to speak to HR and create an official position and go through the proper channels.

"What is the salary, and when can I start?"

More good questions, but he didn't have the answers yet. "I need to speak to someone in HR and get this rolling."

"Next week?" She sounded too eager. Desperate even. "You said this was just a summer job, so I am aware that I don't have long."

Something was bothering her. He recalled the food she'd been taking from that party and made a mental note to himself to pay her handsomely. "Is there something you're worried about?"

She folded her arms. "I would like to start soon. Maybe next week."

"Send me your resume." He scribbled his email address down and handed her the slip of paper.

"Should you not have asked me this to begin with?" Amusement frolicked in her eyes as if she'd one-upped him. He should have, and would have, had he been thinking with a straight head. She pulled a plastic wallet out of her bag and whipped out a sheet of paper which she handed to him. He skimmed through it.

She was twenty.

Twenty-one next week. He was due to turn thirty in December.

Why the fuck was he even thinking about that?

"You will see I have good qualifications, but I didn't study further."

"This looks good." He put it down to go through properly later. As for her salary, he plucked a figure out of the air, the salary that Miranda was on, not stopping to consider that Miranda had been here for a few years, while Eleni was just starting out. Her eyes widened in disbelief, but the shock vanished as quickly as it had sparked.

"Would that be acceptable?"

She nodded, unable to speak.

"Leave it to me." He rose, remembering that he had a conference call with his father and brother. "I'll be in touch."

"Thank you for this. For giving me this opportunity," she said, turning to him at the door, in a rare display of gratitude. The waitress he'd first met had gone. This Eleni was humble and grateful, and some of her feistiness had gone. If truth be told, he missed that part of her.

Linus walked in as Eleni left, and Dominic's blood pressure shot up. Did the man stand by Miranda's desk all day waiting for him?

"Not now, Linus. I have phone calls to prepare for."

"You hired her?"

"She can help with the odd translation issues I have."

"But you have me."

Unfortunately, he did. He not only had Galatis to try to win over, but he also had pain-in-his-butt Linus grovelling at every turn and getting in his way.

He didn't like being questioned so closely by Linus, especially with the waitress due to start work next week—something he would definitely make happen. "I don't want to have to rely on you. You're a manager and your time should be spent on more important things. Not translating for me."

Linus winked at him and waggled a thick finger at him. "She's hot, eh?"

"Shut the fuck up," he growled. Another asshole eyeing the poor girl as an object. "That's not why I hired her."

CHAPTER EIGHT

ELENI

The job offer letter came through two days after the interview.

A man in HR had called her to discuss accommodation.

Accommodation?

Eleni had been prepared to make the long journey to Athens and back each day, but the man at the other end had laughed and told her that the company were putting her up in a hotel nearby, for the duration of the summer.

She'd been at home, doing warmups before her run, and at this news, she'd hit the floor, lying spreadeagled, staring at her ceiling.

A hotel room, for her, in Athens? She could scarcely believe her luck.

Breaking the news to her mother hadn't been easy and she'd waited until she had the letter in her hand.

"A job in Athens? I didn't even know you were looking for work in the city."

Eleni hadn't told her mother, but even if she had, she doubted that her mother would have cared. "I need more money. Cassia doesn't want me back for a month—"

"And you want to climb the mountain. For Jonas." Her mother shrugged.

"Yes, for Jonas."

"And what about you, Eleni? What do you want?"

She wished her mother could be more empathetic. Be kinder, softer, gentler with her. It was as if she resented that Eleni had found love, had been happy, that she'd found someone who had cared for her. "I want him to come back. I miss him." Her lower lip wavered just saying the words. Memories of Jonas came flooding back as tears welled in her eyes. "Aren't you happy for me? *Can't* you be happy for me, ever?"

"Be careful. You've never worked in the city before."

"It's good money Mama, and they're letting me stay there. They've got me a hotel room."

"A hotel room?" Her mother's tone was hard to gauge. Eleni wasn't sure if she was jealous or excited for her.

"Don't you want to know what I'll be doing, or who I'm working for?" Eleni cried, feeling as if she had to prompt her mother all the time.

"You're old enough to take care of yourself now, Eleni."

"That's not what I asked you. You're my mother. Don't you care about anything?" This woman frustrated the hell out of her. Not waiting for an answer Eleni marched into her room, and quickly got changed out of her clothes, slipping into a pair of denim shorts and a loose top. Then she rushed out.

"When do you start?" Her mother called but she was already out of the door and on her way to the taverna.

Stefanos had finished his shift and she hooked her arm in his and led him away, breaking her good news.

"You're leaving?" Stefanos' face fell and he sounded resigned. It wasn't quite the reaction she'd been hoping for.

"Only for a few months, but I'll come back at the weekends sometimes, and you can come and visit." She told him about the hotel room, which was the highlight for her, having her own space and place, away from her mother.

"I'll be sure to do that."

"I can do something new. Something that I've never done before."

"Climbing the mountain?"

"Working in an office."

"When do you start?" Stefanos asked.

"On Monday." It was so different and exciting. Up until a few days ago she would never have imagined such a thing happening to her.

"You must have wowed him on sight."

"What?"

"The billionaire. I bet he hired you on the spot. I bet you looked amazing."

"You don't think he hired me for my brains?" This had been gnawing away at her, and she'd asked Dominic that very question, but the answer he'd given her had satisfied her. And she didn't get those creepy vibes from him. Her built-in radar usually alerted her to such things, and Dominic wasn't that type.

"I don't think your brains came into it, much."

Eleni nudged her friend in the ribs not so gently. "Don't say that. That's nasty." It put the doubt back in her. While she didn't think Dominic felt remotely interested in her, Stefanos was right. Why had he been so eager to give her a job? Maybe he was a nice guy and had a sister and hated what had happened to her?

It was too much of a stretch to believe that.

"Maybe you could ask him if he's got a job for me?" Stefanos suggested hopefully.

"At least let me get my foot in the door first."

"Just be careful, Leni," Stefanos cautioned. "You're gorgeous and you turn heads wherever you go."

"I do not." She laughed and shook her head.

"You do."

She rolled her eyes at him and giggled. She didn't pay much attention to things—until stuff happened, like the incident at the party. Most days, she functioned on a minute-by-minute basis. It was hard to shake what had happened, because memories of Jonas were all around her. Every time she looked at the sea, she remembered the good times and the bad times, and the worst of times. She hadn't been there when the accident had happened; she'd been working, but knowing that he had died in these waters, the same stretch of water that faced her daily, meant that his accident was never out of her mind.

A silence spread between them again, and she could feel the weight of Stefanos' unsaid words and his judgment. "You might think he offered me a job because he wants something from me, but he doesn't. I asked him."

A cruel snort sprang forth from Stefanos's mouth. "He gave you a truthful answer, I'm sure."

"Don't be so judgy. He's not like that. I can tell when guys are ... creepy. Dominic isn't. He's ... nice."

"Nice? He's filthy rich, a billionaire, and you hate people like him."

"He's giving me a chance."

"Sounds to me as if he feels guilty for what happened to you."

"Can't you be happy for me? You're as bad as my mother."

"Sorry, Leni."

"Can't you let me have this? Can't you let me be proud that I have a job? That I might be able to get some experience in something other than waitressing?"

He put his arm around her. "I'm proud of you, I love you, I want the best for you. But be careful, please."

"I'm always careful, but Dominic isn't like that."

"You trust him, do you?"

"I'm doing this for a reason. What's the matter with you?"

"Nothing. Sorry." Stefanos ran his hand through his hair and picked up his cell phone. "I'm jealous and I'll miss you."

"You idiot." She leaned into him as he tightened his hold around her shoulder. "Let's celebrate my birthday in Athens. I'm sure Phoebe and Angeliki wouldn't mind if I celebrated it there instead of here."

"We could make a wild weekend out of it," Stefanos suggested. "Phoebe's desperate for a break. She's been living in her pajamas ever since she gave birth."

"We'll celebrate in Athens," she decided. "I can't trust my mother to behave, and I'd hate for you to hear what I had to." She told Stefanos about what had happened the other night.

He wrinkled his nose in disgust. "Your mother worries me. She's worse than Angeliki, except forty plus isn't the age to be going wild."

Eleni felt a touch of defensiveness. "She's lonely, and she's scared of getting older and not being attractive anymore."

"But walking in and hearing that," Stefanos wrinkled his face in disgust. "That there is already enough trauma to last you a lifetime." The look he gave her was loaded with pity, with a side order of sympathy. "Maybe Athens will be a good break for you."

Stefanos had seen her at her worst, during her darkest times. Those first few days after Jonas' death had been the worst. She hadn't been around to see him get hit. She'd only heard about it afterwards from their friends who were so traumatized they couldn't help but spill the graphic details. They told her of the blood gushing from Jonas' head, of his limp, lifeless body, of how he'd been laughing at a joke, and how he had died instantly.

"I hope so."

"This is a good new start for you, Leni."

"It's only for the summer."

"Being away from your mother can only be a good thing."

It was. It was a very good thing. She and her mother had never been close, which, given that she'd only had one parent, was odd. With her birthday coming up, she was prepared for her mother's mood swings. Her mother had had Eleni when she'd turned twenty-one, and she was prepared for her mother having a hard time coming to terms with Eleni turning twenty-one.

"I'm looking forward to it."

She'd often wished she could be away from here, and now she had the chance to do just that.

I t all happened so quickly. As if she'd blinked and all those secret yearnings to leave the island had suddenly come true.

A breath of fresh air, that's what it felt like, moving away and settling in Athens. The hotel was clean and near to her place of work, and the staff seemed friendly enough. The only minor problem, as she lugged her suitcase up the stairs, was that there was no elevator. Having only three floors in the hotel, wasn't too bad, but she was on the uppermost floor.

Eleni had wondered if Dominic might show her around on her first day at the office, but it was the nice receptionist, Miranda, who introduced her to Agnes and Isidora, the women with whom she would share an office.

She met Linus and a few other people who were on the third floor. The only person she didn't see was Dominic.

Agnes and Isidora were much older than her, even older than her mother and she didn't have much in common with them, but they smiled at her each time she looked at them. There wasn't much conversation.

Two more days passed, and she still hadn't seen Dominic. She only saw Miranda either when she was leaving or arriving at work, or when she visited the water cooler, and with no one to talk to, she soon started to feel off and out of place.

In her skirt, blouse and heels—an outfit she considered just right for an office job—she soon felt hot and sticky. The searing summer heat became too much whenever she went outside to buy her lunch. The sky-high cost of food prices made her blink, and she often returned to work with an apple and a banana and made do with water from the water cooler.

She missed Stefanos and their easy banter, she even missed the taverna and Adamos, and the customers. She longed for the busy long days during which time flew, and the little breaks she and Stefanos took, and the evenings when they'd sit on the beach, talking about life. Sometimes Phoebe, who used to work with them, would meet up, but only when she was boyfriend-less.

Oddly enough, she missed Spetses, and looked forward to returning home over the weekend.

It was on her next visit to the water cooler, that she heard

Dominic's voice, loud and clipped. He was barking orders to someone on the phone as he leaned against the high lecturn that made up part of Miranda's reception desk.

She somehow made it to the water cooler and even managed to pour herself a cup of water without spilling it because her mind was focused on him in his business attire. Charcoal grey pants and a dazzling white shirt. She tried not to look at the expanse of his back, or the way his hips narrowed.

She moved past him again to return to her office, her heart kicking her chest.

"Goddamn idiot," Dominic muttered, sliding the phone into his trouser pocket. He casually glanced over his shoulder, and she didn't even need to look at him to know he was staring at her. "Did Miranda get you settled in okay?"

She pulled back, stopped and faced him. "Yes, she did. Thank you." She nodded at Miranda whose face had turned red and who watched her with a curious expression behind Dominic's back.

"That's ... good." Dominic shuffled the pile of papers he had in his hand. He looked so different in his business clothes. She should have been used to it by now. That first time she'd seen him had been the biggest shock, and she was still having difficulty shaking that image out of her head. Dominic Steele seemed to set the gold standard when it came to wearing sharp-cutting suits with attitude. Who knew a man could make wearing a white shirt be a fashion statement?

Stefanos would have died on the spot to see Dominic the way she could.

"And the hotel?" he asked.

"The hotel?"

"Is it okay?"

"Oh, yes. Yes, it's fine. Thank you."

"Good." He turned and left, leaving her to gawk at his back, with Miranda peering at her. "How did you get this job again?"

Eleni couldn't tell if Miranda was being a bitch, or just asking a normal question out of curiosity. Deciding not to answer that, she swiveled on her heels and left.

Her co-workers stopped talking as soon as she appeared, each of them looking away guiltily.

Her instinct alerted her to something she only now noticed. "Is there something you want to ask me?" She placed her cup of water on the table before sitting down.

Agnes stopped typing. "No. Is there anything you need?"

"No."

Isidora looked as if she were about to say something, then continued to type. Then, after a while asked, "How did you get this job?"

Did you sleep with him? The question blazed in both pairs of eyes. Maybe it was paranoia, but Eleni's cheeks turned red at the idea that everyone might think this.

"Why do you ask?" She didn't know what else to say. "I wouldn't worry too much. I'm not after your jobs. I'm only doing this for the summer."

"It's usually quiet in the summer," Agnes answered. She turned to her friend. "I don't want him to think we can't handle it."

"That's not what he thinks," Isidora replied. They both looked at Eleni again. If they wanted to make her feel uncomfortable, they were succeeding. Her insides twisted into a pretzel.

Dominic had not only given her this job, he'd created something out of thin air for her.

She had no right to be here. She didn't deserve it, and everyone she met knew it.

CHAPTER NINE

ELENI

S he returned home to Spetses on Friday evening and the apartment felt even tinier than she remembered, as if she had somehow outgrown it.

But she had been looking forward to coming back, which surprised her. Even for the celebration which made her uneasy. Her mother had booked a restaurant for lunch tomorrow, the actual day of Eleni's birthday. This was something else Eleni hadn't expected, for her mother wasn't one for celebrating birthdays, not even her own. She didn't like the idea of growing older, or the reminder of another year passing.

"Is this still on?" she asked, pausing in the living room to see what had riveted her mother to the TV screen this time.

"Shush!" Her mother lifted a finger to her lips, then turned her attention to the TV again. It was a soap opera that had been running for years with no end in sight, and a gorgeous looking couple were about to kiss.

Eleni wanted to scream at her mom, that this stuff wasn't real. That spending her time gazing longingly at soap operas with pretend characters having pretend romances wasn't helping her.

But she didn't want to sour the mood.

She'd hoped her mother might have shown an interest in Eleni's first week at work, might have had a few questions and asked how she was doing, but nothing had changed. Her mother was as obsessed as ever with her soap operas. Office work couldn't compare with TV love triangles.

"I'm meeting Stefanos. I'll be back later," she announced, and left. By the time she got to the taverna, Stefanos was waiting for her. Adamos and some of her friends there clustered around her, wanting to know about Eleni's new job and life in Athens. At least they were interested.

Then she and Stefanos walked by the beach before sitting down at their favorite spot.

Stefanos had asked her some more about the job and how she was doing. Even in the telling of her news, Eleni didn't feel enthusiastic. But it had only been a week. People were different. Did she expect fun and games with the two old women in the office? Linus seemed to hate her for a reason she couldn't fathom. Dominic was as busy and as grumpy as ever, but strangely considerate towards her. And Miranda seemed to lose coherent speech and thought around her boss.

"You don't sound excited." Stefanos could see through her bullshit because he knew her better than anyone.

"I'm not sure why he gave me the job." She plucked at a frayed thread in the hem of her yellow summer dress which she'd changed into quickly, getting out of her business clothes.

"Why?" A note of alarm sounded Stefanos' voice. "Did something happen?"

She picked at another frayed thread, killing time before she answered. It was only now that she'd come home that she felt the disconnect and loneliness, and the disappointment in her new life for which she'd had high hopes. "Nobody talks to me. I feel all alone." She told him about the people in the office.

"It's only your first week."

"My first week at the taverna was so much fun."

"You didn't take this job to have fun, Leni. You wanted to get away from here, and this is your chance. That you're working for a hotshot boss, one who came looking for you, is a bonus."

"He did not come looking for me."

"He was here, in the taverna, the next day, waiting for you. I know that because I was doing my best to serve him. I would have gladly served that man in any way, shape or form but... the man is straight. Wasted on women."

"Have you finished?"

"He came here to offer you a job. Be grateful."

"I can't complain."

"And yet, here you are."

"I don't feel like I belong." But that feeling had been with her for most of her teen life and beyond. Apart from the time she'd been with Jonas. He'd believed in her and loved her. He'd needed and wanted her. He'd made her feel she mattered. No one understood what it was like to not matter. She had no siblings, her mother lived for her soap operas, and she'd never known her father.

Stefanos laid a gentle hand on her arm. "You do belong, silly. You always have. But you're getting old. Another year wiser. That's enough to make anyone feel all over the place."

"I'm not *that* old. You're four years older than me."

He rolled his eyes. "We don't need to talk about that." She forced a smile and looked up at him. "You're right. Maybe I am feeling out of sorts. I need to give it some time."

A wicked grin settled on Stefanos' lips. "Do you have much to do with Dominic?"

"I've barely seen him. He's busy and keeps himself to himself."

"Do you don't have any photos of him?"

"Are you insane?" She looked at him as if he were a three-year-old asking for a cigarette. "How, *why*, would I have any photos of him?"

The man was an enigma. He'd been so different on the island to how he was now. She cringed thinking about the way she'd treated him. How disrespectful she'd been. But now she was so much more ... careful. Guarded. And he was being nice. Seeing him in his suit had put her on alert.

It was the first time she'd been attracted to a man since Jonas died. Dominic Steele was the epitome of a young, hot, sexy billionaire, and this was wrong. And weird, and complicated. She lowered her eyes, underplaying the warm and fuzzy feeling sprouting inside her.

She said nothing about him, in case Stefanos noticed anything odd about her and figured that merely talking about Dominic had a peculiar effect on her. She changed the subject. "We're going to have fun next week."

"Can I meet you at work, for lunch or something?"

"No." It wasn't lunch or her he wanted, as much as a glimpse of Dominic.

T he sun warmed her skin, and this view from the terrace,
overlooking the water, would have been wonderful, for
anyone else.

Eleni wondered if she'd ever be able to look at the sea and
not think of Jonas. It was hard to chew, even harder to get her
food down and with her mother sitting across the table from
her, this lunch was turning out to be as difficult as she'd
feared.

But she wasn't the only one struggling. Her mother was
moving her food around her plate. She was always dieting,
going with the latest fads, moving from one new thing to
another.

Turning twenty-one today should have been a happy,
joyous occasion, for Eleni but it was far from what she felt as
she struggled to eat. Ending the misery of the silent meal, her
mother set down her fork, then fished around in her bag for
something.

"Here." She placed a small box on the table. It wasn't
wrapped up and it didn't look brand new. Eleni could see the
scuff marks on it. "What's that?" She set down her fork,
curious, but wary. This was most unlike her mother. Eleni
hadn't expected a physical gift. Her mother paying for lunch
and slipping some money into her birthday card was all she
had expected.

But not this.

"Open it and find out."

A tinge of unbridled excitement fluttered inside her, and
her fingers hovered over the box. She opened it and looked
confused as she stared down at a long thin glittering ...
something. It wasn't a ring, or a necklace or anything
recognizable. "What is it?"

"Take it out and see." Her mother's voice was weighted by weariness. Eleni did as instructed. "A hair slide?" She held it up and the sun glinted off the small gems studded into the swirly shaped clip, spraying a myriad of colors into the air.

"It's for your hair. When you put it up, if you ever do. They're real."

"Real what?" Eleni stared at the tiny gems and the sparkling light dancing off their surface.

"Diamonds." Her mother nodded and Eleni's heart stopped.

"Mama, *real* diamonds ...but how did you—" She jumped up and threw her arms around her mother's neck, a move unfamiliar, and bold, and alien. Her mother's body went rigid, her arms still on the table, as if she'd been frozen in time. "Don't do that, Eleni."

"But Mama ..." She wished her mother would open up to her, at least today of all days. Even this, a birthday lunch, had been hard, but giving her this expensive gift had confused her. Eleni didn't need anything from her mother, especially not anything as extravagant as this. All she wanted was for her mother to love her and show her that she cared. "This is too much, Mama. You didn't need to do this. I don't need gifts; I just want you—"

"Your father gave that to me on my twenty-first birthday."

Eleni's face froze. The chill spread to her limbs and torso, like ice cracking on a river. The cold turning her body rigid. Her mother had never spoken about Eleni's father before. Once, when she'd been about seven or eight, Eleni had asked her about him, but her mother had shouted at her and made her cry, then bought her an ice-cream to make up. Eleni had never mentioned him again.

Ever.

This unsolicited piece of information was welcome if shocking. "My father?"

"He was an extravagant man," her mother said, softly. Eleni stared at the hair slide with new eyes, watching dazed as the diamonds glistened in the midday sun. "He was the love of my life." Her mother snorted and picked up her fork again. "At least I thought he was, but I was young and foolish. What did I know?" She pushed her food around the plate again and with her fork stabbed a sundried tomato.

"Mama—" Eleni had so many questions. All this time she had listened to her mother and not asked, but now she couldn't keep quiet. "Who was he?" All her life she'd had a faceless nameless image of a man, but now she was so close to getting some answers and filling in all the blanks.

"He's not important. He deserves to be forgotten."

"But—

Her mother set her cutlery back down and sat back, her shoulders tense, her face hard. "When I told him I was pregnant, he told me to get rid of it."

"He what?" Something cracked in her chest, as if her ribs had been broken. Her own father hadn't wanted her. It was bad enough that he hadn't stayed with them, hadn't been a part of her life, but to know that he hadn't even wanted her to be born, cut like a serrated knife. Eleni pushed her plate away, her appetite dissolving to nothing. She wished her mother hadn't told her. "Mama, why are you telling me this on my birthday?"

"I want you to know. Men can be monsters, especially the ones who don't look anything like monsters. They're the worst. Your father said he couldn't do this—be with me anymore—and that what we had wasn't fun anymore." Her mother scoffed. "The fun stopped the moment I told him I was pregnant."

"He really didn't want me?"

"He told me to get rid of you. He even gave me money, but I threw it back in his face. I didn't see him after that. I wasn't going to do the thing he asked. I wouldn't, I *couldn't*."

"Mama." Eleni started to get up again, wanting to console her mother, and needing desperately to feel a connection, a hug. But her mother lifted her hand, stopping her.

"Every time I look at you, I see him. You have the same high forehead, the same straight, perfect nose. You have a lot of me, too ... but when I look at you, I see so much of him. He was a beautiful man. *Beautiful.* The way other women looked at him should have been a warning, but I took it to mean that he was a great catch. Some great catch."

So, this explained why her mother had pushed her away. Eleni reminded her of him. The breath caught in her throat. This was too much information shared at a time when she hadn't expected anything.

"I'm over him. I'm strong. You don't have to worry about me. But be careful. Be very, very careful of men who indulge you, who buy you with gifts and show you a good time with money." Her mother looked away, a faraway look on her face as her gaze landed on the sea.

She understood it now, why her mother had been the way she was. Always so bitter and angry. Always so concerned about her looks fading with time. "Mama." She again reached across the table for her mother's hand, but surprisingly, this time her mother didn't move her hand away.

"He told me that he already had a wife and a family ..."

Eleni's other hand flew to her face. Her mother looked far out in the distance. "He said I was just an afterthought."

"Oh, Mama, no." As much as it hurt her to know this at all, she was hurting more for her mother. This bombshell was something she could never have imagined.

"He wined and dined me and took me to so many places; glamorous parties in Aegina and Poros and Hydra. He showed me another life, and I foolishly, believed he was going to take me away from this to a better place."

"We don't need him, Mama." Eleni's heart ached for her mother, and she squeezed her mother's hand gently, both taking and giving comfort from the touch. Eleni looked at the box as if it were a timebomb waiting to explode then put the hair slide back in the box and closed the lid.

The shine had been taken off it.

"I don't want it, Mama." She pushed the box towards her mother who pushed it back.

"I don't want it either, but it's yours. I haven't been able to give you much in life but—"

"I don't want anything, Mama, just your—"

Just your time and attention.

Her mother continued, "It's worth a lot more now. I took it to a shop soon after to have it valued, and to make sure it wasn't a fake, like him. I wanted so much to believe he was the one; he was my first and only love, but he used me. I have pushed him out of my thoughts, but you exist, Eleni. He doesn't know you do, but you do. You're my daughter, and I love you. I always have even if I don't show it to you the way you want."

While her mother had been there for her in the few weeks after Jonas' death, and Eleni had believed this might have been the start of a new relationship for them, a new man had come into her mother's life and Eleni was left alone to grieve. All she'd ever wanted was for her mother to be just that—a mother, someone who gave her hugs and love and dispensed wisdom. But now she understood her better.

She stared at her food, at the box with its shiny, priceless but unwanted hair slide inside it. She wanted no part of it, because it came from a man who had wanted no part of her.

"Get it valued," her mother insisted. "Do what you want with it. It was worth a lot twenty years ago, and it will be worth a lot more now."

CHAPTER TEN

ELENI

The malaise had set in yesterday during her birthday lunch and continued when Eleni returned to Athens the next day.

It followed her into work and stayed with her when she went into the office and Agnes and Isidora gave her that sneaky side eye again.

She stared at the screen trying to make sense of the computer system she was supposed to use. Agnes' tour of it had been so brief and so fast, that Eleni felt she'd been left with whiplash and a feeling of inadequacy that squashed her spirits.

She wasn't stupid, or slow, but the rapid-fire tutorial Agnes had given her had confused her further. She'd tried to get to grips with the system, and to make a dent in her workload but she was lamentably behind.

And today, after the bombshell her mother had dropped

on her birthday, Eleni's mind wasn't at its best. She felt slow, and foggy, her actions like wading through glue.

Desperate to leave the claustrophobic office atmosphere, she went to lunch earlier than usual, and sat at a cafe, needing time alone. She'd finally found out something about her father, but it was something she would rather have not known. There was always something going wrong, her life seemed to be perpetually in ruin, and she'd had to become adept at picking herself up and getting on with things.

The one good thing she had going for her was this job, and the opportunity that Dominic Steele had given her.

He'd seemed like such a jerk at first, a typical wealthy man, entitled and privileged, but she had seen a softer side to him, and he'd been more approachable.

Things weren't so bad, she told herself in an effort to see the good in her situation.

She returned to work, determined to be more upbeat instead of drowning in sadness, but her uplifted spirits soon sank. She'd heard Agnes and Isidor talking as she'd approached the door, but they fell silent as soon as they saw her.

Smiling at them weakly, she averted her eyes, and with focused determination, sat down and stared at her screen, struggling to make sense of it. She wasn't going to make any friends here sitting in an office all day long with two women who hated her. It was so different to the pace and rhythm of the taverna where everyone knew everyone else. And the customers: every day, every hour, every minute, she would see a new and fresh face. Some people were nice, some exceptionally lovely, some picky and petty and nasty. She had become accustomed to meeting a vast array of people from all walks of life and all over the world. In a small way, it made her hanker even more for the mountain trip.

DOMINIC

D ominic stepped out of his office. It was late. Nearly everyone on this floor went home at five thirty and he was often the last one out.

He walked towards the water cooler then stopped when he saw her. Her hair was down, cascading over her shoulders. She was in heels, wearing a pinafore dress with a white shirt underneath. As she bent over, refilling her plastic water bottle, he presumed, he couldn't drag his eyes away from her shapely thighs.

"What are you still doing here?"

He'd startled her. Her body jerked and she spun around. "You scared me."

"I didn't mean to. It's nearly eight o'clock." Didn't she have a home to go to? A girl like her shouldn't have to be working late. Not doing the temporary work he'd managed to carve out for her.

"I was trying to get caught up."

"Caught up?"

"On the system."

"What system?"

"Your computer system, the one we all use—"

That pile of shit. "That's not my system, I assure you. If I had anything to with it, it wouldn't be as shit as it is." He could see by the look on her face that he'd shocked her. "Didn't Agnes show you?" he asked. "She was supposed to."

The woman had a penchant for doing things in her own time and in her own way. He'd judged it wrong, asking her to train Eleni. That was the problem with walking into an office for a few months and taking charge. He didn't know all the people as well as he should have. He had no interest in getting to know them because this was Nikolaos' office, and he would be back soon enough. Dominic had bigger goals to accomplish than ensuring a temporary worker had work that was significant.

He suppressed a smile.

Maybe Miranda could help. Nikolaos' shy but efficient PA was someone he trusted. Someone who was honest and down to earth, and he didn't feel that way about most people.

She would be the right person to train Eleni.

"She did. I just want to make sure I have it right." Eleni chewed her lip, and it immediately revealed more to him than her words had. She sounded timid, so unlike the ballsy waitress he'd first met, the one who'd given Ioannis what he had deserved. She opened her mouth, then closed it again.

"Something you want to say?"

She pressed her lips together, feeling unsure, then, "Was there really a job for me or did you invent one?"

He laughed uneasily. "There's always work here. Do you have any idea how busy this office is?"

"It's quiet in the office I share."

He cocked his head. He should have known that a good deed wouldn't end there, by giving her a job, that it would lead to complications.

"It feels as if I've been put into a role, into an office, and I'm not wanted."

"That's not true."

"I'm taking work away from Agnes and Isidora."

"I doubt it. They're slow and old, and they plod along like dinosaurs. They're scared I'm going to replace them with you. That might not be such a bad thing, actually."

"You can't do that," she protested.

"I can do whatever the hell I like." He paused to examine

her face. "You look shocked, but don't be. I speak my mind, like you."

"I appreciate you wanting to help me, because of what happened, but I don't need your pity, Dominic."

It was different, something he wasn't used to, her calling him Dominic with no reverence, as if they were equals. He shuddered, thinking how much she'd hate him if she knew his thoughts. He didn't mean it like that, but everyone here was so respectful. Miranda had called him Mr. Steele for weeks until he'd told her to call him by his first name. People quaked in their shoes when he summoned them to his office. But Eleni was above all the airs and graces, and he liked that.

"Are your colleagues unfriendly? Have they told you that you're taking their work away?"

"No, but I feel as if I'm not doing anything of value, anything significant."

She wanted to do work of value. How odd, given that she'd come from the catering industry. That she gave a fuck at all. He'd let her down. He'd plucked her off the island and planted her here, then forgotten all about her.

"It's a bad system. There's nothing intuitive about it. The managing director of this office is away. He was supposed to have implemented a better system. It was in the works, but I don't know what happened." Dominic frowned. The Athens office was so different to what he was used to in the US. "He'll get around to it one day, I hope. Don't feel too bad. It's not your fault."

She wiped her slender fingers across her forehead. "Maybe I'm overthinking things. I need to give it a while."

"It's only been a week," he agreed. He'd have to do something. He hadn't checked in on her, to see if she was settling in okay. But these things weren't for him to do. He didn't have the goddamn time, not with Galatis doing his head in, but this was different. This woman was here because of him. He had to do better.

"It has. It's not been long at all."

His cell phone went off. It was Helen. He needed to get this. He lifted a finger to Eleni telling her to wait. "Helen?" He turned his back, and paced around, listening to her. She was talking fast as usual, throwing dates and clauses and contracts at him. She wanted him to read something she'd emailed him.

"Okay. I'll take a look and call you." He slipped the phone into his pocket; his work wasn't done and he'd need another hour or so in the office. "Don't spend too much time here. It's not worth it." He started to head back.

"Then why are you here?"

He turned around, couldn't help but laugh at her innocence.

Because his father was testing him. Because his brother was on standby waiting for him to fail. Because he needed to prove himself. Because there was a lot at stake. "I have things to catch up with as well. A lot of people are depending on me and I have to get results."

"That sounds like a lot of pressure."

He nodded.

"It's not as blissful as I thought it was... being a billionaire," she said. The corners of his lips curved up. She had a laser sharp memory and she had no qualms about saying to him what others never would.

"Don't stay too late."

The next day he stopped by Miranda's desk and asked her if she could block some time out to show Eleni the in-house computer system.

"Me?" his PA asked, turning bright red, the color closely creeping upwards from her neck to her ears.

"Yes, you." He explained that the new hire, Eleni, wasn't familiar with the system, and that Agnes had given her a rough guide to it, but he felt Eleni could do with an in-depth overview. "You know the system inside out, Miranda. You're the best person for it."

"The best? You really think so?" Her cheeks deepened to a shade not unlike a ripe tomato.

He nodded. "Could you show Eleni?"

"Yes."

"Arrange it with her, but sometime this week would be good."

Miranda's eyes looked glazed, and he wasn't sure how much of what he'd said had gone in because she was smiling at him, hanging onto his every word as if he was reading her a bedtime story.

He clicked his fingers. "This week? Eleni? Make sure to show her." Sometimes he wasn't sure what planet she was on, but the work she produced was always of excellent quality, and she was good at it.

Miranda blinked, snapping out of whatever fantasy world she'd been in. "I'll arrange a time with her."

CHAPTER ELEVEN

ELENI

The receptionist smiled at Eleni when she came to work the next day.

"Dominic asked me to show you the in-house system."

Wait, what? Eleni had walked past her and now backtracked. "Were you talking to me?"

"Dominic asked me to show you the system."

"Did he?" The man worked quickly. Eleni was touched he'd already sprang into action. "Would that be okay?"

"It's what Dominic wants."

"O-kaaay," Eleni answered slowly, finding Miranda's choice of words odd. They quickly settled on a time to meet later in the day. Miranda could only make it after working hours which made Eleni feel bad for keeping her at work longer than she needed to be there. But the PA insisted it was fine by her, and once again stated that Dominic had been keen for her to provide the training.

As she entered the office, the two women stopped talking. Eleni ignored them. She was less bothered this time when they looked away guiltily and pretended to be concentrating on their work.

At the end of the working day, Eleni went and sat with Miranda who went through the computer system thoroughly. She was a good teacher, and patient, too. With her there was none of that prickly falseness she'd felt from Agnes, and Eleni felt relaxed enough to learn. By the end of the training session, she was not only more confident about using the system, but had gained a friend, and talk soon turned to non-work related things.

"You're really pretty," Miranda said, out of the blue. They'd been talking about how Eleni was adjusting to her new job and her life in Athens, when Miranda burst out with this little compliment. Eleni didn't know how to respond. So, she smiled instead and said nothing. Miranda had a gorgeous heart shaped face, full lips, and was very pretty. Eleni was all but ready to compliment her in return but felt that it might ring hollow to say this to her now.

"How did you get this job?" she asked instead. Miranda told her that she'd applied for a dozen jobs in Athens, looking for administrative type of work, and had now been in this job for three years. At twenty-three she was two years older than Eleni, but she didn't have the self-assurance that Eleni would have expected. It was almost as if she looked up to Eleni, and there was no reason to, unless Eleni's dealings with Dominic played a part in Miranda's assessment.

"What about you?" Miranda asked. Eleni recounted the story of how Dominic had been at the taverna where she'd worked. "Then later I met him at a party on a yacht."

"A yacht?" Miranda's eyes grew large. "You were at a party on a yacht?"

Eleni burst out laughing. "I wasn't a guest. I was waitressing, serving the food and drinks."

Miranda's shoulders slumped, as if this admission relieved her. "But how ... how did you ... get this job?"

Eleni didn't know what to tell her. She had a sneaky suspicion that Dominic had done her a favor and she was wary of telling Miranda the truth, but her gut instinct told her she could trust her. So, she recounted the story, of how she'd been fired.

Miranda looked shocked. "I'm sorry. Are you okay?"

Eleni nodded.

"Men. Some are pigs, no?"

"Yes."

"Dominic was good to give you a job here."

"It's only for the summer, but it helps, yes."

Miranda sighed, loud enough for Eleni to take notice. "He's a nice man. So much nicer than his dad and his brother."

"He has a brother?"

"Alexander. They come over from time to time, him and the senior Mr. Steele. They come here more than Dominic. This is the longest Dominic has stayed."

Eleni sat forward, her interest brimming. "What are they like?" She was curious to learn more from a reliable third party, which she believed Miranda was.

"Dominic's father, he's ... I don't want to say anything that will get me in trouble."

"You won't. I won't tell anyone. This is between you and me, Miranda. Don't worry."

Miranda looked guilty. "His father isn't nice. He's bossy. He likes to think he's important. I know he is, but the way he talks to everyone else isn't nice. They're all like that, even

Alexander. Dominic is bossy, yes, moody and mean a lot of the time, but he's the nicest of them all."

Eleni was puzzled. She'd seen a little of that behaviour, but he'd been mostly nice to her.

"He's different with you," Miranda commented, when Eleni remained silent.

"You think so?" She was all ears to discover another opinion on the matter.

"He doesn't talk to you the way he talks to everyone else. Are you and Dominic ..." Miranda winced. "Just good friends?"

The way she said 'good friends' indicated something weighty behind those words and when she blushed a few seconds later, Eleni got the drift.

"We're not friends. It's nothing like that!" It was definitely NOTHING like that. "I'm just an employee, like you."

"We should try and get some lunch together one day," Eleni offered. She didn't have any friends here, and that's what was lacking.

"Lunch?" Miranda's face brightened. "That would be nice. How about one day next week?"

Eleni smiled, genuinely feeling happy. "My schedule is free. I can go whenever you want."

"I'm sorry I didn't believe you when you came the first time for your interview."

Eleni thought back to her interview. That moment seemed like a lifetime ago.

"He's such an important man, nobody sees him without an appointment. You can't show up and demand to see him, and that's why I thought ... and... "Miranda visibly swallowed, tuning Eleni in to her discomfort. "You're so pretty and ... I thought maybe ..."

Eleni dipped her head, falling into this unnecessary delusional rumor. "You thought?"

"That you were ... a new friend or something ..."

"A new friend?" She wanted to ask more, but Miranda's face was so red, Eleni was worried she might explode. "Let's talk privately when we meet for lunch."

DOMINIC

"What is she working on?" Linus asked, carrying a wad of papers in his hands.

"She?" Dominic asked, distracted. He rifled through the paperwork Linus had landed on his desk.

"The new person."

Dominic's mind was still on the dinner date he couldn't get out of. It was something he didn't need this weekend, but business was a matter of nurturing relationships. Tomorrow's meeting was at one of Athen's newest restaurants. An investor Dominic was keen on doing business with had invited him to join him and his wife for dinner there.

"Eleni?" Good job he remembered her name.

"What have you got her doing?"

"Something." Dominic was deliberately being vague.

"She's sitting with Agnes and Isidora?"

"And?"

"Is she up to the task?" Linus asked, clearly not happy about the way in which Dominic had suddenly hired her.

"Yes, she's up to the task. Whatever Agnes and Isidora are working on, Eleni is more than capable of doing."

"Are you sure?"

Dominic's gaze sharpened to a knife edge. "What's your point, Linus?"

"My point is you hired her when there was no need."

"I say there was a need."

"Based on—"

"My gut. It seems you have a problem. Do you?"

"Nikolaos always kept me informed. These decisions were always—"

"I'm not Nikolaos." Dominic didn't like the way Linus seemed to think he knew best. Maybe he did, to a degree, but he was not in charge. Dominic was.

Dominic still hadn't forgotten how flustered Linus had been when Dominic first arrived in the Athens office and announced that he would be in charge during Nikolaos' absence.

With his boss away for so long, Linus was always trying to gain favor, always looking to cast himself in a favorable light, as if he were angling for a promotion so that he could somehow slide into Nikolaos' place, if and when the opportunity ever arose.

"Of course, you are not Nikolaos." Linus bared his teeth into the smile Dominic hated.

"And you would do well to remember that."

CHAPTER TWELVE

ELENI

Her head was buzzing; the three cocktails she'd consumed might have had something to do with it.

Her friends had arrived last night, and it had been a late one. They'd had dinner then drinks, and more drinks, before hitting a nightclub and coming back to her hotel room at six in the morning. After waking up late in the afternoon, they lazed in bed and talked for a few more hours.

Later, they somehow summoned the energy to get dressed and went out again. This weekend was about celebrating her birthday with her friends, but as excited as she had been as soon as they'd arrived here, the energy started to seep out of her. By the time they'd had something to eat at one of the fancy booths upstairs, above the dancefloor, Eleni was ready to sleep. She didn't want to hit the dance floor, unlike her friends.

The air electrified with laughter and chatter. Their table

was littered with small plates of appetizers and empty cocktail glasses which a server hastily cleared away. Stefanos had done well to book a table at this new restaurant where bookings weren't available until September. They'd only managed to get a table because of a last-minute cancellation, and it helped that Stefanos had flirted plenty with the guy on the phone, begging for a table. This wasn't the ultra-chic and ultra-trendy, and ultra-pricey, restaurant in the VIP section, which was discreetly cordoned off from the dancefloor, but it was good enough.

"I like this one!" Phoebe shrieked, jumping up as a new track started. The new mother of a two-month-old seemed determined to make the most of her first weekend without a baby stuck to her breast. She started dancing on the spot. Servers rushing to and from tables were no obvious impediment to her moves. Angeliki jumped up and grabbed Eleni's wrist. "Come on, we're all going downstairs to dance before she headbutts a server."

"One more!" cried Stefanos, as another tray of shots was delivered to their table. He handed out the shot glasses.

Phoebe clapped her hands together while still dancing.

Angeliki counted down.

They downed it at the same time. The burn of the liquid slid down Eleni's throat and heated her insides. Her head was light, her body pumped with adrenaline. She felt happy. Filled with a heady buzz that only strong alcohol or pure love could give.

She grabbed Stefanos and the four of them bundled their way down the sleek spiral staircase—it was sheer luck that she didn't trip on her six-inch heels and onto the dancefloor.

She lost herself in the music, in the thumping beat, the heavy bass, the energy fizzing in the air. She danced with abandon, feeling freer and happier than she had in a long, long time.

"Are you okay?" Stefanos's voice in her ear sounded strange, like it was faraway. Suddenly, everything was funny, and she loved everyone. She started hugging and kissing her friends, telling them how happy she was that they were here with her.

"You've had too much to drink," Stefanos shouted in her ear. She threw her arms around him. "I'm having so much fun. I love you," she cried, before moving back into her own space to start dancing again. She blew a kiss to him, overcome with emotion and happiness. Stefanos cared. Her friends cared. They loved her. She wasn't unwanted, and what her father had said didn't matter.

It didn't.

She slapped an errant hand away when it landed on her bottom; the second time since she'd started dancing. Then she turned around to throw a dirty look at the hand's owner. Above them, women danced in little capsules accessible by steps and suspended about ten feet in the air above the heaving crowd.

A dancer vacated a capsule and Eleni quickly dove through the crowd, up the steps and to the capsules. She snagged the empty one. Here, alone with nothing but the music, she danced like a woman possessed.

DOMINIC

G oddamn typical.

Dominic got out of the car with Helen and moved towards the dark glass and silver building.

A tall server in a tux greeted them at the VIP entrance. "Please come with me. I will escort you to the VIP lounge."

Dominic's gut hardened to steel. He hated the place as soon as he heard the music.

"You said it was a business meeting," Helen noted.

Dominic flexed a finger along his collar. At least he didn't have to wear a tie or jacket. But he would rather have done that than come here. "With dinner."

"But it's so loud."

"Beats me." First Galatis and the ancient Greek relics, and now Thanos had gone and booked this of all places to meet. Why these people couldn't stick to meetings in an office was beyond him.

"This is meant to be one of the hippest new places in Athens," remarked Helen, sliding her fingers over the shiny silver and black panelling. "Consider yourself hip and trendy."

"I just want a normal fucking meeting."

She placed a soothing hand on his arm. "Smile, you're in danger of enjoying yourself."

"What is with these people?"

"People?" Helen lifted an eyebrow. "My people, you mean? Or people in general?"

He huffed. "That's not what I meant." He wasn't dissing the entire Greek population. But these men seemed to have a penchant for wanting to do business anywhere *but* around a table.

The elevator opened to reveal a large and busy dining area at one end, and below it he could see the dancefloor.

Not this, please.

They wouldn't hear one another over this racket. His gaze trailed up at the cages suspended in the air. People were inside them.

Dancing people.

He stopped. Stared. Then stared some more.

Was that Eleni?

Dressed in a short black dress, with earrings so large he could see them from where he stood, someone who looked very much like his newest hire was dancing like a wild shaman. He blinked, craning his neck to see if it really was her. A curtain of dark hair tumbled over her shoulders as she moved to the music.

Helen tugged at his hand. "Come on, we don't want to keep them waiting."

He complied but couldn't help looking back one more time.

It *was* her.

ELENI

From inside her capsule, Eleni waved at Stefanos who had gone upstairs to their table again and was leaning over the balustrade looking down at the dance floor.

Looking for her no doubt.

She shouted his name, but with all the noise, he couldn't hear her. Fanning her face, feeling hot, she stopped dancing when the current track finished and got out. There was a bar area outside with tables. That's where she needed to be.

Outside the music could still be heard but it was dulled and not invasive. The fresh air soothed her. The night was hot and dry, and she eyed a group of people vacating one of the tables by the pool. She immediately rushed towards it and collapsed on a seat, desperate to catch her breath. She was hot and sticky, and her dress clung to her like a damp second skin.

Yuk.

But as she sat and people watched, the world around her started to spin. She lowered her head, wanting it to stop.

How many cocktails had they had? Her fuzzy brain couldn't work out how many.

"Eleni?"

She looked up to find Dominic standing in front of her.

Dominic, here?

Their gazes collided and locked, like laser missiles finding their target.

Her heart seemed to be in its own little dancing cage, moving erratically to the music and the sudden appearance of Dominic. She shook her head, believing that she was seeing things. He took a step towards her, lines criss crossing across his forehead.

A black shirt fit over him like a second skin, and black pants she was sure hugged his hard-as-steel butt. Pity he didn't have his back to her. He looked sexy as hell.

She smiled. He was here. *For her.* He'd come to help her celebrate. She got up, felt dizzy then flopped back down again.

"Are you drunk?" He moved towards her, and this close to her she couldn't help but breathe in his strong scent. The noise in the background sunk further away, and all she could sense, feel, hear, was his tone. Deep, sexy, intimate, his words reverberated in a place deep inside her chest. She still couldn't believe it. Dominic, here. She sniffed, closing her eyes as the world threatened to spin again.

"I'm happy," she giggled.

"But under the influence."

She smiled at him. This man was divine. So divine. So delicious. Why hadn't she noticed him before? "Sit down," she motioned at a spot beside her, shifting up to make room for him on the bench.

"I'll stand." He shoved his hands deeper into his trousers. His all-in-black stealth mode clothing unleashed a kaleidoscope of butterflies in her belly.

"You don't want to sit down?" If she focused on him, only on him, maybe she could forget about the width of his shoulders, and the definition of his muscles, even through his shirt.

"I saw you dancing, up in the air."

She squealed uncontrollably, slapping the table with her hand. "You did? It was so much fun. So much fun. You should try it." Her eyes widened. "Do you want to?" She got up and tottered a step towards him, this new idea lighting up all the synapses in her brain. Neural pathways buzzing with joy.

"I think you've had too much to drink."

She followed his gaze and found that the clingy fabric of her dress had ridden way up her thighs. She hastily pulled it down, before asking, "Do you like it?" Her hand touched her bare shoulder. "Angeliki said I should wear this because I might get lucky."

His lips pursed together. Then, "Are you here alone?"

"With friends. They're here, somewhere." She prodded him playfully in the chest, only to find it hard-as-steel. The plane of his muscle had no give. "Dom, you are so hard."

He picked her hand and lifted it away. "Do not call me *Dom.*"

She inched nearer, tottering on her heels. "You smell so *good.*"

"You've had too much to drink." He nudged her back down onto the bench gently.

She stared up at him, her head still light, the moment turning surreal. "You look so sexy in black. You should wear black all the time." She pointed a finger at him, gesturing it up and down. "Now *that*, would give Miranda something to blush about."

He looked around. "I can't leave you here like this."

The same big, menacing looking guy she'd seen a few times before with Dominic now stood behind him again. "Who is that?" Then it dawned on her. "Are you ... is he ... are you with *him*?" Clasping her hands together, she was filled with hope for Stefanos. "Because my friend, the one from the taverna, thinks you're superhot. So does Miranda, in case you hadn't noticed."

Dominic's gaze settled over her again, assessing her as if he didn't know what to make of her. "Eleni."

"It's true."

He looked over his shoulder again. "Can you call your friends?"

"Why? They're having fun. *I'm* having fun. I'm celebrating my birthday, Dom. Let's dance." She tried to stand up again, but the sudden motion made her feel giddy and she promptly fell back onto the bench.

"You're in no state to be dancing."

She didn't miss the muscle flexing along his jawline. And what a beautiful jawline it was too.

"Don't you want to dance with me?" she asked, pouting. "It's been a long time since I danced with someone."

"Dominic. There you are. I was waiting by the waterfall." A glamorous woman, with the style and glamor of a movie star, sidled up to him.

Eleni couldn't take her eyes off the woman's glittering chandelier earrings, or her fitted, cream dress. Eleni felt underdressed. Her gaze bounced between the woman's beautifully sculpted face, and Dominic's.

"Oh." Eleni gasped. The cogs of her brain whirred

furiously fast, the neurons firing and making connections. He was with someone. What was she? His girlfriend? His wife? A date? She couldn't help herself, again. "And you are?"

"Helen." Dominic's one word answer might as well have been 'Quiet,' for all the effect it had on her. She'd heard him on the phone to Helen once.

It now made sense. Dinner on a Saturday night. At this chic new hotspot. With his significant other.

Eleni was lost for words. The shock sobering her quickly. Even in her addled state, floating in her own drunken bubble, Dominic's expression wasn't lost on her. She had embarrassed herself, and he wouldn't forget this so quickly.

Dominic's mouth twisted. "She's had too much to drink. I don't want to leave her by herself." The unnecessary concern in his voice, which might have made her feel that he cared, was erased by Dominic talking in a quiet voice to his girlfriend. Eleni felt like a burden, like a child who no one knew what to do with. Shame branded its name on her, even as she eyed the woman's dainty hands checking to see if she wore a wedding band. She did not.

"Oh, hell-oooooo." Stefanos arrived, with Phoebe and Angeliki on either side.

"Who's this?" cried Angeliki, her eyes on Dominic and completely blind to the woman next to him.

"How exciting to run into you again." Stefanos extended a hand which Dominic stared at for a few seconds before shaking.

Phoebe prodded her breasts and winced in pain. "I need to pump. Where's your bag, Stef?"

"You brought your breast pump *here?*" Eleni asked, aghast. Phoebe had shown no shame in using this in the hotel room, in front of them. Then she'd left the washed contraption to dry on the coffee table.

"It's in the cloakroom," Stefanos answered, smiling at Dominic. "Are you joining us? We're celebrating Eleni's—"

"No." Dominic stared at Eleni, and she stared at the beautiful woman he was with.

"The *pump*, Stef. I need the pump!"

"You're in good hands." Dominic gave her a nod, mercifully ignoring Phoebe. "Enjoy your celebration."

Something sharp poked at her jugular as she watched Dominic and the woman slip away, and she didn't feel so good.

CHAPTER THIRTEEN

ELENI

"My boobs are free again." Phoebe came out of the bathroom smiling and with a wet breast pump in one hand.

"Ewww. That's disgusting." Stefanos made a face as she set the plastic bottle on the side table.

"Don't you care about hygiene?" Eleni asked, shocked.

"I poured it down the toilet." Phoebe made a face as if she was devastated by the wastage. "Good quality milk. Wasted."

A chorus of 'Ewww's went around the room.

"You," Phoebe pointed a long talon at them all. "...have no idea. I was leaking in bed. It's all over my nightshirt."

Everyone's eyes locked on Phoebe's chest. Eleni visibly gagged.

"I borrowed one of your T-shirts," Phoebe told her. "I pulled it out of your drawer while you were sleeping."

"Keep it." She no longer wanted it, and she'd have to get

housekeeping to change all the sheets. Phoebe yawned and climbed back into the bed where Angeliki lay, scrolling through her cell phone.

"Are you going back to bed?" Eleni glanced at the clock. It was past midday. "We don't have long left." Her friends were going back in a few hours' time. "Why don't we have a nice breakfast somewhere?"

"Food is the last thing I want. I've slept three hours each night. I might as well have had my baby with me." She snuggled underneath the sheet.

Angeliki jumped out of bed. "I have a date."

"A date?" asked Eleni.

"Maybe two dates." Angeliki grabbed her clothes and headed for the bathroom.

"Two?"

"From last night."

"And, what? You're going to do them both?" Stefanos asked, stretching out on the sofa bed which Eleni had shared with him.

"Disgusting! I'm not going to *do* anyone."

"You want a longer relationship?" suggested Phoebe.

Stefanos laughed. "One that lasts from lunch until dinnertime."

Angeliki stood in the doorway. "You're horrible. All of you."

"Just be careful," Eleni cautioned.

"I'll have lunch with one, and dinner with the other one. I'm going to get a later ferry back, so you two go on without me."

Stefanos chortled. "Did you mean you'll have one *for* lunch and one *for* dinner?"

Angeliki threw him a steely look. "You're evil. I'm a changed woman. I'm looking for a quality relationship."

"Aren't we all," muttered Stefanos.

Listening to their banter, Eleni couldn't help but think of last night and the absolute fool she'd made of herself. She'd woken up in the early hours thinking about how she could go back to work and face Dominic again. Or ever.

Stefanos nudged her. "It's just you and me, Leni. Let's go."

"Let's." She didn't want to lie in bed, and the room was musty and stale, reeking of alcohol and body odor.

A short while later, they were sitting outside a nice little café, drinking coffee.

"My mother gave me a present last weekend." She'd been keeping that conversation to herself, mulling it over, dissecting and trying to imagine the faceless monster her mother had been in love with. The father figure she had never known. It hadn't gone unnoticed that her mother only told her enough about her father, but had kept much hidden, like his name, and maybe a picture. Surely she would have a picture of him? Because her mother referred to him as her first and only love. "She told me about my father."

Stefanos jolted to attention. "She did what? What did she tell you?"

"Don't get your hopes up. It's not so great." Eleni recounted the conversation, telling him about the hairpin, and everything, except the part about her father wanting her mother to abort her. After, she felt better, as if a heavy load had washed clean out of her system. Her thoughts were no longer festering inside her.

Stefanos was such a good listener and a precious friend. He listened intently, and without interruption, so that she felt heard. He told her she was better off without a man like that in her life.

"I know." She tapped her fingers on the shiny menu, her thoughts a million miles away.

"I don't like this, Leni, you sitting here as if you're at a funeral. Shit..." He closed his eyes hard, cringing at what he'd said.

"It's okay. You are allowed to talk about death and funerals and accidents." She couldn't fall apart all the time. She *didn't* fall apart all the time now. She didn't wake up every day feeling sad. Time passed, and she had learned to come to terms with Jonas' passing. There was a knowing, deep in her heart, that the expedition represented a closure. A milestone. An ending and a beginning. The expedition was a goal post in her mind, something to aim towards, a chapter in her life she was ready to assimilate and be done with.

"This weekend has been good for you."

She smiled. It had been good. She had loved being with her friends again, and letting her hair down. But there was Dominic. And what she had said to him. How she'd behaved. She sucked in a heavy breath.

"What?"

"Nothing." She didn't want to discuss it. "Thanks for organizing it. That club, it's the sort of place I'd never go to."

"But it was your twenty-first, it had to be special."

"It was. I needed to let my hair down."

"You were dancing in the capsules, Leni!" Stefanos chortled, "Was that the highlight or was it when your boss turned up? That man." Stefanos shook his head in disappointment. "He's wasted on women."

And what a woman to be wasted on.

She had been everything Eleni expected. Beautiful, elegant, poised. Enjoying an evening with her lover. She shivered, feeling uneasy. She hadn't looked at anyone in over a year, hadn't had the space or mental clarity to do so.

She sat up with a jolt as Jonas' face flashed by her, and she remembered snippets of their conversations.

She hadn't thought of him much now, not since she'd been in Athens. Guilt stabbed like a hot poker through her. She was forgetting him.

"You noticed him too, huh?" Stefanos examined her face closely.

"Me? No. He's my boss."

"More reason to fantasize about him."

"You're crazy."

"And you're lying."

It was entirely possible that after last night Stefanos could tell. They had all been drunk, but maybe she'd been more drunk than the rest of them? "I am not. He's my boss. I don't have an opinion about him."

Liar.

"Of course you don't."

A server came to take their order, and as Stefanos gave his, Eleni watched the young girl scribble down the order. Things had changed in such a short space of time. For one, she was not a server anymore. And two, she was starting to have feelings for someone again.

———

Her head was bowed low, and her shoulders hunched. She wished the floor would gobble her up and keep her somewhere, until that encounter with Dominic had been erased from his memory.

She didn't even lift her head to acknowledge Agnes when the woman wished her a 'Good morning.'

Had she really told Dominic how good he looked in black? She vaguely recalled asking him to dance. Or had she?

Maybe she'd made that bit up, because she couldn't have been that stupid.

Dominic was not a man who any woman in her right frame of mind would ever say those things to.

Her palms turned clammy, she couldn't sit still or focus on her work. Her chaotic thoughts were giving her a mental block. Feeling restless and unable to tolerate it any longer, she went to Miranda and asked if Dominic was free.

"He's out, at a meeting, but he should be back soon. Is it something I can help with?"

A thought stabbed Eleni hard. She'd broken the girl code. Had she really insinuated that Miranda had the hots for him? And Stefanos, too?

She winced.

"What is it?"

Something you will hate me for.

"I need to see him. Can you let me know when he's back?" she asked weakly, before going back to her office.

When her phone rang a short while later, she jumped, and when Miranda announced that Dominic had returned, her heart started beating faster.

"I told Dominic that you wanted to see him," said Miranda trying to be helpful.

Eleni's heart sank. She'd hoped to go for more of a surprise visit. Now Dominic would be expecting her. He would be ready, with a sarcastic comment or ten at the ready. She shoved her pride deep into her stomach and forced herself to go to him. She knocked on the door, inhaled a long, deep breath, prayed to God, and entered when ordered to. He was removing the cufflinks from his cuffs.

She had been a quivering mess before, and now she was worse as he rolled up his sleeves and flashed forearms she had the desire to lick. Worse than that, a flashback of him all in black suddenly appeared. She didn't dare to go any closer and stood so far from his desk she might as well have been in the middle of the room.

"Do I smell?" he asked. A touch of lightness in that usually stern voice.

Tentatively she inched a few steps forward. "I wanted to apologize about the other night." She started to wring her hands. Her nerves fluttery and ready to take off, make a quick getaway. The evil man was going to make her relive it.

"I wanted to say that ..." Her eyes clamped on his sinewy forearms, and she lost her trail of thought. "That ... uh..." He started to loosen his tie revealing a dusting of golden hairs and the floor turned unsteady beneath her.

"You wanted to say?" Beads of sweat lined Dominic's forehead, and against his tanned golden face his blue-green eyes blazed like jewels.

That was a very good question. What did she want to say?

Foreplay.

No. *Not that.*

Forearms.

Not that, either.

She'd accidentally swapped brain cells with Miranda. It had been a long time since any man had triggered this kind of reaction in her. She didn't understand it. She forced her mouth to work. "I was drunk."

"Is that what it was?" Those greeny-blues stared at her in amusement.

"I was having fun. It was my ...I was drunk." This was painful—like ripping her nails out with pliers. "I might have said something that ... I obviously didn't think through clearly ..."

"Like what?" Dominic placed his hand under his jaw and

looked at her as if she were entertainment. All that was missing was popcorn.

"Don't you remember?" There was hope. Maybe he hadn't heard; the music was loud and there was a lot of noise.

"What did you think you said?"

Maybe she'd been so drunk she'd fantasized and made the whole thing up. It wasn't impossible. Her mother lived vicariously through the daytime soap operas, and maybe Eleni's grief over Jonas had tipped her over the edge? So much had happened to her, it wasn't only the grief, but more recently, the weight of her father's words, a new job, a new city, the heat, and this celebratory weekend. Maybe she'd had a turn. "I met your girlfriend. Do you remember that?"

His mouth twitched. "Helen? She's real, she's definitely real. She was there."

"She's very pretty, and ..." *Stop right there.* Her brittle voice sounded cheap and tinny. Heat crept along her cheeks. She didn't know where to look. Or what he was thinking.

"I'll just ... go." She pointed at the door behind her, putting it down to a bout of heatstroke. She and Stefanos had sat out in the sun for a long time yesterday and it was possible.

She retreated towards the door.

"I appreciate you telling me how much black suited me."

She froze as her hand reached for the doorknob.

"And I don't dance. I have no sense of rhythm. I wouldn't have been able to keep up with you. Those were quite some moves you were making, up in the cages."

Her body stiffened, and she could feel his gaze scorching her back. "Can I go? *Please?*" She couldn't face him. Couldn't bring herself to turn around.

"Do you not have anything more to add?" His voice was low. Intimate. Only for her. As if he might have said this to her over a candlelit dinner.

There she went again. Fantasizing like a maniac. "Are you going to fire me?"

He laughed. "For what?"

"You're not going to fire me?"

"Again, for what?"

There was something different about him this morning. So different that she couldn't at all reconcile him with the man she had first met.

"Please may I be excused? And please can we not talk about this ever?" Her voice sounded tinny and timid, but her insides were glowing with heat.

"Eleni. I would rather not address your back." His voice sobered, an indirect order commanding her to turn around. She turned around slowly.

"It was your birthday. Happy belated birthday."

A simple nod from him told her she could leave.

CHAPTER FOURTEEN

DOMINIC

"Where's Linus? I can't get a hold of him."

Miranda gaped at him with a hapless expression and her cheeks flushed red. "I-I haven't seen him."

"That's not what I asked." Briefcase in hand, he was ready to go to today's meeting with Galatis which was at the Parthenon. "Get him for me," he ordered.

He glanced at his watch again. At this rate he'd have to go alone. He debated what to do as Miranda got on the phone and tried to locate Linus, but Dominic's impatience was wearing incredibly thin. He was a stickler for punctuality.

Then he saw Eleni near the water cooler. Their gazes met, and she looked away quickly. A smile tugged at his lips. He'd enjoyed making her feel uncomfortable when she'd come to apologize for her behavior.

Something stirred in his loins, but he managed to tamp it

down quickly. He could not go there. He swallowed, tightening his hand around the handle of his briefcase. "You'll do." It was most unusual that Linus wasn't here, but Eleni was.

She stared at him, her eyes landing on his lips as if she wasn't quite sure if he was speaking to her, or maybe she was lipreading. A line appeared between her slanted brows. "Are you ... are you talking to me?"

"Do you see me looking at anyone else?" Screw Linus. He would rather not take this woman, but he needed someone just in case, even though he hadn't needed to use Linus' translation services yet because Galatis was still playing around, showing him Greek relics and forcing him to visit all sorts of places.

He turned to Eleni. There was no time to waste. "This way. You're coming with me."

"But what? Where?"

"If Linus turns up tell him I went without him," he snapped at Miranda.

Behind him Eleni asked, "Shouldn't I get my bag or—"

"You don't need anything." He headed for the elevator and expected her to follow.

"But where are we going? You haven't said. Some notice would be good."

"Why? Do you have other meetings to attend?" he snarled, then immediately regretted taking out his anger on her. It wasn't her fault that he was going to the Parthenon, or that Linus was late, or that he couldn't quite shake that image of Eleni in that short dress dancing as if her life depended on it, in a cage suspended in the air.

Her heels clacked along the street as they walked towards the car. Perhaps he had made a mistake. Already the heady scene of her perfume, flowery and fresh, seeped into his skin.

If he wasn't careful, he would be in danger of doing something silly.

"I don't have meetings, but Isidora wanted me to do something for her."

He turned to her. "You are here to work for me, in my employ. I will ask of you what I want, and you will comply. Is that clear?"

Her eyes widened. "Perfectly clear."

His driver opened the door for him and he climbed in, leaving Eleni to totter over to the other side.

"Does that guy follow you everywhere?" she asked, as his bodyguard climbed into the passenger seat.

"He comes with the territory." He opened his briefcase and pulled out some paperwork. In the meetings so far he hadn't needed anything.

Sightseeing would be a more apt term for what Galatis had him doing. In fact, earplugs would have come in handy, because at least that way he could have blocked out the Greek's prideful commentary about his beloved Athens. As if Dominic gave two fucks about it being the oldest city in the world, or the birthplace of democracy. The motherland of western civilization.

So what?

Every time Dominic tried to steer the conversation towards business, Galatis would use his big fat hand to placate him. Then he'd tell Dominic that he needed to be patient, that good things came to those who waited.

The first time he'd met the guy had been at the Acropolis Museum which the officials had to close off to the public for an hour so that the two of them could meet there. Dominic considered this a stunt. Galatis didn't need to boast about his wealth or influence, but perhaps he felt a need to show the younger Steele. His father and Alexander usually dealt with this man, which was why Dominic was biding his time and letting him play his games. As they'd walked around the museum Galatis would boast and point out facts that had bored Dominic beyond comprehension.

The last meeting had been at the Acropolis, and today it was at the same place, the Acropolis, but, apparently, they were going to see the Parthenon which sat atop the hill. The old man couldn't walk for more than a minute without getting out of breath. No wonder these soul-sucking visits were taking forever.

"Here." He placed his briefcase on the space between them. "If I need you, I will call you."

"Where are you going?"

"To meet with him. He's fucking me around and twisting my balls."

Eleni's mouth gaped. "I don't understand."

"I have a meeting with Hector Galatis. Ever heard of him?"

She laughed out loud. "Who hasn't heard of him?" The man was a household name. Revered all over Greece for his many businesses and charmed life, for his rags-to-riches story that was an inspiration to many. Jonas had looked up to him.

"He's one of the biggest billionaires in Greece."

"Then you should like him, no?"

Dominic sneered. "I don't like him. He does my head in. He's a pretentious beast and he wastes my time."

"Isn't it rude of you to talk about a fellow billionaire like that?"

"I don't mean to be offensive to the Greek people. Just this asshole. This is the third meeting with him and we've not discussed an iota of business."

"But why did you bring me?"

He tapped the folder beside him. "You'll need to get that to me if I need it. I'll call you."

"Why don't you take it with you?"

"Because I have to play his game. He wants to waste my time, which is why he has me going to these places, traipsing around in the searing heat, looking at ... things." He glanced at her warily, knowing that he had to be careful about what he said around this Greek tourism ambassador. "If I turn up with my briefcase, he'll know I'm eager to talk business."

"Aren't you?"

"I don't want him to know that."

"Why not? Isn't that the point?"

He stared at her innocent face and those huge naïve doe-like eyes. "He can't see me as being weak."

She shook her head. "And you think taking your briefcase and being prepared is a sign that you're weak?"

"You don't understand the semantics of business, Eleni. It's like a card game where I can't show my hand and have to keep him guessing."

"It sounds like he's keeping you guessing."

She was astute, he had to give her that.

"He's an insanely rich man whose business could help us," he told her.

"Just like the man on the yacht that night."

A muscle pinched along his jaw and he wondered if she thought about that evening a lot, because it slipped out of her mouth quickly. "I wasn't cozying up to Ioannis."

"It's fine. You don't have to explain. You are the boss. I work for you, and I will do whatever you ask."

She was on fire this morning, throwing back his words. Nothing like the demure and embarrassed woman who'd come to his office earlier, apologizing for the night at the club.

The car came to a stop.

"Wait outside."

"In this heat?"

"This isn't a day trip for you. This is work. You need to be vigilant."

She looked at him with loathing in her eyes.

"Keep an eye on the briefcase."

"What's the lock combination?"

"One, one, one, one," he muttered, adjusting his tie and getting ready to climb out of the car.

"Not nine, nine, nine, nine?" she asked, getting out at the other side.

Up ahead he could see Galatis. Hard to miss him, with that huge belly, and the Panama hat. Beside him his bodyguard held out a large sunshade for him.

Dominic's gut hardened at the sight as he prepared himself for a wasted hour talking about culture.

Wait, what had she just said? "Nine, nine, nine, nine?" he echoed.

"I assumed you'd go for the bigger number."

Turning his back to her, he braced himself and headed for Galatis.

ELENI

E leni leaned against the car, then backed off it because the metal was so hot. The heat beat down on her.

This was work?

This was so new to her. This life in the city, away from her mom, and the island, and working in an office. She pictured Stefanos rushing around the taverna and missed their lunches and the little conversations they had between serving customers.

She walked over to the driver's side and knocked on his window. He opened the door instead.

"Aren't you hot in there?" she asked, noting that his face was red and sweaty.

"I am used to it."

"Why don't you turn the air conditioning on?"

"That would be a waste."

"It wouldn't," she cried. "You look so uncomfortable." Then, "I'm Eleni."

"I am Kostas."

"Come and stand out here," she suggested.

"It is as hot outside as it is in here."

"I don't know why you don't put the air conditioning on. I would."

He smiled and closed the door.

Hot and bothered, she looked at her watch to see that not even five minutes had passed. She was going to get uncomfortable standing around like this in the heat. Putting her hand to her eyes, shielding them from the sunlight, she looked up and tried to see what was going on.

From this distance she couldn't make out much because Dominic was now further away. Both sets of bodyguards hovered behind the men, another reminder of how surreal her new life was.

To kill time she ambled around, never straying too far from the car, and always looking over at Dominic and the old man in case she was being summoned. The idea of Dominic having to be at someone's beck and call amused her.

Then, to her surprise, she saw Dominic coming towards her.

That had been quick. Not even twenty minutes. Was this

really what Linus did? She felt sorry for him and this sorry excuse of a job he had. She couldn't imagine traipsing around after Dominic again.

"Your face is red," he remarked and got into the car.

She climbed in. "That was fast." Inside the cool air-conditioned car, her body temperature started to regulate again. Dominic's blue-green eyes pierced through her. He'd tanned a little even in that short of a time span, and he was now a pinky-golden shade. Something in her heart somersaulted. Maybe a beat missed, an army of goosebumps stood to attention under the sleeves of her shirt.

"Galatis was hot. He asked to reschedule."

"Why not have the meeting in an office?" she asked.

"Why not indeed?"

"You must be annoyed." She noted the tightness around his lips.

"What do you think?" His eyes seemed to linger at her hair. "You put your hair up."

"It was hot."

He whipped out his cell phone and began tapping away, ignoring her abruptly. She looked out of the window, glad to have cool air of the air conditioning on her skin.

"So, *that's* Hector Galatis?" she asked. "He doesn't look anything like how I thought he would."

"That's the one." Dominic slowly dragged his gaze away from his cell phone. "How did you expect him to look."

"Powerful."

"And how does he look?"

"Old and in bad health."

"He's not in the best shape," Dominic agreed.

"*He's* the one you called the big, fat crazy Greek?" No respect even for someone as successful as Hector.

"Are you going to hold it against me forever? I wasn't being offensive to your people."

She searched his eyes, so intense in their blues and greens mixing with starburst of gold. "He irritates you."

"I need the deal. I wish we could conduct business around a table, in an air-conditioned office."

"Why doesn't he?"

"Because he doesn't want to make it easy for me. He wants me to run around like a dog every time he throws a bone."

"He's testing you."

"He's making things difficult. I need to make this deal and I don't have much time."

"You sound desperate."

His Adam's apple bobbed. "I have to prove to my father that I can do this."

"He doesn't think you can?"

"He's waiting to send my brother out, to clean up, and finish the deal, but I keep assuring him I'm taking care of it."

"He doesn't believe in you?"

"It would appear not."

How odd that they both seemed to be afflicted with something similar. "That's weird."

"What's weird?"

"That we have something in common." Who would have thought she'd ever say that to someone like Dominic Steele? She slipped back against the seat, letting the soft leather cushion her back. She'd already kicked off her stilettoes, and revelled in the cool air, the soft seat. If this work, she could happily do this and get paid for it.

"What's that?" Dominic asked.

She opened her eyes and stared at the headrest in front of her. "My father didn't really believe in me, either."

"Didn't?"

"Hmmm." She looked out, saw the sea as the car sped by, saw a boat and a paraglider floating in the sky. She didn't want to elaborate and wondered what had possessed her to say what she had.

A low, apologetic sound came from Dominic. "I'm sorry."

CHAPTER FIFTEEN

DOMINIC

Dominic strode past Linus who was talking to Miranda at her desk.

He went into his office and dropped his briefcase to the floor, irritation crawling up his spine. He was tired and hot and bothered.

Linus traipsed in after him. "You saw Galatis without me?"

"You weren't here." Linus's self-importance mingled with a hint of his desperation, and pissed Dominic off more than the heat and Galatis' conduct had. Stripping off his shirt, he reached for a clean one and slipped it on.

"I'm sorry, but my wife is seven months pregnant and my two-year-old was sick with the vomiting bug. I had to stay and look after them."

"It's fine." Dominic did his buttons up and sat down, then

turned the table fan on. The AC here was dire, and he could feel heat starting to creep along his skin.

"It's not fine. I will not let you down again."

He tapped his keyboard and waited for his computer screen to come back to life. A ton of new emails stared back at him. Dominic's eye caught on a slew of them from his father. These were urgent and he needed to tend to them now.

He had a conference call with his father later on. What he didn't need was Linus hovering around asking him a million and one questions. "Don't worry about it."

"The little one threw up all over me before I could call to let you—"

"I said it's not a problem." Either Linus was tone deaf and stupid or he was even more desperate than ever to please Dominic. "Why are you still here?"

"You took the new girl?" The man didn't even bother to hide the condescending tone in his voice.

"Yes."

Linus looked hurt. His eyes going from side to side as he tried to process this. "My mother will come and stay with me. This won't happen again."

His mother coming to stay with him? Jesus. "Such drastic action is not needed."

Linus held up his hands in a placating manner. "It's okay. You are a busy man, Dominic, an important man, and I am available at your disposal."

"There's no need to flatter me. Please stop."

"I'm sorry."

Dominic wished the man would leave. They were done talking.

"You won't have to take that girl with you again," said Linus, never one to get the hint.

"Her name is Eleni, and I will do as I want."

"Of course, Dominic." Linus agreed, a little too quickly.

"I'm busy. Is there anything else?" He prayed not. Linus shook his head. "Then close the door behind you."

Dominic sat back, contemplating the non-event with Galatis. The man had wasted his goddamn time. Talked about his newest grandchild, born yesterday. Had showed him photos of the baby on his phone. Dominic had remained calm, even in the face of such absurdity. Such blatant misuse of his time. It had been short, that had been the good part, but they hadn't discussed business at all, and then the old man had said he was too hot to think. When Dominic had tried to bring up business matters, Galatis had chided him and told him he was too desperate.

It made him wonder if he had sounded like Linus had just now.

He grew pensive, thinking about Eleni. The journey had been less troublesome. Quieter. She wasn't as annoying as Linus who spoke too much and tried to ingratiate himself with Dominic. Eleni talked, but her conversation he could handle. Found himself interested in it.

He had half a mind to take her along with him on the other meetings. It would make a change for her, and it would be better for him.

Linus could cause problems. But Dominic was the boss. He shouldn't have to worry about these things.

Then why was he?

His cell phone rang and the name on the caller ID sent a chill through him. He was tempted not to take it. But he did.

"Dominic." His father's commanding, baritone voice came down the line. "What's the hold up with Galatis?"

Dominic feigned surprise. "Hold up?" His father had a negative way of looking at things, at least it seemed like that to him. "There's no hold up. He's just ... putting me through my paces like you said he would."

His father coughed. "I didn't expect it to take forever."

Neither did I.

"He has me meeting him in all sorts of places," Dominic explained.

"Humor him. Hector is nothing if not trying. He wants you to work for the honor of doing business with him."

"I am working on it."

"I'm expecting good things, Dominic. This deal is a given."

"I heard you the first time, Dad. You don't have to keep repeating yourself." His father could be a patronizing man. Dominic counted to five and breathed in slowly. His father's words and tone and everything about him always riled him up.

He got up, paced around his office, looked out onto the traffic spilling onto the busy streets. Beyond it, much farther in the distance, he could see the sea.

He hated this wild goose chase with Galatis. But more than that he hated the pressure of his father's judgment hanging over his head like the sword of Damocles.

ELENI

She couldn't contain herself.

As she headed out of the office, home, she took her paycheck stub out of her bag and opened it, curious to know how much money she had received from her first office job.

She worked hard at the cafe and the money was good, but

the office work was much easier in comparison, and she was excited to see in writing what Dominic had promised her.

She opened the enveloped and unfolded the white rectangular sheet of paper. The air sucked right out of her lungs. She staggered back a few steps.

It could not be.

They'd made a mistake—the HR department or whoever was responsible for this.

Dominic had quoted her a different figure when they'd discussed it.

This was nearly double what he'd told her.

It couldn't be right.

She blinked a few times, but the number was still there.

The largest number she had ever seen on a paystub that belonged to her.

This was ... more money than she could have hoped for. More money than she'd dreamed about.

At this rate, she'd be able to go on her expedition in two months' time.

She put the slip away. The smile slipping from her face.

Obviously, there had been a mistake.

The next morning, she looked around the office, at Agnes and Isidora, and opened her mouth to say something. But a feeling in the base of her stomach told her this wasn't the way to go about it.

She walked towards Dominic's office, Miranda raising her eyebrows as Eleni sailed past, oozing confidence she didn't feel in the pit of her queasy stomach.

She knocked, then entered when she had been given permission to do so.

Dominic surveyed her as if she'd walked in clutching a hand grenade. They eyed one another warily. It wasn't that she was scared of him, she was just really taken aback by the steely look on his face. "This better be important. I'm about to make a call."

"I'm getting paid too much." She thrust out her paystub, then slapped it down on his desk.

He looked at it, then looked up at her, his face perplexed with confusion. "And?"

"And?" she cried. "I've been overpaid. There's obviously been a mistake."

She waited for him to pick up the flimsy sheet of paper and examine it, then tell her 'Yes, so there has.' And then tell her what the real figure should be. That's what she needed to know, the real figure.

He didn't. He didn't even touch it.

"No mistake." He was calm. Quiet.

She scoffed at the joke and waited for him to drop the punchline. This man could be cruel and vicious. She'd had first-hand experience. Once.

"What do you mean?

"There's no mistake." He stared at her for the longest time, and she wondered if he was daring her to blink, to play that childish game she had played with her friends back at school.

She blinked because her eyes were starting to water.

"Are you complaining that you're getting paid too much?" He sat back in his chair, tapped a pen against the table and appraised her as if she was a specimen from the zoo. "Your honesty is commendable."

"I want you to fix it. I don't want to have money that's not mine in my bank account. It's there. All of it, in my account. I checked last night, and this morning, and it's still there. It's making me nervous."

"You're not listening to me." The corner of his lip lifted,

and raised a hand to his face, his index finger lying across his upper lip while his fingers covered his mouth.

"Are you ... are you laughing at me?" Maybe it would have been better to have not said anything at all.

Immediately, as if he'd been called out, he adjusted himself, and splayed both hands on the table. "It's rare to have an employee complain they were being paid too much, Eleni. You have not been overpaid. This is what I am paying you."

"But ..." This was shocking. Her mother would be shocked. Happy shocked, and Stefanos, he'd want a job here. If she worked here for more than the summer, for a year—she did the mental math quickly—she would be ... richer than she had ever been.

It was life changing. A drop in the big blue ocean to someone like Dominic, but for her, the difference between working to get by, and working and enjoying life.

"But what?" He frowned, lines appearing like magic on his forehead. "You must never undervalue what you are worth. This is the going rate for the job you do, and therefore this is what you get."

"But when we spoke you told me it would be less."

"Well, it's this, now."

"There's no mistake?"

"There's no mistake."

The scream she wanted to let out would have to wait until she got into her hotel room. This. Was. Amazing.

This was something good.

It meant so many things.

She was smiling and she didn't even realize it until she looked at Dominic and he was smiling too.

"Thank you."

"Never underestimate your worth, Eleni."

CHAPTER SIXTEEN

ELENI

Miranda waved at her, beckoning her over from the water cooler.

"You get to go with him again."

"Who? Where?"

"Dominic. He's got another meeting with Galatis and Linus is off sick. His entire family has caught a bug."

Go with Dominic, again? Eleni's insides churned at the prospect of being in close proximity to Dominic again. Just him and her. It was the being stuck out in the heat, she told herself, and waiting on a grumpy Dominic to finish a meeting with the evasive Hector Galatis, *that's* what she was dreading the most. Nothing to do with the way her skin tingled because he was mere inches from her. Or the way his eyes sometimes locked on hers a little longer. "Lucky me."

Miranda looked visibly shocked. "Don't say that. You *are* lucky. What I wouldn't do to have that chance."

Eleni felt sorry for Miranda, and briefly considered getting her to meet Angeliki who would most definitely get her thinking that there were other men available on the planet.

Who was she kidding? Miranda had to be protected from the likes of Angeliki at all times.

"Oh, Miranda. I wish I could do something for you."

Miranda looked at her oddly. "Lunch would be good."

"Sorry." How long ago had they talked about it? Between the two of them they hadn't yet been able to come up with a time and day to suit them both. Not that it mattered because Eleni often passed by Miranda's desk and they managed to catch up many times during the day. So much so that Eleni was beginning to enjoy office life now that she wasn't so alone. "Let's go on Friday. I found this place that does the best dolmadakia."

Dominic appeared just then, creeping out from behind the shadows of the corner, sheet of paper in hand, and the two of them stared at him. But Dominic's gaze settled on Eleni. Miranda might as well have been invisible.

"Can you send these off?" He placed a pile of papers in front of Miranda, who promptly blushed. Without another word to Miranda, he marched off back to his office, leaving Eleni fuming at the manner in which he'd spoken to his PA. But since when had the view of his back caused goosebumps to spring up all over her skin?

He had such an awesome butt. Tight, hard, firm. She could tell just by looking. Her thoughts screeched to a halt when she turned to find Miranda's eyes focused on the computer screen, concentration lining her brow as her fingers flew across the keyboard.

No more. This would have to stop. Eleni headed for Dominic's office, and because his door was half open, she marched right in. He was sitting at his desk, not looking the slightest bit surprised to see her. He raised an eyebrow.

"Please." She folded her arms.

"What?"

"Please."

"Please what?" he growled.

"'Please', it's a word and you might want to use it, occasionally."

"What? Why?"

"Not 'what' or 'why,' but 'Please.' It would be nice for Miranda to hear that word from you when you ask her to do things for you."

He sat back, steepling his hands then resting the index fingers on his chin as if he were thinking. "And you're telling me this, because?"

"You don't speak to her nicely."

"I'm not rude to her."

"You're rude to everyone."

"Am I rude to you?" he asked.

"No, maybe, you were at first." She didn't know why his question stopped her. She couldn't let him derail her. "Miranda would walk on hot coals if you asked her to."

"I would never ask such a thing of her. Can you imagine the court case and the headlines?"

"Is that what you always worry about? Money and your reputation?" She didn't like the way he had casually dismissed Miranda's feelings.

"I'm being serious, *Dom*."

There it was again. The little muscle ticked along his jawline. He started to type something on his keyboard.

She understood.

He had dismissed her, not that she wanted to spend a

moment longer here. Spinning on her heels, she marched towards the door.

"Noted," he said.

She paused, releasing a breath as she turned around.

"I'll try to be better next time." He was still typing away, staring at his computer screen, as if he couldn't bring himself to look at her.

"Good." At least he had taken her advice. Dominic Steele was going to listen to her and become a better human being. She couldn't help but smile as she got ready to leave.

"It's just that ..." He sounded nervous. This was new.

"What?"

"I knew, even before you confirmed it," he said, dragging his gaze to her.

She closed her eyes for a few seconds longer than usual, hating that she'd drunkenly told on her friend, even though he'd already known Miranda had a crush on him.

"I know she'd walk on coals for me. It makes me uncomfortable."

"Is that why you're rude to her?"

"I don't aim to be. More that I keep my interactions with her short and to the point."

"A 'please' and a 'thank you' wouldn't go amiss."

"Noted."

She turned to leave, again.

"Also, I need you to come with me again. Tomorrow. Linus has called in sick, so—"

"*I'll do*, you mean?"

"Pardon me?"

"You said last time that 'I'd do' like I was cement filler or something."

A smile tugged at his lips. "I can assure you that you're nothing like cement filler."

"That's good to know."

"We're going to The Odeon of Herodes Atticus."

"So much Greek culture and heritage to take in. It can't be easy for you."

"I don't hate going to these places, if I were on a sightseeing trip or something. You understand that, don't you?"

"Does it matter what I think?"

He lifted his chin up, looked at her as if he didn't know what to make of her. And all she could see was the way his shirt strained around his biceps.

"Meetings with Galatis make me lose the will to live."

"We wouldn't want that to happen. One less billionaire in the world, that would be so tragic."

He was trying so hard not to smile.

DOMINIC

He heard her voice before her saw her. Eleni was talking to Miranda about food.

"I'm ready," she announced as soon as she saw him. She had her hair up again, and her sleeveless white blouse and pale yellow pencil skirt made him do a double take. He had to drag his eyes away. He nodded, acknowledging her and was about to head towards the elevator when he remembered. "Good morning," he said to Miranda, and looked away as soon as her cheeks turned pink.

"That was nice of you," Eleni said to him in the elevator.

With the three of them inside it, and his bodyguard taking up more than a third of the space, they were a little tight in the tiny space. So tight that once again her flowery scent was impossible to ignore.

That scent would stay with him all day.

"Does he follow you everywhere?" she asked, when they got out and Sven was a good distance behind them.

"Pretty much."

"Even to the toilet?"

He stared at her, raising an eyebrow. "What do you think?"

"I'm being serious. What if someone gunned you down in the toilet?"

"Gunned me down?" Dominic climbed into the Merc and waited for Eleni to get in. "Not a knife or a crossbow?" He got out his cell phone and started typing away.

"I imagine assassins would have guns with silencers, especially for someone of your importance and caliber."

"You're beginning to worry me." He rushed to type an email reply to Helen.

"I'm trying to have a conversation, Dominic. Sorry for boring you."

"You're discussing my death. You sound rather obsessed about it."

"You're not a morning person, are you?" she asked, when no more than a minute's worth of silence had passed.

"I'm not one for chattering incessantly."

"Incessantly?"

"It means all the time."

"I know what it means. English might not be my first language, but we were taught it well in school. My English is probably much better than your Greek."

He huffed out a loud breath. "I suppose it is."

"But do you see what a difference it makes, saying 'Good morning'? You must have made Miranda's day."

"Because that's what I exist for," he muttered.

"There's no harm in being nice. It doesn't cost you anything. Those dollars," she air quoted the dollars, "that you worry so much about, you didn't have to spend any."

"Why are you so talkative this morning?"

As far as he could see, she wasn't wearing any mascara, but her lashes were ridiculously long. Her eyes ridiculously soft. She'd put her hair up again, and his gaze drifted to her ridiculously long neck.

She was stunning to look at it, and he had to force himself to bring his attention back to his laptop. He clicked on the next email and tried to concentrate on its contents.

"You'd like me to be quiet." She smoothed down her skirt. "I can be quiet." She pulled out her cell phone and started tapping on the screen.

In due course they arrived at the The Odeon of Herodes Atticus.

She started to open the car door to get out.

"You can wait in here."

She stared at him as if he'd told her to fly to the moon. "In here?"

"That's right."

"But I came prepared." She pulled out something from her bag and held it up.

A bottle of sunscreen. "And I'm wearing a thin blouse and I have flat shoes." He chose to ignore her. Not least because the white blouse she wore was a little too thin, and he could see the outline of the cami she wore underneath. Maybe it was meant to be that style. Sheer seduction. She'd paired it with a pale yellow skirt and flat nude colored pumps.

He shook his head, wanting to dislodge his thoughts, the errant thought gone as he tried to focus his attention on unbuttoning his shirt cuffs. He started to roll them up slowly, already tensing at the thought of traipsing after Galatis in the heat. At least it was morning, which was some respite. He wouldn't have to suffer the sharp, scorching heat of the noon hours.

"Stay in the car," he told her.

"You really don't want to give me cancer." Her smile was so wide, as if he'd given her another pay raise.

"I'll call you if I need anything."

"But you don't have my number."

"I do. I asked Miranda for it."

ELENI

Eleni sat inside the car and read her texts and email messages. This was work? It was bliss.

She didn't even need to keep looking out of the window to see if Dominic might be on the brink of summoning her. Not now that he had her phone number.

She didn't know how she felt about that, him having her number. It was something personal. Surely he should have asked her for it first?

Slipping off her shoes, she wriggled her toes, thinking how blissful this was, that *this* was now her work; sitting in a car with nothing to do. No rushing around like she did at the taverna, juggling customers' orders and making sure the right food ended up at the right table in time.

Plugging in her earbuds, she selected her favorite music on her phone, and closed her eyes.

Not more than fifteen minutes had passed when Dominic returned, his face like thunder.

"That was quick." She hastily removed her earbuds.

"That was a complete waste of my time," he muttered under his breath. "I don't know why I put up with this shit."

Dominic didn't swear a lot. "What happened?"

"Nothing happened. That's what happened." He loosened his tie and motioned for the driver to go.

"Why do you put up with it? With Galatis disrespecting you the way he does?"

Dominic looked out of the window, his jaw muscles tight enough for Eleni to notice. "Because I need the deal. I have to prove myself."

"I know that, Dominic, but *what* happened?"

"Galatis had something come up. Something more urgent."

"Ah."

"Ah what?" he snapped.

"You're angry because he didn't drop everything for you. Because he had someone else more important than you."

"I'm angry because he wasted my time."

"You're angry because there's someone more important than you."

"I don't know what you take me for, or what you think you know about me, but I can assure you, I have no illusions about my importance. I have my father to thank for that. He constantly drilled that into me that I was never as good as my brother. Alexander is his pride and joy. Galatis wasted my time."

She shifted slightly away and closer to the door, not wanting to be at close range for the waves of anger coming off of him. She wasn't sure how much of the chill in the car was due to the AC and how much was due to Dominic's mood but the temperature had dropped to freezing.

"Dinner," he said finally.

She slowly turned her head in his direction. "Are you

talking to me?" She couldn't tell if he was on the phone, if he might have a cell phone strapped to his other hand.

"Yes I'm talking to you. Who else?"

His harsh tone landed like a slap. An awakening she badly needed. She needed to wisen up and to stop acting as if Dominic Steele was an average guy. He wasn't. He was a very rich man who had important things to do and a man who cared nothing for no one.

"Dinner?" she asked, needing to make sure she'd heard him right.

"Are you free? Tonight. At seven? Galatis is having a soiree and he's asked me to meet with him then."

"And you want *me* to come with *you*?"

"I need you."

She was too speechless to reply. Something fluttered in her heart.

"As a deterrent," he added, as an afterthought.

"A deterrent?" Yes, of course. This was business. He needed... a deterrent?

"It helps me and it looks better," he explained, not making any sense at all.

"Looks better? To whom? For what reason?"

"Don't worry. You're not ..." He waved his big hand between them both, and all she could see was the huge watch, so big, she could hardly *not* see it. "You're not expected to ... we're not together. This is ... it's ... just better for me to..."

"You're stammering, Dominic. I've never heard you stammer before." She blurted the words out because she was so surprised.

"It's better for me to be seen with someone at a social event."

"Why a 'deterrent?'"

"To ward off ... you know ..."

"I don't know." She could feel the wrinkles bunching up on her forehead. "Ward off? You mean keep away?"

"Exactly that."

"What are you hoping to keep away?"

"Other women. Even the married ones have no shame. A woman on my arm is a deterrent."

She sat back. It made perfect sense. Why not. Her heart had sunk a little, and she didn't know why.

They returned to the office and she had her lunch at her desk, hoping to catch up with the work she had missed. But at the same time, she was trying to wrap her head around the idea of going to dinner with Dominic Steele as his deterrent.

She managed to get through the rest of the workday just fine, and then she rushed home.

Dominic had told her he'd come to pick her up in the car and to be ready by 7pm.

Luckily she'd brought a few of her nice dresses with her, when she hadn't been sure what she'd wear for her twenty-first celebrations.

She opted for a black dress, nothing like the short and off the shoulder number that she'd worn on her birthday, but something more sophisticated, in the vein of an Audrey Hepburn outfit.

She slowly got ready, curling her hair into waves. With her heels, and clutch bag, and her hair swept to one side over her shoulder, she looked elegant and understated, not too over the top. The look was perfect. She wouldn't be out of place as Dominic's fake plus one and now found herself looking forward to the evening.

Dominic's explanation for inviting her made her feel safe. She didn't get any creep vibes off him, never had, otherwise she would not have taken this job. She'd met many men, had suffered their rude innuendos and glances, to know that when a man showed an interest in her, it was because he wanted something.

Not so with Dominic.

If anything, he'd always been good to her, which was why his treatment of Miranda had rubbed her the wrong way.

Dominic was too wrapped up in the big deal he was pursuing and nothing else mattered.

Besides, he had a girlfriend.

Why hadn't she asked him about her?

Tonight was going to be a business arrangement, and she would get to see the house of the great Hector Galatis. She would get to see how the rich lived. This was exciting, stepping into a different world, and it beat staying in her hotel room eating a takeout alone.

She was using the curling irons to twirl a wayward lock of hair into place when her phone rang. It was Dominic. In a panic she looked at the time, then breathed easy, because she still had half an hour to go.

"Eleni?" He sounded meek, unlike himself.

"I'm getting ready, won't be long."

"I meant to call you earlier, but I got tied up in a conference call. I won't need you to come tonight after all."

"You won't?" Her voice sounded sad, pathetic. Disappointed.

"Helen's back and it's probably better that I take her."

Too much information. She managed to pull her senses together. "Oh, that's okay, I was about to start getting ready."

Her heart sank. She stared at her reflection in the mirror, all dressed up and with nowhere to go.

He didn't need her, because he'd found someone better.

CHAPTER SEVENTEEN

DOMINIC

The dinner with Galatis and a few other business associates was bearable.

Of course, they hadn't had time to discuss the particular deal that Dominic was after, but at least it had given him time to catch up with Helen while they were shown around Galati's impressive multi-million-dollar home.

Helen had returned from her meeting in Aegina earlier than expected, which was why, when they'd spoken earlier in the day and he'd mentioned the dinner with Galatis, she'd offered to come, even though he hadn't asked her. She said she needed to run something by Galatis, and because it made sense, he'd agreed.

But it still niggled him that he'd had to turn Eleni down at the last minute. It had been far easier to cancel on Eleni, than to explain to Helen that he was bringing a young and relatively new employee with him.

It had been a lousy thing to do to Eleni and were it not for the call from his father that he'd had to absolutely take, he would have called her much earlier.

But he wasn't prepared for the cold shoulder at work the next day. Feeling bad, a sensation new to him, he wandered into the office she shared with the two ogres, a place he hardly ever ventured into, but as soon as he appeared, the two women inside were all smiles. Eleni glanced up, nodded at him and then went back to her work.

He opened his mouth to ask her something then became aware of the women staring at him, waiting and watching. Eleni kept her head down, a steely determination in her posture.

She didn't want to talk to him.

He thought better of it and marched back out.

ELENI

E leni was still stinging with the pain of humiliation at being left behind, being replaced by the elegant Helen, when Dominic entered the office.

The sight of him, looking subdued, wearing a sheepish expression instead of his usual hard-set expression unnerved her.

She wasn't used to seeing him look so ... meek.

Agnes and Isidora greeted him with an enthusiasm she had never before seen in them. But he wasn't looking at them. He was staring at her as if he had something to say, but she wasn't interested in listening.

She didn't even look at him much, and when he

unexpectedly left in the same silent manner in which he'd turned up, she released a long breath.

It shouldn't have felt like a let-down, but it did. It shouldn't have hurt, but it did. It shouldn't have meant anything, but it did.

It was nothing to do with Dominic, and everything to do with where she was at in her life right now.

Almost a year and a half after Jonas' accident and she was still trying to move on. Mount Kilimanjaro was a milestone she felt she needed to reach, but lately, a sliver of guilt had started to seep into her soul. Was it what she really wanted?

Being in Athens was helping to sever the ties to Spetses and her first love. With so much going and adjustments to be made, new ideas and possibilities were filtering through her walled-up defenses.

Dominic, for one, had crept into her thoughts, unwelcome and unexpected.

Dominic calling her to say he was taking Helen instead, had hurt. But it shouldn't have.

She toyed around with flimsy explanations as to the reason why. Maybe it reinforced the idea that she didn't matter; a message which her parents, individually, had imbued her with.

Maybe there was another reason. But she dared not dwell on those thoughts, because it didn't matter that Dominic was nice to her, and that he was being polite to Miranda because of her intervention. It didn't matter that he'd given her an opportunity to change her life, to reach a goal he had no idea about. It didn't matter that he was the type of man she had previously detested.

Dominic had every right to go to the dinner with his girlfriend. It was nice that he had someone.

With a start and a jolt, she realized that *that's* what needled her.

She didn't see much of him for the next few days. Linus returned to work. She'd seen him in the hallway once, and he'd given her an unfriendly smile which she'd tossed right back at him.

Linus returning meant that she would no longer be required to accompany Dominic to his business meetings.

All she needed to do was keep her head down and work. She had to because he was paying her handsomely for it.

"D ominic would like to see you." Miranda's voice was breathless, as if he'd asked to see Miranda instead of her.

"Me?"

"Yes, you."

Eleni hung up, feeling uptight and wary. She marched into his office; head held high. "You wanted to see me?" It had been two days since she'd seen him, since he'd appeared in her office and abruptly disappeared again.

"I have a meeting with Galatis and I'd like you to come with me."

"But Linus is back—"

"I don't want Linus. I'm asking you."

"Is Helen not available?" she asked calmly, even though she was riddled with a category five level of anger.

Dominic's brow furrowed, and he stared at her for the longest time, rather like she imagined he might when Galatis reeled off another fact about the Acropolis of Athens, or the Delphi instead of discussing his beloved deal.

She was afraid that she'd crossed the line and stepped

accidentally into his private life. Immediately she regretted asking him. "I mean, sure. I can come." Her hands turned all fidgety and she pulled her index fingers, first one hand, then the other. "You're the boss. I can come. After all, I work for you, in your employ and you can ask of me what you want, and I will comply."

He watched her silently, while she rambled on like a blubbering fool, repeating the words he'd said to her.

Say something, she wanted to scream, when he was still silent. His inaction unnerved her, and the butterflies in her belly—more like wild bats—didn't help. She was not used to this. This ... this falling to pieces and losing control of her thoughts and her feelings.

"It's an early start tomorrow."

"How early?" It was happening.

"I have to meet with the crazy old Galatis at seven, at some goddamn..." He squinted at his computer screen. "... Temple of...hef—and—esst-aa-ee—stus".

Her lips pressed together. It was commonplace, tourists not being able to pronounce many Greek names, but Dominic, when he did it, it made her especially mad. Gathering her composure with all the might she could summon, "You mean the Temple of Hephaestus. It's pronounced ha-faz-stus."

"And *that's* the reason I'm taking you with me."

"Can you say it, properly? Could you try?"

He seemed surprised. "You want me to ... say it?"

"It's a Greek temple. It wouldn't kill you to get the name right."

His eyes moved from her mouth to her eyes. She could see he was finding it difficult. "Ha-faz-stus," he said, slowly.

She blinked. "You know where I live?" He looked at her silently. Almost guiltily. "Of course you know where I live. I'll be ready." She almost turned on her heel and left but she couldn't help herself. "If you change your mind and decide to take Helen, please let me know earlier, so that I can go back to bed."

And then she turned and left, her face heated.

"Your stationery order is here," said Miranda, stopping Eleni in her tracks.

"What?" A pulsating between her legs had thrown her mind into disarray. She stopped. Miranda was shoving a small package in her hands.

"Thanks," she said, absent-mindedly.

"What happened in there?" Miranda whispered, her neck craning as she peered closer.

That man. This hadn't happened in a while, not since the time when she'd first set eyes on Jonas. He was so handsome, dark hair, dark eyes, olive skin, and the heart of an angel. He'd been her everything. He'd loved her from the get-go.

And now ...

Now she wasn't thinking of him so much. Tears welled up in her eyes.

"Eleni." Miranda rose in her chair, her eyes growing large with worry. Eleni shook her head, not wanting to talk about it. That bossy, miserable, mercurial man in there, a man she could not read nor understand, he made her *feel* things. Made her experience emotions she'd kept suppressed for a long time. He was to blame for the way her heart was flapping, like the wings of a frantic bird.

All he'd done was ask her to accompany him again, but he'd said nothing about the dinner where he'd stood her up. The one he'd ditched her in favor of taking Helen.

"Can we go to lunch today?" she asked, desperately needing some good female company.

CHAPTER EIGHTEEN

ELENI

As soon as Dominic called her Eleni grabbed her bag and left her room, flying down the stairs. She'd been ready way before time, not wanting to give him a reason to be angry or late.

She climbed into the sleek black Merc, and her nostrils filled with the scent of musk and maleness.

"You managed to wake up early, then?"

"Just about." She'd been up for two hours, hadn't slept well and had woken up at the crack of dawn. A glance in the mirror and she'd been shocked to see how tired she looked.

He made a sound, then got back to looking through his paperwork.

It became so unbearably quiet that she seriously considered taking her headphones out of her bag and listening to music. Dare she do it—sitting in such close proximity to her boss? A man so wealthy and so important, that doing so, ignoring him, would be like giving him the middle finger.

Yes, she would.

She dipped her hand into her bag and fished around for the small pouch containing her ear pods when Dominic spoke up. "I'm sorry about the other night, about letting you down at the last moment."

He'd surprised her, not only by what he'd said, but that he'd mentioned it at all. She didn't know what to say. He must have mistaken this for an acceptance of his apology, because he continued. "I should have called you sooner. You weren't dressed, I hope?"

She tried to remember what she'd told him. Putting on a brave voice, she lied. "I was about to start getting ready. It was a good thing you called when you did."

"Helen ... she's my lawyer," he said, his face pensive, his hand on the car door, which he hadn't yet opened. He stared at his trousers, then turned and looked at her. "It made sense for her to be there."

She was startled to hear him explain. "You don't owe me an explanation. You don't have to apologize."

"But I am."

She wasn't sure why he was telling her this, and she had no idea why her heart was beating faster.

He hadn't said girlfriend, he'd said she was his lawyer. Just a lawyer and nothing else.

Thankfully Dominic left the car before she could say anything, and she was left in the awkward silence. She was glad that there was a window between them and Kostas, and that he couldn't hear anything.

Settling back in her seat, she felt lighter, as if a great weight had been lifted from her chest. No idea why. She didn't allow herself to get too comfortable, because she expected today's meeting to be over as quickly as the last one had, which meant Dominic would be as moody and as miserable as ever.

She braced herself.

DOMINIC

D ominic slipped on his aviators and trudged towards Galatis, wondering why he was at another Greek temple. Again.

On the bright side, he'd left Linus out of the loop, even though he'd returned to the office. This was not a bad thing. It was easier to have Eleni with him. She was low maintenance. She talked a lot, but she didn't ask a million silly questions. She didn't suck up to him.

She intrigued him, whereas Linus was a constant thorn in his side and now that he'd brought Eleni along with him, he had no intention of asking Linus to accompany him ever again.

"Hector." Dominic held out his hand which Galatis shook. His bodyguard stood behind him with a sun umbrella sheltering his boss' whale-like body from the sun. His own bodyguard was a good distance away, just how Dominic preferred it.

Being early morning, the sun wasn't in full force yet. Dominic felt reassured that he would be fine, for a while. He wouldn't burn to a crisp just yet on account of having no umbrella to shield him.

The old man adjusted his glasses and motioned for Dominic to follow him.

"Are we sightseeing again, Hector?" he asked, goodnaturedly.

The old man laughed, the rumble deep in his chest. "But of course."

Dominic attempted a laugh and struggled. He had to slow down his steps so that the old man could keep up. "I'm only here for the summer. How about we discuss the terms of the deal?"

"Did you know that the Temple of Hephaestus is the best-preserved Greek temple in the world?"

"That's ... remarkable," Dominic answered slowly, as he reached deep within him to pull out an ounce of enthusiasm.

"And did you know that Hephaestus was born to Hera by parthenogenesis?"

"I had no idea." He had no idea what parthenogenesis was either, and he didn't really care.

Galatis continued, unperturbed. "She was so horrified to find her son lame and crippled that she threw him off Mt. Olympus. And that's when Hephaestus later took revenge by entrapping her and making her a prisoner."

For the love of Christ. Dominic swiped and shaking hand through his hair and adjusted his aviators. "That sounds ... tragic... all round. It ... it really does."

"Family is important, Dominic."

This was not the natural leap in conversation that Dominic was expecting. He wasn't sure how to respond, so he didn't.

"Tell me something, Dominic, your father, he is passing the torch to Alexander already?"

"My father isn't stepping down yet, and Alexander isn't taking over, neither am I."

If the old man had meant to ruffle Dominic's feathers, he had.

Dominic hated comparison to his brother. He straightened his spine, as if standing taller might give him an edge of superiority he felt he needed. "The Steele Corporation is booming, Hector. You don't need to worry about who is taking over or not. However, we welcome the opportunity of working together with Galatis Industries."

"All in good time, Dominic."

Dominic allowed himself to blink slowly. "While I love this scenic tour of Athens, it would be good if we could sit down and iron out a deal that works for us both."

Galatis waggled a finger at him. "That is the problem with you, Dominic. Always so serious, always in a rush, always needing to move from one deal to the next. Some things need careful thought."

Galatis stood beside him and stared at the temple, a loud appreciative sound coming from his throat. "Hephaestus was the ancient god of fire."

Anger seethed quietly inside Dominic's chest. He did not care, but he counted slowly to five before asking. "Is that so?"

And so it began. A running, useless, waste-of-time commentary with Hector Galatis as his own personal tour guide. With great force, Dominic somehow managed to keep himself from exploding into a fit of rage, not that this would have been any good for his blood pressure.

They had been here for what seemed like hours.

Did this man not tire?

Granted that the ground was level. This wasn't the Acropolis with its hill and crumbling ruins.

But Galatis often surprised him when he least expected it.

"We will meet again," the old man said as they returned back to the point where they had first met.

"Like I already said, Hector, I only have the summer."

"I can see the desire to get this done on your face,

Dominic. You shouldn't give it away, your impatience. Alexander is in Europe. Maybe we can all meet together."

How did Galatis know?

His brother had called from London yesterday. He'd said he was over for business and Dominic half expected him to show up at any time. This was the type of thing Dominic's father and brother excelled in, stealth manoeuvres. But for Galatis to know that Alexander was already here worried Dominic. It meant that his brother had spoken to Galatis directly. He'd overstepped his mark and sidelined Dominic and in doing so made Dominic look weak.

He doubted that there was any real business reason for Alexander to be in London. The real reason, Dominic was sure, was to check in on him. His brother would make it look like he'd casually come to Athens, was just passing by to say 'Hi'.

"Alexander doesn't need to attend these meetings." Dominic smiled. "If we're done for today, Hector, I need to get back." He put his hand out for the old man to shake.

"Say hello to your brother."

"You take care. Hector."

He needed to call that dumb assed brother of his and find out what the heck he was doing speaking to Galatis in the first place, let alone what he was doing here.

He flung open the car door and climbed inside, sinking his back into the seat. He closed his eyes, needing a moment to calm down.

Sweet baby Jesus.

That man was going to be the death of him.

ELENI

D ominic returned an hour later looking visibly vexed. When he sat in the car and closed his eyes, remaining silent, Eleni said nothing. Whatever had happened between him and Galatis must have been bad.

After a few moments, Dominic opened his eyes, sat upright, then ordered Kostas to drive. Quiet moments passed and still he looked as stressed as ever.

"This is madness, Dominic," she said softly, watching him run a hand over his neck before wiping his face with a tissue. She was about to ask why he put up with the old man's games, but she already knew the answer. Dominic was trying to strike a deal to prove something to his father, and she didn't want to rile him up further, so she said nothing.

They drove on. The silence weighted by something heavy. When enough time had passed and she assumed he might have calmed down, she asked him if he was any nearer to getting the deal he was after.

"No. Fuck, no."

Okay.

Don't ask another question.

"Galatis wants my balls."

She didn't know how to respond to that, so she smiled weakly. Any talk of Dominic's private parts, hypothetically or not, seemed inappropriate.

"You're always so angry, Dominic. Have you ... um ... ever considered getting therapy for your anger issues?"

"I don't have anger issues."

She smiled weakly at him. *Don't say it.* "The people around you don't walk, they tiptoe."

He stared out of the window and she examined his beautiful side profile, could sense, more than see, the bunched-up emotion under his skin, making those sculpted bones of his even more remarkable.

"I don't mean to be an ass." He turned to her, his eyes blazing as if they were on fire. "But the pressure of trying to get results when the people you love are waiting for you to fail, is hard to ignore."

"Are you referring to your father?"

"My brother was always his favorite".

"And you?"

"My mom's, maybe, but she has no say in the business, not much, not in a way that counts, and she's okay with that. She likes the social privileges she has, being patron of charities and museums."

"Sometimes, you have to let it go, Dominic. Just breathe and give it up. Being angry isn't going to get you anywhere."

"Be like you, you mean? A ray of sunshine, believing everything is going to work out."

"I am not a ray of sunshine. Don't you remember that first day we met?"

"I'll never forget it. Are you prone to tripping?"

"Only around you."

"Right. Only around me."

But she truly felt sorry for him. For once a wave of sympathy came over her. A lot was riding on Dominic's shoulders. The pressure to perform and get results. To be responsible for so many people, to have to answer to shareholders and his family.

It was only her mother's approval she sought, and that was hard enough. She wanted to make Dominic feel better. "You may think your father is being harsh on you, but at least he wanted you."

"What do you mean?" he asked, quietly.

"Just that ...my father didn't want me."

Dominic stared at her quietly for the longest time, as if the sentence didn't make sense. "What do you mean he didn't want you?"

"My mother told me that he wanted her to get rid of me when she told him she was pregnant."

Dominic's mouth opened, and then closed again.

"She was in love with him," Eleni continued, grateful that she'd managed to get his attention and not have him focus on his problem. But with his rapt attention, and his gaze tender as he listened, she now wasn't sure about oversharing. "I think he might have been her first love, I don't know because she never talks about him, so when she did finally open up about him, I knew it had to be something important, and that's when she told me that when she announced she was pregnant, he told her to get rid of it. To get rid of me."

"What? That's despicable. What makes a man say something like that?"

"Already having a wife and family would do it."

He looked visibly shocked. "Fuck. That's cruel. That's appalling. I'm sorry."

"What do you have to be sorry about? At least now I understand her better. All this time, I wondered why she hated me ..."

"Your mother hated you?" He moved closer, raising his hand as if he was about to cup her face, but stopped himself before his hand touched her skin.

The breath that she had been holding slowly released. "We don't have a great relationship. She was a young mother, and I feel like I messed up her whole life for her."

"A young mom? How old is she?"

"Forty-two."

"She's not that much older than me."

Shock wrapped itself around her, like a sheet of ice. "How old are you?" She'd often wondered.

"I'll be thirty this year."

She grinned. "You *are* old. Ancient, like many of the temples Galatis has you visiting."

He cracked a smile.

"But you're not anywhere near my mother's age. She had me when she was twenty-one. My mother told me this, about my father, a few weeks ago, right after I started here."

"Jesus."

"So, you see. You're not alone, Dominic. We both have not-so-great relationships with our parents, but at least you have a father. That must count for something? And at least you know who you are, you have an identity. I only know half; the rest is a mystery and its left me with so many questions."

"I can imagine." He looked sad for her, or maybe he felt sorry for her.

"The people I love die. Not just that, but the people who *should* love me, they don't. My father didn't want my mother to have me, and even though my mother went against his wishes and had me, I think sometimes that she regrets it. I've spoiled her life. She was a beauty, and she had this wonderful life ahead of her, but I ruined it all."

"That's not true."

"It is. I don't matter."

"You do matter. You matter to a lot of people ... I imagine."

She looked at him, something flashing through his eyes, and something else she couldn't decipher. She looked away, and wished she hadn't opened up so much, wished she'd reined in her words, but lately, it was becoming harder to keep her feelings to herself, especially around Dominic.

"You've never met him?"

"I've never met him and I have no idea who he is. I don't want to ever meet him. He broke my mom's heart. I never knew him so it doesn't matter. It's not like he came into my life and then abandoned me. I don't spend a lot of time thinking about him because my mother never talked about him and early on she made it clear that it wasn't okay to talk about him."

Dominic's mouth twisted as if he was about to say something, but he didn't. What could he say?

The tenseness in the air loosened, and she didn't want to dwell on her sorry past anymore. It wasn't right to be confiding so much in the man for whom she worked. Yet, it didn't feel wrong either.

Talking to Dominic like this, now, the hierarchy between them fell away, perhaps it had never really been there in the first place.

"You may think your father's being harsh on you, but at least he doesn't sound like the monster who is my father. Yours cares about you, and he wants you to be your best, that's why he's testing you."

"My father is a tyrant, and my brother is following in his footsteps. Maybe some of their hardness has rubbed off on me."

"Maybe it has, although you've mostly been nice to me."

CHAPTER NINETEEN

ELENI

E leni was talking to Miranda over by the PA's desk when Dominic barged out of the elevator and stormed into his office. It was the blackest mood she had ever seen him in.

She and Miranda stared at one another and it was a moment before either of them spoke.

"What was that about?" Eleni whispered. "Not another meeting with the great Hector Galatis?"

Miranda moved closer, like a co-conspirator about to drop a huge bombshell. "Alexander is in London."

"And?" This was hardly the stuff of blockbuster news.

"He's been talking to Hector behind Dominic's back."

Now *this* made sense.

"What a snake."

Miranda nodded, the weight of the world on her shoulders, as if she were bearing Dominic's pain.

"I told you he was mean."

Mean wasn't the word Eleni would have used. "No wonder he's angry," she said, softly. After their conversation in the car a few days ago, she felt oddly closer to Dominic, as if she understood him better. The sins of the fathers perhaps did have some bearing on what the children grew up to become.

Everything in her life, everything she was, the way she reacted to and dealt with events, was part of her upbringing. She had been shaped by her mother and by her life on the island, but the absence of a father figure must have had a bearing.

And so it might have been the case with Dominic. Having a successful father with great expectations, must have been difficult.

She felt sorry for Dominic and had opened up to him in a way she hadn't with anyone, not even Stefanos. She hadn't even told Stefanos about what her father had said.

Dominic had listened carefully, and he'd empathized with her. In those moments she forgot the blurred lines between them; that he was a billionaire boss and she was the girl from the island he'd felt sorry for.

He'd helped her, with this job, and his generosity, and now the man was hurting. She held up a finger to Miranda and waltzed towards Dominic's office.

"What are you doing?" Miranda hissed.

Eleni knocked on the door and heard a grunt, then sailed in only to find Dominic shirtless.

Shirtless.

Her mouth fell open, and her brain cells froze; each and every one of them now imprinted with an unforgettable image of a topless Dominic.

With his back to her, he strode forward and reached into a

cupboard close by, his thick amply muscled arm pulling out a shirt.

And then he turned and saw her, his face red, from anger or the heat, she couldn't tell, nor did she care because her gaze slowly, inch-by-delicious-inch, raked in every dip and valley of his torso.

"I didn't hear you knock." A scowl dressed his face as he slipped on a pristine white shirt.

"I did," she said, or she thought she did. Her ability to think evaporated as did the reason for her coming to see him.

His hair seemed damp because it was a darker shade of brown than usual. Luckily, she had the presence of mind to close her jaw, pressing her lips into a line in a determined effort to keep her mouth firmly closed.

"This damn heat," he seethed, doing up the buttons of his shirt before tucking it into his pants.

"I knocked," she said, attempting conversation.

"I didn't say 'Come in,' he growled, reverting back to the other Dominic. Boss man.

"I heard you say *something*, otherwise I wouldn't have ... come ... in". Her voice trailed off at the end. "I ... I just ..."

Wanted to see if you were okay.

Faced with this angry man, with all traces of the person she'd confided in earlier, gone, she hesitated. "Good day?"

"Fucking ridiculous."

She stepped back, as if he'd dealt her a physical blow. He so rarely swore, that when he did, she took it as an accurate barometer of his rage level. But there was something else heating and winding its way inside her belly, twisting and snaking at the juncture of her thighs, a simmering heat, that he seemed to be suffering from but which she now felt herself.

She was going to ask how he was, and mention something

about Alexander, but it didn't seem the sensible thing to do anymore.

She rushed out, made her escape to freedom. It wasn't healthy that Dominic's moods, that angry look, one stern word, could raise her blood pressure, turn her white with anger, and clammy with desire all at the same time.

"Do you want to go to lunch again today?" she asked Miranda.

Thirty minutes later, she and Miranda were sitting outside having lunch again and Eleni was thankful for Miranda's company. She seemed to need it more with each passing week, as her interactions with Dominic grew, and her emotions dipped high and low.

Miranda sat across from her, eating a salad. Around them the traffic rolled by, cars roaring, horns honking in the searing heat.

Eleni was too pent up to eat.

"What happened in there?" Miranda asked.

"Where?"

"You know where. You know what I'm asking. Your face was so red I thought I was looking in the mirror."

Eleni couldn't help but giggle at her friend's self-awareness. "Do Dominic and his brother not get on at all?" Eleni was curious to know.

"They are like a messed up rich family. Think of all the drama and then multiply it by ten."

"Will he come here do you think? Alexander, I mean."

"I heard Dominic on the phone with him earlier. Dominic was angry that his brother spoke to Hector Galatis without telling him. That's all I could make out before Dominic stormed out for a meeting."

No wonder Dominic was annoyed. "That's a low blow. Dominic is working on a deal, or trying to."

"It's not good," Miranda agreed.

"He had a meeting," Eleni remarked, hoping to glean some information. Maybe he'd gone back to taking Linus with him again.

"He was meeting some other people from another company, and Helen went with him."

Eleni tipped her head to the side. "She was here?"

"Earlier this morning."

"Does she come here a lot?"

"She's the company lawyer, so she's here sometimes, and then all the time, and then we don't see her. It depends on whatever deal is going on."

Eleni sank back against the chair in relief.

"But," Miranda shrugged. "I don't know if that is all there is between them. I've made dinner reservations for them on weekends."

Maybe not.

A knot tied inside Eleni's stomach. It might even have been her colon. Dominic had expressly told her that Helen was his lawyer. As if he'd wanted to clarify that point. But Miranda seemed to have other ideas. "It is possible to have business meetings outside of work," said Eleni."

"I'm not so sure. They're so comfortable around each other." Miranda shrugged. "I could be wrong."

Now she'd gone and planted seeds of mistrust and jealousy inside Eleni's head. If anyone would have an antenna for watching interactions between Dominic and other women it would be Miranda.

Eleni shifted uneasily in her seat.

"You haven't touched that," Miranda stared longingly at the chicken souvlaki on Eleni's plate.

"I'm not hungry. You have it." She'd picked at the fried

potatoes but couldn't bring herself to eat anymore. She pushed the plate towards her friend. Miranda chewed her lip. "I shouldn't. I'm supposed to be on a diet." She skewered a cucumber with her fork and held it up, staring at it.

"I shouldn't be putting temptation in your way," answered Eleni. Miranda was voluptuous, more than anything. "You're gorgeous, Miranda. You have a beautiful figure."

"Like a Greek goddess?"

"Like that."

"You are too nice." Miranda set her fork down and contemplated the food on Eleni's plate.

"Go on, I don't want it."

She'd lost her appetite even more now that she wasn't sure what role Helen played in Dominic's life. She wished she hadn't gone barreling into his office, worried about his foul mood and attempting to see if she could calm him down.

Calm him down?

Who was she to calm him down?

She was a nobody.

It would have been better for her sanity to not have seen him in the flesh. His waist tapering to a V at the hips was none of her business. Neither was the way his abs dipped and rose.

Absolutely none of her business.

It wasn't that she ran out of the room because he scared her, it was that she was starting to wonder what it might be like running her fingers across that wall of chest. And feeling his lips on her mouth.

He was older, and there was a good chance he wasn't single.

Wait, what?

No, no, no. His status was of no concern to her.

At least, it shouldn't have been. After all, she was lonely

and prone to fantasizing. She hadn't had sex in over a year and a half.

That's what was going on.

Sitting back, she focused her attention on Miranda enjoying every morsel of her food.

CHAPTER TWENTY

ELENI

E leni paced around her room, her nerves jangling as she waited for Dominic. He'd emailed her yesterday just before she left work, to tell her she would have to accompany him again to another meeting.

Sure enough, at seven on the dot, he called her.

"On my way." She sprang into action, shoving her feet into her flat sandals, not bothering to pull the thin strap up around the back of her ankles.

She grabbed her bag, phone and keycard, and rushed out of the door, flying down the stairs at breakneck speed, conscious of his OCD about punctuality.

Her heart racing, she was nervous because there was the not so small problem of sitting beside him in a car having seen *that* body.

His naked torso flashed into her head and ... she went flying down the stairs, missing a step and tripping over herself.

She cried out in pain as she landed awkwardly, and in a heap, on the floor, sprawled on her butt with one leg folded to the side and the other akimbo. Pain shot upwards from her foot.

A hotel assistant came running to her side. She gasped, as the pain came in waves, intense and fast.

"Thank you," she managed to say on a whisper, when he gave her his arm and tried to help her to standing. She winced, not wanting to make a scene, or be fussed over, but thankful that she could stand.

Then her phone rang again, and she saw it lying face up, her bag and keycard scattered around. Along with one of her sandals.

Dominic was calling her.

She tried to stretch and reach it, but her left foot hurt, and when she stared down, her ankle was purple and growing larger.

"You shouldn't move," the assistant told her as her phone continued to ring. There was no point in answering it.

She *couldn't* move. "Could you please go outside and let the man in the black Mercedes know that I've fallen? Please hurry. He has a temper."

"Let me help you to sit down at least." The man helped her to the stairs, and eased her onto one of the steps. As he ran out, she scanned her body, quickly checking the damage. There was no blood. That had to be good. There was no pain anywhere else apart from her left foot. She examined her injury, hoping she hadn't broken any bones.

Surely, she'd be howling in pain if that was the case?

Dominic would be furious.

"What happened?" He rushed to her side, staring down at her, his face ashen. His eyes trailed to her ankle and he crouched down.

"I tripped."

He touched her foot, and she would have flinched, wanting to move it away but it hurt too much. "How?"

"What do you mean how?" she cried. "My broomstick hit the wall. How do you think?"

"How bad is the pain?" his fingers trailed gingerly over her ankle which was turning darker fast.

He wasn't angry with her?

"Bad, but I'll live."

"It doesn't look fatal. You can't sue me."

"Is that all you care about?"

He grinned. "I care that you're hurt."

"I don't think I've broken anything, but I can't go with you," she said, trying to gauge his mood. "I'm sorry."

"No need. At least you didn't break your neck."

Trust him to think of the worst case scenario. "It didn't occur to me that I could have. I would have definitely sued you then."

"You couldn't have. I don't own this hotel."

"Killed in the line of duty," she offered, watching the corners of his mouth twitching.

"Are you naturally always so clumsy? You're always tripping."

"Only when you're around."

"I was in the car. How did this happen?"

"I was rushing so as not to be late."

"Do I have an effect on you, is that what you're implying?" His long fingers trailed gently over her ankle.

"I rushed because I didn't want you to get angry. One of these days I think you're going to kill me."

The hotel assistant stood by, looking at them both.

At least Dominic didn't appear to be angry. But he didn't need to hang around. She would go back upstairs to her room and stay at home today, raise her leg, ice her foot, whatever the solution was once she'd Googled it. "You should go. You'll be late. You don't want to keep Galatis waiting."

"Fuck Galatis," he muttered under his breath. She allowed herself the luxury of ogling him in his suit before reaching for the handrail. She tried to lift herself to standing again.

"What are you doing?" Dominic cried, putting his arm around her waist and making her sit down again. "You've injured your foot."

"Oh, really?"

He rolled his eyes and ordered the assistant to hold the door open. Her eyes widened with shock and horror when he ordered her to put her arm around his neck.

"What? No?" Not after she'd seen him shirtless. She didn't want to be within an inch of his body. Otherwise who knew how many more sleepless nights she would have?

"Stop being so stubborn."

But stubborn was her middle name. She was rooted to the step. "I'll take the day off and go upstairs to rest. You go on. I can make my own way up."

"How?" he growled. "On your broomstick?"

Through her pain, she still managed to narrow her eyes at him. "It's an electric broomstick."

"You're nothing like a witch," he said quietly. "I wish you'd stop using that reference."

Oh. *Was that a backhanded compliment?*

"You really don't have to worry about me, Dominic."

"I'll carry you upstairs then." He moved as if he was going to scoop her up from the step. Her body hardened as if rigor mortis had set in.

"I'll ask the hotel guy. He'll take me upstairs."

"Over my dead body."

As the shock of Dominic's words landed, he did it. He

scooped her up, lifting her easily as if she were a flimsy rag doll.

"Dominic," she whimpered, feeling shy, and embarrassed, but liking the feel of his hard-as-stone arms, one across her shoulders, the other under her thighs. The scent of his cologne washed over her. She could get used to this; being in his arms and inhaling his scent as if it were the most addictive of drugs.

He was taking her to her room. She would have to suffer this for three flights of stairs. By the time she reached her room she would be a trembling, shaking mess in his arms.

She would rather die.

"Put your arms around my neck," he ordered. "Don't want you falling again."

"What? No."

"Do it."

She tentatively put both of her arms around his neck and, as if she were a full-blown junkie and could not resist, she took a sniff of his neck.

He stopped, angled his face at her. "Did you ... sniff my neck?" He stared down at her.

"What? No. I'm in pain. *Terrible* pain." She winced and sighed on cue. Dominic moved carefully, but instead of heading for the stairs, he moved towards the doors. "I can't go to the meeting with you, Dominic. I can barely—"

"We're going to my house." He moved towards the car, and Kostas opened the door for him.

"We're what?"

"We're going to my house."

Óh Theé mou. "What, no!" She could not.

"You've said that three times already."

"Why are you counting?" she cried.

He gently shifted her into the seat, and placed her other sandal which she hadn't noticed him pick up, back on the floor. She hadn't even noticed him picking it up. He ordered her to sit sideways with her legs up, her back against the car door, but she refused to, not wanting him to see her feet, especially not now with her grossly swollen ankle. "And why are we going to your house? Why?"

The man had gone mad. There was no reason she needed to go to his house. Why couldn't he leave her here to recover in her hotel room?

Instead of answering her, he made a phone call, leaving her in dazed confusion and bewilderment. The hotel assistant brought her bag and other belongings.

Dominic got into the car. "My private doctor will assess you at my house."

This man had gone too far. "I don't need a doctor."

"Says the medical doctor herself."

"Dominic. My foot is not broken."

"Are you sure?"

"I know so. It doesn't even hurt that much."

"We'll find out soon enough."

But he had a meeting with Galatis. "You can't waste time on me," she said. "You have more important things to do."

"I will do as I please."

"Drop me off at the hospital if you're so concerned. I don't need your private doctor to see me."

"I don't need the drama of arriving at the hospital, but if he thinks you've broken it or fractured it, and we need to go to the hospital, we will."

"It's not broken, Dominic."

"How do you know?" he asked, glancing at her foot.

"Because I'd be crying if it was."

"Would you? You're a tough one, Eleni."

"Dominic, this is insane..." But it didn't matter what she said to the man, Dominic wasn't listening to her.

She winced as she tried to slide her foot into her sandal but she couldn't. Not only was her ankle growing bigger, the pain was getting worse. They had been driving for a while and she looked out of the window to see where they were, and nearly choked to see the sea, a sandy beach and palm trees outside.

"You live near the sea?" she blurted out, knowing the answer even as she said it. Because, where else would Dominic live? His family ruled when it came to bigger and best-isms.

"I need peace. I cannot stand busy crowded places."

He had the money. The man could live on the moon if that option ever became available.

The car pulled up outside a large three story, white stone house. It was surrounded by what looked like a tropical garden.

"Are we here now?"

"Yes."

"I could have been resting in my hotel room." It had taken twenty minutes to drive here.

"You'll be better off here."

"Your house has three levels!"

"And you can have the ground floor to yourself."

She tried to make sense of these words, and this new world he had thrown her into as he came around to her side of the car to help her. But his phone went off, he pulled it out looked at it. "I have to take this," he muttered to his bodyguard. "Help her."

"I can walk if you support me," she said, hastily, not wanting the six-foot four-inch tank to carry her.

But he ignored her and scooped her up in the same way Dominic had, taking her past the beautifully kept lawn with its perfectly kept shrubs and flowers and into the house where he set her down on a big velvet draped couch. The gorgeous decor comprised of rich greens and wood tones with rugs in jeweled colors adorning the honey-colored floors. Glass lamps and lighting gave it a contemporary yet stylish touch. There was light everywhere. The space and light filled with beautiful high-end furniture and art pieces. Objects she was accustomed to seeing from the parties she'd waitressed at.

She expected nothing less from this man and his family. She'd only been sitting for a few moments, soaking in the interior when she heard Dominic talking to someone and then a man she'd never seen before entered the room.

DOMINIC

"Dr. Georghiou," said Dominic, introducing the middle-aged bald man with reading glasses. "Tell him how you fell."

That was fast. Did Dominic have a doctor on standby? She was left to explain to what had happened while Dominic moved away and started talking to someone on the phone.

The doctor examined her foot carefully. "It doesn't look broken." He pressed a finger lightly against her swollen ankle. "It's a mild sprain, you're lucky."

"That's mild?" Dominic returned and was standing around staring at her elevated foot, making her feel self-conscious. Thank goodness she'd had the foresight to paint her nails a few days ago when she'd been bored one evening.

"You were lucky. You could have broken or fractured it, falling down the stairs," the doctor told her.

"Are you sure she doesn't need an x-ray? What if it's fractured?" asked Dominic. The crazy man should have been more concerned about Galatis than her foot. The doctor stood up. "It's a mild sprain. Don't put any weight on it today, elevate it, ice it and go easy on it for a few days. As the swelling goes down, short walks will be good for your recovery. No sports or running for a few weeks."

"No running?" exclaimed Eleni. Her preparation for the expedition required a moderate level of fitness.

"As if you run," laughed Dominic.

"I do," she exclaimed, annoyed by his dismissiveness. "You're not the only one who keeps fit."

"You noticed?"

She could feel her face turning red. Doing a Miranda.

"I wish you a speedy recovery, young lady." The doctor nodded at her before shaking hands with Dominic who thanked him.

Dominic looked down at her.

She tried to slowly stand up.

"Where do you think you're going?" he asked as she looked around for her sandals.

"I'm going back to the hotel." This was wrong, so wrong, on a million different levels.

"The one where you have to trudge up three flights of stairs because there's no elevator?" he cried.

"Stop reminding me of that."

"I've heard you complaining about it enough times."

"That's not true." She'd mentioned it to Miranda once, maybe twice. Okay, maybe a few times. Had he listened to their conversations while passing?

"You should hear yourself." He moved closer to her. "Stay here and rest up. The doctor said for you to rest up for a few days at least."

She struggled to get up, but the moment she put weight on her foot, it hurt too much.

He continued watching her hobble and flail. "You can't go

anywhere. You can't work, not like that. I wish you would listen."

She collapsed back on the sofa. There was no point in arguing with the man. She had to begrudgingly accept that he was right. He seemed to be annoyed at her.

"This wasn't my fault. I rushed to get downstairs because —" She stopped.

"Because?"

"No reason." She couldn't think straight and was in danger of saying something that would embarrass her. But one thing was certain, she could not stay here.

"I'm going to meet with Galatis. You have the house to yourself. Take it easy. You heard the doctor. No running or aerobics either."

She made a face. "Very funny."

"Rest up, and maybe this evening, or tomorrow, I'll see that you go home."

Because he turned and left, he didn't see her mouth hanging open.

This evening?

Tomorrow?

God, no. Not tomorrow. She'd be out of here by sunset at the latest.

CHAPTER TWENTY-ONE

DOMINIC

Dominic ignored Miranda's questioning expression when he returned from his meeting alone.

But it was the sight of Linus, standing around, talking to her, that really pressed his anger buttons.

"Don't you have work to do?" he growled at Linus, unable to stop himself. It was wrong of him to be speaking to a manager in that tone, and especially not in front of another employee but Galatis had wasted his time, yet again, and Dominic was pissed. Again.

Linus looked fearful. "I was waiting for you. We have a meeting, and you are late."

Shit. Another meeting. Dominic blew out a weary breath, then raised five fingers at the man, indicating that he needed a few moments. He entered his office and let out a groan. His day was falling apart. The room sloped as the shock hit—most days were like this. He had nothing to tell his father.

Lately, his life seemed to be a clusterfuck of meetings that served no purpose and wasted his time.

He'd called Galatis this morning, while the doctor tended to Eleni, and asked to reschedule the meeting they planned, but the old man had insisted he was fine to meet and it didn't matter if Dominic was running late.

Dominic was running late. The detour to his house and tending to Eleni and summoning his private doctor had cost him time. Not that he would have done things differently. But he'd later rushed to the Erechtheion, another ancient Greek temple, to see the old man, but Galatis barely gave him ten minutes of his time.

After taking a short but slow walk around the temple dedicated to both Athena and Poseidon—a fact which he knew only because Galatis had thrown it at him—the old man had suggested they meet again because he was busy. He had something he needed to deal with.

"That's why I called to reschedule, Hector," Dominic had said, through gritted teeth.

The old man had tapped him on the shoulder. "We meet again. I get my secretary to arrange another meeting."

Another Greek site. Another useless meeting. Another hour or more wasted. And to make matters worse, he'd mentioned that his nephew was getting married. It was his sister's son, and Hector invited Dominic to come. It was only when he casually mentioned that the wedding was in Santorini, that Dominic's ears pricked up. Some of the shock and surprise at this news must have traveled up from Dominic's gut to his face. Galatis hadn't even finished gloating about the beautiful young socialite his nephew was marrying, when something hardened in Dominic's belly.

Because, in a day of clusterfucks, why wouldn't this man's

nephew be marrying Demi Laskaris, the woman Dominic had once dated briefly?

Dominic said nothing to Galatis, but smiled, and steered the conversation to their PAs talking and setting up the next meeting. He'd had enough of the man stringing him along for a ride that went nowhere, playing games, and dragging this out unnecessarily.

He'd already been worked up before the meeting knowing that Alexander had spoken to Galatis behind Dominic's back; a dirty move made by his scheming brother—a move his father had probably suggested. His family didn't trust him to see this through. By the time he'd left the so-called meeting, he was even more irritated.

He picked up the phone and called his brother again, but it went to voicemail, again. He didn't leave a message.

This entire week had been a clusterfuck of epic proportions, and to top it all, this morning there had been the episode with Eleni.

It wasn't her fault she'd fallen, but Jesus, he could have done without that drama.

He toyed with the idea of calling her to see if she was okay, but Linus knocked and came in carrying a thick file. "You said five minutes. It has been five minutes." Linus looked apprehensive.

"I'm sorry I snapped at you," Dominic said, in a rare moment of making an apology.

"You did not look happy. How was our friend Hector?"

"He was fine."

"Did he make a decision?"

"Not yet."

"You took the new girl again?"

"Eleni, yes."

"She didn't return with you?"

"Are you watching her every move?" It pissed him off that this guy was so concerned about his business.

Linus laughed, giving another wolfish smile. "She is taking my job, no?"

He was suddenly defensive. "She's not taking your job. She's not. Don't say stupid things like that." Linus had a problem with Eleni, and Dominic had a problem with that.

The man nodded, a half hearted acknowledgement. "I can come with you for the next meeting," Linus suggested.

Eleni would be out of action for a while, and if Galatis had another meeting soon, Dominic had no option but to take Linus with him the next time.

"Let's go over last quarter's figures," he said, prompting Linus to open the folder.

They had barely gone through the first few pages when his cell phone rang. Seeing Eleni's name spring up, he grabbed the phone and answered it on the first ring. "Yes?" and in a lower voice, "What's wrong?"

"Why would you say that? What do you think I've done, burned down the house?"

His mouth twisted. "You have a strange fascination with death." From the corner of his eye he watched Linus diligently looking at the paperwork, but he didn't put it past the wily man to be listening carefully to his conversation. "All is well, I trust?"

"Yes. Nothing is wrong. Don't raise your blood pressure unnecessarily."

Her silky voice soothed him. He got up and paced around the room, getting as far away from Linus' supersonic hearing as he could. "That's a relief to hear."

"You sound uptight, Dominic. What's wrong with you?"

Something about her tone, her demeanor, her voice, was

lighter. Relaxed. Friendly. As if being at his place, being away from work, had changed the dynamics between them.

"All is good," he answered, holding the phone closer to his ear, glancing over his shoulder to find Linus turning the pages of the folder.

"You can't talk. Are you in a meeting?"

"That would be affirmative."

She giggled, the sound rich and flowing, like a river. A boon to him after his day so far. "Have you been nice to Miranda today?"

He wiped a hand over his face. "I believe so."

He chuckled to himself, hardly believing the conversation they were having. "How many painkillers have you taken?"

"Two. Why?"

"They seem to be having quite an effect on you."

"I'm relaxing and taking it easy, like you told me to."

"Good."

"You're even less talkative than usual," she remarked. "Who's in there with you? Is it Linus?"

"Yes."

"Let me guess. He's there, at your desk, staring up at you."

"Not sure. It's difficult to assess." He needed to hang up. As much as he was being careful, he wasn't sure what Linus was hearing. But he didn't want to hang up. This was … nice. Easy. Addictive.

What he needed after the morning he'd had.

"You're standing with your back to him?" she asked. He could almost see the grin on her face, could hear the teasing in her voice. "Your psychic abilities are frightening."

"I should add that to my skillset, along with the waitressing."

He cleared his throat, killing a laugh. "I'm in a meeting, so if there is anything …"

"I'm hungry. Is it okay for me to go through your cupboards and fridge?"

"There was a point to the call after all."

"You don't think I called you to chat, did you?"

"You're sensible enough to know not to."

She giggled.

"Of course you can go through the cupboards. Eat what you want. I have no idea why you would even ask.

"Because, Dominic ... you left me in your house." She had a way of saying his name that felt cosy, as if they were more than people at work. As if she woke up and it fell from her lips with ease.

"There was a reason for that," he managed to say, trying to clear his mind of the visual that had slipped in there.

"I don't want to be shot or arrested by the police for going through your things."

"There goes that fascination with death again." He stopped, the smile falling from his face. What an insensitive thing to say. She'd lost her boyfriend in a tragic accident. He coughed. "They don't do that here, last I checked."

"That is true. Only in America, but I wasn't sure if your place was wired up to the local police station or whether your bodyguard might be trigger happy."

"Sven is aware of you and would not do such a thing."

"That's good to know. I can rest easy."

"That was the plan." He was waiting on her to end the conversation because he could not bring himself to.

"The plan is working. I feel much better."

"Good." He needed to wrap this up because he could sense Linus growing impatient.

"Are all of your cameras on?" she asked.

"What? Yes. They are. That's the whole point."

"Can you see me? Should I wave?"

"I haven't looked, and no. Do not."

She giggled again, and her laugh was so lovely. So infectious, he would hear it in his head all day, like a catchy song on the radio that played on repeat.

"So I don't need to put back all the expensive watches and cufflinks I've swiped?"

He snorted, then lowered his voice. "You went to my bedroom?" The idea of her in there made his cock twitch, and he immediately hated himself for it.

"I would never do such a thing."

"That would be wise."

Linus looked up at him, and Dominic stared at the floor. "Was there anything else?"

"No. Maybe I just wanted to hear your voice."

If only.

"I'm joking."

He pressed his lips together. "I fear the injury has affected your brain."

That made her laugh. How he loved that sound.

"I should let you go back to Linus, and meanwhile, I will investigate the inside of your refrigerator."

"Please do."

"I won't find any severed body parts, will I?"

He almost choked. "I would hope not."

"Because, you can be quiet and moody, and you know what they say about quiet and moody people."

"I do not know."

"That's a conversation for another time," she said.

She was so talkative. More than she'd ever been. It wasn't only that, it was the way she was talking, the things she was saying. It was a conversation he didn't want to end.

"Thank you, Basilia."

"What?" she shrieked.

He forced his lips into a straight line, cancelling out the smile that threatened to break out, and hung up.

It was a few moments before he could compose himself enough to turn around and face Linus. The man's gaze burned into him. Dom scratched his chin as he tried to switch off from Eleni and direct his attention back to the matter at hand. But it wasn't easy. Eleni had done a number on him and that conversation had been quite something. He didn't care two hoots about last quarter's figures.

He was starting to think of her more often than he should have. After every Galatis meeting where she accompanied him, her flowery scent would linger with him all day.

But he couldn't go there. He couldn't be that man. He *didn't* want to be that guy, like every other sleazy guy who'd hit on her, like Ioannis had. Mixing work and pleasure was something he frowned upon, but more than that, he couldn't give his family more ammunition to confirm their beliefs about him.

He had to get his head back in the game.

"Everything okay?" Linus asked, prying for information.

"It was my housekeeper." Dominic schooled a somber expression as he studied the figures in front of him.

"She had an injury?"

"You were listening?"

Linus bared his teeth into a smile. "That is one thing I cannot do—close my ears." He folded his arms, sighing. "Believe me, I would love to because my wife cannot stop giving me orders."

"She's pregnant. I don't blame her. Shall we continue?"

———

ELENI

Eleni's grin deepened as she hung up the phone. Dominic was in a playful mood, and she hadn't expected that. The man had a sense of humor she hadn't expected.

Feeling joyful, she swiveled on the barstool a few times, before coming to a stop and admiring the view.

The kitchen was bigger than the house she shared with her mother. The house was gorgeous. More beautiful than anything she had seen in her mom's glossy celebrity magazines.

What a wonderful existence moneyed people had.

Cameras staring down at her from the walls had made her paranoid and she'd wondered if Dominic could see her in the bathroom. To find out, she'd gone against the doctor's advice and hobbled around the downstairs area, not wanting to be nosy, but wanting to make sure that Dominic's presence in the house wasn't all seeing and all knowing.

Thankfully, she'd discovered no cameras in any of the three bathrooms on the ground floor. She didn't dare venture upstairs in case she set off an alarm or something, and besides, it wasn't in her nature to snoop around. So mindful was she of not overstepping the line, especially at the home of the billionaire, that she'd needed to check with him before she searched around for food.

Now that she'd called the boss and gotten permission, she could go through his cupboards and fridge freely. She was starving especially since she'd not eaten since this morning.

As expected, there were no severed body parts in the fridge. She made herself a sandwich with some cheese and grabbed an apple from the fruit bowl before sitting down at the kitchen island to eat.

Dominic was funny, and charming, and kind. He'd been

so good to her, and he didn't owe her a thing. The thought comforted her because it had been a long time since she'd felt that anyone cared. Stefanos cared, as did her friends, but this, with Dominic, was something new; something warm, soft and bubbly teasing her heart out of its dormant slumber.

Working in Dominic's company, it was the closest she had come to feeling wanted, *needed*. To being of use. Him dragging her to meetings, made her feel as if she was doing something. Even if she hadn't actually *done* anything of use.

She didn't like being stuck in the room with Agnes and Isidora, though they were making more of an effort with her ever since they'd discovered she was going to meetings with Dominic.

She didn't even care if they thought she was sleeping with him.

CHAPTER TWENTY-TWO

DOMINIC

Eleni was sleeping on his sofa when he got back from work in the evening, earlier than usual.

For a few moments, Dominic watched her. Her foot was elevated on a cushion, and by her side lay a book which she'd taken from his bookcase.

Not wanting to rouse her, he started to move away, pulling the loosened tie from around his neck, when she turned to her side then made a moaning sound. Her eyelids fluttered open. Large brown eyes stared back at him. Then they flew wide open and she bolted upright, as her senses seemed to return. "Oww!" She cried out in pain, reaching for her ankle.

"You okay?" He stared at the swelling which seemed to have gone down somewhat.

"I forgot about my ankle."

"Sleep will have that effect on you." He removed his

jacket and laid it on a chair before removing his cufflinks. She watched his every move, her eyes glazed and in that dream like state between sleep and wakefulness. She stared at his forearms as he slowly rolled up his sleeves,

"Is that a man's equivalent of taking off a bra?" she asked, yawning.

"Excuse me?"

She opened her mouth, then closed it. Then opened it again. "Nothing. I didn't say anything."

"You okay?" he asked, wondering if she might also have a bout of concussion.

"Great." She placed a hand on her mouth as she yawned and stretched some more. "How long was I out for?"

"I don't know. I just got back. I wasn't watching you on CCTV the entire time."

"You were what?" Alarm filled her eyes.

"I'm joking. I haven't looked at the camera footage. That's not my job. I'm not a creep, Eleni."

"I should make a move." She stared down at her feet, as if she were assessing how much pain and effort it would take.

"You're not supposed to walk today."

"I can't stay here."

"You can."

The easy familiarity that they'd had on the phone earlier hung precariously in the air between them. She seemed guarded as she slowly tried to lift her injured foot and set it on the floor. The look of pain on her face told him all he needed to know.

"This is a big enough house, Eleni. I don't need all ten bedrooms."

Her jaw hung open. "Ten bedrooms. You live here all alone?"

He could imagine the thoughts going through her mind.

He knew. It was insane. They barely used it, and even then, only one or two of them, whoever was over for the summer or for work. "It's the family residence here in Athens, so whenever my brother or my father ..."

"In Athens? You mean you have other homes?"

Would she crucify him if he told her the truth, that he had many, and not just in Greece, but all over the world? Real estate never failed as an investment. "Yes."

Wide eyes stared back at him. Eyes filled with trepidation. He tried to gauge her thoughts.

Fear? Was she wondering if he had ulterior motives for making her stay here? Because he didn't. He wanted to help her, but he wasn't after anything.

Even if his manhood begged to differ. An uneasiness seeped into his skin at the thought. He was seeing her differently, thinking of her differently, and though he had tried to battle against this unseemly attraction with all his might, it was becoming impossible.

Eleni's appearance had been easy enough to ignore and dismiss because he'd experienced enough drama with airheads who were beautiful but had nothing else to them. There was so much more to her. She had a heart and knowing what he did about the tragedy she had suffered, he found himself drawn to her despite trying to stay away.

But having her in his house, and most likely overnight, was wrong. He had to be careful. It wasn't that he couldn't fight temptation, he could. Besides, Eleni wasn't remotely interested in him. She was still in love with her boyfriend, or the memory of him.

He hoped she would lose the stubbornness and listen to him, and if she did, he couldn't stay here tonight. "There is plenty of room. You're not in the way or anything."

"I should go back, Dominic. Think how this looks "

She was worried about that, too? "We're not doing anything wrong. You've hurt your foot."

"I don't have a change of clothes."

"I'll give you one of my T-shirts. I can show you to your room. It's the one two doors down from the kitchen and you won't have to climb any stairs."

She seemed to be considering it. "If I stay, I'll have to go back tomorrow."

"You can work from home tomorrow. I'll have Kostas pick up your laptop from work and bring it to you."

She stared at him in horror. "And tell everyone that I'm staying at your place?"

He made a noise in his throat. She had a point. He didn't want to think what Linus might have to say about this. "Nobody needs to know. You can't walk, Eleni. Even if you went back to your hotel, you'd make your foot worse by going up those steps. You'd be trapped inside."

"I'll be okay, Dominic. You worry too much."

He paused, unsure what to say in response.

"Why are you so nice to me?" she asked.

He hesitated to answer. He could tell her part of the truth. "You fell down while rushing for my meeting. I'm responsible."

"But I'm not your responsibility."

"Your family and friends are in Spetses, so they can hardly help. I dragged you all the way out here. Stay tonight. I'm ... I'm seeing Helen, so I'll be out late." In case she was worried about being stuck with him at home.

To his surprise, her expression went blank, but he couldn't work out if she was disappointed or relieved. Or something else. "Helen?"

"I need to eat first," he replied, not answering her question deliberately, "and so do you. I presume all that sleeping and doing nothing has given you an appetite?"

"I am hungry. I could get used to this life."

He smiled at her. Not wanting to make her uncomfortable, and aware of what had happened to her before, he'd already decided to leave her in the evening, hoping she would see that he didn't have any underhanded motives for keeping her here.

ELENI

She was hungry. There was no denying that.

And she'd slept for hours. She had no idea how it was the evening already. She'd only just sat down to read after lunch, finding a book on one of the bookshelves, and then she'd fallen asleep.

By the time Dominic had returned, the day was still bright, but it was much later in the evening. It made sense for her to stay.

She didn't care so much about being trapped in her room as she did about the thought of Dominic carrying her all the way up three flights of stairs at the hotel to install her in the bedroom.

There was no point going home now. If she'd had any fears or reservations about being here, Dominic had allayed them. He was going to see Helen. There was more to it than he had first let on. Miranda had been right. The tingling feeling which had started in the base of her stomach earlier when they'd spoken on the phone, soon petered out. There had been a change in how they were with one another. It was as if they'd gone to a different frequency, and the wavelength on which they were now talking made her more relaxed than ever around Dominic.

He gave her a choice of cuisines to pick from, menus, but had no menus to show her. "Surprise me," she'd said, and he had. When the food arrived, there was enough for a feast.

"You eat this much food, Dominic?"

"I didn't know what you liked, so I ordered a bit of everything."

"You should have asked me." There was food there for ten people, and she didn't eat much at all.

"You told me to surprise you."

"You already have." She looked into his eyes and something warm melted inside her, a reassuring feeling that she was being cared for. That, in this moment, as surreal as it was, Dominic was looking after her.

Why was he always so good to her?

It wouldn't all fit on the small table, so he laid it out on the larger table on the side and told her what the various dishes were.

"I had my lunch on the island. We can eat there," she insisted, trying to get up, but the pain started as soon as she put weight on her foot.

He moved a small coffee table to her and insisted on bringing the food over. "Sit down, Eleni."

She paused to gape at him, taking in everything he was doing for her. "You're very kind, Dominic."

"Enjoy it while it lasts. This is a rarity. Either that or I must be coming down with something."

She giggled.

There were two sides to this man; a harsh, unrelenting, serious side—the one most people saw and which made them tremble. But she mostly saw his softer side, and she had no idea why.

While he'd given her this job out of pity, because of what had happened on the yacht, it didn't make sense for him to still be so tender and attentive to her.

"Why are you doing this for me?" she asked again, his answer from earlier not satisfying her curiosity.

He gave her a pointed stare. "I told you why," in a weary tone that suggested he no longer wanted to discuss the matter.

But he was doing too much. Far too much.

He plated the food she asked for, then filled his own plate up before joining her on an adjacent sofa.

They ate quickly and quietly, and she even had seconds. When they had finished eating, she felt emboldened, nourished, better.

"I think I could hobble back to the hotel, Dominic."

"Not this again."

"I could even jog back."

"I didn't know you were a runner."

"That's because I didn't tell you." She wasn't sure she wanted to tell him now that she was training. She didn't want to talk about Jonas, wanted to keep him in her heart tucked away in a small special place. Talking about Jonas to Dominic didn't feel right. "It's a hobby, something I do to keep fit."

"I didn't know."

Why would he? They weren't supposed to have that type of dynamic. But here she was, sitting in his home, on his sofa, having food he had plated for her. What a turnaround.

But why?

And how?

It seemed so unreal to her, and yet Dominic Steele now watched her with amusement.

"What?" she asked, feeling self-conscious. She hoped her feet didn't smell. Or that the dolmades, the stuffed vine leaves she so loved, weren't stuck between her teeth.

"Nothing."

"You don't have a housekeeper or a chef?" She'd half-expected to see them and had been surprised that when he'd left her alone, she'd been truly alone.

"I don't like having people around. I like my space and I'd hate to have a live-in housekeeper."

"But *I'm* here in your space."

"That's different. You're only here for a day or so—"

"Just for tonight," she insisted.

"It's not like you're going to be here regularly."

"No. And what about your bodyguard? Isn't he in your space?"

"He patrols the house from the outside. He's not in my space."

"Who's Basilia?" He'd mentioned a name earlier which hadn't made any sense.

"My housekeeper."

"So, you do have one?"

"She comes every few days. She cooks and cleans." He waved a hand at his surroundings. "You don't think *I* keep it this immaculate."

"You're a very tidy person," she noted.

"There's only me, and I'm hardly going to make a mess. It's not like there are children running around."

She wondered what that might be like. Dominic with children.

The deep lines on his forehead relaxed. It was the only thing that reminded her of his age. A man like him, as old as him, she shuddered to think of how many women he'd dated. Rich, too, with those looks and all that wealth. Her stomach recoiled at the idea of the many nameless, faceless women who would have thrown themselves at him.

No, she wasn't in any danger of him making a move on

her. Men like Dominic weren't interested in women like her. "Given that you hate having unnecessary people around you, I should consider this an honor."

"You should." He shifted his position on the couch. Laid his arms to rest on top of the backrests. Made it impossible for her not to stare at his chest.

Christé mou.

"Why did you rush into my office that day?"

"What day?"

He paused a moment before replying. "That day you saw me without a shirt."

She tried to regulate her breathing. "You're asking me about that now?"

"I was going to ask you earlier today, but then you fell."

He was asking her now, and she was at a disadvantage because she couldn't scamper away. He demanded an answer and she had no choice but to give it.

"You were in a bad mood," she said, fighting with her mind to not go back in time and recall that particular scene.

"It had been a difficult day, what with Hector and my brother, and … the state of things, really."

"He really stresses you out, doesn't he?"

"Alexander? Or my father?"

"Both, but you mentioned your brother just now."

"He's in Paris, or he was when I spoke to him that day. I dread to think where he is now."

"You're worried he might appear?"

"I'm pissed that he's talking to Galatis behind my back."

He got up and started to pace around the room, his hands in his pockets as if he was making a business decision. "I know why he's doing it, though he denies it. He's checking up, maybe opening a second channel to Galatis."

"Wouldn't that undermine you?"

He stopped and looked at her, his piercing eyes like lasers. *Ó Theé mou.* Dominic was so handsome. But he was even more so when he was angry. He was intense. Her heart flipped a few times just staring back at him.

"That's exactly my point. My brother wouldn't see it as that. He'd see it as him doing the right thing by the company."

She heard her breath, in and out, short and shallow. That mouth, those lips. It was wrong, so wrong, but she wondered what it might be like to kiss those lips.

"They don't trust me to do this, and Galatis isn't making things easy for me, not that he should, but with my family breathing down my neck, Alexander is the last complication I need."

"How is it that you have a shipping business here at all, with your family being in the US?"

"My father. It's his doing. It just happened."

"Happened?"

"In the sixties, my father met a man in a bar in Piraeus—he hadn't gone there to do business, he didn't even realize it was a worldwide maritime centre—or maybe he did, but he wasn't there for that reason. He'd just ended up there by mistake, and he met a guy in a bar. They got on instantly, they just clicked, my father said. Before the night was over, they'd decided to go into business together.

My father took a risk. He had money, not as much then but enough to finance this operation, and the man, Simos Pappas, had the know-how, and he was Greek, and he lived there, so it worked just fine. Together they set up this company in Athens. It was the perfect location for keeping an eye on our fleet and subsequent maritime operations. And that's how this transatlantic operation was born. They built the business up slowly over time and it would come to mutually benefit both parties, My father's first fortune came from that."

"First?"

"We have other businesses, but the shipping part of it, my father just fell into it."

Was he being deliberately vague? Trying to play down just how wealthy he was? "It was fated, then?"

"What?"

"How they met. It was meant to be, your father ending up there by mistake."

"Perhaps. But Simos died around fifteen years ago, and that's when The Steele Corporation took over the entire business. It's a good thing we had everything in place, because our core business is tech, real estate and finance."

It seemed to pain him to disclose this to her. So she dug deeper. "Is that all? Just those three?"

"We're a big company."

"I expect everything about you to be big, Dominic. What do you call it over there? Supersized." She stifled the grin.

"We like making money. Nothing wrong with that, but to answer your question, that's why we have a presence here. My father had considered selling off this company, it doesn't make sense to focus when we're just a minor player in the market."

"Ouch!"

"What is it? Do you need another painkiller?" His gaze fell to her ankle.

She laughed. "Ouch as in that must hurt, you being a minor player. Not dominating."

The tiny knot that had formed between his brows slowly vanished. "Shipping is dominated by the Greeks, and now China, Japan and Hong Kong are prominent players, too, not to mention South Korea and Norway. But the business makes money, so ..."

"Of course, why else would you do anything, if it didn't make money?"

"Exactly."

"Why is Galatis even giving you his time if he has the biggest fleet? Why should he partner with you?"

"Because like a dinosaur, that fleet might be big, but it is becoming outdated and soon it will die out. He hasn't done much to bring it into the modern era, and we've identified an opportunity. We specialize in tech, and we can help Galatis. He's still living in an old world, but the world has moved on. There are huge challenges in the shipping industry, new environment regulations, security risks, cargo loss due to containers falling overboard—it happens, believe it or not— and tech and digitalization are more important than ever—"

"It feels as if you're giving me the presentation you should be giving to Galatis."

"You did ask."

"I did."

"I'll shut up then—"

"No!" she cried. "Please continue."

"Where was I?"

"Your containers were efalling overboard."

"You were listening?" He sounded surprised.

"Yes, I was listening. Continue."

"Compliance, safety—maritime shipping lines need to focus on that, and things like improved shipping procedures, risk assessments, better cybersecurity and training, these things are increasingly becoming important. We believe making alliances is the way forward. We can offer Galatis a way to do business with us. Ninety percent of goods are transported by container ships. Shipping isn't going anywhere, nor will it be replaced, but if Galatis doesn't move with the times, his business will die and other savvier companies will dominate. We might not have the fleet size, but we have the know-how for pretty much everything else he needs. We can share vessels, and we can invest heavily in his business, providing resources and know-how, to help him upgrade his fleet. Shipping is going through a digital transformation and we're at the forefront of tech. We can create the tools Galatis, and others, need. We want to increase our market share, and this is the perfect way to do it. And, partnering with Galatis allows us to enter the sea transport market on a much bigger scale."

"But what's in it for him? Maybe he's just giving you the middle finger, and he's not really interested, so he's playing with you instead."

"We can offer so much in return."

"It sounds to me as if you need him more than he needs you."

"He needs us, he just doesn't know it yet. He thinks he can resist change. He can't. Don't even get me started on things like the greenhouse gas emissions. Shipping companies are moving toward carbon neutrality and we've invested heavily into research and development on that front, looking at alternative fuels and zero emission vessels in the future. But Galatis hasn't done much on this at all. He knows what we're offering, he has the proposal I worked so hard to put together. We're perfectly placed to do that. My father is aware of the old rivalry between many of the shipping magnates. They don't like each other. They're bitter and jealous. He's not going to partner with a Greek company because of old wounds, but The Steele Corporation, the parent company behind the shipping business, is huge. In the US we're a major player. Galatis is interested, but he's giving me a hard time because I've come to him. I'm already at a disadvantage."

"But why are you going only to him?"

"What part of what I told you doesn't make sense?"

"Don't use that tone with me Dominic. I'm not Miranda."

He cocked his head. Dipped his brows. The pain killers were having an effect on her not unlike that of a few cocktails. Her tongue was loosening fast.

The apology obviously wasn't coming. "I just don't understand why you're so desperate to do business with him when he treats you with such contempt. Why can't you seek out smaller alliances, and then you can spread the risk, and you have more experience at your disposal. That's what we did at the taverna. We used to have only one cook, then Adamos hired another one, and it was better."

"That would explain the waiting times," he muttered.

It took her a while to understand but what he meant. "It's very sad that you're still upset about how long you had to wait before someone took your order."

"Given that it was you, I'd say the wait was worth it."

Her heartbeat came to a screeching halt, like a horse suddenly reined in by its rider. This, she liked. This openness. This niceness that was so not *him.*

She tried to steer the conversation back to safer pastures. "B-but ...you are brothers, you and Alexander. You must have gotten along at some point in your lives?"

"We did. But he's very competitive. Thinks he knows everything. Thinks I'm just his kid brother. He's opinionated, uptight and a bit of a snob. You would hate him."

This made her smile. "I don't hate you, and I would have said you were all of those things when I first met you."

"Oh really?" The words were wrapped in sarcasm.

"But it turns out that you're actually very sweet."

"Or maybe that's how I am with..."

He didn't finish the sentence. They looked at one another. He blinked. "You still haven't told me why you walked in to my office that day."

"I ..." It sounded too presumptuous, the real reason, but he was staring at her as if he wouldn't let her move until she told him. "You looked upset and I thought ... foolishly... I mean, after we'd been talking the other day, in the car ...I ... I was worried and I wanted to see if you were okay." She winced, because saying it out loud it sounded even more presumptuous than it did in her head.

"You were concerned about me?"

She blinked back at him.

"You were worried, Eleni?"

Her mouth turned desert dry, and her chest started to beat faster, abnormally faster, enough to make her fear for her health. Maybe it wouldn't be a bad thing to have a hospital stay for a few days, get away from Dominic. "You're always so angry and uptight, and ..."

Who did she think she was? The only woman who could calm him down?

"I'm sorry if I took it out on you."

"You didn't."

"I'm sure I did, when I was doing up my shirt buttons. I'm sure I snapped at you."

Shirt buttons. Did he have to go there now, in this moment?

"It doesn't matter."

He looked away. "No, I guess not." He reached for her plate and cleared the table. She tried to stand up, feeling guilty that he was doing this alone, but she needed a moment to still her beating heart.

They'd spoken so much, but she was still left feeling that their conversation had been full of unsaid things.

She waited for him to return from the kitchen. "We could watch a movie," she suggested, feeling perky. Watching something would ease the simmering tension that had suddenly crept in. Her heart was doing that strange, fluttering, fast-beating thing again. Maybe she had a condition her mother wasn't aware of. Maybe it was something on her father's side?

Dominic returned and reached for his jacket. "I'm going to see Helen. I might not be back until the early hours, so don't wait up."

In her euphoria, she'd forgotten all about the other woman. Her chest tightened, making it harder to breathe as she watched him leave. There was more to what he and Helen had. "Don't rush back on account of me."

"Goodnight, Eleni." But he didn't turn around to say it.

"Goodnight, Dominic," she said to the back of his head, hating that he was going to his friends-with-benefits lawyer because it was so boring for him to stay here with her.

CHAPTER TWENTY-THREE

ELENI

T he sun streaked through the windows when she woke up with a start.

Eleni opened her eyelids and stared at the bright white ceiling, confused. It took a few seconds for it all to come back at once—where she was.

In Dominic's house.

In his bed.

No, in a bed in one of his ten rooms, in his house.

Óh Theé mou.

She got up, wearing only the T-shirt which he'd left on the bed along with a new and comfortable pair of flip flops. She reached for her phone.

Eleven o'clock? She was so late for work! But as she rushed to get out of the bed, she cried out in pain when the full weight of her body came down on her feet.

Her ankle.

It was a dull ache at first, which throbbed through it, but then the pain turned sharper and stronger.

She'd sprained it and no way was she well enough to walk out of here. She flopped back onto the bed, her head sinking into the big downy pillow as she considered her options. She couldn't go to work, not like this, not today. Unless she took a few pills.

But she couldn't stay here either. Not for another day. It slowly started to come back to her about last night and she wondered if Dominic had come. Or had he stayed at Helen's?

Helen's just a lawyer, he'd told her once. But he'd gone over to her place last night, and it couldn't have been for dinner, because he'd eaten with her.

If not for dinner, then what?

Another shot of pain lanced through her. This was Dominic's house, and if she hadn't been in the way, he would most likely have asked Helen to come over for the night.

No, Eleni could not stay here and get in the way. She needed to get back to her hotel, and fast, and then she would figure out a plan to work from home.

For a fleeting few seconds she debated calling Agnes and Isidora to let them know that she wouldn't be coming in to work today, but they didn't care whether she did or not. So, she decided against that.

But she couldn't just leave. She had to tell Dominic who was obviously at work. She sat up slowly in bed again then reached for her cell phone and rang his number. Just like the last time, he answered on the first go.

"Are you okay?"

"I'm fine. Thanks." She chewed her lower lip, her thoughts running rampant about his whereabouts last night and what he might have been up to. "I overslept. Sorry. I don't think I can come to work today—"

"I wasn't expecting you to."

"I was thinking that I need to get set up for working from home for a week..."

"Don't worry. I'll get someone in IT to set you up."

"Thanks. Um ..." *Don't ask him. Don't.* "I didn't hear you come back last night. I was probably out of it."

"You probably were."

She considered probing further, not satisfied with the answer he'd given her.

Don't.

"I have to go. I'll talk to the tech guys." He hung up.

At least he'd saved her from making a fool of herself. But had she detected a hint of evasiveness? He didn't seem to want to tell her when he'd come back.

Why did it matter?

She groaned loudly, hating this.

It *did* matter.

She was consumed by the need to know, and not in a good way.

Something had changed. For her, at least. Something about Dominic and the way she saw him.

Which was why she could not stay here another night. She decided to take a shower, clean up the bedroom, have some breakfast and then get a taxi back to her hotel.

Slowly and carefully, after taking a couple of pills, she was able to spring into action. After her shower, she managed to hobble to the kitchen, make herself a bowl of cereal and pour a cup of coffee. She enjoyed a leisurely breakfast, taking longer than normal because she didn't want to leave, and because this was a once in a lifetime opportunity, having a sleepover at a billionaire's place. She couldn't wait to tell

Stefanos about it, long after she'd left the company. He would ask her too many questions. He would worry too much.

And nothing had happened, or was going to happen, but Stefanos wouldn't believe her anyway.

She stacked the dishwasher, then got her belongings together, packing the T-shirt Dominic had lent so that she could wash and return it to him. She put her sandals in there, because the flip-flops were so comfortable and she couldn't wear anything else.

As she searched on her phone for the number of a local taxi company, the sound of a car made her look up.

Dominic?

What was he doing home so soon?

She hadn't even made her getaway. Why had she taken her sweet time having breakfast?

She peered through the windows and saw a black SUV.

It was a different car. She worried about what had happened to the Merc, and worried even more that he had come home. She wished she'd left earlier because Dominic wouldn't let her leave now.

She snuck another peak through the windows and saw the car door open. A man got out, but there was something different about him. He looked similar to Dominic at first glance, but the way he moved was different, more of a cocky swagger, where Dominic's gait was more purposeful. This man's hair was different, too, lighter, more blond.

And then it hit her like a bolt of lightning, straight through her chest.

He wasn't Dominic.

Alexander?

She jolted away from the window, then couldn't resist another peek. He was pacing around talking to someone on the phone.

This. Was. Alexander.

Óh Theé mou.

She couldn't be seen here. This man was opinionated, and uptight and mean, a hundred times more than Dominic had ever been, judging by the way Dominic had described him. She looked around for a place to hide, the house was big enough for her to.

But the sound of voices outside the door made her freeze. She stood frozen in the large living room, and wished she'd woken up earlier so that she wouldn't be in this mess.

It was too late to hide, and too late to leave.

She was stuck.

She rushed into the utility room and set her bag in there, then looked around in panic.

Dominic's judgmental older brother couldn't see her. Not like this. He wouldn't believe her excuse of a sprained ankle, or that Dominic was being kind to her by letting her stay the night.

No, Dominic's older brother would have a thing or two to say about her, a temporary employee, being here overnight. He'd presume the very worst and think she and Dominic were having a summer fling. Then he'd relay everything back to their father. She couldn't let that happen to Dominic.

She eyed a duster, then some more cleaning materials. An apron or two. She reached for them all, pulling the apron on and tying it around at the back. Then she hobbled out, forcing herself to walk as normally as was possible, towards the noises. Thank goodness she'd popped a couple of pills.

She could so do this.

The key turned in the lock, ratcheting her already frayed nerves. She focused on the dusting and prayed for an easy exit. More loud noises followed and she heard the sound of two men talking, then they stopped.

She spun around, made an exclamation of surprise then rambled something in Greek. The other guy looked like Dominic's bodyguard in height and stature. They might as well have been twins. While the dim recesses of her mind tried to answer the question of why each brother had a bodyguard, her nerves were on alert.

"Who are you?" The brother's voice had tones of Dominic, interweaved with a touch of sharp, crisp and condescending. In answer, she waved her duster. "Ah, you speak English?" As if she had no idea who he was. "You are?" She stared at the man, forming an opinion of Dominic's brother in an instant. He looked at her as if she were a lump of shit on his shoe.

"I asked you first. "Who the hell are you?" Alexander repeated.

"The housekeeper. Again, I ask *you*, who are you?" She didn't like that man one bit.

"*You're* the housekeeper?" His eyes went up and down her, making her skin bristle. "What the hell happened to Basilia?"

"She is not well. I am helping for now, but I am finished now, so I must go." She put the duster up against the wall, and started to undo her apron as she tried to walk, as best as she could, back to the utility room to get her bag.

She could feel his eyes burning through her back.

"What's wrong with your foot?" he shouted out after her.

"I hurt it."

The man snorted in shock. "And my brother still made you come in and clean the place? What an asshole."

She returned with her bag over her shoulder, and hobbled past them in pain so excruciating, she was sure she'd faint.

Dominic's brother whistled as he stared at her foot. She presumed it was his brother because he still hadn't answered her question, but he so fit the description she'd been given, and he resembled the nicer Steele brother, that she no longer needed his confirmation.

"It looks painful."

"It is." As painful as talking to this asshole.

CHAPTER TWENTY-FOUR

DOMINIC

T he first inkling that possible trouble was brewing, was a message he received mid-morning when he came out of a meeting.

Alexander had left him a voicemail saying that 'he was on his way.' What this meant, Dominic had no idea. His brother could be enroute from London, Paris, Rome, or ... anywhere. He could even be on his way home from the airport.

He grabbed his cell phone and called him again, only to reach his voicemail, again. He decided to call Eleni, to warn her, when his cell phone lit up.

"You traded in your housekeeper for a younger model."

Jesus. *He was already here.* Dominic scrubbed a hand across his forehead. "My what?" And then it hit him like meteor. He'd met Eleni. "You're at the house?" Of course, he was. Alexander turning up at the house unannounced was a very Alexander thing to do.

"Got here about twenty minutes ago."

"You could have told me before. Like the day before." *So that I could have been prepared.*

"I left you a message, bro."

"When?"

"An hour ago."

That sounded about right. "I've been in meetings all morning."

"You sound pissed, Dom. Are you?"

"You seem to be all over the place, lately. Are you checking up on me?"

His brother snorted. "As an older brother, I thought I'd swing by, seeing as I'm here."

"I'm not a child. I don't need anyone to see how I am." Alexander was, without a doubt, checking up on him. "Where's El—" he stopped himself in time before he said her name. "...the housekeeper?"

"She left in a hurry."

In a hurry? That didn't sound good. Not with her injury. He could imagine Eleni's reaction, those soft brown eyes filled with terror when his brother turned up.

But what had made her lie about being a housekeeper?

"What happened to Basilia?" Alexander asked.

Christ. As if he had any idea. "She's ... not well?" He hoped that's what Eleni might have said.

"Such savage working conditions, Dom. What are you doing to the poor girl?"

Wait, what? "What are you talking about?" he growled, hating that he was so uniformed and had no clue about what had been said between Eleni and his brother.

"She limped away. Said she tripped. Was that your doing?"

Dominic knew Eleni well enough, and he was sure she

wouldn't have said anything of the sort. Alexander was probing and shit-stirring as usual.

"How the hell is that going to be my fault?" He swiped a hand across his brow. "I must go. I have another meeting, but I'll be home soon. Stay put, don't go anywhere."

"I won't. I'm here for a few days."

Something tightened in Dominic's neck. "What for?"

An uneasy laugh rolled across the line. "You're pretty paranoid, aren't you?"

Sensing defensiveness, he asked, "Did dad put you up to this?"

"Like I said, I was in the continent, so I thought I'd pay my little bro a visit. Why do you always have to assume there's something sinister about my visits?"

"Because I know there always is. You failed to tell me that you spoke to Hector." His gaze fell to his open door where two of his managers were sitting on the edge of their seats, watching him.

"Hector? How the hell is he?"

"I'll have words with you later." Dominic slammed the phone down.

ELENI

Eleni hobbled into the building and saw the smug receptionist—the one who'd given her such filthy looks on the day of her interview—staring at her flip flops in amusement.

With as much dignity as she could muster, Eleni made her way slowly to the elevator, cursing that she couldn't go any faster.

This morning had been enlightening.

Her first impression of Alexander had been everything Dominic had told her he would be. With him staying over, Dominic was going to be busy and she didn't want to get in the way. Or give his brother any ammunition to use against Dominic.

She needed to get herself set up to work from home, which was why she was here. She'd already called and spoken to someone in the IT department to get her set up with everything she needed to work remotely. All she needed was to get her laptop.

Miranda's shocked face greeted her the moment she hobbled out of the elevator. "What happened?" she cried, standing up and gawking at Eleni's feet. Eleni limped forward, her gait odd and uneven. "I fell."

"You fell? Eleni!" Miranda rushed to her side. It was the fastest Eleni had ever seen her move. "Fell where? It looks so painful."

"It is very painful." Eleni stayed on the spot, not wanting to move. The pills she had taken earlier were wearing off and the pain in her ankle was starting to get worse. It had sapped all of her energy, trying to be as normal as was possible when Alexander had arrived, and making her way into work had only made things worse.

"Come and sit down." Miranda took her by the arm and started to lead her towards her seat behind the desk.

"No. I can't. I've only come to pick up my laptop. I'll be working from home for a few days until I can walk properly again."

"Why are you even thinking of working?" Miranda stared at her as if she'd turned into an elephant. "Just take the time off."

"I can't do that. I need the money." And temporary workers didn't get paid for time off.

"How did you do it?" Miranda wanted to know. Eleni placed her hand on the desk and swallowed a sigh of relief at finally being able to shift the weight off her foot, then recited her story again.

"*That's* why Dominic returned without you yesterday," Miranda said slowly.

"You didn't know?"

Miranda shook her head. "I called you but you didn't answer."

Yes, that. She made an apologetic face. She'd seen the missed calls, but she didn't call Miranda back because she'd been in too much pain; and she'd assumed that Dominic might have told her. Now she wasn't sure what to say. Not wanting to lie to Miranda in case she asked further questions Eleni winced as she tried to walk again. "I should get my laptop."

But alarm bells went off in her head at the sound of a door opening nearby. A door she couldn't see but knew was around the corner from Miranda's desk. A door she knew belonged to Dominic's office.

He appeared in the next second, about to push one arm through the sleeve of his navy-blue suit.

Her heart melted like butter. It took for her to see him again for her to remember how devastatingly handsome this man looked in his white and blue number.

He stopped as soon as he saw her, his gaze falling to her feet. "What the hell are you doing here?" he growled. His voice was stripped of all the softness it had last night as they ate dinner and talked.

"I ... I..." It startled her, his gruffness. She didn't understand his rage. On one level, her brain guessed that he must have found out about his brother, but why was he taking it out on her?

Miranda scurried back to her desk and began typing away at the speed of light, as if she was trying to set a new Olympic record for typing speed.

Eleni's chest tightened. Hopefully a plate of steel armor was going up around her chest. After her lapse in judgment these last few days, she needed to be strong and never forget. Nice Dominic had vanished, and the asshole was back. "I came to get my laptop."

"I told you I was going to sort it out."

"Why are you angry at me?" she cried, not caring that Miranda could hear.

"My brother's here." He swiped a hand through his hair.

"Yes." She wondered what he'd told Dominic. They had obviously spoken.

"In my office, now."

"Don't talk to me like that," she snapped. The pain in her ankle was getting sharp again. Miranda stopped typing, her gaze ping-ponging between Eleni and Dominic.

"In my office, now, Eleni. *Please,*" Dominic pleaded.

She slowly moved into his office.

"Sit," he ordered.

"I'm not sitting. I need to go home."

He pulled out a chair for her. "Your foot. You need to rest it. *Sit.*"

"I'm not—"

"For fucks' sake, will you listen to me and sit down? Quit being so stubborn."

"Do not swear at me." She sat down in a huff, then regretted her dramatic descent as the pain shot through her ankle again. "If you're angry with your brother, take it out on him. I am *not* your emotional punching bag."

"You're not. I'm sorry. Why did you say you were a maid?" he asked.

Was he mad about *that?* "I was trying to help you." This was not going to be easy; his shirt sleeves were already rolled up. Naked forearms on display.

God help her.

She shifted her focus up and surveyed his face slowly.

"Explain."

"You said your brother was an opinionated jerk. You made him sound not so nice, you said he was checking up on you. How would it have looked if I told him you'd let me stay over?"

Dominic pinched the bridge of his nose for the longest time, as if his fingers were glued to it. "You didn't have to belittle yourself like that."

"Who says I was? Working as a maid is good way for some of us to make money."

He stared at her, his expression hard to read, but the line between his brows softened and slowly disappeared. "You've worked as a maid?"

"Most people aren't born to billionaire parents like you."

He looked as if he was going to say something, but she beat him to it. "I need to earn money and I do whatever it takes." This man didn't need to know why she needed it. What she needed was probably the equivalent of what one of his suits cost. It sickened her, now that she was confronted by it, how vast the void between them was. How different they were, even if she sometimes thought they had so much in common.

Something hot and lava like melted through her insides, running down her belly leaving a painful burning sensation it its wake. She couldn't believe that this man in front of her, the man at the root of the complications springing up in her life, the man she tried to help, by *lying*—because he had helped her, was angry at her.

She wasn't too happy with him either. He'd spent the night with Helen, after making her, Eleni, feel so special. He'd been so good to her, letting her rest at his home, getting his private doctor to see her, then making sure she ate, and just when they'd got talking, he upped and left.

She didn't know who he was. Sometimes he was nice and kind, and soft, and other times, like now, he looked at her as if he wanted to tear her apart.

"How did you get here?"

"On my broomstick."

"You think it's funny?"

"Can't you take a joke?"

"I'm not in the mood for jokes," he growled, whipping out his cell phone.

"I still don't understand why you're so mad at me. Take it out on Alexander, don't take it out on me."

"Sorry." He turned his back to her, giving her an unforgettable view of his back in a white shirt ... broad shoulders going down to slim hips.

"Fuck," he hissed.

"Bad night with Helen?" She really should have kept her mouth shut. She really, really, really should have. He spun around, that great, big, Herculean body of his now facing her. She couldn't help the way her greedy eyes swallowed him all up. One night at Dominic's place and she'd turned into a raving mad sex lunatic. How could she not?

"Helen?" His voice was quiet. The verbal equivalent of a pin being taken out of a grenade. There she went again with her preoccupation with death and destruction. Maybe she needed to see a therapist, more so now that she'd worked with Dominic Steele.

He bent down, his face level with hers, his cologne intoxicating her again, rendering her brain incapacitated. He inched closer, his face tanned, his eyes a kaleidoscope of gold sparkling in a sea of green and blue. He searched her face, and then ... he moved in a little bit more.

He was ... he was going ... to ... Kiss. Her. She licked her lower lip instinctively.

His gaze dipped to her lips. "You think I'm angry because of Helen?" His voice was a rumble deep in her chest.

"It's just ... a guess ... you were ..." Her brain had folded into itself, she struggled to think through the fog of her thoughts. His lips so near, his body so close she could feel the heat. He consumed her.

"I was?"

He stared at her, filling her body with ideas, and hope and even more longing. She parted her lips, wanting, wishing, imploring him to do the thing.

Focus.

Think of Jonas.

"You were happy when you left me." She managed to sound normal. As if Jonas had thrown a bucket of cold water over her. "I'm glad you told me everything about your brother. I was prepared."

She'd burst the bubble, and she would never know if he'd been about to kiss her. Standing up straight, Dominic turned away from her, whipping out his phone and ordering his driver to be ready. Then he called Miranda to fetch Eleni's laptop and bring it to his office.

She started to get up, noting that he hadn't answered her question. "You don't need to do that for me. I can take care of it. I managed to get here, didn't I?"

"I'll see you back to your hotel."

Dominic? Accompanying her to her hotel room? No. No. Never. "That's not necessary—"

"It's not your choice. The last thing I want is for you to fall down again and break the other ankle."

I do, I do have a choice. She would normally argue her point, but ... her brain, her racing heart, her damp panties. He might as well have kissed her for the effect he'd just had on her.

"It's not broken. It's sprained."

"Whatever."

She thanked Miranda for her laptop and gave her a final parting glance as she got into the elevator with Dominic.

She could already see the questions in Miranda's eyes.

Miranda who was in love with Dominic, a fact that her boss was aware of and did his best to ignore, now looked at her like a rival.

This was so messy all around. They descended in silence, and once out of the elevator, Dominic ordered Sven to help her into the car. He was aloof, and didn't talk to her in the car, to the point that she wondered why he'd come along at all.

When they reached the hotel, she got out slowly, trying not to wince too much as she put her foot on the ground. The first move always hurt after she'd been stationary for a while.

"Thank you," she said, when he came over to her with her laptop and bag. "I'll come up with you."

"There's no need."

"You're going to climb three flights of stairs with a laptop in your hand?" he retorted.

"Why are you doing this?" She didn't understand him at all. He could have sent Sven to do what he was now doing.

"As if you have other alternatives."

They entered the hotel and immediately the contrast dawned on her. The three-star rickety little hotel, with its cheap linoleum flooring, and dark interior was such a contrast to Dominic's home. It seemed a timely reminder of the differences between them.

"I can carry you up the stairs," he threatened. She couldn't tell if he was joking or not, first the aloofness, and now he was being friendly. She'd rather fall back down the stairs than that.

"You don't have to. I can manage." She flashed a smile that was only possible because she knew she'd take two painkillers as soon as she got to her room. "I'm feeling a lot better. The doctor said walking is good." She started the slow climb up, holding onto the handrail and hoisting herself up step by step. It helped that Dominic carried her belongings. He climbed with her, slowly, silently, until she got to the top and then made it into her room.

He ran his gaze around the room, before examining the small desk by the window and setting her laptop down. "Call me if you need anything."

He left abruptly, closing the door behind him.

After spending so much time with this man, she was still none the wiser as to who he was.

CHAPTER TWENTY-FIVE

DOMINIC

His brother might as well have draped an "I'm home!" banner across the front door.

Dominic's gut clenched at the sight of the black SUV outside his house, especially knowing who was inside. He was still trying to get over what had happened between him and Eleni in the office earlier.

The way he'd lost his mind and his senses. The mistake he'd almost been about to make.

Her lips, full, luscious, like everything about her. He'd been tempted to kiss her.

What the fuck had he been thinking? The woman now lived in his head rent free. He couldn't bring himself to look at her in case he did something else that was stupid. It had taken restraint to walk her up the three flights of stairs then leave her.

Now he had to deal with this. He hated that Alexander

had turned up unexpectedly, but more than that, if he were honest with himself, he hated that Alexander's arrival likely hastened Eleni's exit. And *that* was something he detested above all.

He opened the door, preparing himself. His brother wasn't stupid. Basilia had been their housekeeper for years. They knew her family. They knew Eleni wasn't a part of that family.

"Hey!" Alexander's voice came from the direction of the kitchen, and when Dominic entered, his brother was sitting on a bar stool around the island, stuffing his face with the leftovers from last night's takeout. "This is good shit." He stood up and wiped his mouth before giving Dominic a bear hug.

Dominic fought the desire to throttle his neck. "It's not shit."

"Damn right it's not." Alexander quirked a brow at his brother. "You don't usually get takeout."

Dominic breathed out slowly. "I must have known you were on your way." How many more things would he have to lie about with Alexander around?

"Have you already finished for the day? I wasn't expecting to see you until late this evening."

"I came home to see what you were doing here. Would have been nice to have some notice."

"I wanted to surprise you."

"You have." Dominic wiped a hand over his face, an image flashing through his head of Eleni meeting Alexander. What would she have thought? She'd obviously been smart enough to come up with a reasonable excuse for her being here. "What are you doing here?"

"Like I said, I was in the continent, so..."

"Doing what?"

"I had some business in London, then a couple of things to take care of in Paris. And while in Paris, it was easy to come here and see how my little brother was doing. Quit always being so uptight."

"You shouldn't have bothered."

Alexander looked suitably taken aback that he stopped eating for a few seconds. "Are you pissed about something?"

"No, really. You shouldn't have wasted your time." Dominic counted to five slowly, then hit him with it. "You've been talking to Hector."

"That again ..." Alexander rolled his eyes before refilling his plate.

"As if that doesn't suck on its own, hearing it from Hector first sucks big time."

"I was going to tell you."

"The fuck you were. Why would you do something sneaky like that?" And then it hit him like a bolt of lightning. "You're here to meet with him."

"I'm not." The defiance was too strong, too forced.

"Dad put you up to this?" Dominic demanded to know.

Alexander got up and strode over. "I'm not, I swear. We've known the man, we've done business with him before, we move in the same circles. I'm allowed to call him and see how he is."

"Spare me the bullshit. Hector isn't someone you casually invite to have drinks with. You reached out to him to find out what's going on with the deal." His progress with Galatis had been so unbelievably slow that it was practically zero. Alexander suddenly appearing wasn't a coincidence. He was here to make things happen. Dominic could guess at the conversation between his father and Alexander.

Alexander gave a half shrug. "It was dad's idea."

"I fucking knew it. You both don't think I can pull this off."

"But only because Hector can't be trusted, and we need this deal. Dad's worried about him, not you."

"Bullshit." Dominic shrugged off his brother's hold. "You and dad still think I'm the useless younger son of *the* Robert Steele. Well, I intend to prove you both wrong."

Alexander placed his hands on Dominic's shoulders. "Listen to me. That's not true, but, now that you've mentioned it, how's it going?"

Dominic bore down on his teeth. What could he say?

The man has me running around after him at all these goddamn places.

But instead he kept his mouth firmly shut, Alexander's question was all the proof he needed. "You're a really bad brother, but you're an even worse liar."

"Okay, fine. If you don't want to tell me then don't. You're mad at me, so let's leave it."

"How long are you here for?" Dominic asked suspiciously.

"A few days. I'll be out of your hair in no time."

"Just back off on the Galatis deal."

Alexander's mouth twisted. "I will, alright. Chill." Then, "Cute maid. You hitting that yet?"

Dominic's fist almost jumped to his brother's face, but by some miracle he managed to keep it by his side. He didn't need to give his brother a reason to suspect anything. "Don't be so fucking stupid."

"'Cause I sure as hell would. She's hot, got a gorgeous—"

Both of Dominic's hands fisted, and it took all of his focus to not have them connect with Alexander's jawbone. "Shut the hell up."

"Something wrong, bro?" Alexander's eyes twinkled.

"Something you want to tell me? Demi's wedding getting you all riled up?"

"That's the furthest thing from my mind." Demi's wedding was so low down on his radar, that he hadn't given it much thought until he'd realized she was marrying Galatis' nephew.

He felt restless. Couldn't stand around talking to Alexander in case his brother said something else that would irritate him.

How quickly things changed. Yesterday Eleni had been here, and that had made for an interesting, and pleasant, evening. But today with his brother, all he could do was play defensive. "I want your word."

"For what?"

"To keep your nose out of my business. No calling Galatis or arranging to see him behind my back."

"As if I would."

"You would. You so would."

For the next few days, Dominic kept a watchful eye on his brother and made sure he dragged him along to the office with him.

In addition, he was curious to know how Eleni was doing, but he didn't dare call her. Their exchange in the office had been intense and now things felt strange. Off. He didn't trust himself and knew he needed to keep some distance between them.

Late one afternoon, his cell phone beeped. Eleni had messaged him. A quiver of excitement shot through his chest:

Eleni: I hope your brother hasn't put you in a worse mood than usual.

He looked around, made sure Alexander was still working away on his laptop, and replied:

Dominic: He's under observation in my office.

A dart of exhilaration shot through him when she texted back a few moments later:

Eleni: Poor man. Is he getting the Dominic death stare?

Dominic: Is that a thing?

Eleni: It's a thing

"Let's go get some drinks," Alexander announced.

Dominic looked up. "It's early for that."

"It's never too early for drinks. Linus is coming." Alexander closed his laptop and stood up. "Helen said she might join us later."

Dominic frowned. His older brother had a tendency to create a social event out of nothing, and he'd invite anyone and everyone. It was a wonder he hadn't asked Miranda.

"Come on. I'm going home tomorrow. That should be reason enough for you to celebrate."

He wasn't wrong. Dominic's mood lifted. "That is a reason to celebrate." He stared at his phone, conscious of the fact that he hadn't replied to Eleni. He felt a pull in his chest, an urge to reply to her. "Give me a few minutes."

Dominic: My brother leaves tomorrow. I'm going for drinks with him and Helen and others. How's your ankle?

He waited a few moments, and then some more, and when Alexander hollered for him to hurry up, he turned off his computer, slipped his phone into his jacket pocket, and left.

CHAPTER TWENTY-SIX

ELENI

She had been enjoying the flurry of messages right up until Dominic had mentioned that he was going for drinks with Helen and a few others.

Reading that message helped cement Eleni's decision to go home for the weekend.

For the past few days, she'd managed to keep her thoughts in check, but sitting in the hotel room and working from there, had driven her mad. Staring at the same old four walls, ordering take out and not seeing anyone, had been like a prison sentence.

What could she do but think about Dominic?

Solitary confinement with a laptop should have kept her mind off her boss, but as the days passed, her thoughts drifted to him.

Not being at work, and therefore not in the same building as Dominic, there was no possibility that she might run into him, and robbed of any chance of seeing him, her mind had filled in the gaps. She'd thought of him the entire time.

More so because she'd recently spent so much time with him. Sometimes, it seemed like a dream.

Miranda had come over yesterday evening and they'd ventured out for something to eat. Eleni had been grateful for the fresh air and long walk, and Miranda's company made her feel better. Her friend had casually mentioned that Alexander was working in Dominic's office for a few days.

Eleni wondered how that was playing out. She wondered about it a lot. Today she'd made it through lunchtime without doing anything about it, but a combination of boredom and curiosity eventually got the better of her.

So, naturally, she'd dropped Dominic a message. It seemed only right for her to want to know, given that she'd met his brother, and was aware of their relationship.

She hadn't expected him to reply immediately. They exchanged a few messages, each giving her a dopamine hit, making her feel happy.

At least, she *had been* happy until she found out that he was going for drinks with Helen.

She had returned to Spetses later that evening.

That's what Dominic's reply had done to her. She didn't want to feel jealous, didn't like feeling miserable, and yet she did. It wasn't right for her to have an attraction for her boss, but, again, she did. She needed space, *more* space. Because even though she'd not been in the same physical environment, thoughts of him still lurked everywhere in her mind.

Believing that a change of scenery would help, she'd gone home. Her mother, noting her ankle straightaway, started fussing over her. This was new, something Eleni wasn't used to, and she accepted it, and enjoyed having her mother act like a mother. She cooked for her too, and Eleni was grateful for some home-cooked food after days of eating takeout.

Later the next evening, after Stefanos finished work, they found a quiet little corner of the beach and caught up, watching the sun setting.

Stefanos had a heap of questions about her job and how she was getting on, and he wanted to know how she'd hurt her ankle. She told him about meetings she accompanied Dominic on, the ones where she did nothing but sit in the car and wait for him. She told him how she'd tripped and fallen down a few stairs and sprained her ankle, but she told him no more than that. Then she hurriedly explained about the eccentric billionaire Hector Galatis, and the way he had Dominic traipsing around the Greek temples and ruins. And how Dominic usually came back from these meetings annoyed and frustrated.

"Why does Dominic put up with this?" Stefanos asked.

"He's trying to show that he can put up with this game. Galatis really is crazy," she told Stefanos. "In the heat of the midday sun, poor Dominic is out there, getting burned."

"Poor Dominic?" Stefanos gaped at her.

Heat scampered up her cheeks, and she was glad the sun was setting, and that they were both facing the sea. She couldn't bring herself to look at him. "I feel sorry for him. Dominic wants this deal so badly, and that man makes him run around all the time."

"What's he like to work for, this gorgeous billionaire hunk?"

"He's ..." She didn't know how to answer that because so much had changed. She didn't even see Dominic as a boss because of the way they'd met in the beginning, but then he'd mesmerized her when she'd seen him in a business suit that first time. If he had treated her like he did the others, she would feel differently, and she would be able to answer Stefanos' questions. But it was all so very different. Dominic was nice to her.

"He's okay," she said, not wanting to divulge much because Stefanos could see right through her. He would notice the wobble in her voice, or the expression on her face. He would know that something was up. She'd never been able to hide anything from him. "But the money is the best part of it all."

"Yeah?"

She nodded; her glee uncontainable. Her salary was the most she'd ever earned anywhere.

"You can go and climb that mountain now?" Stefanos asked. "You'll be able to cross that off your list."

"I guess I will." Her mood turned pensive. She'd done this for the money, for the mountain climb, but she hadn't even thought about the expedition much. Only now that Stefanos brought it up.

"When?"

"I haven't even thought about that." Tears welled up in her eyes. "I haven't been thinking about Jonas much, either."

Stefanos leaned forward in concern. "It's okay," he said softly.

"How could I forget?" she whispered. It was Dominic who was starting to occupy the place in her heart and mind that Jonas once had. "How could I do that?"

"It's okay to not think of him all the time. You're not expected to."

"But I loved him."

Loved him. She'd never talked about her feelings for Jonas in the past tense. She lowered her head, overcome by a crushing sense of guilt and sadness. Stefanos put an arm around her shoulder. "It's okay, Leni. It's okay."

But it didn't feel okay. It felt like she was starting to forget Jonas. Her cell phone pinged and she glanced at it. A message from Dominic had just arrived. She hadn't replied to his last message, and this being a weekend, she hadn't expected to hear anything further from him. Her heart rate surged. She hadn't even read the message, but the mere sight of Dominic's name was enough to give her palpitations.

Dominic: When are you coming back?

How did he know she'd gone home? She hadn't mentioned it. She'd only told Miranda.

Her heart missed a few beats. Maybe this wasn't a continuation of the flirty messages, but something work related. She got worried.

Eleni: In a few days

She didn't want to make the journey back to Athens just yet and working from home here seemed like a good idea.

"Who is it?" Stefanos asked, as she tried to bring the phone closer to her face so that he couldn't see her message.

"Miranda." She placed the phone by the side of her leg, then stretched out her legs, flexing and pointing her toes gently. "I should get back. My mother is cooking dinner again tonight, and she wants us to eat together."

"She misses you." Stefanos got up slowly, and together they folded the large blanket they'd been sitting on. "Let's get something to eat with Angeliki and Phoebe tomorrow. Angeliki has man problems."

"A new man or the one she met in Athens."

"She's gone through a few more since then."

Eleni gasped. "But it's only been—"

"I know." Stefanos' expression was the epitome of disapproval.

"We need to see her." Eleni did not like the sound of that. Her phone buzzed again and the high she got from seeing Dominic's name flash up caused her to break out into a huge smile. She quickly schooled her expression, but it was too late.

Stefanos was watching her closely. "What's she saying now?"

Dominic: That's vague. Care to be specific?

Eleni thought fast. "She wants to know when I'm coming back."

"When are you going back?"

"Maybe in the middle of the week. I overdid it with my walking and my ankle feels sore again."

"We can hang out for a few more evenings?" Stefanos was excited.

"Yes." She smiled in acknowledgement. The idea of being at home and hanging out with her friends again filled her with happiness. She tapped an answer out quickly on her phone.

Eleni: Maybe Wednesday. Are you missing me?

She'd hit SEND too fast, getting carried away in the double conversation with Stefanos.

Her phone buzzed straightaway.

Dominic: Do I miss you? Impossible not to.

Her heart leapt. She swallowed. Something ignited in her belly, stirred her senses.

Stefanos moved towards her with one side of the blanket in his hands, and together they folded it in two and two again.

"How about we try eating out tomorrow, the four of us?" She searched around for her slippers and heard her phone buzz again. She found one, and then the other, buried under some sand which she shook off, flapping her sandal in the air.

"You lied." Stefanos had grabbed her phone and held it out for her. He wouldn't have been able to get into it without a PIN code, but the heading of Dominic's message flashed up for a few seconds right along with his name.

Eleni snatched her phone. She opened her mouth to say something, but closed it again. There was no point in telling a white lie to hide an existing one.

"Does he talk to you like that all the time?" The hard edge to Stefanos's voice cautioned her to watch her reply.

"Who?"

"I'm not stupid, Leni. Dominic Steele, who do you think?"

There was nothing she could say.

"You're flirting, the pair of you?"

"No!"

"You have something to tell me, Leni?" If looks could kill, she'd be as dead as the starfish she could see behind his shoulder.

"No." It was true. There was nothing romantic between her and Dominic. *Nothing.* Nothing had happened. It might have come close to happening ... unless that time in his office was all in her head.

She wasn't even sure. Too many painkillers had muddled her mind. "We're not flirting." She backed away, holding the blanket for security.

"Does he usually talk to you like that?"

"He's only asking when I'm coming back, Stefanos. Why are you getting so worked up?"

"Oh, I don't know. Maybe because I'm trying to work out why you lied and said it was Miranda?"

She sighed loudly, then stopped to face him. "I knew you would give me a hard time about it."

"Obviously, you knew there was something for me to give you a hard time about."

"Wait, what?"

"I worry about you, Leni. I've seen guys make a move on you."

"Dominic would never do anything like that. He's a gentleman."

"I'm not talking about him making a sleazy move. He's too refined to do anything that vulgar. I'm talking about him falling for you."

"That's not going to happen!" This was Dominic Steele. He wasn't about to fall for someone like her, no matter how many tricks her mind played on her to make her believe otherwise.

Stefanos shook his head, but she waved her hand, dismissing any crazy ideas he had. "Nothing is going on. It's just a message."

"Some message," Stefanos grumbled, and then became unusually quiet as they headed back. The last thing he said to her before she went into her house was to be careful. He told her he didn't want to see her get hurt.

She'd laughed it off, pretended he was being silly and that she didn't know what he was talking about. But once inside her home, and without Stefano's scrutinizing gaze, she was confused.

She read the message again and couldn't believe her eyes, or ignore the furious beating of her heart.

Dominic: Do I miss you? Impossible not to.

She was attracted to this man in a way she'd never felt attraction before. Excitement pulsed through her, and her heart threatened to burst through her ribcage. She held her breath and considered her next move.

Why would Dominic say such a thing? Why had she asked him such a thing in the first place?

Her insides turned gooey like marshmallow. She didn't know what this was, this emotional connection between her and Dominic.

She'd been relaxed, and in a conversation with Stefanos, and therefore not paying proper attention. She'd been excited, and happy that Dominic had texted her. Maybe it was the notion of the distance between them, and her knowing that she wouldn't have to face Dominic anytime soon, that had made her bold?

There was no other way to explain her forwardness.

After dinner with her mother she disappeared into her room and dissected her and Dominic's texts as if they were cryptic crossword hints.

With a racing heart, and butterflies in her stomach, she lay on her bed and typed out her reply, without alluding to his message.

Eleni: Sorry for the delay

She waited breathlessly.

Dominic: Reason?

Eleni: I'm not a loner like you. I have a life and friends.

Dominic: Meaning?

Eleni: I was out with Stefanos, sitting on the beach, reflecting on life

Dominic: Conclusion?

She paused a moment, contemplating his questions and wondering what had gotten into him.

She couldn't wrap her head around it. The fact that Dominic was texting her.

Like this.

Again.

She wanted honesty. To get to the bottom of it, because this was so unlike him. She worried that Alexander's stay had profoundly affected his mental health.

Eleni: Are you drunk?

Dominic: Had a meeting with Hector, a proper one. At his house. Drinks were involved.

She gasped with worry.

Eleni: Did you embarrass yourself?

Dominic: I can handle my drink. Unlike some people

She grinned.

Eleni: That's good to hear, because you seem pretty drunk to me

He didn't reply immediately, and she missed the rapid fire of text messages. She hadn't realized how much she'd missed him until now and this texting back and forth between them.

Dots appeared on her screen, then stopped, and a moment passed, stretching out longer, making her wonder what he was writing, or deleting; what it was he wanted to say, or hide.

She waited. And waited. And waited.

Her fingers hovered over her phone. She hadn't touched a drop of alcohol, and yet she felt ... daring, light-headed, awash with euphoria. It was heady, flirting like this was so much easier, so much more daring than talking face to face. He'd stopped typing and it didn't look like he was going to message her. So she did.

Eleni: You said you missed me

Her heart hammered with excitement, or maybe it was fear, or even downright stupidity.

This was not appropriate. Dominic was her BOSS. She squeezed her eyes shut, enjoying the high. This was so much fun. It lit her up from within when she'd been dead inside since Jonas passed ...

Dominic made her smile again. He made her heart gallop, he stirred something inside her that had lain dormant for so long.

He didn't reply straightaway, the gut-churning delay making her wonder if he was drafting up a letter for her immediate removal. He could fire her for inappropriate conduct, even though he was as much a party to this as she was.

A message flashed onto the screen.

Dominic: I did not say that. In those words

She breathed out. Then saw he was typing. Then stopped again. Then another message flashed up.

Dominic: Don't put words in my mouth

Her insides turned to a watery mush. Thoughts swirled and swooshed through her mind, before breaking into little pieces like confetti.

Don't do it. Do. Not. Do It.

Eleni: I'd love to put something in your mouth.

Their messages had crossed, because his message flashed up instantaneously. She was hyperventilating as she read it:

Dominic: I have a wedding to attend. My ex's. I might have had a few glasses of whiskey

She shouldn't have done it. She shouldn't have said *that* to him. Big mistake. Big. Sackable. Deplorable. Sluttish. Mistake.

She buried her face in her pillow, humiliation burning not just her cheeks, but her entire body.

I'd love to put something in your mouth.

There was no buzzing sound on her phone. No reply. She imagined Dominic to be disgusted and ashamed on her behalf. She waited for what seemed like ages, but only eight minutes has passed, according to time on her cell phone.

There was a chance he hadn't read her message. She

would act as if she hadn't sent it, and prayed that he would act as if he hadn't received it.

She glanced at his latest message again and tried to read between the lines. He had a wedding to attend, his ex's, and he'd had a few glasses of whiskey. There was a story here, and if she dug deep enough she would find it. Pushing her embarrassment away, she texted:

Eleni: You sound sad

He didn't answer straightaway. Then:

Dominic: Not sad at all

Eleni frowned. This man sounded as if he was drowning his sorrows. Either he was lying, or there was something he wasn't telling her. She didn't know what to say. There were questions she wanted answers to, but ... without prying further ...

Eleni: You sound as if you still like her

Dominic: I do

A heaviness settled in her chest. She considered turning her phone off, not wanting to feel more pain. But another message popped up from him:

Dominic: But not like that. I'm happy for her

Eleni: Thank goodness. I'd hate to see what you're like when you're sad

She regretted sending that. But this was good, for her, it gave her hope that he'd missed her text completely.

Dominic: We parted on good terms.

Eleni: Good

Eleni breathed a sigh of relief. Okay. This was good. Maybe he wasn't crazy about his ex. They were friends. This. Was. Good. This she could take.

Dominic: She's marrying Galatis' nephew. Small world.

She almost fell off the bed. *What? Galatis' nephew?* So, it was true. These billionaires all mixed in the same circles. She had more questions.

Eleni: Then why are you drinking like a sad man?

Dominic: She wanted to know who my plus one was, for the table settings

Eleni: And?

Dominic: There is no plus one

Her heart did a somersault inside her chest.
Why was he telling her this?

Eleni: What about Helen?

She bit her lower lip. Had she learned nothing? Bringing up Helen's name turned Dominic into a rabid dog.

Dominic: She's my lawyer. How many times do I have to tell you?

She couldn't tell if he was angry or sad, the way he'd fired off that reply so quickly.

Maybe Helen was just a friend, and not a friend-with-benefits? But it still didn't make sense why Dominic would drink more because of a table arrangement setting. Was he ashamed to go alone? Was that why?

Maybe it was jealousy, maybe he wanted to show his ex that he was doing fine without her. An idea sprouted in her mind, and because her recklessness was in full swing, she sent him her reply:

Eleni: If you need to make the bride jealous, I'll go as your fake date

She'd gone too far. Crossed that line between employee and boss. Worse, she'd made the mistake of thinking that he had feelings for her, just because she did for him.

A reply buzzed through, and she jumped off the bed, staring at her screen, afraid to read what he'd texted.

Dominic: I don't

She swallowed. Okay. This was good. He'd ignored her offer for what it was. Ludicrous rubbish. Dots appeared on her screen and she held her breath.

Dominic: need to make her jealous

She sighed with relief, and quickly typed a reply.

Eleni: That's good

Their messages criss-crossed again with his flashing up at the exact same time.

Dominic: That's not a bad idea. Why don't you?

She watched more dots appear on the screen, then:

Dominic: come along, that is.

She dropped the phone. Alarm kicking her stomach into her throat. What was she supposed to say to that? He'd asked her to come with him ...

She fanned her face, wondering how she'd gotten herself into this mess. At the same time, another part of her brain was trying to process the fact that he'd called her bluff and asked her to come along.

What should she say? What could she say?

He was her boss.

She couldn't go to the ball, or rather, the wedding.

Who did she think she was?

Cinderella?

CHAPTER TWENTY-SEVEN

DOMINIC

What was he?
Needy?
Desperate?
Thirteen?

Dominic slammed his whiskey glass down on the table and let out a loud groan. Eleni hadn't replied. He'd gone too far.

Shit.

He'd said too much.

He'd lost control of his emotions and his senses, something which had been happening ever since he'd met Eleni. Something had been happening to her, too. Something which had prompted her to make a lewd comment back to him. Knowing her, he was certain she was dying from humiliation. He wasn't going to mention it.

The effect she had on him was intoxicating. He didn't

need alcohol when he was around her. He stared at his cell phone, waiting for her to reply, panic knotting his insides.

But there was nothing. Nothing to indicate that Eleni was typing a response, either.

Answer me.

Several minutes passed, and still there was nothing.

It didn't look as if she was going to reply, and he couldn't blame her. His behaviour was nothing short of him making a verbal pass at her. He should have known better; he'd managed it so far. It hadn't been easy, but he'd managed it.

Nothing like a few glasses of whiskey to throw his self-control out of the window.

Asshole.

She was an employee, a temporary employee at that, someone he'd bypassed the usual hiring process for in order to get her to join the company.

And now he'd asked her to come to a wedding, as his plus one. Or rather, *she* had asked, and he had accepted her offer.

Disgusted with himself, he was about to switch his phone off completely—not wanting to be lured in by the sound of more texts coming through—but he couldn't bring himself to do it. That would require going cold turkey, and he wasn't ready to do that. He threw the phone onto the empty armchair, instead.

He felt like a juvenile; unable to rein in his emotions, and his feelings about Eleni were getting completely out of control.

At work the next day he kept his head down, locking himself away in his office. At least Alexander had left; that was one less thing to worry about.

If any more meetings came up with Galatis, he'd have to suffer taking Linus along with him again just as he had a few days ago. No more Eleni accompanying him. No more having Eleni within a two feet radius of him.

The last meeting had been fruitful. Galatis had actually listened to what Dominic was proposing and things were starting to move ahead.

As for Demi's wedding, he simply would not go. A part of him had ignored the invite altogether and pushed it to the back burner until Galatis had mentioned it.

One morning as he made his way to work, he'd stepped into the elevator and pressed the button to the third floor only to find Eleni and Miranda slip in after him.

"Oh ... hey ... Dominic." Miranda blushed her usual shade of bright red, while Eleni's face drained of color.

"Miranda." He nodded at his PA, but his gaze returned to Eleni.

"Hi." She smiled, but it was a weak smile, a half-assed smile.

The journey from the ground floor to the third lasted a lifetime.

When the elevator doors opened, the women left first, and he released a deep sigh.

Heading straight into his office he sat down, collapsing into the chair with relief, glad to be in the safety and sanctity of his own private space.

ELENI

She returned to work in the middle of the week, and as she surveyed the building, it felt as if she'd been away for much longer than a few days.

A lot had happened in that time. Messages had flown

back and forth between her and her boss, and which she now regretted. Back then, in the easy comfort of her bed, she'd been finger happy, firing off texts. A familiarity had developed and deepened, to the point that she had made the mistake of forgetting who Dominic was.

Anxiety clawed in her chest. She hadn't replied to his last text, and she had no intention of doing so. They had ceased all communication and it was for the best.

Just as she was about to set foot in the building, Miranda screeched out her name. Eleni was so pleased to see her friend that she threw her arms around her and hugged her as if she were a long lost relative.

They caught up quickly, talking over one another, but when Eleni stepped into the lift and saw Dominic, her heart stopped.

She didn't know where to look and barely managed to say 'Hi.' When the elevator doors opened, she had never been happier to get out of there and escape into the office. The co-workers who usually ignored her now greeted her as if she were a long-lost friend. They fussed around her, offered to fetch her water from the cooler and to get her lunch for her, even though her ankle had healed, and she was walking like normal.

Eleni offered them a plastic smile, no longer caring for their so-called friendliness which was too late in coming.

But inwardly, her heart was on a hamster wheel, furiously racing to get ahead and imagine a better future. One in which she could accept that Dominic was her boss and nothing else. But after a long, gruelling hour of trying to focus on her work, she couldn't take it any longer. She couldn't forget the things they'd said, the things *she'd* said.

It was time to confront him.

Looking straight ahead, she sailed past Miranda's desk,

her muscles tense, her words prepared, ready to face Dominic no matter what mood he was in on the other side of the door. She knocked and entered when ordered.

His eyes widened when he saw her and something told her he wasn't ready.

"I'm ...uh ..." She fidgeted with her hands. A terrible thought coming to her. While she'd been panicking and dissecting their communication, what if Dominic had been so drunk he wouldn't even remember what they'd said? The man was busy running multi-million dollar companies. What made her think he even remembered what had happened?

"You're back," he commented.

"We met in the elevator just now, of course I'm back."

"It was a rhetorical question."

"A what?"

"I said it for effect. I wasn't looking for an answer."

"Why would you do that?"

He stared at her. This wasn't getting any easier. She overlooked the language differences and dove in. "I'd taken too many painkillers when I ... when I offered to be your... your ... fake date." She scratched her hands and added, "The other day."

He closed his eyes for a few seconds, as if she'd dredged up something he'd rather have left far behind, as if memories of that evening were too embarrassing for him to talk about. "I'm sorry for texting you when I was under the influence of alcohol."

Her lower lip parted. She allowed herself to breathe. "Okay."

"It's not okay. I shouldn't have said what I did."

This was good. They understood one another, they were at least talking about it which meant the awkwardness could go, eventually. She took a step towards his desk, her hands clasped low against her belly. "I shouldn't have suggested I'd be your fake date. I made the offer, Dominic, not you. You didn't do anything wrong."

"You didn't reply." He looked at her, and for a fleeting moment, she caught something strange in his eyes. He coughed lightly, then looked at the papers on his desk and picked up a pen. "I wondered if something had happened when you didn't, that's all."

"I felt silly. I was out of line, making that suggestion. I didn't even have an excuse because I hadn't touched a drop of alcohol."

"But you'd popped plenty of pills."

She forced a laugh. "I was heavily drugged up."

"It seems we both were under the influence." He started signing the letters on his desk, his dismissal like a pain shooting across her chest, letting her know she wasn't important and occupied no part of his mind or his time.

"At least that's been cleared," she said, something breaking in her voice.

"We're good, Eleni. Close the door behind you."

Once outside, she leaned against the door for a second or three. Her desire for this man knotted around her heart like a barbed wire fence, holding it captive.

CHAPTER TWENTY-EIGHT

DOMINIC

For the second time in the meeting, Galatis picked up the double-sided sheet of paper which comprised of the deal Dominic was pushing for, and examined it carefully.

"I have contemplated this in great depth."

These were sweet words to Dominic's ears. "And?"

"The profit share you suggest is not something I can agree to. You're being arrogant, Dominic. I have the biggest fleet, and you have ... nothing in comparison."

Dominic released a welcome breath. They were making headway. Discussions, at long, fucking last. "We have the means, the technology and resources to help you to upgrade your old fleet, and we can also help to maintain it. Let's face it, Hector. Only those companies who embrace smart shipping will succeed. Steele Shipping is at the forefront, and we can help you, but help comes at a cost."

"I need to think about it some more."

Dominic forced a smile. "You've only had the summer."

Amusement lined Galatis' face. "And in that time I gave you a grounding in Greek history."

"You certainly did. I have been educated."

"The pleasure is mine." Galatis' thick brows lifted in amusement. "I will discuss this further with my people".

"Please do." He prayed the man would move fast, this time around.

"We will meet again and discuss further."

"That would be great. Let's meet here again," Dominic suggested, with a nod at the surroundings. A meeting inside an office, around a desk—only because Galatis was suffering from a chest infection—had been far more productive than any of the previous meetings. Who knew?

"Alexander has gone back?" the old man asked.

"He has."

"It is a pity we did not meet."

"He was busy," Dominic replied smoothly.

Galatis tapped his fingers on the table. "You are eager to please your father, eh?"

"Aren't we all?" Dominic smiled sweetly, but it was a smile he didn't feel.

The old man started to cough. A low, dry cough that soon turned into a thunderous, rumble. He thumped his chest, and an assistant rushed to his side with a glass of water.

He took a few sips, wiped his mouth with a handkerchief another assistant passed to him. He sat back, his breathing heavy and labored. "Old age is a killer, Dominic," he chortled, then burst out into a fully-fledged laugh.

Dominic smiled. "You have many years ahead of you yet, Hector." He was anxious to get this wrapped up because after weeks of slow-as-a-snail progress, things had suddenly taken shape and had momentum. "Why don't we schedule a meeting now for next week?"

"Next week I am busy. My nephew is getting married. My sister's boy. You remember?"

Dominic nodded. "How could I forget? We should schedule something on your return. When will that be?"

"It's in Santorini, and it will take me a while to get back to work." He lifted his heavy hands in a can't-be-helped gesture. "It is a Greek wedding, and there will be much celebrating. You are coming, no? I invite you."

Dominic couldn't hide it any longer. "We live in a small world, Hector. Your nephew is marrying ..." he chose his words carefully, "a friend of mine, as it happens."

"Demi Laskaris? You know her?" Galatis' squirrelly eyes probed Dominic's face for answers.

"Yes. Like I said, it's a very small world and Demi has also given me an invite." The man didn't need to know that he and Demi had had a short, passionate summer fling.

"Two invitations." The old man slapped his thigh and laughed. "You are in big demand, eh?"

Dominic nodded. He didn't care to elaborate on how he knew Demi, and he prayed that Galatis wouldn't ask.

"Excellent. We will talk there. You are lucky, Dominic."

"Why is that?" he asked, feeling uneasy. He'd been about to say that he wasn't going.

"At a family celebration, you will get me at my best. If your luck is good, and I am very drunk and very happy, we might even seal the deal. What do you say, eh?"

Hell, no. He had no intention of traipsing after Galatis at a wedding. He stared at the man blankly. "I ..." He was about to tell him he had no plans to attend. But if Galatis was saying they could finalize the deal, he *had* to go.

"We will meet there, my friend," said Galatis. "I look

forward to introducing you to my family. They don't know you as well as they know your father and your brother."

Dominic opened his mouth again.

"Are you single, Dominic?"

Such a direct question required a direct answer. "Single and proud of it."

"No wife, no girlfriend, eh?" The old man steepled his fingers together. "If my half a century in business has taught me anything, it is that behind every successful man is a strong woman. I will make sure you find someone perfect." Galatis tapped his fat index fingers together, a contemplative expression on his face. "I have some *beautiful* nieces. My own daughters are happily married but my nieces ..." He did a chef's kiss with his fingers. "It would be a good union. The Steele name and my sister's family. They are half Galatis ... it would still be a very powerful union."

Dominic laughed uneasily. "Oh, I have someone."

Galatis surveyed him. "You told me you were single and proud of it. Did you lie?"

Jesus. "No," he replied quickly. "Not at all. I have someone in mind. Someone who ... who is special. It is new."

Galatis nodded, his smile one of satisfaction. "A good woman grounds you. She will stop you from making mistakes."

"Mistakes?" Dominic didn't understand.

"A good woman will stop men from thinking with their balls instead of their head."

What was this crazy old fool talking about?

"I don't understand."

"You know how I built my empire, Dominic? How I came from poverty such as that you could never survive, and I went from that to this ..." Galatis waved his arm around the wood paneled walls of his office. "Because I had a reason to make something of myself. I had a family who needed security, food and a roof over their heads. My hunger to win at all costs is what I am known for, and it was all because of them, my family. I had to do what I did, because of them. Family is everything."

The old man started another coughing fit, while Dominic looked on helplessly, wondering what he had talked himself into.

As Galatis' assistants fretted over him, he could only wonder how in the world he'd gone from not going to a wedding, to now attending with someone 'special.'

As the car drove back to the office, he contemplated Galatis' words. He would ask Helen to come with him, if only to appease the old man. Galatis had met Helen and knew she was the company lawyer. He would buy it, that they were together.

Being this close to getting the deal done, he would rather die than let anything get in the way.

CHAPTER TWENTY-NINE

ELENI

Things were back to normal. For her. Maybe for Dominic they were the same as they had always been.

Eleni doubted that she had ever been a blip on his radar, but for her, Dominic had been rooted in her mind for a long time.

But now there was no texting, no messaging, no meetings among the Greek ruins. There were no further interactions with Dominic and this was probably for the best.

"So many people," Eleni gasped as they entered the large outdoor seating area of the restaurant.

"I told you it would be fun! You'll get to meet other people from the company. Everyone knows Anna."

I don't. Eleni felt like an imposter attending the farewell party of a woman who had been at the company for forty years and was now retiring. It was someone she didn't know, but Miranda had insisted that she come along. "It's free food and drink. It will be fun."

She needed fun, more than the food and drink. She needed something to take her mind off the intense rollercoaster ride she'd been on with Dominic. This was the only reason she'd come. As her eyes scanned around the place, she could see it was brimming full of people. The company was so much bigger than she had at first envisaged.

Sitting on the third floor and isolated, she had never set foot on any of the other floors and had no idea as to the number of employees who worked here. She only ever saw a handful of people. The same people, all the time.

At least Dominic wouldn't be here. He hated parties, and an event like this was one of his worst nightmares. They had stayed out of one another's way, and he'd had a few meetings with Galatis—she knew this because Miranda updated her on everything—and had learned that he'd taken Linus with him. She had been replaced, but she understood why.

It would have been awkward.

"Do they do this for everyone who leaves?" she asked. The place was packed.

Miranda laughed. "No. But Anna's been here since the beginning. Management makes it a big deal when it's someone important like that." She waved to a group of people hanging around the bar. Eleni dutifully followed her friend around, noting that Miranda was more at ease here, and obviously in her element. It was a refreshing sight to see.

For the rest of the evening Eleni stayed by Miranda's side, letting her friend introduce her to new people. She had fun, too. It made for a distraction, being out and meeting new people instead of suffering the pain of unrequited love and drowning in angst between the four walls of her hotel room.

But her ears pricked up when someone mentioned that

Dominic would be making a speech. Something heavy dropped in Eleni's stomach, her reaction to this snippet of news catching her unawares. She had tried to push Dominic to the back of her mind, but she seemed to be failing. Everywhere she went, he turned up.

From that moment on, she'd been on edge, unable to concentrate on any conversation, her stomach churning as her eyes and ears were on high alert for signs of Dominic.

As the evening wore on she grew impatient and nervous, and killed some time by having a few slices of pizza. She had half a mind to leave, and yet a part of her was curious to stay.

"There's Dominic," someone said. She was standing in a group with Miranda.

The hairs on the back of her neck straightened, and something tingled in the base of her belly. A silence descended on the crowd and everyone looked in one direction. She turned to find Dominic a few yards away, his eyes burning into her.

This man had an effect on her which she didn't understand. Even when she had her back turned to him, her body could sense his presence.

"He's with Helen again," Miranda said in a voice low enough so that only she could hear.

"So he is," Eleni remarked, trying to normalize her shaky voice.

Standing on the side a few meters out of sight was Helen. Eleni couldn't avoid staring at the lawyer, couldn't stop herself from making the comparison of that beautiful woman and herself.

But Dominic's eyes were on her. His face tanned and golden, his eyes more intense than ever, sparkled under the shimmering light of restaurant lamps. He started to talk about Anna and the decades long contribution she'd made to the company, but every so often, his gaze would find its way to her.

And when that happened, it didn't matter how many people were around, for her, it was just the two of them.

DOMINIC

He had managed to persuade Helen to join him for the farewell drinks of one of their longest standing employees who was finally retiring.

He hadn't wanted to come. He hated social gatherings, but it was important for him to make an appearance. He had to deliver a speech, because Anna had worked here from the first day his father had set up this branch of the company.

What he hadn't expected was to see Eleni here. It was like a punch in the stomach, and once their gazes had locked, he hadn't been able to take his eyes off her.

What in God's name was he doing, spending his waking moments thinking about her, a much younger woman who was still grieving for her boyfriend? He recoiled in disgust each time he thought of what she might think if she ever found out how he felt.

Yet sometimes, he wondered if she felt the same, after all, she was the one who'd sent those suggestive messages.

He forced himself to look away and deliver a heartfelt speech, because working here for forty years was a huge accomplishment. By the time he was done talking, Anna had tears in her eyes. He beckoned for her to come up, and then took out a small envelope from his jacket pocket. "On behalf of the company, our sincere thanks and gratitude for your service, Anna."

The head of her department had already given her flowers and a gift bought from the proceeds of a collection contributed to by employees. Anna looked at him, her eyes filled with gratitude as she accepted the envelope.

And then it was over. He released a breath hoping to ease the tightness across his chest, and returned to Helen, because he couldn't go to Eleni, no matter how much he wanted to.

But even as he listened to Helen talking about her day at work, it came to him: the problem that kept him awake at night and weighed heavily on him during the day, had a solution, and he'd been staring at her throughout his speech.

He had considered other options and drawn a blank. Helen was going away with her boyfriend and would not be free on the weekend of the wedding. He could have hired a discreet escort, but he didn't want to make polite conversation with a woman he didn't know. Attending the wedding and making small talk with the guests would be draining enough.

He glanced at Eleni, sucked in a breath, and mentally prepared his proposal.

ELENI

"You're staying?" Miranda asked as she swiped two glasses of champagne off the table and handed one to Eleni.

"I'll stay on a bit longer." Eleni had been planning to leave, but now she had a reason not to. She sipped her champagne and tried not to look in Dominic's direction, but from her peripheral vision she could make out that Helen was still glued to his side.

She tried to keep her attention to Miranda who was laughing and joking with her friends.

"Enjoying the party?" Dominic broached the circle. Everyone in the group turned and stared at him. As did she. When he lifted his bottle of beer to his lips, her attention turned to his mouth and stayed there. A murmur of 'Yes's' floated in the air, and Miranda turned quiet, staring at him, slowly blushing.

Someone asked Dominic how he was doing, and Eleni could see Dominic visibly blanch. He didn't like things like this. She looked around for signs of Helen, and didn't find her.

And then she wondered why he'd come to this group of people, why not Linus, or some of the managers?

Why here? Where she was?

Did it mean something?

Her heart thundered inside her chest as Dominic smiled and made pleasant small talk—something she knew he detested.

And it vanished, all of her hard work of trying to forget him had been undone in less than two seconds now that this gorgeous, tanned, wide-shouldered man in a crisp white button-down shirt stood in front of her smelling of ocean breeze. He always smelled so clean and refreshing.

She remained silent, letting the people in the group talk to him, while she listened. Every once in a while he would glance at her and her insides would turn molten.

Then, slowly, one by one, people started to leave. Fraternising with the boss in a social setting wasn't a great way to have fun. Miranda left, too, but probably for other reasons. Eleni needed to make her escape but she sensed, or wished—it didn't matter which because her logic meter stopped working whenever Dominic was around—that he wanted to talk to her. Because never in a million years would this man have willingly come and joined his employees, let alone spent time conversing with them.

"And you," he said, to the one person who remained standing with her. "How are you enjoying the party?" His tone was slightly sneering, slippery as ice, hard to gauge. Not surprisingly, the man he'd addressed his question to—the guy who had asked Dominic how he was—mumbled something she couldn't clearly make out before quickly disappearing.

It was just the two of them left. She had trouble looking at him, and tried to think of something to say, a question to ask, a prayer to recite.

"How is your foot?" Dominic asked.

"All healed now." Ba-boom ba-boom ba-boom galloped her heart. "How's your brother?"

"Overseas, mercifully."

She looked up at him, saw the tightness around his eyes and wondered what had happened. "Did you two fight?"

"Not physically." Dominic looked away, giving her a rare opportunity to gawk at his face. She greedily drank in every inch of him. His short answer told her that he didn't want to talk about it. "It's not like you to mingle with your workers," she remarked, changing the topic.

"I had a speech to make," he replied smoothly. "I didn't know that you knew Anna."

"I don't. Miranda dragged me here."

"Dragged?"

"I didn't want to come."

"Because I'd be here?" His voice was low again, intimate, for her ears only, as if they were lovers talking about their lives and little disagreements.

"I didn't expect you to be here. So, no. Not for that reason. I don't know many people here, and Miranda said it would be a good opportunity to get to know people."

"Is that what you were doing? Making new friends?"

Her eyes scanned over him. "Tell me you didn't come over here to interrogate me about being sociable."

That muscle, the bulging, popping little tell-tale sign along his jaw indicated his unease. "I don't suppose you're free this weekend?" His eyes were dark, and she couldn't read him, couldn't work out if he was being serious or not. Couldn't determine what he was asking, or why. Couldn't be sure if her ears had misheard or her brain had wrongly communicated.

"What did you say?"

He chewed his lip, something this man never did. He looked uneasy, again, something this man never was. Something was up. Was it possible that he was on tenterhooks like her?

Maybe it wasn't entirely in her head.

"I need a favor."

She stared at him. She had definitely misheard. "A favor?" But if not ... she would help him. Of course, she would. Dominic had always helped her and she would do whatever he asked.

"This will sound strange ..." He lowered his voice and looked around slowly, then leaned in, as if he had a huge secret to tell her. "What you once suggested ... about being my fake date..." His voice turned to a whisper so that she had to inch nearer to hear him. "Is that something you ... uh ... you might consider—" He was stammering again. A sign that he was uneasy.

"I'll do it."

"You don't even know what it is."

"I'll do it anyway. It won't be illegal. I know that much. I know you're a decent man, so, I'm not worried."

He let out a huff, which she couldn't decipher.

"I want to help you because you've helped me, Dominic."

"Hmmm." He made an agreeing sound, then, his voice still low, and bending towards her, "It's inappropriate of me to ask you this but—"

"You wouldn't if you weren't stuck. I understand." Him needing her help made her feel powerful.

He coughed lightly, his eyes darting around as if he were looking for spies. Eleni understood his caution. "I asked Helen, because the optics would have been better—Galatis has seen us at meetings," he said quickly, "but her boyfriend is taking her to Venice." He gave her a pointed look as if to press this point.

Trumpets blasted and confetti rained down from the heavens in the back of her mind. Her heart did the salsa.

Helen had a boyfriend and it wasn't Dominic. So, it was true. They were just friends. Not friends with benefits. "Lucky woman," she answered slowly. She would file all of this away—tonight, and what was yet to come—and put it somewhere safe to analyze carefully later.

"I considered asking Miranda, but I was afraid she might rupture a few blood vessels in shock. Also, not appropriate." His lips quirked upwards.

"No," she agreed, though she wanted to know how him asking her was any more appropriate.

"But ... I trust you, and I don't see you as an employee."

"You don't?" A wave of surprise crashed over her.

"Because of ... situations and circumstances."

Situations and circumstances.

Her insides were doing the Sirtaki. Dominic didn't look or sound drunk. He was sober and normal. Talking to her on an equal level.

"I need to get this deal done. I don't know what I'll be more relieved about, getting the deal done, or never having to meet with Galatis again, at least, not for a long time."

His words were a reminder that after this he would be gone, returning to his life back in the US.

"How will this help you with the deal?"

"Because Hector intimated that he might be more relaxed and easier to deal with during his nephew's wedding."

"His nephew?" She didn't understand. "But you said it was your ex who was getting married? Are we talking about a different wedding altogether?"

"Small world. My ex just happens to be marrying Galatis' nephew."

She let out a shriek. "What?"

"It's true. She is. Small world."

Eleni couldn't comprehend it. "Was it her goal to find an 'aire?'"

"A what?"

"A millionaire or billionaire."

"Very funny."

"I don't think it's funny at all," she retorted. "I don't think it's a good sign that she's looking at bank balances."

"It seems to indicate a pattern," he remarked.

"I'll do it."

They smiled at one another. Talking to him, like this, just the two of them, was like old times, like reclaiming some of the closeness they'd had before. It felt like settling against a soft cushion draped in velvet and was so lovely that she could have stayed here all evening.

Dominic glanced at his watch. "I should get back."

"It's not that late." She looked up. The sky wasn't dark but slowly painting itself in darker hues. "You make yourself sound ancient."

"You must think so."

She stared at him, allowing their gazes to tangle, to imagine a future which could never be. Nine years lay between them, but they were still in the same decade, in their twenties, though sometimes, like now, Dominic seemed to be much older.

"And here you are, in charge of a company and in a position that would take others decades to reach."

"I'm not sure if that's a compliment or not."

"It's a compliment."

"A backhanded compliment," he remarked drily, before adjusting his tie. She could tell that he was hot and bothered, that if he were at home, he would loosen it and take it off.

She knew so much about him, and the bits she didn't, her imagination filled in the gaps. Always, lately, Dominic was taking up too many of her thoughts.

"I'd better get my ancient self off to bed. Goodnight, Eleni."

"Goodnight, Dominic."

CHAPTER THIRTY

DOMINIC

He was already panicking.
Eleni hadn't even needed time to think about his offer and she'd accepted it before he'd even finished telling her what he needed from her.

Now he wondered how he would survive that weekend.

Eleni had no idea.

No goddamn idea at all how much she affected him.

She charged into his office early the next morning. "Where is it? The wedding?"

"Close the door please." He watched her sashay back to the door, wearing a pale yellow sundress and nude pumps, then forced his gaze to his paper diary as she sat down opposite him.

"Santorini."

"Santorini?"

He nodded, his head feeling wooden, like a certain part of

his anatomy had been when he'd woken up this morning.

"I've never been there," she cried, happily.

"No?" How the heck was he going to get through it with her by his side? It wasn't too late to hire an escort. The trivial conversation wouldn't kill him as much as an unattended, weekend long, hard on would.

"I've been to many of the Greek islands, but I've never been there," she chirped happily, completely unaware of his uneasiness.

"Hmmmm." If she was going to be this excited, and look this gorgeous, he was going to be in big trouble. "It's not just a wedding. There will be parties and dinners and drinks going on."

"And you intend to go to them all?"

"The Laskaris family like to flaunt their wealth. They'll put on a lavish event." He hadn't yet decided if he would attend all the fancy events, but he planned to be wherever Galatis was. He could sense Eleni's reticence. "As long as you attend the wedding, we'll be fine."

"Aren't you worried about how this looks?" she asked, waving a hand between them. "About you and me being a couple?"

"I won't be announcing it in the company's newsletter," he assured her. "And in Santorini who would know?"

"Your friends and acquaintances. Doesn't that bother you?"

Her worry confused him. "Why should it?"

"Because I work for you."

"Nobody knows that."

"What about Galatis?"

"I don't think he's seen you. You were always at a distance or in the car, and even if he did, so what?"

"So what?"

"I don't care if Galatis thinks I'm dating my ... *assistant*." He threw his hands up in the air, unable to come up with a better word.

She seemed to ponder over this, then, "At least you can show your ex that you're not sad and single."

"We're ... not ... dating," he reminded her.

"But she won't know that."

"That's not the reason I'm going. I'm not taking you to make her jealous. I'm taking you so that Galatis doesn't pair me off with one of his nieces."

He told her about Galatis' 'behind every successful man is a good woman' speech. "But more than that, he threatened to set me up with his nieces."

Eleni giggled helplessly.

"What's so funny?" He'd never seen her laugh so much.

"You should have started with that. What you need is a deterrent. You're so uptight and wooden, Dominic. You hate crowds, and people and all the socializing. Galatis trying to set you up with someone ..." She started giggling again. "That's your worst nightmare. No wonder you were desperate enough to come to me."

He gazed at her in silence. She really had no idea at all.

When she left he contemplated what the hell he'd done agreeing to go to a wedding he hadn't wanted to attend, with someone he'd been trying to keep his distance from.

This was not a good idea. Not a good idea at all.

Having Eleni by his side solved some problems, but it would create many new ones, too. He'd always tried to be a thousand times more careful, never wanting to be like the others, the ones who dropped their cheesy pick up lines, the ones who pawed her. He'd always done his best to keep his distance, until it became impossible to do so.

Situations and circumstances.

And now here they were.

He prayed he didn't live to regret it.

ELENI

Demi Laskaris. *This* was Dominic's ex?

Eleni had waited to get home that evening to have a good snoop at Dominic's ex online. Her eyes raced over an article about this socialite beauty who was marrying the nephew of Hector Galatis in a lavish ceremony in Santorini. Pictures abounded of the happy couple, but Eleni gaped at the beautiful woman who had once been Dominic's girlfriend. She looked like a model. Even Helen looked like a model, though Dominic had taken pains to point out to her that there had never been anything of a romantic nature between them.

Still, Demi Laskaris and talk about the Galatis family and the lavish weekend of wedding celebrations gave her cause for concern. She was already an outsider and couldn't imagine fitting into that type of lifestyle. She had no idea how she would smile and make polite conversation with the very group of people she despised; the reckless, having-fun-no-matter-the-consequences type of people who ruined lives and did not blink an eye.

The wedding was next weekend and she had nothing to wear. She rifled through the closet, but the only remotely passable outfits she had were the cocktail dresses she'd brought for her birthday. They were all short dresses, nothing elegant or smart—though she had her Audrey Hepburn ensemble which Dominic hadn't seen. She needed to find something else because she was determined not to let Dominic down.

She flopped onto her bed, her heart thundering in her ribcage, just thinking about this new world she would be stepping into.

A world in which Dominic belonged, and she clearly didn't. Always the waitress or the maid, never a participant in the world of the wealthy, and now she'd have to pass as Dominic's girlfriend.

She couldn't tell Stefanos, or Phoebe or Angeliki, because they wouldn't understand. She couldn't even tell Miranda because she and Dominic had agreed to keep this a secret between them. As if freaking out about the clothes and etiquette wasn't bad enough, she also had to consider what it might be like to spend the weekend with Dominic.

After another sleepless night, she went to see him in his office again the next day.

His door was half open, so she marched right in, closing the door behind her. "I wanted to check on something."

"More questions?" He looked at her in amusement. She was sure the corners of his mouth twitched before he cupped his chin and covered his lips with is index finger. "Or are you having second thoughts?"

"Not quite."

"You have other plans?" he suggested.

"No, no, I'm free. I can come." She wasn't sure how to broach it.

He looked perplexed. "I will pay you."

"For what?"

"For your time and inconvenience."

She stepped closer to his desk. "This will be like a vacation for me. I've never been to Santorini, I told you."

"I *will* pay you for your time and effort. It's not negotiable, Eleni."

"If it makes you feel better." More money? She'd never had so much money in her life.

"It would."

If he wanted to throw money at her, she wasn't going to argue too much about it. She glanced around the room. "It would help with the expedition."

"The what?"

"The ... uh." She chewed the inside of her cheek, buying time and a way out of this conversation.

"Did you say *expedition?*"

She hadn't wanted to talk about this. Not to Dominic of all people, but his eyes were on her, a mixture of surprise and awe. She couldn't very well lie. "I ... I've been saving up for ..." She didn't want to tell Dominic about Jonas because the guilt was overwhelming. These days she didn't think about Jonas unless something prompted her to, and here she was in her boss's office agreeing to go away with him for a weekend and be his fake date.

"A friend of mine died, tragically." *He wasn't just a friend ...* That was the item of information to not hold back on, surely? "My boyfriend, actually." She couldn't bring herself to look at him. Noticing a paper clip on the floor, she picked it up.

Dominic mumbled an apology or something.

"We were going to climb a mountain. Kilimanjaro, would you believe." She put the paperclip back into his desk tidy, and still she couldn't look him in the face. "He, my boyfriend, Jonas ... it was his dream. We'd been planning it and ... and then he ... he was ... he died."

Her heart sagged and sunk lower in her chest cavity. The remembrance of that time weighed on her heavily each time she thought about it.

"I'm so sorry for your loss."

She picked at something on her skirt. "I've been saving for it because it costs a lot, but I'm not so sure now." She looked up at him.

"Of what?"

"Of still going through with it. It won't be the same without him."

"I'm so sorry, Eleni."

She tried to regain her composure because she hadn't been prepared for this. She had kept Jonas' memory close to her heart. Telling Dominic had just seemed so ... wrong. "I should get back to ... to work."

Her legs couldn't move fast enough out of Dominic's office.

DOMINIC

He swiveled around on his executive chair and huffed out a sigh.

She was still grieving the tragic passing of her boyfriend.

Now he finally understood her need to earn money. The two jobs, and the reason she couldn't afford to lose her income.

She was doing it all for an expedition that she and her boyfriend had planned. She was still in love with him.

He had to focus on his own goals. Galatis and the wedding. If he could close the deal, his mission here would be accomplished. Nikolaos was due to return next month and Dominic's job here would be done.

The only other upside of attending the wedding with Eleni was that Demi would see that he had a plus one.

Even if she was just a fake date.

CHAPTER THIRTY-ONE

ELENI

"The family jet is in the US, so we won't be taking that."

Eleni looked at him as if he were an alien. He'd said it so matter of factly, as if everyone had a private jet at their disposal.

"Do you only have the one?" she asked, as calmly as she could.

"The other one's out of commission."

That told her. She blinked a few times.

Looking unfazed, Dominic slipped an envelope across the table to her. "I've booked tickets. We fly out and come back on different days."

She was relieved to hear this, though her mind was still trying to come to terms with the one jet being in the US and the other one being out of commission. She'd gone shopping one day after work and had managed to find something affordable and decent, but it didn't stop her from getting worked up about her outfits, the shoes and accessories, and how to do her hair and make up.

Whether she would fit in. Or stand out like a sore thumb.

Even learning about Dominic and his family, it hadn't hit home, not even when she was being chauffeured around with him in the Merc. She'd become so used to his bodyguard skulking around always within reach, that he'd become invisible to her.

But now, because of this mission, each new thing she learned about Dominic's world, especially about the women in his past—the smart, wealthy, upper class women—troubled her and made her even more uneasy.

And now this. That he didn't travel the way most people did, he had a private jet. Every new fact made her retreat into her shell.

He gave her a lengthy stare. "Eleni? You zoned out. Are you still okay to do this? Because this isn't like coming with me to one of Galatis' meetings around Athens."

He didn't need to remind her that this was a society wedding in the world of billionaires, a place she didn't belong in.

"I ... I ..." she faltered for a small second, but determination steeled her resolve. He was still the man she'd thrown orange juice over. A man who had been just another annoying tourist.

And one who had paid her handsomely so that she could fulfill Jonas' dream.

Wasn't it her dream also?

Dominic sat up looking worried. "You're having doubts."

"I'm not. You're the reason I can do the mountain climb, for Jonas. You're the one who's made this possible for me."

His Adam's apple bobbed and something in his expression darkened, something she didn't understand. It only served to remind her that this man and his moods could change in an instant.

"I want to do this," she continued. "You've been to all these Greek monuments you don't like—"

"I never said I didn't like them. It was the company that frustrated me, and I had a goal to achieve. It's not that I don't like the Acropolis or the Temple of Ha..ha..hafa—"

"Hephaestus."

He pointed a finger at her. "That one."

She had the urge to roll her eyes so hard they'd be permanently stuck that way.

"I'm sure if I were going sightseeing with someone..." He looked away and picked up the pen. "It might be fun ... "

"I'm grateful for all that you've done for me, Dominic. I can do this."

And now the real reason she'd come to see him. "I ... I was umm ... going to ask you where it is, the wedding, so that I could book a room at a hotel nearby—"

"We would need to book into a room together. We're dating, remember."

Together? She felt physically weak.

A room. A bed.

With Dominic in both?

Her heart bumped around in her chest, the shock frying her nerves. She couldn't look at him a moment longer, otherwise she would be no better than Miranda, revealing her growing infatuation to him so clearly. "I had forgotten about that."

She had.

For all the freaking out about the wedding, she'd been so worried about looking out of place that she had completely lost sight of the more fundamental issues; that they were supposed to be a couple.

Which meant they would have to be together.

And pretend to be in love.

And share a room.

And a bed.

And ... her stomach turned queasy, as if she'd eaten bad prawn saganaki.

Dominic sat back. "I sensed it might be awkward for us to stay together in a hotel room for two nights ..."

Sweat stuck to her underarms and clung to the back of her neck. She was uneasy, and sick, and worried.

"Don't worry. I've take care of it," he answered smoothly.

"Oh." What did that mean? She had no idea of where she was going, what the order of events was. She didn't even know what time the wedding was.

The being a couple and staying together the entire weekend—night and day—clouded every brain cell she possessed.

She needed to get out of his office. *Now.* "Thank you," she managed to say. There were more questions, obstacles and problems brewing. It was so much more complicated than she'd at first contemplated. This was going to be nothing like staying in a hotel room with her friends.

This was going to be torture. She got up and like a robot managed to put one foot in front of the other enough times to make it to the door.

"Eleni?"

Her insides were still in free fall and any moment now she expected them to fall to the floor.

"You've forgotten your plane ticket."

Miraculously, she managed to make it back to his desk to retrieve the ticket, without having a full-blown panic attack.

"Are you okay?" Dominic's eyes flashed with concern. She raised a hand to her forehead, knowing that she looked like the picture of someone who was coming down with a sickness, a fever, the bubonic plague.

"I'm fine. I'm ... excited..."

So excited that it had sent her into shock.

She was anything but fine.

DOMINIC

Two nights in Santorini with a woman he could not stop thinking about.

A woman who was still pining for her dead boyfriend.

At least now he had another reason to distance himself.

But he had to stop thinking of her. Fat chance, given that they would be spending a weekend together.

They would be staying at the family residence in Santorini. He'd been about to tell her but she'd weirded out before his eyes and he was worried this news might tip her over the edge.

Staying at the family villa, a place so big that he and Eleni wouldn't cross paths easily, was the perfect solution.

If Eleni was freaking out about this trip, he was faring no better. The things he put himself through for Galatis and the goddamn deal.

He couldn't wait for the wedding to be over and done with.

CHAPTER THIRTY-TWO

ELENI

"Are you in trouble?" Miranda asked, looking at her oddly as she left Dominic's office.

Ever since Anna's farewell party Eleni had been in and out of there a few times, and it shouldn't have surprised her that hawk-eyed Miranda was keeping a close watch.

"No. It's all good."

She sailed past Miranda's desk and headed straight for the washroom. When she finally looked at her ticket properly, she saw that it was a first class ticket.

First class?

She'd never traveled in first class in her life.

Nor would she ever.

She hadn't even left the country, but this, a first class ticket to Santorini, was beyond her wildest dreams.

She wanted to call Stefanos and tell him. She wanted to

shout it from the tops of her lungs. She wanted to tell Miranda, but everything about this trip was top secret.

The next few days passed in an uncomfortable haze. She'd been restless, and had gone on more runs than ever in an attempt to calm her nerves. Packing her suitcase had proved especially difficult, and had her questioning her sanity.

Then, the day finally arrived. When she left work at noon, she felt so uneasy lying to Miranda about going to Spetses for the weekend, that she couldn't look her friend in the eye properly.

The short plane journey was over all too soon. It had taken less than an hour, with Eleni closing her eyes for most of the trip, wanting to cement and savor every last little soufflé of pleasure so that she would never forget it.

Dominic had told her he'd send Kostas to pick her up from the airport. She was so happy to see him when she got out of the baggage area that she hugged him.

Her heart thumped as she gazed out of the car window, her nerves fraying like threads from a hemline. She fretted over how this weekend would go, and how she would survive two nights under one roof as Dominic's fake girlfriend.

She saw blue domed churches, whitewashed houses, a few candy-colored ones sprinkled in, against a backdrop of sparkling turquoise blue waters. She opened the window and gazed out at the deep blue sky, inhaling the scent of summer. It was beautiful. Words couldn't do it justice. She tilted her head, hearing the sound of Greek music playing faintly, but it soon disappeared as the car sped on.

"Where are we going?" Eleni asked, as they left a strip of hotels behind them. She'd thought they might be staying there. Dominic had told her that he'd taken care of it, but she was none the wiser.

"To Mr. Steele's house."

"He has a house here as well?" *What house?* He hadn't told her a thing.

Kostas laughed. "They have many houses."

"I'm sure they do," she muttered to herself. After a while, Kostas announced that they were nearly there.

Her heart thumped with fear and excitement. If things became awkward between her and Dominic, she needed to be able to get back home easily. Dread settled in her stomach. She didn't know Dominic that well.

What if he was a psycho?

What if ... her imagination took her to the darkest of places.

But then a huge beautiful white villa came into view, with no other homes nearby. It was a majestic, sprawling building with balconies along the upper floor.

"Is *this* it?"

"This is it. You will enjoy it here. It is paradise."

It certainly looked like it. The villa was spread out like a giant octopus, and looked so exotic, so beautiful, she couldn't believe she was going to spend two nights here.

How the wealthy lived.

"Who else is here?"

"Mr. Steele and Xenia."

"Who?"

But Kostas had already climbed out of the car and was reaching into the trunk to get her luggage. Eleni grabbed the handle of the small roll on luggage trolley. "Thank you, but I can get this."

"Mr. Steele asked that you make use of the facilities. Xenia will show you around. He said you can take any room on the ground floor."

"Uh-huh." She absorbed this information as calmly as she could.

"Good afternoon, Miss Trakas." An elderly woman appeared before her. "I am Xenia. Let me take that for you."

Eleni stared back at the woman with salt and pepper hair wrapped up in a neat bun. This must be Dominic's housekeeper, at *this* residence, she assumed.

She tightened her grip on the handle of her luggage trolley. "It's okay. I've got it." She smiled and followed the woman into the house.

Eleni followed the housekeeper who gave her a tour of the villa, but she soon lost count of the number of rooms she was shown, and just when her mind had absorbed the beautiful large kitchen area something shimmered, catching her attention outside. A glittering aquamarine pool whispered her name.

"A pool", she cried, leaving her luggage by the door. Dominic hadn't said anything about a pool. She immediately regretted not packing a swimsuit.

"Would you prefer this room, Miss Trakas?"

"Oh, please don't call me that. I'm Eleni." This woman was older than her mother. Eleni would not have her calling her Miss Trakas.

"Yes. This is great! Thank you." It was closest to the kitchen and had a perfect view of the pool.

"I have prepared a light lunch for you."

"For me?" Eleni looked over her shoulder to double check that the housekeeper wasn't talking to anyone else. Kostas. Dominic even.

Xenia smiled. "Yes, you."

"You didn't have to do that. I would have made myself something."

"Mr. Steele insisted."

"He shouldn't have."

"Even if he hadn't, I would have made something for you."

Eleni smiled at the Xenia, and placed a hand across her stomach. A warm feeling spread out from her belly at the idea that she was being so well looked after. "That's ... that's very thoughtful of him ... of you ... thank you."

"I will leave it in the kitchen. You may take it where you please. Mr. Steele will be back in the evening. He wants you to enjoy the house."

"In the evening?" Eleni's eyes widened. Miranda had informed her that he'd flown out yesterday. That much Miranda knew—that Dominic was attending a wedding in Santorini. It was Eleni who would have to lie the most about this weekend. Why hadn't Dominic told her these things himself?

Walking into her new bedroom, Eleni stood still and took in the room, the size of it and the gorgeous décor. She pinched herself that this was real, not a dream.

If only Stefanos and her friends could see now. If only her mother could. She would take lots of photos later, so that she could show them all one day when this was long behind her and it would no longer matter if this secret came out.

She was tempted to jump into the pool in her underwear, but didn't want to take a chance that Dominic might come in, unexpectedly and see her. She immediately whipped out her cell phone and texted Dominic.

Eleni: This place is beautiful. I never want to leave!

Kostas and Xenia were so discreet that she didn't see them, and it felt as if she had the entire place to herself. She started to unpack, slowly taking out her clothes and hanging them in the closets.

When she finished, she surveyed her room and the shimmering pool from her window, then she collapsed onto the bed, hugging her chest, feeling pure, unadulterated joy.

What a life.

What a world.

And it would be hers for this glorious weekend.

She reached for her phone, puzzled to find that Dominic hadn't replied. Unable to contain her excitement she sent him another text:

Eleni: This is paradise! I'm going to have such a wonderful weekend. Can't believe you're paying me for this. I would have done it for free.

After lunch she lazed by the pool reading a book, and then, when it got too hot, she took a nap in the bedroom.

When she awoke a short while later, she floated around the ground floor of the house again. The villa was simply stunning. Something from the magazines of the rich and famous—which Dominic clearly was. She really shouldn't have been so in awe of it all, and yet she was. Jaw-droppingly in awe.

But where was he?

It was a glorious day, sun streaming, cicadas clicking, a landscape so pretty it stole her breath. It was perfect. But she was alone, and savoring things alone, as she had discovered after Jonas, wasn't satisfying.

She'd brought her running clothes with her, so she slipped into her sneakers and changed into her running shorts and tank top. Donning a ball cap, she set off, determined to keep up with her runs. A short run around here would help her to get her bearings.

Half an hour later she was back, dripping with sweat and overheated. She jumped into the shower.

It was a shower like no other. A wide-as-a-steering wheel overhead shower giving a torrential downpour.

She changed into a comfy T-shirt and pair of denim shorts.

And waited.

And waited.

And waited.

She'd expected Dominic to show up by now. She assumed he must have been extremely busy because he hadn't even replied to her texts. With nothing to do to pass the time, she read some more by the pool. A few more hours passed and the sky turned a rich purple shade.

A delicious aroma wafted out from the kitchen. Eleni went to investigate and found that Xenia was cooking something. She offered to help but the housekeeper told her that everything was done and she would be back tomorrow.

"You don't stay here?" She'd been relieved when she first saw her, thinking that it wouldn't just be the two of them, her and Dominic, stuck here alone this weekend. Then she remembered Dominic telling her that he didn't like sharing his home with others.

"I have a family I need to get back to." She smiled. "I will be back tomorrow."

Xenia left and Eleni found herself all alone in a beautiful house, sitting by a pool which glittered under twinkling lights which automatically turned on.

Hunger made her irritable, and she was nervous and jumpy that Dominic still hadn't shown up. She felt silly and inconsequential sitting here in this beautiful setting, all alone with nothing to do and no one to share it with, and she worried that he might be having regrets about asking her here.

Or maybe he was out with the other rich and well-heeled people? Surrounded by beautiful women somewhere? Beads of moisture sprang up along her hairline, prickling her scalp. She had been a fool to come here, a fool to want to help him.

What made her ever think he'd want to spend time with her outside of the wedding?

He'd brought her for a reason. To be seen with her. At the wedding only.

Not on a night like this when champagne and pretty ladies beckoned.

With hunger gnawing at her belly, she decided to give up waiting on Dominic and to eat before she died of starvation. She filled her plate with the orzo that Xenia had made. Feta and olives garnished the rice-like pasta and smelled so delicious, her earlier unease soon disappeared.

She sat outside, by the pool again. The villa at night was even more gorgeous than by day, with its fairy lights and garden lamps turned on. She had lit one of the big chunky candles she'd found inside the kitchen, and now its flickering flames created an intimate ambiance, *for one.*

She'd only taken a few mouthfuls when she heard footsteps. Dominic was home. The house was so big, she hadn't even heard the car pull up. She forced herself to stay calm.

Then, finally, slowly, Dominic came into view.

Tall, gorgeous and in a tux, he pulled his bowtie off. His eyes glittered as he stared at her. "Hello." One word, so low, so sexy in that voice that was unusually gravelly.

"Oh ... hi."

"Eating alone?" He moved closer, each step nearer

making her heart rate rocket. Even though she was eating, her stomach emptied, turned hollow and light.

"I waited for you." In the eerie silence, only punctuated by the sound of cicadas, she tried to slow down her breathing.

Seeing him in his business suit was bad enough—the man jolted her each time she saw him, the image of his pants hugging those supremely sculpted buttocks, the way his cotton fabric strained just enough at his biceps, holding her attention until she forgot to breathe. Every time. But now, in his tux, this was a dapper Dominic, suave and devastatingly handsome. It would take weeks for her to dislodge this image from her head.

She blinked ... then prayed silently that she wasn't doing a Miranda.

"I should have texted to let you know."

"Why didn't you?" That sounded angrier than she'd intended. He cocked his head as if appraising her mood. "Xenia made you something to eat."

"It's delicious. You should have some."

Dominic waved a dismissive hand, as if he wasn't fazed. He pulled out a chair across from her and sat down, sitting casually, with his arm draped across the empty chair next to him, and one of his legs lazily out, his foot pointing towards her. She tried not to look, to not make it so blatantly obvious that she was dying to rake her eyes inch by inch all over him.

The fork she was about to lift to her mouth went back onto the plate. She didn't like people watching her eat, especially people she was attracted to.

Like this man watching her across the table. Her skin started to tingle, the way it had started to recently whenever Dominic was around.

The Steele tingle. It was fast becoming a thing.

She's made a mistake in coming here and offering to be his

fake date. They'd only spent five minutes together and it was already torture. Here in the villa, away from work, he'd already reduced her to a lust addled wreck. The ambiance, the lights and pool, the intimacy of just him and her in this huge place, was frying her brain.

It took all her reserves of steely determination to keep her eyes level with his, and her voice casual. "You're ... you're not hungry?" she managed to say, forcing herself to breathe slowly, to try to show a modicum of composure, to hide the combustion taking place inside her.

"I had some canapes."

"Canapes?" Her insides spiraled. It was so obvious that he'd been to an event. Without her.

"A pre-wedding party. I was hoping Galatis might be there, so that we could get the business stuff out of the way."

He'd gone without her. "You didn't think to take me?" The neediness in her voice made her ashamed. "One of the reasons you brought me along was for Galatis. You flew me first class ..."

He frowned. "Because I didn't have the jet at my disposal."

She shook her head. They were on different continents, literally and metaphorically. "You're missing the point." She was forced to eat, because the silence, waiting for him to say something, weighted the air with foreboding.

He stared at her pointedly, a brow lifting. "I didn't think you'd want to come along."

"You didn't even ask me."

"Are you annoyed I didn't ask you?"

I was here for a reason.

Maybe he regretted her being here. Maybe being around his peers changed him. Maybe the wedding of his ex rekindled old feelings. Maybe he was ashamed of having her by his side.

Maybe that was why he hadn't asked her tonight.

"I'm supposed to be your fake date." This place, him, it was all too much. She forced a smile. "I want to make sure that I'm fulfilling my end of the deal." She lifted another forkful of food to her mouth but it was getting harder to swallow. Her mouth was bone dry, her appetite slowly vanishing. The orzo that had been so delicious a moment ago, now felt as if she were forcing dry hay into her mouth.

"Eleni."

Her eyes went to his arm as he moved it from the chair, resting both hands on the table. He looked as if he was about to stand up.

Or give her a lecture.

"I didn't mean to upset you—"

"You didn't."

Her lie hung heavy in the air and mercifully, he looked away, scratching that beautiful angular jawline of his.

"I assumed you'd be tired. It's not a long flight, but still, traveling and getting used to a new place can be exhausting, coming after work as you did. I assumed you might want to enjoy the house and have some time to yourself."

Don't ask. Don't ask what time he went there, or say that you could have met him there.

Don't be that desperate woman throwing herself at him.

She didn't fall for men like him. Her experience with rich men had completely turned her off this breed.

There was the tragic past she could never forget. The yacht and the party and those drunken revelers who'd taken one life and destroyed many others. The compensation to his family, no matter how big, could never bring him back.

She despised these people, and she needed to remember that.

"You should have stayed there, Dominic. It's early even for someone of your age to be coming back so soon." She forced her lips to curve upwards, but inside her heart was heavy.

"I didn't want to leave you alone."

She didn't want him to leave the party on account of her. She didn't need looking after. She waved her hand dismissively. "I'm enjoying the evening. I like my own company. Go back to your friends."

He frowned at her. Those little creases appearing on his brow. "I'm here now."

"You're dressed the part. You should relax and enjoy yourself now that you're finally on vacation. You're always such a workaholic." Her voice was oddly cheerful. She didn't know how she was going to get through tomorrow, surrounded by the likes of Galatis and other high socialites.

Her, a waitress, so out of place, out of her element. She had no right to be here.

"Are you trying to get rid of me?"

"I was about to go skinny dipping in the pool, since I forgot my swimwear."

She heard a sharp intake of breath from him, then he wiped his face with his hands. "Don't let me stop you." He stood abruptly.

"You're going back to the party?"

"I'm going to bed. If you want to enjoy the pool, Eleni, you go ahead. My room is upstairs, and I'll pull down the blinds. Don't worry. I give you my word that I won't look."

He was always such a gentleman to her, even if he had no idea that he elicited so many other emotions in her. Jealousy, and anger, and sadness. "Shouldn't we work on our story?"

She suddenly remembered that they hadn't discussed this important topic.

"Our story?"

"Of how we got together. How we met, in case your friends ask."

"Do we need to?"

"Don't you think we should get our stories straight?" What if Galatis asked her how she met Dominic?

"Maybe we should. I need to get out of these clothes. Give me ten minutes."

She pushed her plate of half-eaten food away. Dominic getting out of those clothes, or *any* clothes, for that matter, was something she shouldn't think about.

She banged the table lightly, unable to tolerate the torture of such sultry thoughts.

CHAPTER THIRTY-THREE

DOMINIC

Eleni was going to go skinny dipping in the pool?

The wild and wicked thought clung to Dominic like a leech as he quickly got out of his tux and into sweatpants.

He felt guilty as soon as he'd found her sitting alone by the pool eating dinner by herself. He should have asked her to come with him to the pre-wedding cocktail party. She tried to make out it didn't matter, but he could see that he'd hurt her, and that had been the last thing on his mind.

He'd spent most of the day talking about business, first over lunch, then over drinks later. Demi had been thrilled to see him and had introduced him to her fiancé before inviting him to the cocktail party.

Knowing that Eleni had landed, he hadn't planned on staying too late but unfortunately, the soon-to-be-married couple had insisted he stay a bit longer.

So he had.

In a way, it helped him to keep his distance from Eleni. It was why he hadn't replied to her text messages. As much as it had pained him, he'd forced himself to ignore them because he didn't want to get sucked up in an exchange which might turn flirty.

That would be dangerous, and he couldn't afford for that to happen now.

But she had plans to go skinny dipping.

He recoiled, burned by a sense of shame for holding the image her words had drawn for him.

Even now his sixth sense told him to go back to his room, but his legs moved towards Eleni. He poured himself a glass of whiskey on the way out to the pool where Eleni had cleared the table and was sitting in her shorts and tank top.

God help him this weekend.

A muscle twitched along his jaw. He was so used to having women throw themselves at him, that this was a new and unfamiliar feeling, wanting the one woman who didn't want him.

"Let's discuss." He sat down, next to her this time, and noted that she moved her chair away a few inches.

Keep your shit together, Dominic.

"Okay." Eleni steepled her fingers together. "Let's do this. How did we meet?"

"Why don't we just say what really happened?" Telling the truth was always the best option. It avoided the need for inventing the hundred and one white lies which usually followed a big lie.

"You mean when I poured juice all over you at the taverna?"

He laughed at the memory, and so did she. "It's a good story," she insisted.

He agreed. "It *is* a good story."

"It's the type of story people would want to tell their children, or grandchildren." She blinked rapidly a few times, as if she'd made a mistake; had said too much and wanted to walk it back. "If this wasn't a fake dating situation."

"But it did happen in real life," he remarked, rather soberly.

"You know what I mean." She waved a hand between them. "If this were real."

He wished it could be real. Everything about her, about being with her.

"But it's not." Her left shoulder lifted. He hated that she could so easily dismiss it. That she wasn't wrapped up in the angst which consumed him every time he thought about her.

"Fine. We'll say we met at the taverna." He tapped his fingers on the table.

"What if people find it strange that I work for you?"

"What if they do?"

"It would be a problem, no?"

"Why would it?" It was his company, well, his *father's* company, but he could deal with it.

The question was, could Eleni?

She'd already told him that the women she worked with, and Linus, weren't too fond of her. "Maybe for you it might be difficult," he said, softly. "I would hate for people to talk about you behind your back."

She laughed. "But this isn't real, Dominic. People can say what they want."

It wasn't real, and he had to accept the truth. "People won't ask such in-depth questions. We shouldn't stress about this too much." His gaze swept over her. She had long, long legs. He couldn't help but notice them in the shorts she had on, and that figure hugging T-shirt that outlined her body so clearly. What was she trying to do to him?

Don't go there.

He shook his head and forced his gaze to fixate on the pool behind her. "Most of the people you will meet will be more interested in themselves than you or me, Eleni."

She chewed her lower lip thoughtfully.

"Is something worrying you about this?" Because he didn't want her still to be worrying.

"Not this." Once again she waved her hand between them. Did that mean anything? She seemed to be at ease, with only the two of them sitting and talking the way they were.

He certainly was.

He could sit here all night, could happily spend the weekend with her, sitting by the pool and talking, just the two of them.

"We have to know things about each other. What do you know about me?" she asked.

He sat up, swirled the glass of whiskey and contemplated. "Your favorite color is pale yellow, I'm guessing, based on the number of times I've seen you wear it."

Her mouth fell open.

"And dolmadakia is your favorite Greek dish, one of them, I think."

"You're observant, or nosy."

"You like tequila, and you dance without inhibition." He felt a victory coming on, given by the shocked expression on her face.

"You are a ladies' man, aren't you?" she threw back. "A charmer, paying attention and listening."

That wasn't the response he'd hoped for. "No."

She stared at him as if he were a puzzle she couldn't decipher. "You know so much about me."

"I've shared more car rides with you than any other employee. I've walked past Miranda's desk to get to my office —and the two of you don't always talk in whispers."

"I can't work out if you're very perceptive or if you have very big ears."

He grinned. "Go on, hit me with it. What do you know about me?" He was eager to find out. She stared at the table, scratching her arm, bringing his attention to her body, making it hard for him to look away.

"That you like whiskey, and ... it's common knowledge that you hate social events, and people ..."

He didn't disagree. "Is that all?"

"And ..." She seemed to be struggling.

"You can't think of anything." He was disappointed.

"You're bossy, and demanding, and moody. You're grumpy and you hate people and idle chatter. But you've always been so nice to me."

Everyone knew this. "What else?" he demanded, wanting to know if she'd learned anything else about him.

"Why?"

"Why what?"

"Why have you always been different with me?"

"I haven't."

"You have."

This had to end right now. "Maybe because of the way we met," he said slowly.

"The story we'll tell our children, no?" She giggled. But he did not do the same in return. Instead, he stood up. "I have emails to reply to."

"You're working? Even now while we're on vacation?"

"*You're* on vacation." He slipped a hand in his pocket while the other one curled around his whiskey glass. "The wedding starts at two in the afternoon, so you have the morning free."

"Did I say something?" she asked, looking perplexed.

"I have work to do. I always have work to do."

"And the work will never end. Stay a while, Dominic. Isn't this nice?"

"It is. I wish I could, but I can't." He gave her a rueful smile as he left.

CHAPTER THIRTY-FOUR

ELENI

It was the sunshine streaming through the bedroom window that woke her up.

She hadn't bothered pulling the blinds down because she wanted to see the lights around the poolside area from her bedroom window. It was such a pretty sight to look at as she lay down to sleep.

But now a new day had dawned; a day she dreaded despite Dominic's attempts to make her feel at ease. She worried more than ever about the new dress she had purchased, and of it not being worthy.

Getting out of bed, she pulled the garment out of the closet and examined it closely. Now she was worried that it might be too risqué. The sleeveless, beaded, corset top was too fitted, the full-length satin skirt with a fishtail too figure hugging.

It had looked glamorous when she'd tried it on at the shop, but now she wasn't too sure.

The last thing she wanted was to look like Dominic's cheap date. She wanted to do him proud. Wanted to slip into his world and feel a part of it.

She'd found it touching that he had been more concerned about how people would treat her—people like Linus and Agnes and Isidora—if they discovered that the two of them had been here together. She'd had to remind Dominic that they were only playing at dating.

It was *fake,* right?

She put the dress away and got showered and dressed into casual clothes before venturing into the kitchen for breakfast. The house was empty. No sign of Xenia or Dominic.

Too restless to eat, she decided to go for a run to calm her nerves. Training for the expedition was always at the back of her mind, lurking like an anchor around her ankles.

A run in the morning would kill some time, especially with the wedding being in the early afternoon and Dominic had said he would be working.

She ran a scenic route, past the beach and then some shops, a church and a bus stop, then jogged all the way back. Hot and thirsty, she headed straight into the refrigerator for a carton of orange juice.

Hearing a rippling noise, she looked out of the window to see Dominic swimming lengths in the pool.

His face was in the water like a professional swimmer, his thick arms, strong and powerful, cutting through the water with ease as he glided serenely.

She watched him, mesmerized, unable to take a sip of the juice which, only moments ago, she'd been thirsting for. He was so elegant, so silent, and majestic, that she could not take her eyes off him.

He stopped when he reached the end of the pool, wiping the water away from his face and smoothing his hair back. He still hadn't seen her, and seemed to be in a flow state, aware of nothing and no one as he swam to the other end of the pool. Then he climbed out looking like an Olympic gold level swimming god.

Eleni's jaw dropped open as she moved towards the door. Perspiration trickled down the back of her neck, along the sides of her face. Whether this was because of her run, or from watching Dominic, she couldn't tell.

He walked towards her. "You're going to spill your juice." He nodded at her glass which was in danger of tipping over. She tipped it upright just as his eyes traveled down her length. In the dim corners of her mind, it struck her that he was watching her with the same intensity that she was him. "You went for a run?" His voice was a raspy whisper.

"I've gotten lazy with my training for the expedition."

"Ah, yes. The expedition." He reached for a towel and the world slowed down, giving her ample time to take in his glistening wet body. Rivulets of water trickled down his large expanse of chest, lower, lower, lower, just like her gaze.

His swim shorts hugged his hips ... and she could only imagine the riches that lay beneath that fabric. Fireworks exploded in her mind, and she forced herself to stare at his face because she was in serious danger of drooling like a baby if her eyes lowered.

Dominic moved the towel over his hips, shielding himself from her. He swiped a hand over his jaw, bringing her attention to those angular bones she had come to know so well.

Their gazes held in a moment buzzing with promise. Something sparked in the air between them, something she could feel thrumming along her skin, coiling low in her belly.

"We should start getting ready," he told her. "We leave in ninety minutes."

CHAPTER THIRTY-FIVE

DOMINIC

He traipsed upstairs to his room and stripped off his trunks, but now he had a raging hard on he had to get rid of.

His control, his ability to distance himself and not give a shit, had been eroded. His guard was dropping faster than his patience.

It had been easy to hide his feelings when he only saw Eleni from a distance, in safe areas, like at Miranda's desk or in his office. Even being in the car was safe because his driver was a third wheel.

Their roles in a work environment kept the barriers in place. But now he was in the battle of his life, trying to act disinterested when his feelings, his emotions, his heart, and his dick, were telling him otherwise.

This could not happen.

This would not happen.

You'll be no better than the others.
He got into the shower.

ELENI

She closed the door behind her and let out a long breath, the one that had been stuck in her chest ever since she'd seen Dominic climb out of the pool in all his Herculean gorgeousness.

That sight of him, with water running down his bare skin, was an image branded on her soul forever. One thing was certain—she'd be dreaming about this man for a long time to come.

She glanced at the clock on the dresser. Time was ticking by. She had ninety minutes and she couldn't spend most of them fretting about her dire situation: stuck with Dominic in a beautiful villa. She was starting to sound like a whiny, ungrateful brat.

She quickly showered and washed her hair, then quickly dried it. Then paced around the room in her underwear, staring at the dress hanging up, wondering, worrying, becoming more anxious by the moment.

She wanted something that would catapult her from waitress to socialite. Would this dress do it? Would Dominic like it?

She had to remind herself that she wasn't dressing for *him*. She was dressing for herself, so that she could exude the confidence that seemed to have deserted her.

This was business.

She chewed her newly painted fingernail, then promptly stopped. She didn't want to ruin her nails. She needed all the glam help she could muster. Painted nails, a touch of make up, the diamond hair slide she had remembered to bring. At least it would come in handy here. Taking her time to get it right, she put her hair up into a messy French twist, letting tendrils loose to frame her face before she fixed the hair slide in a little to the side of her twist.

Her reflection in the mirror made her heart race faster. She didn't look bad at all. That was an understatement.

She looked ... stunning.

Different.

She had been transformed. Lifting her chin, and angling her face from side to side, she decided in that moment that she would do.

She would more than do. She would fit right in. She was suddenly excited to put the dress on.

"Eleni!"

Dominic's voice floated to her from the hallway. She stared at the clock.

Where had the time gone?

"How much longer will you be?"

"Almost ready!" she yelled back, and quickly climbed into the long satin skirt before putting on her corset.

Moments passed before, "Eleni!" Sharper, louder, the urgency in Dominic's voice panicked her.

"I just need another five more minutes!" She slipped her arms through it then froze as her hands went to her back to do up the hooks. With horror she realized she couldn't do them all the way up. At the boutique the store assistant had helped her.

"I hate being late. How long?"

What was wrong with the man? "I'm coming!" She rushed to the door and shouted for Xenia. With no response forthcoming, she rushed into the kitchen in her bare feet, with her corset half hanging off. "Xenia?"

"She's not here." She heard Dominic's voice around the corner before she saw him, and then it was too late to hide. Panicked, she turned around, so that he couldn't see her bare back.

"But...but she said she was coming today."

"She's been and gone..." A sound, something between a gasp and admiration fell from his lips. Dominic stared at her as if she were the most beautiful thing he had ever seen. "You look ..."

"I need her ..."

"For what?" His heated gaze traveled slowly up and down her length.

"For ... something."

"I'm here."

"But I need *her*," she whimpered. Her heart missed a couple of beats, maybe ten, as she took in his appearance. He was dressed in the inkiest darkest blue suit, with a white shirt, cufflinks, and tie. He stole her breath away and she, she was in danger of swallowing her own tongue, of hyperventilating if he moved any closer.

Why was it that this man took her breath away just because of the clothes he wore? They both mirrored one another's awe. Reflected back in his expression was the sure sign that she had dazzled him, as he had her.

"What's the problem?"

How could she ask him? She had no choice. "I can't ... I can't do my back up."

"Let me help you." He moved towards her, and her heart leapt into her mouth.

"No." The idea of Dominic doing up her hooks at the back set fire to her already heated skin.

"We need to get going, Eleni. I don't want to be late."

He was angry, and impatient, and concerned about the timing. She was concerned about her body and how she might just fall into him. "I have another outfit I could—"

"This. I want you in this." His eyes were a liquid, shimmering darkened blue and there was something about his voice. Something strong. As if he'd issued an order. As if she had no choice but to wear this. For him.

An electrical pulse charged through her. Angry Dominic was one thing, but this, him being commanding and sexy, he turned her into a wanton wreck. She moved so that her back was to him, and her breath hitched in her throat when his fingers grazed her skin, slowly moving down.

"These things are fiddly ..." He sounded different. Not as assured and as confident, and he seemed to struggle with the hooks, his breathing heavier than normal, his fingers clumsier than usual.

"I shouldn't have worn this—"

"This is the perfect dress. It is so very you."

She was tempted to ask him what he meant, but she couldn't string a sentence together. Dominic unleashed in her a torrent of emotions, flooding her already overloaded senses. With one touch he had turned her molten.

She swallowed, trying to still her breathing. Every time he was around her, the air became scarce, and she struggled to fill her lungs.

"That should be it. You're good to go."

"Thanks," she managed to say, as she turned around and thanked the heavens that her strapless bra was padded. That he wouldn't see the way her breasts had peaked, just because of his touch.

His gaze raked over her slowly, causing her to clench her pelvic floor muscles, her stomach, and hold in her breath while her body—already a tingling, vibrating mess—absorbed his heated stare.

"You look ... you look ..." The expression on his face told her more than mere words ever could have. She put a hand to her French twist, praying that it would hold, her fingers gingerly touching the hair slide. "You like it?"

"Yes."

"I was worried that I might ..."

He lowered his face, curiosity mingled with a slow burning desire as he stared at her. "Might ...?"

"Might let you down. All of your girlfriends, they're so ... beautiful and elegant and, I didn't want to..."

He touched his finger to her lips as if to silence her but all it did was reignite the dying flame. "Girlfriends? It's Demi, and we were nothing but a short summer fling."

"She's beautiful."

"She can't hold a candle to you."

Had he just thumbed her lower lip? The touch of his skin against her lips made her flinch. This thing between them, this invisible hum, it was of another frequency, a different channel. They were changed. In this moment, they weren't the same Dominic and Eleni from the office.

They were a possibility of what a new future could be.

His hand held there, making her breathing labored, making her use all of her restraint to not tilt her face up to him, or lick her lips. Her body was preparing for something ...

But he wrenched his hand away quickly, as if he'd burned it. "We should go."

"I need to put my shoes on..." She rushed back to the room, taking a moment to catch her breath, to still her heart. She laid a hand on her chest, as if that might help. Her body was a riot of feelings, desire ratcheted up to dangerous levels, pretty soon all her emotions would be in disarray.

He was waiting by the front door, staring at her as she walked towards him, setting her heart ablaze. Never in all her twenty-one years had she ever felt on the verge of falling apart, just because of the way one man looked at her. His gaze was loaded with so much pride, her heart was ready to climb out of her mouth to do a victory lap.

Dominic helped her climb into the car. "Sorry," he mumbled, as his hand brushed the curve of her bottom when he slid the fabric of her skirt under her so that it wouldn't crease when she sat.

It was so thoughtful of him.

She had passed the test. Dominic liked her dress.

They were silent during the journey. She was lost in thought, still recovering from the fact that he'd helped her get dressed, still remembering the look on his face when he'd seen her.

She lost track of time and had no idea how long it was before the car came to a stop. Dominic helped her out; his attentiveness so tender, she was starting to think he really meant it.

"We should hold hands," he suggested, and a few awkward moments ensued, as they looked at one another.

"Now?" she asked, nervously. A flood of emotions assaulted her senses, and she was overwhelmed by the opulence of her surroundings as well as Dominic's attention.

"No, when the wedding is over."

She frowned. *He's trying to make you laugh.* "Now," she tried to smile, the array of cars and finely dressed people coming out of them made her jittery. She'd seen people like this before when she'd been a server at events. When she'd been on the other side.

Deep breath.

As if he'd sensed her unease, he placed his hands on her

shoulders, his fingers pressing gently against her skin. "Don't be nervous. You look beautiful. You belong here, and for today, you're with me."

The words, the promise in them, rippled through her, reassuring her.

"Eleni?"

She needed a moment to gather her thoughts, because his fingers on her shoulders made her lose track of everything, she forgot to reply because her vocal chords had rendered her speechless.

"Ready?"

As ready as she would ever be.

Grasping her hand firmly in his, he set about working the room, introducing her to various people. More than once she detected their gazes bouncing from Dominic's face to hers, then back to him again, and mostly everyone, every woman, gave her the side eye, surreptitiously taking in her outfit, from top to bottom, their faces plastered with too much make up, their smiles as fake as Botox.

When they'd made it through a lobby full of people, Dominic stopped, then bent down, his lips barely caressing her earlobe.

"Are you okay?" His breath was warm against her skin, his voice so low and familiar she felt the reverberations in her chest

"Y-yes." Something blossomed in her belly, something deep and fulsome, like a flower blooming from a bud. She felt dizzy and light, as if she were floating on a cloud high above and looking down. It seemed surreal.

He moved his face away, then, glancing over her shoulder, moved his face close to her neck again. "Have I told you how beautiful you look?" There it was again. His warm breath kissing her skin, his sea breeze scent filling her personal space.

"You're tickling my neck," she cried, flinching at his closeness, at her reaction, at the effect of him being so close.

As if to tease her, his lips brushed her earlobe and her heart jumped in her chest.

Her legs threatened to go on strike which meant any moment now she'd hit the floor. "Is this really necessary?"

"Hector is watching," he murmured. His fingers skittered across her bare arms, reawakening the hot desire she thought she'd safely locked away for now. She didn't care who was watching, all she could absorb was the feel of Dominic's fingers across her bare skin, the low whisper of his voice, his breath against her ear.

And then she snapped out of it.

Hector Galatis.

The reason for this façade. Dominic could make her believe that this was real, that he was starting to want her, given the intensity of the attention he was giving her. But it was a ruse.

Never forget that.

She steeled herself as his hands slid slowly down her arms, sprouting goosebumps in their wake. His fingers wrapped around her wrists possessively for a few seconds before he lowered them, then his fingers intwined with hers and she forgot to breathe.

"Smile, Eleni." He did it again, swooping in and whispering directly into her ear. The heady combination of his closeness, his breath, his voice a deep rumble she felt deep in the echo chambers of her heart.

"I'm trying," she whimpered, caught up in the fog of emotion swirling around her. She smiled back at him like an obedient little imp.

In this moment, she would have done whatever Dominic asked of her.

CHAPTER THIRTY-SIX

DOMINIC

E leni seemed more nervous than he'd expected her to be, and it surprised him.

This environment wasn't new to her. She'd worked on the yachts and at parties of the wealthy.

With her beauty, and sassy attitude, he'd expected her to deal with this just fine, so when her discomfort was palpable, it threw him for a loop. Wanting to put her at ease, he'd done his best, taking her hand, reassuring her, trying to say the right things—but he wasn't sure it had worked.

But something else was happening, for him at least. Taking her hand did something to him. It wasn't only her soft skin, or her small hand that fit so well inside his big one. It was more than that; complicated in a million different ways it didn't need to be, because of who he was.

He'd caught Galatis staring in his direction, the old man's sad dog eyes flitting between him and Eleni. It had been the reason why Dominic had leaned closer to Eleni and put on a show of affection for the man to witness.

True to form, the old hulking beast of a man was slowly making his way towards them.

"Dominic," the old man greeted him warmly.

"Good to see you, Hector." They shook hands, and by his side, Dominic could feel Eleni's nervousness. The old man's gaze fastened on Eleni, his eyes slowly taking in her face, inch by inch. "Who is this delightful young lady?"

"This is Eleni." He didn't say *who* she was.

"It is a pleasure to meet you." Hector introduced his wife, whose hand Eleni shook gently. She complimented Eleni on her dress, and Eleni warmed to her instantly.

Hector was all smiles and softness around his wife. A different man altogether. Dominic was reminded of Hector's words about what had motivated him to be successful, of how he had done it all for his family.

He squeezed Eleni's hand even more firmly, willing to speak up for her and the workplace romance, should the need arise.

"Shall we take our seats?" Hector's wife asked him.

"We will speak later, Dominic." With that the old man and his wife left them, leaving Dominic to lead Eleni to one of the seats a few rows back from the front. "That wasn't too bad, was it?"

"He didn't recognize me." She let out a breath.

"I wouldn't have cared even if he had." He motioned for Eleni to take a seat first. She seemed nervous again as she looked around surveying the crowd.

"Are you okay?" he asked, his mouth near her ear. A flowery, clean scent wafted over him.

"You keep asking me that."

"I want to keep making sure that you're okay."

"I'd tell you if I wasn't," she whispered back.

"Would you though?" He raised an eyebrow, doubting that she would.

She smiled in response, and he was undone, thinking of her in a way that was guaranteed to bring trouble.

A few moments later Demi walked past on the arm of her father—a man who had been bitterly disappointed when he and Demi had broken up—but it wasn't Demi he was looking at.

Eleni smoothed down her skirt, placing her clutch over it, her hand going to her hair slide and adjusting it. He observed her in awe, wanted to put his hand on her to reassure her, but he could not move and was content to sit and take in all of her while she was unaware.

The way she'd done her hair suited her and showed off her long neck and perfect little nose. Her eyes, large and brown, wide like a doe's, with lashes extra thick and long today, and a thin satiny line of eye pencil on the upper lids. Her lips, full, cherry red and glossy.

He knew all this in detail because he couldn't stop looking at her. With her cheekbones high and sculpted, her skin smooth and velvety, he could only imagine his lips skirting across that skin.

A shiver rolled over him.

Jesus. No boner in here. Please.

Eleni turned to him. "She is stunning..." she started to whisper, but it was too late; she'd caught him staring at her.

The color rose to her cheeks, her hand going to her neck before fluttering to her lap. She seemed embarrassed, and looked at her lap, then up ahead.

If anyone was going to have trouble today it was him. His heart pitter pattering beneath his ribcage was a sign of danger. Eleni made him feel things that he struggled to keep suppressed. She looked so glamorous, all dressed up, especially in that dress.

That dress.

Those hooks.

The sight of her bare back, the clasp of her bra—the things he had tried not to think of—had been thrust in his face unexpectedly.

Life was testing him severely.

ELENI

She had survived the wedding. Just about.

Seeing Dominic's ex-girlfriend up close had been torture. It had been an epic, monumental moment which had ground her down, seeing the tall, elegant and beautiful woman moving gracefully down the aisle.

Eleni had felt like a garden gnome in comparison.

But then she'd turned to Dominic and caught him staring at her. It was a moment she would never forget. *She* was the one Dominic had been staring at, not his ex. He'd stared at her the way she had probably been staring at him, eyes full of longing and desire. Her breath hitched in her throat just thinking of that moment.

The wedding was over, and the guests spilled out of the blue domed church where the newlyweds were quickly surrounded by well wishers. She and Dominic got their chance to congratulate the happy couple, but this time Eleni didn't feel inadequate or out of place.

A short while later, they got into the car and drove to another stunning villa by the sea. This was where the wedding reception was taking place, Dominic told her.

His hand on the small of her back guided her towards different groups of people as they mingled around, the sound of happy chatter as uplifting as birdsong.

She was having a great time and feeling more relaxed than ever. The faces in the crowd that had been nameless earlier were now people with whom she was having friendly conversations with.

At one point she caught sight of Hector's wife who was standing alone at one of the buffet tables, her handbag on one arm preventing her from easily getting the food.

Eleni excused herself and went over to her. "Let me help you," she offered, taking a plate from the table. The older woman beamed and told her that Eleni reminded her of one of her daughters. Eleni then leapt into waitress mode, helping to plate the food for her.

They made casual conversation about the wedding and the new couple, and then Eleni excused herself and would have returned to Dominic. "Come and sit with me," the older woman insisted. Eleni's heart sank.

"I should let you eat in peace." As much as she liked this kind lady with her soft features and gentle ways, she was enjoying her day with Dominic even more.

This was a rare occurrence, being away from the work environment, just the two of them. It didn't even take a gargantuan leap of faith to pretend that this was something it wasn't, because as far as fake dates went, this felt real.

Everything that had happened between them today was real and intense, so perfectly raw and full of possibility that her nerve endings hummed, a low, thrumming vibration keeping her on edge. Even now, away from Dominic, she could feel him.

"Come," Mrs. Galatis insisted. "You remind me of my middle

daughter, and—" the old woman made a clucking noise with her tongue, "not one of my children has come home this summer to see me. Not one. Sit with me for a while. I like your company."

Eleni looked over her shoulder and found Dominic staring at her. A shiver rolled through her. Was that a yearning in his eyes? Or something her imagination had just made up? He nodded beckoning her to come back to him, and she gestured that she had no say in this. But then a beautiful woman, not Demi, but someone else, sidled up to him and he turned his attention to her.

That hadn't taken very long.

DOMINIC

Another woman whom he barely remembered from his days with Demi had managed to collar him.

Dominic forced himself to have a halfhearted conversation with her, but his insides plummeted in shock when Eleni stayed by Hector's wife's side. He looked around for Galatis only to find the man laughing with a huge group of people. Dominic didn't want to interrupt.

The woman by his side, someone whose name he couldn't remember, kept talking even though he barely paid any attention to her words. When he could stand it no longer, he shot up from his chair and excused himself, not caring what she thought.

He searched out Eleni again, his gaze darting back to the table where she had been sitting with Galatis' wife. Only, Eleni had disappeared.

Frantically scanning the crowd in hopes of finding her, he

still couldn't see her. He summoned his bodyguard who was hovering close by. "Where's Eleni?"

"She went into the ladies lounge."

Dominic marched off in that direction, eager to find her and have her by his side again.

Just her and no one else.

ELENI

The pink and cream marble washroom with white lilies in silver vases, was the prettiest ladies lounge she'd ever been in.

Eleni tidied her hair up then applied a touch of her lipstick.

Admiring her reflection, she smoothed down the front of her dress and stared at her reflection in the mirror.

She smiled because she had managed to look as spectacular as she'd wanted to.

A woman fit to grace Dominic Steele's arm.

She was on heightened alert, all her senses shiny and new, like that of a baby. The tingle in her body, the shot of adrenalin in her blood, excitement coursing through her veins, all because of one man.

She'd been sitting with Mrs. Galatis for some time when Hector came with his sister, giving Eleni the perfect excuse to leave.

Overcome by a sense of possessiveness, she was determined to go up to Dominic, no matter whether he was deep in conversation with a beautiful woman or ten, and make it be known that he was with her today.

Opening her clutch bag she slipped the lipstick in, then

strode out feeling confident and on top of the world when a hand grabbed her arm. Rough and hard.

"I remember you. The waitress, eh?" Hard, glinty eyes stared back at her. The sickly smile brought it all back. It was the man from the party on the yacht, the one she had kicked and who now gripped her wrist like a vise.

She winced. "Let go. You're hurting me." She tried to free her hand, but his hold was firm, and painful.

"You're looking very beautiful and very different." The man smiled at her again and loosened his fingers a little, but still held her captive. "Are you with the American?"

She ignored his question. "Let go of me." Her eyes searched for Dominic.

"You don't like Greek, eh?"

She tried again to wrest her wrist away from him but failed, panic climbing up her throat like a tarantula. Her insides were in freefall, that even now, dressed like she was, this man could treat her in such an appalling manner.

"You are a waitress. What are you doing here, looking like *this*?" His greedy gaze devoured her outfit and left her feeling dirty.

"Leave me alone," she said, willing herself to sound brave, even though she didn't feel it. What she couldn't do was show fear. A man like this one would smell it and know he had won.

"You do extra work on the side, eh? Charge by the hour?" He smiled, perfect teeth, cosmetic white and blinding.

"Get. Your. Hand. Off. Me," she bit out, tempted to kick him again, but refraining, not least because her dress wouldn't allow that range of movement, and because she couldn't do that here of all places.

"You are very pretty. I like you."

"I don't like you. Let me go!" Her heart rattled inside her

ribcage, clamoring to break free. She glanced over the man's shoulder in vain, desperate for Dominic to find her.

His face turned ugly. His lips a sneer. "You little slut. You are a temptress."

A surge of hatred erupted inside her. "Let me go!" she cried. "You're a disgusting, desperate man."

"I am what you see. But you," he motioned at her with his hand, "...you are trying hard to be someone you're not."

Try as she did, she couldn't free her wrists from his tight hold. He had her trapped in a corner.

"Are you here with someone, or are you providing 'entertainment?'" Another wolfish smile formed on his lips, revealing sharp white teeth.

"I'm not looking for anything, least of all someone like you." Her mind was spinning, fury climbing up her throat like Medusa. She wanted to lash out, but he held her back, his strength overpowering her.

He pinned her with a sleazy gaze. "I have seen you at parties before. Not just this summer, but before. A face like yours is hard to forget."

"Get your disgusting hands off me," she hissed, her voice trembling with rage. Even here, dressed up and finally feeling special, this man had seen through her.

"I saw you with Dominic Steele. Does he have you for the hour, or for the night? Because I want my turn. Or do you only fuck Americans?"

She lashed out, the force of her anger balled up in her fist, but she couldn't reach him. His hands still shackled her wrists.

"He will use you and throw you away like toilet paper." The man sneered. He was enjoying this.

Her face burned with disgust. "You're hurting me." Tears prickled in her eyes.

"Be nice to me, and I will be gentle with you."

She pulled back with all her might, but he pulled her roughly towards him, until she could smell his breath in her face. Recoiling with disgust, she yanked her hand hard, the force sent her reeling backwards so hard that she hit the wall. Pain spiked up her back and spliced through her right shoulder blade. She could have sworn she saw stars, and then Dominic's large frame appeared in front of her.

She was seeing stars.

She heard it first, the thud as the man's body hit a wall and he slumped down slowly, like a cartoon character. She slowly straightened herself and stood taller.

"Get. The. Fuck. Away. From. Her." They weren't spoken words, or hissed. They were deadly, silent warnings with the promise to draw blood.

The man scrambled to his feet and Dominic stood ready, his fists balled by his sides, his body rigid like a warrior getting ready for the kill. Even from behind she knew his face looked like thunder.

He glanced over his shoulder, and she must have been in pain, or making a face because his fist was raised, as if any second now, it was going to break some bones in the man's face.

But just like that he let it drop. One step and Dominic was by her side, his hands framing her face. He looked into her eyes. "Are you hurt?"

"I'm okay," she murmured.

His thumbs caressed her cheeks. "That motherfucker Ioannis," he raged. "I should have found you sooner."

"I went to the ladies lounge. I was talking to Hector's wife, and I was going to come and find you but he ..."

"It's okay." He pressed his forehead against hers, and it

was the most intimate moment between them. "I wish I'd been here. I shouldn't have let you out of my sight."

He didn't seem to notice that they weren't alone. That a crowd had started to form around them.

She shivered, because he still held her face in his hands, concern spilled over from his colored irises, his face so sad and yet filled with a tight fury.

She caught sight of a couple of guests looking over, past the barricade that was his bodyguard who was preventing people from approaching them. But Dominic seemed lost to everything but her.

She lifted her hands to his and brought them down gently, hating that they were here, that their own secret little bubble had to be broken. "People are watching, Dominic," she whispered. "I don't want to make a scene."

He examined her hands, his face tensing when he saw the ugly red marks staining her wrists. "The son of a bitch." He went to pull away, but she grabbed his arms to stop him.

"Don't make a scene, Dominic. He's not worth it. Hector is here, and you want to set a good example."

She let out a sigh. Something was hurting, but there was too much going on for her to focus. Shock and pain mingled with a bone deep tiredness that had suddenly come over her.

Sven picked up Ioannis, handling him roughly, then took him outside.

"What's he going to do to him?" Eleni asked, alarmed."

"Give him a warning, if he's lucky. I want to punch his fucking face. Kick him hard in the balls like you did before." Dominic's finger stroked her cheek. Anger still raged in his eyes, and she doubted that he was even aware of what he was saying. "I shouldn't have let you out of my sight."

"Hey, don't worry about that now." She was about to raise her arm and touch his face but her shoulder was hurting.

"What do you want to do?" he asked, loosely holding her hand, his fingers half intwining with hers.

She wanted to go back to the villa, get away from here. She wanted to be with Dominic and no one else, but she had come for a reason. "Should we work the room?" she whispered. "We could go outside?"

Dominic scoffed. "Neither."

"We should stay for as long as you want. You have to—"

"I don't care about any of that. What do you want?" he asked again.

"I want whatever you want." She looked at him and tried to read the expression in those now darkening eyes.

"You have no idea what I want."

Her heart missed a beat or two. Her insides turned light and fluttery. He was such a charmer. He said all the right things, looked at her as if she was the only one for him. Made her think she was Cinderella and he her prince. "I'm okay to stay here, Dominic. I'll never have a chance to be a guest at an event like this again."

"You want to stay here? You expect me to believe you? I've studied you well, Eleni and I can tell when you're lying."

She might have been nervous a few seconds ago, but with this man by her side, she felt invincible. "You've studied me as closely as one of your contracts?"

"You have no idea."

He was so intense, she had to smile to lighten the atmosphere.

"I pay attention, Eleni, because you are worth paying attention to. You matter."

His words vacuumed the air clean out of her lungs. This man lifted her up and made her feel special. He always had.

He showed her that she wasn't 'just' a waitress. She wasn't 'just' anything. She was special, and had worth, and was valued. But most of all, he made her believe that she was as precious as the air he breathed, and he needed her for his survival.

No one in her life had ever given her the right to feel valued. And now, this knight in his aviators was in her life and she was determined to cherish the short time they had together.

"How is it that you're such a busy man, running your empire, and yet you still have time for me?"

He tapped her on the nose. "I will always make time for you."

CHAPTER THIRTY-SEVEN

DOMINIC

God help him if he ever caught Ioannis within an inch of Eleni.

Something had twisted deep in his gut when he'd seen the man grabbing her by the wrists. Fury had blinded him, but somehow he'd made it over to her side, not before he'd sent the motherfucker flying.

Some men were the scum of the earth. All he'd wanted, all he'd tried to do, was to make Eleni feel at ease, but Ioannis had smashed all of that carefully built-up confidence in a second.

Men didn't do that. Not *real* men. Cowards, men who were weak and afraid of rejection, resorted to those bullying tactics.

Resentment simmered beneath his skin. Contempt and hatred, too, that yet again, Eleni had been subjected to such an assault.

His natural reaction had been to protect her and keep her

safe, but Eleni didn't need his protection. She didn't need anyone to take care of her. She'd taken care of herself against this type of predator before, but a kick to the balls would have been an impossibility given her dress.

And what a dress.

He couldn't focus on the journey back. A hot numbness swept over him. He tried to think, to separate his emotions, from the way he felt about Eleni this morning when he'd helped her with her dress, to how he'd been shaking all over when he'd found Ioannis pestering her again. It had been like a fist to his throat, he couldn't breathe, couldn't swallow.

He'd wanted to shed blood. Ioannis' blood.

Eleni was the only thing that mattered. He didn't want her to hurt any more than the poor girl already was. And when they arrived back at the villa, he came to her side of the car, to help her out.

"I'm not injured, Dominic," she said, lifting up her skirt with one hand as she climbed out, revealing more of her leg than was good for his health. "I can get out of a car unaided."

She was a stubborn mule, but a beautiful one, and he cared for her more now than ever.

"Take my hand anyway," he insisted. His voice shaky, as if he couldn't trust himself to sound normal. Her soft hand clasped his and he tugged her gently noticing that her wrists were still red.

That asshole.

He didn't let go of her until they were back in the house. But once they were in the hallway, Eleni moved her hand out of his.

And just like that, the spell was broken.

Cinderella was back home, and it was past the stroke of midnight.

There was something he wanted to know. "I didn't ask

you but it's eating away at me. What did he say to you? I could see that he was saying something. What was it?"

"It's not important, Dominic. Let's not talk about that."

"Did he remember you from before?"

"He remembered that I was a waitress."

"Tell me what he said." It killed him, the not knowing.

"I don't want you to get angrier."

"Then tell me and put me out of my misery."

"Your misery?"

"He hurts you, he hurts me."

She looked confused, as if she didn't understand. How could she have any idea of how he felt about her? "Please, Dominic. Leave it be."

"The piece of shit," he snarled, and wished he'd landed a punch across the man's jaw.

ELENI

While she was thankful to be back at the villa, and it was good of Dominic to return with her, she didn't want to stand in his way.

"You should go back, Dominic. It would be a shame for you to leave early."

His mouth opened and emerald green eyes stared back at her. He cocked his head slowly, as if she were speaking in another tongue and he didn't understand what she was saying. "Go back?"

It was still early and the party was going to go on all evening until the early hours of the next morning. "You can still meet your friends, and find Galatis and have fun, even if you don't actually have fun at these events. I'll be okay here.

This is paradise for me. I want to make the most of my last night here."

A vertical line formed between his forehead, the look he fixed her with made her insides melt. "I'm not leaving you."

She feared he might feel obliged. "I might go back later … I need some time alone."

"Alone?" He shoved his hands in his pockets.

That filthy man's words still resonated in her ears. Hard to shake, even harder to forget and impossible to erase.

Stepping into Dominic's world had been enlightening, and for a few hours, she'd even felt a part of it, but Ioannis had been right. She was a fake. She did not belong. When she was with Dominic the world was hers to take and own and conquer. But Ioannis had reminded her that she was living a lie.

Dominic wouldn't be her champion for much longer, and what had just happened was a way for her to come down and hit reality, hard.

But he was now refusing to leave her and return to a wedding he hadn't wanted to go to but had changed his mind about, because Galatis had hinted he might be amenable to making a deal. She could not get in the way of that.

For all she knew, Dominic didn't want to leave the party and be stuck here with her, but he had done so out of a sense of duty.

"You might be able to catch Hector. You said it would be good for you to talk to him if he's in a good mood."

"He's with his family, and he's busy. I'm going to let him enjoy his nephew's wedding. I got talking to his wife earlier, and she told me she liked you. She said you were a lovely person. Told me I was a lucky man."

Eleni raised a hand to her neck and grinned. "She's a wise woman."

"She's a woman who fell for it." Dominic's hands still in his pockets, his stance widened, as if he were waiting for her to make the next move.

"It worked," Eleni murmured. People had fallen for their fake dating, but not Ioannis.

Dominic examined her face as if he was weighing up his options. "I'm not going back. I don't want to. Therefore, we are stuck here."

Her heart blossomed. "I wouldn't call it being stuck, Dominic."

"I guess not."

"I should get out of these clothes," she said, feeling suddenly very tired.

"Me too."

She managed a smile, and turned away, because if she'd spent a second longer gazing into Dominic's eyes she wouldn't have wanted to move either.

In the safety of her room, away from Dominic—and the danger of letting her feelings flood out—she leaned against the door and winced. She'd done something to her back when she'd hit that wall. Lifting her arm she reached for the pain point on the back of her shoulder.

Apart from that incident, by all other accounts, today had been wonderful.

A dream.

She had a feeling that Dominic was glad to be back, too, or maybe she hoped he was. The idea that they could spend this evening together, that he didn't seem to want to go back, filled her with hope.

But first she was desperate to get out of the dress. Kicking off her high heels, she let out a loud sigh and sat on the bed massaging the soles of her feet. Then she undid her French twist, taking out the bobby pins and the hair slide. She hadn't worn any other jewelry except for this diamond studded accessory, preferring a minimalistic style, in stark comparison to many of the other women who dripped with diamonds and pearls. Shaking out her hair, she ran a hand through it, feeling an overwhelming sense of relief.

She needed to get out of this corset and skirt. Reaching back, she undid the first hook at the top, but then she stopped, unable to go further. She remembered. For a paralyzed minute, her muscles turned rigid because there was no way she could get out of this by herself.

Her mind churned over the possibilities of what she could do but there was no way out of it, no avoidance of the fact.

She needed Dominic's help.

Her heart somersaulted dangerously. Anymore and it would spring right out of her chest. What a mess she was in. Dominic touching her again was going to make her fall to pieces.

Lifting her skirt with one hand, she nervously tiptoed into the hallway, and stood at the foot of the stairs, looking up. "Uh...Dominic ..." Her voice was weak, unsure. Pathetic. She cleared her throat, her mouth turning sand dry, her pulse racing. "Dominic."

"What is it?"

She jumped at his voice behind her, and spun around, her eyes going wide. The top two buttons of his shirt were undone, his tie off, his collar loose and revealing a dusting of hairs behind the shirt opening. He'd discarded his cufflinks and rolled up his sleeves. Her gaze dropped to his veined forearms. She clenched her insides. Her brain chose this moment to retrieve her safely stored away vision of him from this morning in his swim shorts.

"Eleni?"

Her gaze settled on his lips, before slowly moving up to

his nose, his eyes, every little feature that made up that gorgeous and beautiful face of his. So angular it might as well have been carved out of stone. "I can't undo my ..."

"Oh, right." He nodded, his expression blank, his tone calm, as if she'd asked him what time it was. "Turn around."

Her jellied legs managed to obey. She turned around, thankful that she could rest her hands on the bannister and support herself enough to remain standing.

"Sorry ... to ... bother ... you," she murmured, forcing her mind to focus on the childbirth videos she'd been shown in class as a teenager in high school. Images which had scarred her forever.

"It's no bother." His touch was electric, making her jolt. He moved her hair to one side, exposing her neck and back, and goosebumps scampered along her naked arms. In that second, she forgot to breathe.

"What the fuck?" he cried, rage pouring out of him. His fingers lightly touched the part of her shoulder which was hurting. That was where she'd hit the wall. "Is it bruised?"

"It's grazed and bloody. Fuck that son of abitch." His voice spiked with rage.

She turned to face him, already imagining the torrent of thoughts flashing through Dominic's minid. "He didn't push me. I fell back when I pulled my arm away from him."

But Dominic was quiet, and she couldn't even read the reaction on his face. Then he disappeared, leaving her with a burning sensation on her skin, not from the graze, but from where his fingers had been.

He returned a few seconds later, with a small medical kit, which he set on the staircase.

"What are you doing?" she cried. "It's just a scratch."

"It's not."

She watched as he poured something out of a bottle onto a pad of cotton wool.

"Dominic!" This was overkill. "I'm not dying."

He stood behind her again, sending those sizzling sensations hurtling through her body, putting her receptor cells on high alert. Her heart leapt and twirled like a ballerina in love.

"This might hurt," he warned, before sweeping the ball of cotton gently over her wound. She didn't even feel the pain, her nerves were so drunk on the touch of his fingers, her mind awash with whimsical fantasy, he could have stitched her skin together with knitting needles and she would have been fine. "That should help keep it clean. I won't cover it. Let it breathe."

"Thank you, Dr. Steele."

"I should have punched that bastard when I had the chance."

She faced him again, alarmed by the rage in his voice. "Dominic, stop. Please, stop. Don't get so worked up about him. He's gone. I won't ever see him again."

"No, you won't." He looked deep in thought, a scowl on his face. "I'm sorry I wasn't there to protect you."

"Dominic." He was overreacting, saying things that made no sense. "You don't have to be sorry. It's not your fault."

But his face showed otherwise. "I should have let Sven watch over you. No one's going to do a fucking thing to me, but you. *You're* the one who always gets the assholes."

"Shhhhh." She put her hand on his arm, hoping to silence him. But instead her fingers started to move along the plane of his arms, moving further up to his biceps. She let out a sound, something between a giggle and a squeak. "You're a wall of steel. Hard all over."

They stared at one another; the innuendo suspended in

the thick air between them. He touched her face, then dropped his hand as if her cheek had been on fire.

The air charged and cackling, snapped with tension, and something else. Something hot and sultry that had been between them all day long.

"I need to ... your hooks. You have to ..." He scratched his ear, motioning for her to turn her back to him again, his voice once more sounding different, knotted and tight.

It was when she turned her back to him, that she heard him sigh. For a few seconds he did nothing, and then his fingers moved down her back as he undid her hooks slowly, one by one. The moment was soaked in intimacy, caressed by unseen kisses.

"There. You should be able to do the rest."

She reached behind with her hands, felt along far down and nodded. She didn't trust herself to turn and look at him, but waited instead for his footsteps to peter away.

CHAPTER THIRTY-EIGHT

DOMINIC

He changed into a loose T-shirt and swim shorts and made his way outside to the pool.

On the way he took a jug of Xenia's homemade lemonade out and two glasses in case Eleni decided to join him.

She said she wanted alone time, and he respected that. He hated that she had had more than her fair share of having to deal with men who behaved like feral pigs. His blood boiled thinking about women having to deal with such unwanted attention.

But the fact that it had been Eleni, intensified everything. Twice now she'd suffered the worst of men in situations that he knew of, but he sensed it had happened many times and it made him want to protect her and keep her close more than ever.

No way did he want to return to the wedding celebrations. No way was he going to leave her alone now.

But he was not in control of his feelings. He'd been shaking when he'd helped her with her dress, but how much of that was due to the rage that still engulfed him, or him being nervous around her, he wasn't sure.

It had required all of his superhuman powers to undo her hooks and not press his lips to her skin.

And he'd hated himself for even thinking that way.

Jesus fucking hell.

How had it come to this between them?

He'd gone from trying to keep her at bay, to *this*.

And now he was suffering for his sins.

With hard ons galore.

Sexy, porn-level fantasies playing in his mind.

He hated himself for every single one of them.

Men couldn't hold back around Eleni, and he didn't want to be that type of man, ever. There was a world's difference between him and Ioannis. He had to tread even more carefully around Eleni because this weekend she was all he could think of and he didn't want it to be that way.

She'd seeped into his skin, sunk deep into his DNA. Being around her was hard on his soul, hard on his heart, and even harder on his dick. This was why a part of him hoped she would stay in her room for the rest of the evening. Tomorrow she'd be gone.

He was staying on for a few more days hoping to have a few business meetings, hopefully with Galatis if the man could get time away from his family celebrations.

He sighed, sitting back and sipping the cold homemade lemonade and reflected on his weekend. Being here, with Eleni, not at the wedding, was perfect.

He was checking the messages on his phone when he heard the flapping of flip flops. Eleni in denim shorts and a tank top, her face scrubbed clean of make up, and her hair trailing down her back, appeared in view. The image went directly from his visual senses to his dick.

What was she trying to do to him?

Give him another tortured night?

A heart attack?

Blue balls?

His heart jumpstarted and he set his phone down so fast, so carelessly that it scuttled across the table and landed on the floor with a loud smack.

Another phone damaged.

Eleni snorted a giggle and bent over to pick it up, giving him an eyeful of her breasts straining over her bra; yet another image that he could do without.

She handed the phone to him.

"Thank you." He examined it with exaggerated concentration, needing something to focus his attention on other than Eleni's delicious body.

Did she have to wear those shorts? And that top? He crossed his legs and wished he'd had head to toe body armor to hide the growing erection which would soon be impossible to hide.

"Is it broken?" she asked, pouring herself a glass of lemonade. She kicked off her flip flops and bent one leg under her as she sat, making herself comfortable, a feeling he didn't share.

He tapped away uneasily on his phone, his cock pulsating as if it had a life of its own; a disobedient teen ignoring his request for calm. "The screen is damaged, but it still works."

"Phew." She made a gesture as if she were wiping the sweat off her forehead. He would have licked it off given the chance.

For the love of Christ keep it together.

"You decided to come out?" He needed to know that she

was okay. He tried to hold it in, but it was an impossibility around this woman.

"I didn't want to stay in the room all evening. That's what I do every day in Athens."

He gripped his glass hard and lifted it to his lips. "I'm sorry your day was ruined."

"It wasn't." She surveyed him quietly, a question in her eyes. "This part is nice."

"This part, here by the pool?"

"You're not so bad to be around, Dominic."

He lifted an eyebrow. "Not *that* bad? Should I be upset or pleased?"

"I can't imagine you ever being upset. Angry, yes, but upset? That would imply you had a heart." Her luscious lips curved up into a smile. A smile he adored and a face he thought of most nights before he went to sleep.

"Most people are scared of you, but I'm not."

"I like that you're not. It's not my intention to scare people, but I don't suffer fools and in my experience a lot of people are fools."

"There you go with your self-aggrandizing manner."

He wasn't trying to brag, nor did he consider himself as all important. "I'm being truthful, and most people can't handle the truth."

She took a sip and set the glass back on the table, but it was the red marks around her wrist that enraged him. He reached out and touched them. "That fuck—"

"Don't, please," she begged, leaning forward. "Let's not ruin this evening."

He forced himself to sit back and calm down.

"What happened back there, and on the yacht, it doesn't just happen to me, it happens to my friends. It happens all the time, at the tavernas, at bars, whenever we're out."

His stomach twisted. "It must suck to be a woman."

"Not as much as it must suck to be a man," she countered. "The audacity of imposing yourself on a woman who clearly doesn't want you. I don't mean *you* ..." she said quickly, "I mean—"

"I know what you mean. I agree. The audacity. We're a horrid sex ..." He flinched inwardly and wished he hadn't mentioned the S-word.

"I know what you mean." She did it again—a smile curved its way along that beautiful mouth of hers.

Fuck.

He shifted uncomfortably in his chair, placing his hand over his ever-growing erection.

"We shouldn't have to be afraid each time we are out late or walking home. We shouldn't have to watch what we wear. We shouldn't have to suffer the shameful catcalls and advances of desperate men."

"No, women shouldn't." The irony of his situation. He wholeheartedly agreed with her—he disliked those men, too— but he was sitting here with a boner, for her. And it was so wrong. It made him feel so wrong, so dirty. He wanted to fly back to Athens tonight.

"Not all men are like that," he countered, trying to speak up for the good ones.

"That is true. I have met some real gentlemen."

He nodded.

"I wish parents would teach their sons that women aren't objects and deserve to be treated with respect."

He lifted his glass to her. "That's exactly it. It all starts with your upbringing."

"I can handle myself well."

"I know you can. Your martial arts skills are legendary."

They exchanged a knowing smile in solidarity.

"I couldn't do that this time, with my dress, and the heels, and it being that wedding. I didn't want anything to reflect badly on you."

"Nothing you could do would reflect badly on me. It was an honor having you on my arm."

A flush crept up her cheeks, fanning out all over her face. She pulled her lower lip with her teeth, a smile quirking on her lips. "Then I did what I was supposed to. I saved you from Galatis' nieces."

"You did. You fit right in, Eleni." She was smart and funny, clever and sharp. She was so much more than the women she felt inadequate next to, and he wished she could see it.

The damage that a lifetime of not being valued—of being told she didn't matter and being rejected by her father—damage like that could be irreparable. The only way to counter it would be to shower her with so much love and attention that it would forever erase all the bad things.

He eyed her, and it took a forced effort to not let his gaze wander down the length of her body. Never before had he experienced such a problem with his vision. "I'm sorry it's coming to an end."

She waved at their surroundings. "I will never forget this. I've had such an amazing weekend."

He marveled at her ability to bounce back, but he shouldn't have been surprised, knowing what he did about her past. "You can say that even with what's happened?"

"I try to focus on the good things and not dwell too much on the bad. There are always bad things, but it's the little moments of happiness that add up and make life bearable again." She looked away, and he wondered if she'd gone there again, to the past, to the accident. He wondered about that a lot more now, that even with her tragic past, she wasn't as bitter as he would have expected.

The huge buffalo in the room, the ghost of her boyfriend, loomed large and full before him. "Is climbing the mountain a way to focus on the good things?" he asked, softly.

"It's something I must do."

He didn't understand it, her devotion, her desire to keep their dream alive. "You must have loved him very much."

She looked up, looked unsure, hesitated. Then, "We'd been together since I was seventeen. He was my first proper boyfriend. The first one to show me what it meant to be truly loved."

His jaw tightened and he did a rough calculation in his head, she'd been with him for two and a half years. And now, all these months later she was still pining for him.

His first love had been a girl he'd met one lazy July in the Hamptons. It had lasted about as long as the summer, and he'd never thought about her much after that.

Eleni looked down at her legs, scratched something on her thigh. He was so engrossed in watching her that it startled him when she looked up and caught him gawking at her. "What about you? You must be quite a catch in the US. You must have a lot of kiss and tell stories."

He was surprised by her forthrightness. This was new, her probing for answers when she'd never been so inquisitive before.

"Why did you and Demi break up?" she asked.

He flinched. "I don't want to talk about Demi."

"But you asked me about Jonas."

"I asked you about your mountain climb."

The air chilled to minus five degrees, or thereabouts.

"She's beautiful," Eleni remarked, obviously unwilling to let it go.

He tried to understand what she was getting at. "So are you."

She made a noise in her throat. Dismissive, perhaps. "You know so much about me. You know where I came from, what I'm doing. You know about my past; you even know about my ... about Jonas and that I'm climbing the mountain. I know next to nothing about you." She'd completely ignored his compliment.

"What do you want to know?"

"How did it work, with you being in the US and her being here?"

"It didn't."

"Why not?"

"Because it was a short summer fling. It was over by the time I returned home."

"But if it had..."

"Had what?"

"If it had been long distance, then what?"

He didn't want to talk about Demi. She was irrelevant. He didn't want to talk about his fleeting relationships, or the fact that he'd broken up with his last girlfriend nine months ago. He didn't want to talk about anyone because all he could think about was Eleni.

And he couldn't talk about Eleni because she was in love with the man who'd died so young and so tragically.

Most of all, with his erection so large and throbbing, he couldn't sit here and look at her a moment longer, nor could he excuse himself and turn in for the night, because he wouldn't be able to sleep. Chances were he'd be jerking off all night.

So, he did the only thing a man in his situation could do.

ELENI

She didn't understand why when she'd asked him about his girlfriends and past love interests, he gave her nothing. But he'd told her enough: that long distance relationships would be tough. A rock, heavy and solid, sank inside her.

"You've been staring at the pool all evening," Dominic commented.

"It looks so tempting." She couldn't help it. She'd been thinking about jumping in and cooling off in the water ever since she'd arrived here.

Much to her jaw dropping surprise, Dominic stood up and stripped off his T-shirt. Her thoughts were in complete disarray seeing him naked from the waist up. Staring at his steel hard abs and muscles sent a tsunami of shivers rolling along her spine.

Before she could take a breath, he dove into the water, coming up when he was halfway in the pool, rising up, broad shoulders, arms thick and corded. The only thing missing were tattoos, but somehow, Dominic wasn't a tatted type of guy. She couldn't imagine him with a spot of ink on his body. But she still drooled at the thought. Her legs threatened to crumble under her, as if her bones were made of feta.

He swept his hair back, lifting his arms, and she felt as if she were watching a slick aftershave commercial.

"You tease," she mumbled, her voice shaky. She'd bored him. Seeking distraction, something to do, she lifted the glass of lemonade to her lips and took a long gulp, biding her time, deciding on what to do. She'd expected them to sit here, talking all evening and all night, and into the early hours of the morning. Around him, she felt so at ease, as if he were a friend.

But watching him in the water tempted her more than ever. She ran a hand along the back of her neck, the dampness sticking to her skin. She longed to cool down.

"Nothing stopping you from getting in," Dominic shouted.

"I don't have a swimsuit. You should have told me there'd be a pool."

"There's always a pool."

She got up and walked around, because her body was buzzing. Her cells were a vibrating, shaking mess, her nerves jangling and dancing, dizzy for joy. It was impossible to sit still and watch him.

Feeling hot and sticky, she instinctively lifted her arms and swirled her hair up into a bun. When she gazed at the pool, Dominic's eyes were on her.

He swam away and when he reached the far end of the pool, he turned and swam back. Then he repeated it all over again, swimming lengths in silence, making her feel as if he was done with the talking.

Putting her hands together, she shouted, "Show off!" He lifted his head briefly to give her a half grin of acknowledgment before he continued swimming.

She couldn't take it anymore. Irritated, tempted, frustrated and hot, she jumped in, fully clothed.

CHAPTER THIRTY-NINE

DOMINIC

He couldn't risk her seeing his trombone sized erection. So he'd jumped into the pool to hide his boner, but Eleni had only gone and jumped in after him. He backed away from her as if she had a contagious disease.

"You jumped in fully clothed," he managed to say, stating the obvious.

"Would you rather I took everything off?"

Fuck, yes. NO.

What had possessed her? He wondered if Xenia might have accidentally added vodka to the lemonade. "You can swim in your shorts?"

"They do feel kind of heavy."

He backed further away, scared she might strip them off and come for him. She had suddenly turned into a seductress. She moved towards him, and he moved back a few steps away until they were walking around one another, their steps slow and cautious, him eyeing her as if she were a predator.

She lifted her arms and made an exaggerated show of sniffing her armpits. "Do I smell?"

"No." He backed away a few more steps until he was in the middle of the pool. She had him trapped.

"Then why are you trying to get away from me?"

Eleni's doleful eyes searched his face. He'd seen that look in women's eyes. It was pure want. He scrubbed his face, unsure if the water was blurring his vision.

"I'm not. It's hot." There was no explaining it, so he began to swim again, taking long, purposeful strokes from one end of the pool to the other. The easy-going conversation from earlier now replaced by a prickly silence. After two lengths, he stopped in the middle of a stroke, a few yards from her. "Why don't you swim?"

She leaned back, splaying her slender arms out on the pool ledge. "My shorts feel tight and heavy."

He swallowed, wishing he could erase her words and the visuals they imprinted on his mind. She was breaking his balls and she had no idea.

He swam away again because his lust-hazed brain was struggling to stay calm. When he turned around to do another length, she waved at him, with her denim shorts in her hand.

Oh. *Fuck.*

She threw them on the pool ledge and started to swim while he stared up at the sky and prayed that she'd keep her tank top on. He felt like he was in danger. Uneasy with her proximity. She wouldn't be able to see his hardness, but if she stared at him long enough, she'd be able to tell and he would no longer be able to hide the effect she had on him.

So, he continued with his lengths. The silence and the swimming saved him. With his face in the water, he was vaguely aware of Eleni doing her laps on the other side, but he forced himself to concentrate on every stroke as he glided through the water.

When he next came up for air, he saw that she had stopped swimming and was standing still in the pool, the water coming up to just under her breasts. She was panting, sweeping her hair back from her face. Her knot had come undone and her dark mane clung to her skin. It was impossible to miss the rise and fall of her chest.

Jesus fucking Christ.

Was she deliberately trying to give him death by blue balls?

"We were having a conversation," she stated, her eyes a question mark. "Then you got up and started to swim. Did I bore you?"

He had never heard her sound so needy before. Maybe something else was going on. Something that the prickass, douchbag Ioannis had done ...

He allowed himself to move a few inches closer. "I didn't get a chance to do my exercise today."

A line formed between her brows. "You were swimming this morning."

Surprise opened his mouth. So he had. This morning seemed so far away.

He tried to find another explanation. "Swimming calms me down. Takes away the tension."

It was true.

He was tense, so jacked up and ready to erupt from the sexual tension simmering beneath his skin, that he needed another outlet for his fizzed up frustration.

"Why do you feel tense?" Innocence poured from her gaze. "I thought ... I thought we were getting along fine."

And that was the problem. They were getting on fine.

Too fine.

He had feelings for her he couldn't extinguish, and that was a problem as huge as his erection.

"You should have gone back to the party, Dominic. You don't have to babysit me. I'm not a child you need to take care of."

"I'm not babysitting you. I'm only taking a goddamn swim, Eleni. Don't be so dramatic." The struggle to stop thinking about her, the constant fight in trying not to desire her, was killing him. It had turned him into an ungrateful prick, and he wished he could take his words back, but it was too late.

She had climbed out of the water and no matter how much he tried to *not* look, he couldn't shift his gaze from her tiny black panties or the slim span of her waist. He wanted to bite that pert little bottom. Lick her all over, explore every nook and cranny of her body.

Jesus, no.

He squeezed his eyes shut.

Don't be a douchebag like Ioannis.

He climbed out of the water, thankfully with his back to her, and grabbed a towel to cover the tentpole extending from his shorts.

ELENI

He'd had made it bitterly clear to her that he didn't want to be around her.

She got the message.

She'd seen him surrounded by beautiful women earlier.

His world. His people.

She'd believed him when he'd reassured her and told her she looked beautiful, that she would be fine. She was fine, by his side, *with him*. Dominic made her feel special. Dominic had made her believe she belonged, but now, all of a sudden, he no longer wanted her company.

He'd tired of her.

She'd accomplished what she'd set out to do, what he'd paid her to do, to be his fake date. And now he didn't need her anymore. She'd noticed it from the get-go, as clearly as if he'd given her the middle finger.

As soon as she'd jumped into the water, he'd backed away. Something had twisted in his emerald green eyes as he'd held her gaze; something she couldn't grasp.

Had it been fear? Or something else.

He moved away from her each time she walked towards him and in doing so had made her feel as worthless as that guy had.

Maybe she had imagined it all—the tender way in which he'd unhooked her corset and the way he'd gently tended to her wound. And maybe she had crossed a line jumping into the water like that, then taking off her shorts.

You charge by the hour?

Ioannis might have been vile and repugnant in the way he put her in her place, but he'd been upfront about who he was. He'd reminded her of who she was, in the same way that Dominic was doing now that he no longer needed her help.

She didn't have to stick around and suffer the humiliation.

This is what men did. It was true what her mother had said; men used you and when they were done, they discarded you.

She walked towards her bedroom door, a hasty plan unfurling in her mind. She'd take a shower now, then pack her suitcase, then go to bed. She was on the first flight out tomorrow.

"What are you doing?" Dominic had an uncanny knack for sneaking up on her when she least expected it. Her hand stilled on the doorknob. Her heart beat wildly in her chest. Emotions swirled around inside her, humiliation scalding her heart.

She'd gotten it all wrong. What he felt was nothing like what she did. "You want to be alone, Dominic. I got the memo." She opened the door, not wanting to face him.

"Is that what you really think?"

She was a blubbery weak mess. "Just go," she pleaded, her shoulders slumping as a tired exhale escaped her lips. "You should go."

He placed his hand on her shoulder. "I don't want to."

"It's late and I have to pack." She tried to take a step towards the door, but his hand remained, the heat emanating from his skin, sending shockwaves through her body.

"Eleni."

Not this. Not now. Not anymore.

"Look at me, *please*." The man didn't beg, not in the real world, but here in Santorini, this was not the real world. This was a slice of make-believe heaven.

Curious, she did as he asked. "What?"

He scrubbed his hands over his face, wiping the water away from his eyes. A hint of anxiety in his voice was the only indicator that he was on edge, because the rest of him, that wall of muscle in the water, signalled nothing but strength and calmness.

"Don't be angry."

"You couldn't get away from me fast enough in the pool just now."

Silence, and then a deep exhale from him. He didn't even

bother to deny it. Exasperated, she spun around, ready to go into her room but his hand went to her should again, halting her.

"That's not entirely true." He sounded sad, or had she mistaken that for weariness? His thumb gently swept over her skin, sending her nerve endings wild. He was so close behind her that she could feel the heat rolling off him. But it was more than just his body heat. A current fizzed through the air between them.

She turned around, needing to read his expression. "We were sitting and talking one minute. I thought ..." She stopped herself from blurting out girlish words which would only embarrass her.

I thought we were getting on well.

A man like Dominic was used to women throwing themselves at him. Never in all her wildest dreams had she ever imagined she'd be one of them, but ... here she was.

"You're upset. I can see that now." His hand reached up to cup her face, a touch she had been yearning for for so long.

"I am not." But her tone gave the truth away. She stared at the floor, becoming acutely aware that her wet clothes were sticking to her, and that her shorts were still by the pool and she was standing here in her panties. Water trickled down both their bodies, the falling droplets landing on the floor and creating a pool of wetness where they stood.

The space between her legs throbbed. A dull thrum of possibility, an ache that had been there for a long time, steadily growing stronger.

"I can read you like a map, Eleni. You're upset, and I think it's because of me."

What a clever man he was. All that expensive school education hadn't gone to waste. "You flatter yourself." She tried to block him off, but her need for him was so intense she could no longer hide it.

"Do I?" He lowered his hand away from her face. "You think I don't want to be around you, but you're so wrong. So very wrong."

"Then why do you move away from me each time—" He put a finger to her lips. It singed, the heat so palpable, she felt the burn.

"Because ..." He let out a groan, deep in the base of his throat, as if he was fighting to keep something in. "Because I care about you, Eleni. I don't want to see you hurt or upset."

"You upset me just now when you couldn't get away from me fast enough."

"That's what you thought."

"What else was I supposed to think?"

He did it again, pressed his lips together, his nostrils flaring. "I want to stomp all over that man's face each time I remember what he did to you, before and now. I can't get it out of my head."

"Then don't think about it." She paused. "Why *are* you still thinking about it?" A muscle jumping in his jaw was her answer. "You can't even bring yourself to tell me the truth," she whispered softly, then squeezed her eyes shut. She'd managed to hold it all in, the way she felt about him, but the weariness of keeping it to herself was too hard.

The summer would soon be over and they would go their separate ways. She wanted to tell him how she felt. Love ... lust ... longing ... whatever it was ... he needed to know. She ventured a glance at his face. "You make me feel special, Dominic—"

"Because you are."

"You make me feel it in a way no one ever has."

"No one?" He looked at her as if he was completely

clueless. He looked puzzled. Completely bewildered. What did he not understand?

Her heart had started to feel again, after a long time. It had taken a while to warm up to this uptight, miserable, and moody man. He had managed to make her put Jonas behind her, to feel something new, and she was left with a bittersweet infusion of guilt and longing.

"A woman like you should be cherished. I would cherish you ...the way you deserve to be cherished."

"You?" she asked, the need desperate in her voice. After all this time together, she wasn't sure, but this, this was a flicker of hope.

"You see yourself as your mother sees you. Maybe being abandoned by your father has left you with scars. How can it not? But I see a woman who is beautiful, and smart and funny and who has a heart of gold. You deserve so much, and I want to give you everything."

She tilted her head, trying to understand. "Why would you want to give me everything?"

His eyes dropped to her chest before zipping back up to her face again. She stepped closer to him, lifting a hand to his face, her thumb sliding across his damp cheek. "You can't even answer that, can you?" The bitterness in her voice was a contrast to the heat and longing she felt inside. It dawned on her that he wanted to be a friend. Nothing more.

"Why would I want to give you everything?" he echoed. "Because I can."

"Then give me something now," she dared him.

His eyes widened, and she thought they were going to come out of their sockets. "W-what ..." He cleared his throat. "What do you need?" He reached out and tucked a damp lock of hair behind her ear, his hand lowering to her neck, making all her cells tingle

Her heart was full and warm and fuzzy whenever he was around. Just being near Dominic made her happy. "I want to *feel*, Dominic," she whispered. "It's been so long ..." She leaned her face into his palm, which now splayed out against her cheek, but instead of returning the gesture, he seemed to freeze. She glimpsed hesitation in his eyes. He cared for her, but not like *this*.

It was like dying a slow torturous death, to discover that this was one sided. Her hopes shattered like confetti bombs.

Maybe this was a language not understood in words. Dominic had his fill of women, but after Jonas, she'd only met the worst of men. There was a world of difference between them and in their life experiences.

This was her chance, and she was going to take it. She tiptoed up and leaned in, pressing her lips against his. No sooner had her lips touched his, than his hand slipped like shackles around her waist, pressing her to him, her body flush with his, no room for escape. His tongue swept into her mouth, taking possession, owning, tasting, commanding, and that was when she felt it, a sharp poke, hard-as-steel against her belly. She had excited him.

They kissed as if they were drinking from one another, tongues dueling and tasting, appreciating. She had often wondered what it might be like to kiss Dominic, and now that she finally had the chance to find out, to experience it ... it was like receiving a hard-earned reward. In the deep, distant edges of her mind, she became aware that he was hungry, and hard, and in this moment, he wanted her.

She clung to him harder when his hands skimmed over her tiny panties, over the round of her bottom then lower to her thighs. In the next breath he scooped her up in one easy sweep. She wrapped her legs around his waist, grinding into him, trying to feel the friction against the hardness of his cock.

Still joined at the lips, they kissed hard. All she could feel was his mouth on hers, and she ground against him lower down. So much feeling concentrated in such small areas. She closed her eyes, savoring him.

He walked into her room, with her legs still wrapped around him, his mouth suctioned to hers. Bending down, he placed her carefully on the bed, before joining her again. Their frenzied kisses filled the air filled with groans and sighs; she didn't know if they were hers or his.

"Dominic," she murmured, as he propped himself up on his elbows on top of her. He stared at her lips as if he wasn't done.

Reaching down between them, she found him, hard and wet and gloriously thick. Lust licked her heated core, the idea that she could have him making her reckless and bold. She rubbed him over the fabric of his swim shorts, appreciating the groan that fell from his lips. "You're so hard."

His lips curled up at the corners. "It's your fault."

She stared at him, dazed and hopeful.

"Why do you think I jumped into the water?" he rasped.

Her smile spread from ear to ear, the understanding unleashing joy inside her. She licked her lips, needing him inside her. "You're also very big."

His lips turned up even more. "Yes."

She hungered for his touch, for his cock, for all of him. There had been no one since Jonas, and no one before. She hadn't thought of intimacy ever since Jonas had passed. She could have become a nun, but then this man had crossed her path.

Slowly snaking her hands into the waistband of his swim shorts, she wrapped her fingers around him. He groaned even more as she slid her thumb over his slippery tip, but he caught her hand in his and stopped her. "*No*, Eleni." It sounded like a man's last dying breath.

He was stopping? Why? Confusion ripped through the haze of her arousal. "But ... I want to ..."

Did he not?

Because his body said otherwise.

Dominic pressed his forehead against hers, looking more weighed down than she'd ever seen him. "We can't."

He lifted his head, tiny spots of moisture lining his brow. Even now she could feel him poking against her hip. Hard as steel.

"I need you," she moaned.

"I can't do this. It would be wrong ..."

"For whom? I want this, Dominic. Please, don't make me beg for it."

CHAPTER FORTY

DOMINIC

He wasn't going to make her beg for it.

Could she not tell that he was ready to oblige? Her fingers had been wrapped around him, making it impossible for him to do nothing.

He lowered his head, resting his forehead against hers, torn between heaven and hell.

"Don't you ... want me, Dominic?"

He grunted something, he wasn't sure what, in response. A shudder fell from his chest. He wanted her more than he had ever wanted any woman but fighting her was had sapped all his restraint. She grazed her fingers lightly over his nipple, sending a shiver through him. Their lips were so close together, he could taste her sweet breath. She had dismantled his resolve.

"I want to have memories of this weekend ... of you ..." Her large brown eyes made him melt.

She filled him with hope, but her eyes were glazed over, heat and desire clouding those dark irises. More desire concentrated in his cock. He'd wanted her since before tonight and telling himself anything else was a lie. But he didn't doubt it was her boyfriend who was on her mind.

Something broke in his heart, and then he licked her lower lip, because he couldn't stop himself. She arched her back, thrusting her breasts into him.

He wanted to fuck her, to eat her, to do unspeakable things to her.

"Kiss me," she begged. His lips claimed hers again, and his tongue slipped into her mouth, tasting, feeling, thrashing against hers.

Fuck. She felt so good.

Her soft fingers hooked around his neck, pulling him flush against her chest. Even through her damp top he could feel her bullet-like nipples against his skin. Her hands splayed out, her nails lightly scratching his back.

Oh, boy.

She had no idea what she was doing to him. Kissing her, hearing her sighs and moans, smelling the scent of her arousal. He was so desperate for her.

He let out a guttural moan, needing to possess her, to make her his, to fuck her so that she'd never think of anyone else but him, ever again.

Restraint held him back, kept him from going further, but he was losing the fight by the second. She was hot and silky, still damp to his touch in her tank top and panties.

His hand dipped lower, and he plucked at the waistband of her panties, his fingers hovering around that area and not delving deeper.

The last remaining shred of his resolve hung delicately in the balance, but Eleni's fevered kissing stoked the flames of fire. She tugged his hair, revealing the state of her desperation.

He gasped, unable to stop himself, and slipped his hand down between her legs before pulling the wet fabric to one side. Her eyes grew wide with daring as he slid his fingers over her swollen lips, her lower lip parted, and a mewl fell from her mouth. Her bedroom eyes dark as the night as he slipped a finger into her hot, tight little channel, and then another one. She arched off the bed when his thumb slid over folds slick and swollen.

"Dominic." Her head rolled back against the mattress, her neck a wide and open expanse of silky soft skin which he covered with long wet kisses.

She was so turned on; her arousal was all over his hands. He'd been hard for so long, he was desperate for a release. Lust and greed comingled, his desire to possess her turning him to frenzy.

He thrust in another finger and worked her clit in circles. An animal groan fell from her lips and she bucked against his hand. To think that this woman he'd met at the taverna, who had irritated the heck out of him, was now the woman he couldn't get out of his mind.

He blinked. His fingers stopped pumping. His thumb stilled.

The taverna.

The yacht.

He had become the very man he didn't want to be.

He pulled his fingers out, saw her eyelids flutter open. "Why have you stopped?" He moved off her, sat upright, the smell of her arousal hanging in the air. He couldn't do this. He'd asked her here to help him, and now he was behaving no better than the filthy pigs who hit on her.

He shook his head, logic dueling with lust, and winning.

He moved off the bed. Eleni propped herself up on her elbows, her tank top riding up and revealing a sliver of her midriff. But her panties were still pulled to the side, and he caught a glimpse of her glistening folds. The sight made his mouth water. It was an effort to look away.

He reminded himself of the facts.

She was still heartbroken and grieving.

Over someone else.

She'd begged him to make her feel something, but he wanted *her* to want *him*. Not some past love she was still pining for.

"You don't find me attractive..." It was a statement, a fact she believed. If only he could tell her. He stared down at her, made himself look at her face, not anywhere else. Her dark eyes filled with sadness.

"You're the most beautiful woman I know."

Her eyes turned round and large. "You're lying."

"I'm not."

She looked at him in disbelief. "Then why did you stop?"

Because it's not me you want.

"I can't do this, Eleni. I would be no better than the men who want a piece of you. The deadbeats who wish they could have you."

"You *can* have me, but you don't want me."

"Any man would want to be with you."

"You don't."

"But..."

I do.

He took a step back, not trusting himself to say or do anything gentlemanly near her. Her brow creased. "Can't you pretend that I'm Demi or Helen? Would that help?"

"Why would I do that?" His voice was a snarl, his eyes vicious. "Why do you keep talking about them?"

"Because—because I wonder if you would comply if they asked you."

"I told you. I have no interest in them. I wish you would believe me."

"Don't I interest you, Dominic? Don't you want me?"

Could she not see that he did? "What about what you want?"

Confusion cast a veil over her heated face. "I told you. I want you ... it's been so long since I ..."

Tension rolled along his chest. She reached out with her toe and stroked his cock. A grunt fell from his lips, a growl rumbling deep in his chest.

"If that's what you want," he said, resentfully.

"It's what I want."

He'd been given the green light. She'd convinced him to do what she asked for. He wasn't taking advantage of her, and if she wanted to dream about her boyfriend, so be it.

His need for her was most urgent, and when his gaze fell to her panties, to her, wide, open and wet for him...

Fucking. Hell. On earth.

He could barely wait to dive in. "Relax," he soothed, then tried to slow himself down, as he lowered to the floor, inhaling the scent of her.

He could comply. Whatever it took to make her feel.

He lowered his head between her legs, ready to feast like a man who hadn't eaten for months.

ELENI

D ominic had looked like a man tortured. A man in pain. But then something in him suddenly switched. In an instant he was on the floor, hooking his thumbs in the waistband of her panties and unveiling her nakedness, inch by inch.

With his hands on her knees, he gently parted her legs. She tried to close them but he wouldn't let her. When she moved her hand down in an attempt to cover her dignity, he moved her hand away. And then he dove in, but just as his face touched her wetness, she tried to clench her legs together. "No ..."

He raised his eyes at her. "Why not?"

"I don't ... like it..."

He looked puzzled. "No?"

It was okay. Nothing great. But she was more worried about how she looked, what he thought, how she compared to the others. She felt vulnerable like this, her legs wide open and completely bared to him.

"Please," he begged. "Let me ... and if you still don't like it, I'll stop."

Her mouth was a firm line.

"You wanted me to make you feel something ... I promise you this will ..." He didn't move but a pleading look in his eyes made her relent. It was better that she let him get it over with. With Jonas it had been quick and clumsy. She hadn't felt anything but a burning shame.

But something else fuelled her unease this time. Dominic Steele, her boss, the object of Miranda's desire, had looked like a man starved and had practically begged her to let him. He wanted this.

"Relax," he coaxed, his eyes still on her. But she couldn't.

Her muscles clenched, and her breath held. She should just let him try for a bit, and then she'd tell him to stop.

He moved his thumb over her clit, making circles, right at the spot which drove her insane. He licked her slowly, his tongue, flat and thick, pressing hard against her most private part. She couldn't help but let out a long moan, the feel of him doing *that*, taking her by surprise. It felt … *so* good. He did it again, licking in broad strokes from the base all the way to her tip.

She sighed, then groaned, arching her back, her legs loosening and falling open at the knees, all the fight, the uneasiness, her inhibitions gone. Dominic pumped a finger inside her again, then another. Her legs flopped wider still as a delicious slow heat snaked inside her. Her nerve endings tingled. Everything between her legs vibrated. A coiling sensation began to build with each stroke of his tongue, each thrust of his fingers. Her head rolled back, sank further into the bed, a loud, pent-up sigh released.

Her muscles gave. She lowered her hand, threading her fingers in his hair. It had never been like this for her, before. Ever. Dominic was a magician, and he worked magic with his fingers and tongue. She could not wait for him to …

A feral noise came from deep within Dominic's throat. As if sensing her coming undone, he threw her legs over his shoulders and lifted her hips, angling them just so, opening her up even more before latching his mouth on her again.

"Mmmm." He feasted on her like a man possessed, enjoying her as if she were a four-course gourmet meal made by a Michelin starred chef.

She bucked, and squirmed, and was vaguely aware that she needed to protest. Do something for him. "Don't you want to … do something else?"

"No." He lifted his head. His eyes glazed.

"Could I do something for—"

He'd lowered his head, his nose brushing against her clit. His mouth latched to her lips, his hot, wet tongue probing her channel. She'd never known it could be so … wonderful. She didn't care that she was laid out for him like a buffet, his to take as he pleased. He wanted *this*. A throb of delicious excitement tasered through her. It felt so … wet, and so pleasing, so joyous.

He hooked his middle finger inside her, then another one, and pumped her, the motion making her buck. Just when she couldn't take it anymore, his lips fastened on her clit and he sucked. He grabbed her hips holding her firm, not giving up on the pressure as waves of pleasure consumed her. She grabbed the sheets, shrieking banshee-like howls, noises she didn't recognize. He slowed down the pace, unlatched his mouth, let her rest for a second or two, before hooking his finger inside her again. Hitting that sweet spot. The one that took her to the edge.

She had never felt this before; this unravelling, melting, falling apart. This sensation of warmth, and tenderness, the appreciative noises he made. Like a man who enjoyed this more than she did. A man who knew what to do, how to make her feel.

She lost her mind, her body acting of its own accord. Heat spreading all over her body. Noises, thick and dirty, came from the base of his throat. It was too much, she was in a place she'd never been, floating, falling, shuddering. Dominic's moans, deep, guttural yet somehow appreciative, slipped into the background.

"Dominic … oh… oh … *Christé mou…*"

He stopped. Looked up. "What?"

"W-what?" She was on the edge, almost there.

"What did you say?"

No conversation. This was not a time for ... "Oh my god," she screamed. He buried his face in her wetness and the air filled with the sound of her moans. She came undone, falling apart as her orgasm ripped through her, and still he guzzled greedily, his tongue washing over her, relentlessly lapping and licking, refusing to give her respite.

"Dominic!" she cried, her voice weak, her body lazy as she convulsed against his mouth. His hand reached for her breast hungrily, then roughly, when he couldn't easily get under the tight damp tank top.

He came up for air, his mouth and nose wet with her arousal. "Did you like that?" His voice was raspy, thick with need.

"Yesss." She was liquid, wet and soft as she slowly came down from her orgasm.

He kissed her thighs, leaving a forest of kisses all over them, before brushing his lips up her body, from her belly to her chest.

"Take off your clothes."

She couldn't move if she tried. "Ummmmm." Her voice was dreamy, faraway. "I need a moment." She was spent, her heart racing as if she'd run the four-minute mile.

Her eyes fluttered open for a few moments, and she watched him stroke himself. It was erotic. Intimate. Something she hadn't expected to see, and yet Dominic was baring himself to her, showing her his need for her. She could only see the motion, could tell that he was pumping himself, as he crouched on the floor. Her jaw dropped as he pressed his chest right up against her softness, and she flinched at the thought of his chest coated with her wetness.

A hunger mushroomed in his eyes. She sat up and took her top off, before reaching for him, her small hand clasping around his shaft. "You're so ... thick."

He grasped her breast, rubbing his forefinger and thumb around her nipple. She grabbed his cock, desperate to touch him, but her hand there unleashed the stallion in him. His mouth suctioned to her breast, swallowing all of it. Animal sounds dripped from his lips. She cried out for him, told him she wanted him, when he planted his mouth over hers, hushing her. She clung to him, kissing him as if her life depended on it. They were a medley of possessive hands, searching mouths and tongues, exploring one another's bodies with the wanton abandonment of wild animals.

"Please," she begged, pumping him harder and harder. With one movement, he stilled her, placing his hand over hers. "Slow down, otherwise I'll come all over you."

"I want you to come all over me, come inside me, wherever you want, Dominic. You can do what you want to me."

He blinked slowly, his lips wet, and mouth open, then rested his sticky forehead against hers. "They are unspeakable, the things I want to do to you."

Oh, yes. Yes, yes, yes. "Please," she whimpered.

He closed his eyes for a few seconds, as if he was the bearer of bad news. "We ... can't ..." He sounded like a man in need. A man who was not yet sated. But a man broken.

"You can't stop now." She had yearned for this moment, had longed for this man. She was desperate for him.

What was he waiting for?

DOMINIC

The salty smell of sex filled the air.

He had watched Eleni come apart slowly before his eyes, and his hard on had mushroomed.

"I want you to come all over me."

Fuck.

Did she have to go and say *that?* "We can't do that, Eleni." He wanted to fuck her. Of course he did. He was a man, not a monk. He wanted to fuck her hard and long, wanted to grind out his pent-up frustration. Wanted to ruin her for all men so that she only wanted him.

But he could not. There was a line, and he would not cross it. It would be irresponsible, and professional suicide for him to even go there.

"Please, Dominic. I want this." Her hot breath kissed his face as she lay beneath him. The need in her breathless whisper was like a mating call to his dick. He tried to hold off, but she begged him for more. Her pebbled breast made him salivate. He couldn't help but reach out, thumb first one nipple then the other while he tried to slow down time, get his thoughts in order. But his cock was hard and ready, inches from her.

"We shouldn't. *I* shouldn't."

"Why?" Eleni cried.

Because it killed him that he wasn't the one she wanted. "You'll hate me if we do this."

"I'll hate you if you don't."

"You might like me a little more if I behave like a gentleman."

"I don't need you to be a gentleman right now."

He squeezed his eyes shut while his cock screamed obscenities at him. "Eleni..." He was fighting a losing battle.

"Take off your clothes," she whispered. "I want to see all of you."

That much he could do. Standing up slowly, trying to make a decision through the fog of his brain, he yanked his shorts down. Her hand flew to her mouth, her eyes on him, wide and hungry. "You're so ... big and ... meaty..."

A smile of pride broke out on his lips. "You're objectifying me. Not that I object to the description."

She giggled.

"And, thank you. But are you really that surprised?" A little humor took the edge off his frustration, and he liked the way she was staring at him.

At *it*.

She licked her lower lip. "I want you."

His shoulders sank. "Eleni." He was her boss, goddamnit.

A boss who was standing in front of her with his cock hanging out, no less.

She chewed her lower lip. "I want you like I haven't wanted anyone... it's been so long ..."

He believed her. She hadn't had sex since the tragedy. And if that was what she needed, he was a lucky man that she was begging him to oblige. "I don't have protection."

Her gaze was still riveted on his penis, and the more she looked, the more he hardened. Not that it was possible to get any harder. He was so ready. Holding back was like not breathing.

"I have birth control." Her eyes lifted to his face. "I ... have a heavy cycle and it helps."

It took a while to sink in, what she was telling him. "You shouldn't trust me, Eleni."

Great answer. That would do it. Not.

For a man who was ready to explode the moment he sank inside her, he was doing a good job of trying to put her off.

"But I do." She licked her lips again. "I trust you. You've only ever been good to me, Dominic. You've always looked out for me."

He swallowed. "Then you should know I haven't been with a woman for nine months."

"And you should know there has only been Jonas for me."

I fucking know that.

ELENI

Anger flashed through Dominic's already heated gaze. She was trying to get a read on him. His body told her he wanted her. But his face looked like it did when Linus was around.

"Are you sure about this?" The hard edge to his voice cut through her sex-haze enough for her to snap to normality.

"Don't you want to?" Maybe he needed her to reciprocate. She'd been greedy. She started to sit up, but the flat of his hand settled under her breasts, forcing her back onto the bed.

"Where are you going?"

"To do something for you." Many other women would have happily obliged.

"You don't ..." He let out a groan. "You don't have to do that. I thought we'd established that you want me to fuck you."

"I do. And I wish you'd get on with it but—" He didn't look happy. "Are you sure?" Maybe her breasts were too small, she wasn't his type, he couldn't bring himself too, despite having the biggest hard on she'd ever seen. She didn't want him to do something he didn't want.

"I'm surer than I've ever been." He reached out, grabbing

all of her breast, massaging, owning, possessing. His fingers squeezed her nipple hard. It hurt, but it was a good kind of hurt. A shot of desire whipped through her.

Dominic licked his lips as he looked down at her, and once again, she couldn't read his expression.

She couldn't tell if he wanted to do the deed because she'd begged him, or if he really wanted to.

Her eyes trailed down to his cock, and she no longer cared. She wanted him. This. *Now.*

He lowered himself down on her, lifting on his elbows so that his big, heavy, beautifully toned body wouldn't squish her. A low growl sounded deep in his throat as he lined himself up at her opening and stayed there. His wet, thick shaft nudging against her. His lips went to her neck. "Are you sure about this?"

He was asking permission even now? How much assurance did the man need? She lifted her hips in answer, desperate to swallow his manhood, and failing. "Dom ..."

That did it.

"Do. Not. Ever ..." He thrust inside her and she tilted her hips, welcoming all of him. His thick shaft slowly inched inside, sinking into her wet heat. He filled her completely, making her stretch, the friction a little on the side of uncomfortable, but then ... ah, yes ... sweet. She gasped, feeling full to the hilt, and yet he wasn't all in.

"Dominic." She stared up at him, his eyes closed, his face tense as he let himself linger. His lips parted, as if he were savoring something intensely. "I'm too small for you."

His eyes burst open, a line forming on his brow, then vanishing completely. He lowered his mouth to give her another mind clearing kiss. Heat rolled over her as his fingers dug into her hips. He angled her just so, and thrust out then back in, the friction so delicious she loosened instantly. And then he was in, all those long, thick beautiful inches of him. He was in so deep, she couldn't tell where he ended and where she began.

It was beautiful. This oneness. His chest pressed against her breasts so that their heartbeats were synced.

He panted against her ear. "Does it hurt?"

"It hurts so good."

He lifted his head, frowning. And stopped thrusting.

"Don't stop. I told you ... it's been so long since ..."

That was all it took. He slammed into her, making her gasp with shock at the fullness of him inside her, occupying every inch of her. A warm, wet, fulsome feeling blossomed in her chest as he started to move in a rhythm. Their eyes locked, each watching the pleasure on the other's faces. Dominic pulled out slowly, a pained expression on his face, before he slid back in again slowly. He set up a rhythm, slow and steady, gentle, then not so gentle. And then he sped up, tenderness replaced by his fast, urgent, desperate thrusting. Making noises, wet and messy, each time he slammed into her.

They were panting, as if air was in short supply. Her body vibrating, pulsating, something building deep within her. He lifted her leg, his heavy hand moving up the underside, cupping her calf up in the air. He rocked into her, moving his cock inside her, rubbing it around, making friction. She cupped his face, helpless to do anything but take it. And it felt *so* good.

A little typhoon of pressure coiled in her belly and started to spin out of control. "Dominic." She smiled at him, full of love and gratitude, drowning in aching bliss, her body starting to convulse. "Oh, Dominic ... this is so ..."

His lips turned up at the corners, not quite making it into a full smile. He seemed to lose control. Biting his lower lip again, before he thrust into her harder.

"Oh, yes," she moaned, her voice gravelly with need. Oh, yes, yes, yes.

He rammed into her harder then, goaded on by her. She wrapped her legs around his waist, clenching her muscles, gripping his cock with all her might. He groaned. "You're killing me."

"I love this. This is what I ... *needed* ..."

He stared at her, his eyes so dark, nothing like the shade of sea she was so used to. He rubbed her clit, between the thrusts, taking her to the edge.

She huffed out a breath, a groan, a sound. He kissed her, his tongue down her throat, hard and hot, the way his cock was impaled so far up inside her. They were joined, connected, one.

She was falling for this man, so deeply, so fast, so unexpectedly. Couldn't imagine a world without him in it. As he grunted and rocked above her, and she gazed at his beautiful face. His angular jaw, his closed eyes, with lashes so long it was a sin for a man to have. That full, ripe, magical mouth. A mouth that showered her with kindness and satisfied her desires.

He tugged his lower lip between his teeth as if it was too much, He closed his eyes, and grunted. Feral and wild. Cursing, saying her name over and over. Fucking her, telling her how good this was. How good she was.

He liked it, he liked her. She laid her palm against his face. He opened his eyes, dark, and hooded, stared back at her. "Eleni ..." He gave her one hard thrust and then spilled inside her, shuddering and trembling in her arms as he emptied himself into her.

She fell apart under him, seeing stars and white light, going to another place.

·   ·   ·

They'd been lying together, cocooned for how long, she had no idea.

She basked silently in her little love-dream with her back against his chest, feeling content and blissfully happy, not wanting this night to end. Not wanting this to be the last of them.

Dominic's arm was wrapped around her waist, his manhood nestled just below her bottom, wet and soft. He snuggled his face into her neck again. Her heart flapped its happy wings. This was the most romantic thing for her, lying like this with their bodies fitting so perfectly.

She dragged his arm tighter over her, feeling possessive, as if she laying a claim to him, even if just for tonight.

"I always wanted to ask you something..." he said, dreamily.

"Ask me what?"

"Those appetizers you were putting away, that day on the yacht. You never took them. I always worried that you might have gone hungry that night."

She turned her head into her pillow, grinning. "Is that what you thought? That I was stealing out of desperation and hunger?"

"You weren't?"

She tried to stifle her giggle. "No. Stefanos and I would go and sit by the beach at the end of the night, more like the early hours of the morning by the time the parties ended, and we were tired but still full of adrenaline, and we didn't want to go home, so we'd have those fancy nibbles and talk."

He kissed her shoulder blade. "And there was me thinking you'd gone without food."

"Why did you come into the kitchen that night?" She had often thought about that. He had been such a difficult customer, and then all of a sudden he'd been nice and friendly to her.

"I told you." He dropped another kiss. "I hate parties, and I didn't want to be there."

"You must have been bored, because you were so nice and friendly. It was like your twin had turned up instead of you."

"I don't have a twin."

He pressed his lips against her skin and sucked hungrily. She'd have a tell-tale hickey or two to show for it tomorrow.

He rolled her onto her back. "Are you okay? Not too sore?"

She chortled. He was always so concerned for her well-being, always so considerate. Nothing like the side of himself he showed to his other employees.

"Are you asking me if I'm ready to go again?"

He cupped her face, making her feel like a precious jewel. "I am ready any time you are." His voice filled with hope. "But it's been a long day. It's not been easy for you. Thank you for putting up with all the crazy." He leaned down and pressed his lips against hers.

"I would do anything for you, Dominic." It sounded like a pathetic declaration made by a weak woman, but she meant it with all her heart. For Dominic, she would do anything. He stared at her, and she couldn't make it out, the question in his eyes. The silence hummed with unsaid words.

She meant what she said. Dominic represented the best in men. The very best. He made the Ioannis' of this world look a million times worse than they were.

He ran his fingers over her lips. "Why so sad?"

She shook her head, not wanting to taint their night with talk of Ioannis.

You do extra work on the side?

Charge by the hour?

You little slut.

You temptress.

You only fuck Americans?

You are trying hard to be someone you're not.

He will use you and throw you away like toilet paper.

Her eyes prickled with tears, and she blinked quickly, hoping to stem them.

"Eleni." Dominic's face softened, but his eyes filled with hurt. "Do you regret this?" He started to move away, but she put a hand to his shoulder, stopping him. Gave a slight shake of her head. "No."

"Then why the sad face?" He traced a finger under her lashes, soaking up the tears which were welling up.

She wasn't going to ruin this moment with the truth. "I'm happy. I'm feeling emotional. I've never come like that before."

He peered closer, as if he was fishing for the truth. "If there's something else, you'd tell me, right?"

She nodded.

"Do you want me to sleep in my own bed?"

"I want you to stay with me tonight," she whispered, sliding a hand around his neck, gently nudging his face to hers. She cupped his chin, noting that he was still on his side, trying to move his growing hard on away from her each time it touched her. "I want you to make love to me again, Dominic."

Surprise shot through those flecks of gold, and he lifted himself back on top of her again, positioning himself between her legs.

You are trying hard to be someone you're not.

He will use you and throw you away like toilet paper.

It wasn't true. Not the way Dominic was looking at her. His gaze so tender, every touch so sublime. "Tell me again," he begged, as she reached for his hand and kissed it.

"Tell you what?" His magic fingers were on her clit again, her brain was turning to mush.

"Tell me you want me, Eleni. Say it's me."

She didn't understand. "Of course it's you. I want you, Dominic."

He entered her slowly, their eyes locked on each other. Clumsy kisses fell from tired mouths that didn't lock tightly this time, soft mewls falling from their lips. They were breathing in one another's air, as he slid all the way inside her slick pussy, before pistoning back and forth, slow, slow, slowly. It was a deliciously long and gradual build to the precipice from which they would fall together.

CHAPTER FORTY-ONE

DOMINIC

I t was the heat in the room which woke him up first, the sheets were on the floor, and the bluish early morning light filtered through the window.

Eleni was between his legs, her head bobbing, her mouth over him. She looked up when he stirred, observing him through her thick lashes. "Is this good?"

Was the earth round?

He nodded, his breath sharp, serrated. He was going to explode into her mouth if she didn't slow down.

Something niggled at him. She'd been uneasy about him going down on her, but she was doing *this* for him? He lowered his hand to her head. "You don't ... you don't have to ... do this," he bit out between pants.

She pumped him with her fist, her tongue darting out and licking the tip. "I want to."

"You don't mind doing this?"

She shook her head. "Am I doing it right?"

In answer, he rolled his head back, his eyes rolling back in their sockets.

Jesus christ.

She had no concept of herself. How amazing she was. How gone he was for her. How hard he'd tried to resist her. How his desire had burned out of control, like a ravaging, unstoppable bush fire. The almost one year abstinence from sex might have had something to do with it.

But this weekend had been his undoing. He'd been horny as hell, hungry for her. She was hard to resist with her gorgeous face, her long black hair, her seductive eyes, her olive skin, her funny ways.

Endearing ways.

Her ability to make everything be sunny and good. She, of all people, who was already swimming in a sea of tragedy, was somehow able to see the good in everything.

He groaned as she took him further into her throat, and he watched her in fascination. "You ... didn't want me ... to ..."

Goddamnit. She was so good at this. She pulled away, her hand taking over and moving along his cock. "To what?" she asked, her lips wet.

"To go down on you."

"I won't stop you the next time... if ...there is ..." She looked embarrassed and bent down again, taking him in her mouth. It was exquisite, the way her mouth worked, how her magic tongue and lips had a mission of their own. How well they fit around him. He couldn't help but fist her hair in his hand. "Jesus. Eleni." He couldn't take his eyes off her. It made him harder, the sight of her with her swollen lips, sucking him. She was naked too. On all fours on the bed, her pert little butt high up in the air, her elbows digging into the bed, her breasts spilling onto the mattress.

He moaned. Could get off just on that visual alone. "You're so fucking good."

"You like it? Yes?"

Incoherent words tumbled from his mouth, his voice low and gravely, full of gratitude. He pressed his head back into the cushioned satin headrest. "I'm going to ..." He tried to warn her, tried to pull out, but her lips were suctioned to him. "I'm going to ... uh ..." He couldn't help it, couldn't hold back.

She was still sucking him after he exploded, crashing into a cosmic universe where he floated out of his body and was heat and white light. It took him a while to regain a sense of himself, and there she was, still on all fours, head down, lapping away at him gently. A ragged groan fell from his lips. "Good girl."

She was. She was the best.

Not because of tonight, but everything about her. He could barely speak, could only watch as he tried to still his galloping heartbeat. She sat up slowly, wiping her mouth, observing his reaction.

"Fuck, Eleni. You're ..."

You're so amazing, he wanted to tell her. It wasn't just the sex, but how she made him feel. What she did for him. He hoped he'd made her feel the same.

There was nothing fake about what they'd just experienced. She moved up the bed and lay against him. He held her in his arms, pressing her to his chest, enjoying the feel of her nuzzling her head in the crook of his shoulder. With her finger she gently traced along his abs, which only made him instinctively flex them harder.

He lay back, enjoying the feel of her fingers, the feel of her. She fit against him like a piece of the puzzle he had never found. They were sticky and hot, but perfect together.

"I've never had a night like this," she whispered, her voice soft and sleepy.

His ears pricked up. Pride filling his body at the compliment. "Yeah?"

"Hmmmm. It was *soooo* good, Dominic."

"Good?" *Which part, when?* He needed specifics, so that he could file them away, and know that he'd achieved something with her. That maybe he'd given her something she could remember him by, something that would stand out and not be erased from her memory. A fragment of him she could hold on to, the way she held on to the memories of her boyfriend.

She yawned. "You were right ... when you ... when you did that thing ... I liked it. I liked it very much."

He knew she would.

He was ready to make love to her again, but this time he wanted to go slow and be more tender. The thought of sinking into her stirred his loins. He cupped the side of her face. "Are you ready for another round?" She didn't answer. "Eleni?"

Her heavy breathing told him she was asleep. Brushing her damp hair away from her face, he let his fingers trace gently over the contours of her face. He wanted to remember every little detail about her so that he could cherish the memories of their time together.

He pushed the thought away.

The weekend wasn't over yet.

There was still tomorrow, and maybe more than that.

———

It seemed instantaneous. He'd barely closed his eyes when he woke up abruptly to find Eleni closing a suitcase.

The sight smashed into him like a twenty ton juggernaut.

"When did you wake up?" Disbelief mixed with anger at the sight of her all calm and getting ready to leave.

Her brown eyes met his. "An hour ago. I didn't want to wake you."

"You should have. I thought ..." The words died on his lips. *I thought we had more time.*

"You were fast asleep, Dominic. You were snoring." She laughed, and her eyes lit up. She stared at him for the longest time, almost as if ... as if this was goodbye. Wearing a pale yellow summer dress, she was like a splash of sunshine first thing in the morning, only there was nothing sunny or warm about this.

"You should have woken me up." Disappointment weighed heavy, but now he was filled with regret. They had run out of time.

Even worse, Eleni hadn't considered the alternative, the one he'd fallen asleep thinking about; not just staying in bed for most of today and having more sexy times, but he was going to suggest she change her flight to a later time, or even move it by another day or two. Whatever she felt comfortable with. He was here for a few days more, and what could be better than having her here with him?

He didn't care what people in the office thought, or if the truth came out. He stomped out of bed, noticed her gaze trail south and settle on him for a few seconds.

Every fiber in his body commanded him to go and claim her, hold her in his arms and take her again. Do dirty, unspeakable things with her, and to her. His cock twitched at the thought.

But she'd already made up her mind.

"You didn't have to go," he said, not bothering to cover his nakedness.

Her eyes danced south, and he could feel himself getting hard again. He looked around in vain for his swim shorts.

"My flight leaves in an hour. I have to go."

That's all she had to say? Nothing about last night?

"I'm still here for a few more days. You could stay a while." His voice sounded coarse, like rough sandpaper. He was in danger of begging her to stay. He looked around for his T-shirt, remembered that it was still out by the pool.

"I couldn't, Dominic. What would people think?" Her gaze ran rampant over his chest, then his face, then his chest again. His hopes lifted, maybe she was having second thoughts.

"I don't give a shit about that."

"Well, I do."

"At least have breakfast." Catching sight of his swim shorts on the floor he reached for them and put them on, to save his modesty if nothing else. "Have breakfast with me. At least give me that."

"Dominic ..." And there it was. A hesitation in her voice and in her eyes. The sparkle, the surprise, the wildness of yesterday, was gone.

Did she want to pretend nothing had happened?

"I have some business meetings, but we can spend the rest of the—"

"Dominic ..." Her head lowered. She couldn't bring herself to face him. "You're the *boss*."

What was this? An outpouring of regret?

"So what? Why are you bringing that up now? I was the boss last night. The one you begged to fuck you."

Hurt flickered across her eyes.

And then he knew exactly what it was.

Guilt.

A huge landslide of guilt. She'd suddenly remembered her

boyfriend. To be fair to her, he'd had to suffer her talking about him last night, but she had begged him to fuck her.

This was ... sex. That's all it was to her.

"Kostas will drive you to the airport."

"Thank you." She smiled, tucked a curl behind her ear. "What day do you get back?"

"Does it matter?" His tone was sharp. Like a rebuke.

"Don't be like that."

He was silent. A long pregnant pause hung in the air.

"You could have stayed," he told her, but she wasn't even looking at him, and all he wanted to do was never stop looking at her. They could have done so much, or nothing at all. Just had a few days with only the two of them in their own private little paradise.

Last night had meant something, he'd been so sure of it. Having her come hard, shudder under him. There had been a connection between them. It couldn't only have been *just* sex.

"It's ... it's better that I go now." She moved towards the door and gave him one final sad look.

Whatever intimacy they had shared last night, feasting on and enjoying one another's bodies, had vanished. They stood like two strangers facing one another across the room.

"Maybe it is."

ELENI

Mixed feelings made her stomach roil with unease.

She had woken up this morning and found Dominic fast asleep, his beautiful face, his gorgeous naked body in her bed.

She would never forget last night, the things they had said, the things they had done. The way he'd cherished her. Things she would never forget. But as she gazed at the sleeping man who had worshipped every part of her body so intimately, she wondered if he might come to later have regrets.

She was the one who had begged him last night. He'd been the gentleman, the reluctant one. She'd pushed him to his limits.

Then when he awoke, she'd tried desperately to read him, to work out how he felt and what he was thinking. Their goodbye had been awkward, strained.

He'd asked her to stay, and as much as his request surprised her, she wondered if he was asking her because he wanted *her*? Or because it had been nine months since he'd been intimate with a woman, and they'd had a great night of sex? As always, in the back of her mind was the fact that she was just an employee who worked for him.

So, she had declined his offer, and then gone through the motions—getting on the plane, no longer in awe of being in first class. All through the flight she'd been stuck in a time warp, last night playing on repeat in her mind, over and over, putting her in a state of arousal that had left her damp between her legs, her breasts tingling for Dominic's touch.

By the time she landed in Athens, what she remembered the most about the weekend, wasn't the wedding, but what had happened *after*.

On the taxi ride back to her hotel, her mind, every cell in her body had been consumed by Dominic. The feel of his steel hard body, the things he'd done to her, the way he'd possessed her body and soul.

She was exhausted, emotionally and physically, but she couldn't stop thinking about him and the night they had shared. The chill of this morning had vanished. Being without him, having this distance between them, had freed her up to want him again. And now she missed him. She yearned for him. Needed him.

Arriving back at her hotel, she unpacked, needing to have something to do, otherwise she would spend even more time going through every single scene in slow motion.

She wanted to call Stefanos. But she couldn't. He would not approve.

She wanted to call Miranda. But she couldn't. Her friend would be hurt and feel betrayed.

Eleni had no one to confide in, and no Dominic to talk to, either.

Could she ever talk to him about this?

Could she ever face him in the office again?

She could feel him on her skin even now, even though she had showered; the scent of him was everywhere, not just wrapped up in her dirty clothes.

He wouldn't be at work tomorrow. Not for a few days, he'd said. At least that would give her time to compose herself.

Unable to settle, she went for a run. Training for the mountain climb. A mountain climb she was no longer sure about.

In her grief and misery she only remembered the good things about Jonas, but now it was starting to come back; there had been bad things too. She and Jonas had rowed, like normal couples. He had flirted with girls a few times. He hadn't cheated on her ... but it hadn't been as idyllic as the memories she cherished.

And now, she didn't even think about him. It was Dominic who walked in her thoughts in the twilight hours, whose tenderness wrapped around her heart during the day.

Still feeling restless, she tried a soak in the bathtub—her go to as a last resort when she was stressed—but it didn't help. She still couldn't sleep.

She would message Dominic.

In that way, she'd be able to gauge his mood. She would apologize for this morning. That would be a start.

She sat up in bed, turned the lamp on, and reached for her cell phone. Her fingers itched to type out what she felt, the things she remembered, the thoughts which lingered in her mind.

She missed him.

Texting would be a back and forth. She needed to hear his voice. Unable to hold back, she called him and waited. She had expected him to answer on the first ring—the way he'd always done with her in the past—but the call went to voicemail.

Dominic wasn't thinking of her anymore. He had moved on, and it was naïve of her to think otherwise.

CHAPTER FORTY-TWO

DOMINIC

The empty villa reflected his mood. Hollow and silent.
With Eleni gone, Dominic was stuck in a weird type of limbo; one which he desperately tried to claw his way out of.

He had seen the way in which Eleni had left so easily. She hadn't looked sad. Nor distraught. She had put last night's events behind her. Guilt and shame might have had something to do with that.

Her desire for him last night had been a reflection of her needs and nothing else. It was his dick she'd needed, not his heart.

In a fit of anger, he slammed his laptop shut, likely damaging yet another device. He'd messed up. Instead of catching Galatis at a good time and securing the deal, he'd been too busy focusing on Eleni.

Alexander would love this and his father would quietly

disapprove. Dominic would feel his father's disappointment all the way across the Mediterranean Sea.

He'd been frustrated by this deal which had no end in sight, but now he had been reduced to a weakling with a heart that beat for Eleni, and a desire for her, the likes of which he hadn't before experienced. He'd even slept in her bed last night, the scent of her in her bedsheets lingering in the air, making him reminisce.

Toughen up, dipshit.

This would not do. His father would expect results as soon as Dominic returned to the office.

He would touch base with Galatis' on his return to Athens. Thankfully, the old man would have seen that Dominic had 'a strong woman to ground him'.

For now, he had people to see and meetings to attend. He got up, ready to leave for a lunch meeting when Xenia knocked on his door.

"The young lady left these behind. I have washed and ironed them." She held out Eleni's denim shorts.

His breath dried up. He couldn't speak. So, he nodded and took them from her.

He was still holding them in his hands and reminiscing, when Kostas informed him that he would be late for his meeting if they didn't leave now.

ELENI

"You caught the sun," Miranda commented as she and Eleni went out for lunch the next day.

"Did I?" Eleni touched a hand to her cheek.

"Did you go to the beach with your friends again?"

Eleni stared at her blankly.

"You left early on Friday," Miranda prompted.

"Oh, yes. Yes." It was all coming back now. She'd told Miranda she'd gone to Spetses.

"You really did catch the sun." Miranda stared at her with a worried look on her face. "Are you sure it's not heatstroke?"

"What? No, it wasn't. It isn't. It's nothing. I couldn't sleep." That part was true. She hadn't been able to. Subconsciously she'd been waiting for a text or a call from Dominic, and when nothing happened, she'd spent hours shifting in bed wondering why he hadn't contacted her.

She was aware that Miranda's crush on Dominic hadn't abated, and even if there had been no need to keep the weekend a secret—in some alternate universe where she and Dominic were together and happy—it would be wrong for her to confess what had taken place between her and Dominic. She couldn't do that to Miranda. It would be like twisting a knife into her heart.

"How was your weekend?" she asked, desperate to change the subject.

Miranda warbled on about the things she'd done, the family get together she'd had to suffer and the copious amounts of food that had been eaten. "Next time you go for a run, take me with you. I could do with some exercise."

Eleni hadn't told her friend why she was running, or anything about the expedition, because she didn't want to tell everyone she met about Jonas and what had happened.

But she'd told Dominic.

But she and Dominic had slept together.

She wasn't sure what that meant or where it left her.

"We should get together on the weekend," Eleni suggested, taking up her friend's suggestion. "I was thinking about going back home this weekend." She longed for

Stefanos' company, to sit in their small spot by the beach and watch the sun set. But first she was anxious to see what Dominic would be like on his return. Unease clawed at her throat. The man could be mercurial and moody, and the intimacy of that night might be something he now regretted. She dreaded falling victim to his silent wrath.

"Again?"

"Huh?" Eleni's lack of sleep was making conversation difficult.

"You just went home."

"I mean in a few weeks' time." She rushed to cover her tracks.

"According to his diary Dominic was in Santorini for a wedding," said Miranda, conspiratorially.

"Was he?" Eleni couldn't bring herself to meet Miranda's gaze. She picked at the tomato in her wrap. "They shouldn't bother rolling these up for me. I always end up picking bits out of them."

"I wonder what he did this weekend," mused Miranda. "The wedding was just one day but ..."

The tomato stuck in Eleni's throat and held there. She choked, coughing uncontrollably, thumping the table until Miranda came over and thwacked her on the back.

Miranda had worked it out.

Eleni wiped her mouth, coughed, and placed a hand to her chest, then took the glass of water that Miranda was holding out to her. "Thank you," she said weakly.

Miranda looked pensive. "I called Helen's office this morning to check on some contracts Dominic needed, and her secretary—I know her well—told me that Helen's away and back tomorrow."

Relief swept over Eleni like a silky veil. "And you think ...?"

"I think what a lucky woman. A weekend with Dominic in Santorini."

"But Helen's in—" She stopped and shut her mouth. At least Miranda didn't suspect her. "When is Dominic back?" she asked, picking out a piece of succulent meat.

Given that her phone call had gone straight to his voicemail, indicating that he might have turned his cell phone off, she wasn't sure her call would even have registered as a missed call on his phone. In which case he wouldn't have known she'd tried to contact him. But it still didn't explain why he hadn't contacted her.

Did he not miss her?

Or remember what they had shared?

"According to his schedule, tomorrow evening."

Eleni's heart sank. Miranda might as well have said next month for all the waiting it involved. Three days felt like a lifetime, and the absence of Dominic endeared him to her more than ever.

She couldn't focus on her work. Her thoughts weren't here in the office; they were all the way in the villa, in bed, with him.

Their night together was so vivid and real, so potent that the mere remembrance of his touch and his kisses made her aroused.

CHAPTER FORTY-THREE

DOMINIC

He arrived back in Athens late in the evening, his time in Santorini had been highly productive.

But, at the back of his mind was Eleni. She still stole moments of his time throughout the day, between meetings and swimming and working out at the villa—whatever he tried to distract himself with wasn't working.

He'd wanted to call her, had wanted to see how she was, but he'd reminded himself that Eleni was the one who'd left. She was the one still hung up on her boyfriend. What they'd had was only sex. If she'd thought about him, she would have called him.

The ball wasn't in his court.

As the plane took off in Santorini, he briefly flirted with the idea of going to her hotel room, but it would be late in the evening, too late to make a casual visit. There had been nothing casual about their time together. What would he say to her?

But there had been no communication between them since she'd left, and he couldn't get her out of his mind. He needed to know; did she feel the same way?

No, asshole. She already told you.

On his first day back at the office, after almost a week away, he stopped by the reception desk to collect urgent messages and mail from Miranda. He wanted to be left alone, uninterrupted, locked away in his office.

"You... you've got a tan," Miranda commented, blushing more than ever. He scowled at her as he reached for the batch of postal mail she had for him. A part of him wondered what Eleni might have said to her.

"Yes?"

"It ..it ... suits you," his PA continued.

He lifted an eyebrow but said nothing as he rifled through the pile.

Miranda lifted her chin. "Was the wedding good?"

His eyebrow shifted up even more. He hadn't said a thing to her about it. It was in his schedule, because he always had to state where he was and how long he was away for, but he hadn't actually talked to her about it. "I never mentioned it."

"You did once." Her voice was short and breathless, as if she'd run a mile and stopped.

He'd wanted to keep the wedding quiet. No good having rumors flying around this place, especially now that he had good reason to be wary.

What had Eleni said? The two of them were good friends. Maybe she'd let something slip.

"Mr. Galatis' secretary has been calling since yesterday. Mr. Galatis is most anxious to see you."

He was perplexed. This was interesting. But Dominic had

no intention of being at the man's beck and call. The only reason he was in this mess—the only reason he'd taken Eleni to the wedding—was because this crazy old fool had hinted that he was slowly inching towards a deal. Dominic didn't hold it against him that he'd been busy with his family, but he wasn't ready to see Hector yet. "Can't do it."

Miranda blinked at him. "But you *always* see him."

"Not today. I don't want to be disturbed."

He marched into his office and dove straight into getting caught up on emails and phone calls.

His father had called not even five minutes after Dominic had sat down. The pressure was mounting; his father wanted an update on the weekend, on Galatis and the deal. Information and progress that Dominic had nothing to report on, but he'd skilfully managed to deflect the conversation to the new business deals he'd made recently and was able to end the call with his father sounding somewhat appeased.

He took a few moments to sit still and contemplate, and in the solitude of his room he was reminded of who he was again —Dominic Steele, a member of the billionaire Steele family. A man who had come here for a specific reason. Not to lose his head over a woman.

Eleni was here in the same building, maybe even in the hallway right now, talking to Miranda. His gut tightened and his body filled with dread at the thought of running into her again.

Forcing himself to forget about her, he started to go through his most urgent messages, but not an hour had passed when a loud knock on his door disturbed him again. He slammed his hand on the table. "I said I was not to be disturbed."

The door opened and Miranda's red face peeked around

it. She opened her mouth to speak, but Dominic beat her to it. "I said I didn't want to be disturbed," he growled.

"But ... it's—"

"No buts, Miranda. For fucks sake can't you take an order from me?"

Miranda's face turned white. But the huge frame of Hector Galatis' slowly moved past her as she flattened her body against her door.

Dominic rose slowly, his insides in upheaval. He wasn't ready to see this man. Didn't want to see him. Ordinarily he would have been excited, humbled even, to have this man in his office.

But today?

Today he was already struggling to focus. He did not need this. Miranda rushed away and closed the door, leaving him and Galatis staring at one another.

"This is most unexpected, Hector." Dominic strode towards the old man. "We barely spoke at the wedding." He beckoned the man to take a seat and pulled out a chair he hoped would be big enough to accommodate him. Then he waited, his foot at the ready to block the chair in case it moved as Galatis slowly descended his weight upon it.

"I ... was ... busy." Galatis puffed, out of breath already as he pulled a handkerchief out of his pocket and wiped his face.

"I could see that." Dominic smiled and slipped his hands into his pockets as he waited. Something was up. Galatis always made Dominic come to him. Not the other way around. "I was hoping we'd have a meeting or two at the wedding," he mentioned casually.

"It wasn't the place."

"It wasn't. You have a large family, Hector. You were working the crowd and enjoying yourself, as you should." Dominic sat down. "Can I get you a drink? Something cold?"

he offered, but all the while his brain was theorizing, trying to work out why he was here.

Galatis shook his head, then closed his eyes for a few seconds. "How do you know her?"

Dominic watched the man's face and waited for his eyes to open. This was most peculiar. "Who?"

"Your girlfriend."

"Eleni?" Unease trailed up his spine like an army of ants. "We should have had this conversation at the wedding, Hector. You could have asked her yourself."

"I'm asking you now."

"I met her at a party," he replied, evasively, but not altogether lying either. As far as he was concerned it was none of Galatis' business. "Why do you ask?"

"I am curious."

"Eleni and your wife were talking. Your wife seemed to like her."

"She looks familiar."

Galatis' questions confused him. It was possible that the man had caught a glimpse of Eleni at one of the meetings. Did it matter to him that Galatis was bizarrely interested in Dominic having 'a thing' with an employee? Eleni had been worried about that. "Is there a reason you're asking me so many questions?" He attempted a laugh to ease the tension in the air. The mood turned dark and heavy, and he wasn't sure why, but something was off. Galatis turning up unsolicited in his office was off. Asking questions about Eleni was off.

When the old man didn't reply, Dominic ventured another smile, unsure where this conversation was going. "This is a surprise, Hector because I got back to the office late last night and I wasn't going to take any meetings today—"

"That clip in her hair." Galatis gestured with his crepey leathery hand pointing to his head. He averted his gaze and looked at a point behind Dominic, on the wall, the expression on his face faraway and distant.

"What about it?" Dominic struggled to understand. Galatis appeared dazed and confused and wasn't making much sense. He suddenly became worried that the man might be on the verge of having a stroke.

"I had something similar made once. It was a custom piece I had commissioned a long time ago."

Dominic stopped breathing. Eleni's words hit him like shrapnel.

I haven't met my father. I have no idea who he is.

He told my mother to get rid of me when she was pregnant.

He already had a wife and family.

His eyes locked with Galatis' in a new understanding and he quickly rewound back to the wedding, and now this sudden visit the moment Dominic had returned to the office.

Could it be possible that ... Hector Galatis was Eleni's father?

The layers were peeling off, the snake shedding its skin, and underneath it all, a snake was still a snake.

This was the man who had lectured him about the virtues of family, the man who had proclaimed that behind every successful man was a strong woman.

This snake?

A married man, cheating on his wife, a man who had family, a man who'd had an affair with Eleni's mother.

A man who then wanted his lover to abort their child.

And Eleni had no idea.

"Have you come here to talk about hair slides, Hector?"

"Who is she?" the old man asked.

"She is someone I met at a party, I told you."

"I want to meet her."

"You had plenty of opportunity at your nephew's

wedding, Hector." There was no way he was going to let Eleni walk into the lion's den. He hadn't been able to protect her before, but he sure as hell was going to now. He swiped a hand over his face, unsure of what to do, or how to tell Eleni. "You've caught me at a bad time, Hector." He lifted his paperwork and shuffled it into a neat pile. "I was hoping we would have been able to discuss things further at the wedding, and to come to an agreement, but I realize now that you were surrounded by family, and quite a large family at that. It was never going to be possible. That's fine, we can meet later in the week. As you can appreciate, I have a lot to catch up with right now."

The old man stared at him for the longest time.

Dominic scratched his jaw, trying to guess at his thoughts. The real reason why he was here. "I recall Eleni saying that her aunt gave her that piece." He prayed that Eleni had an aunt. Or that Hector would not remember either way.

"Her aunt?"

Dominic nodded. "That's what she said."

The thick vertical line in the centre of Galatis' forehead softened. He snorted, as if he'd come to some sort of conclusion, before pushing down on the armrests and slowly hauling himself to standing. "You must invest in some good seating, Dominic."

Or you could lose some weight and get fit. Not be a walking heart attack risk.

"Send me your recommendations, Hector. I'll make sure to accommodate you better next time."

"Please do. There will be a next time. You will be pleased to know that I will be meeting with my lawyers this afternoon to draw up my response to your proposal. I don't like the figure you mention for sharing profits. Perhaps we can find a figure that suits us both?"

"Your fleet is old, Hector. It's not the prize jewel you think it is."

The man lifted his head, his eyes narrowing. "The name Galatis means something in this business. I have made a fortune and I have a legacy that will never be forgotten."

"The name Galatis will be forgotten if you don't move into the new era. Steele Shipping can help you."

"We shall see, Dominic."

He walked Hector Galatis to the door, and felt a sense of relief, not because the man seemed to be moving closer to accepting the deal, but because he was glad to see the back of him.

CHAPTER FORTY-FOUR

ELENI

The idea that Dominic was in his office now gnawed away at her already frayed nerves.

As if it wasn't bad enough that her stomach had been in knots ever since she'd known he'd landed.

Dominic had shared her bed and her body, but the wedding belonged to another time, another universe. She would do well to remember that.

On one of her many trips back from the water cooler, Miranda hissed to get her attention, and when Eleni walked over to her, announced that Hector Galatis had just left Dominic's office.

"He came *here?*" Eleni was shocked. This was the man Dominic had been trying to see in Santorini. That he had come here, to the office, was nothing short of a miracle. "They must have agreed on the deal." Dominic would be ecstatic. He'd accomplished his mission.

Her heart bloomed at the thought.

"I ... I need to see him about something on the system." She gulped down the entire paper cup of water, threw it into the waste basket and prepared herself mentally.

Miranda looked nervous. "He said he didn't want to be disturbed."

Eleni couldn't wait a moment longer to see him. "It's important. Agnes and Isidora can't help. Give me a notepad."

"What?"

"A notepad, papers, anything." So that she looked as if she had a reason to see him.

"Why?"

Because she might need a shield, in case Dominic reverted to his usual grumpy self. She clutched the paper pad Miranda handed her to her chest.

"Are you sure about this?" Miranda still looked dubious, as if Eleni was stepping onto a landmine. "He's not in a good mood."

Eleni smoothed down her blouse. Just like she had missed him, the chances were high that Dominic had missed her, too. She had been a bundle of nerves every day, waiting for his return, and if she could have turned back time, she would have stayed with him in Santorini when he'd asked.

That was the benefit of hindsight. Consequences became clearer after the event. That night had meant something to him. *It had.* Otherwise why would Dominic have asked her to stay?

"I won't be long, and I'll take the blame for it." She sailed into his room not even bothering to knock.

He was on the phone with his back to the door. "I don't know if you should—" She'd made enough noise opening the door and marching in that he swiveled around in his executive chair mid-sentence and glared at her. Her heart hammered in her chest.

"I'll call you back." He slammed the phone down, his face turning hard the more she stared back at him.

"Hello." She hadn't expected a fanfare, or him leaping over his desk to come to her. But she hadn't expected him to sit there looking as if she'd brought the plague with her. The butterflies which had fluttered around in her stomach promptly died and fell to her feet.

A heaviness settled over her. She'd never seen Dominic's face look so thunderous.

His shoulders stiffened, along with his mouth. If his body language could form words, his would be a screaming news headline. "I gave Miranda strict orders not to be disturbed."

"She warned me but—"

He looked at her. "But?"

He was breaking her heart just by looking at her. His cold eyes stared her down, as if he dared her to go there—to that happy, blissful place she'd been basking in since that night. She couldn't erase knowing him, sharing such intimacy, unless she'd had a lobotomy.

But he was back to being the Dominic she had first met. Cold, hard, and with the emotional empathy of a serial killer.

"Sorry, I ..."

What? What had she expected from him? She took a few tentative steps back. His gaze fell to the notepad in her hand.

"What is it? What do you need to show me?" His voice was brittle, thin. Full of contempt.

This wasn't how she'd expected a lover to be. "It's nothing important ... it can wait..."

Another step back.

"It must have been important for you to march in here, despite Miranda telling you I didn't want to see anyone."

Anyone?

Up until this moment, she hadn't thought of herself as just *anyone*, especially to Dominic. They had *had* something together. But she couldn't reconcile the hard, cold businessman before her to the tender man she'd shared her bed with.

Her eyes prickled with tears, and she looked away, blinking and trying to staunch them. "It's nothing, really." She forced herself to look at him so that she would not forget how little she was in his eyes, in his estimation. How she was so insignificant.

He stood up slowly. "You've wasted my time with your interruption. So, go on, what the hell is it?"

His words hit her like physical punches but hurt for much longer because, unlike punches, the words sliced into her heart and splintered inside her.

This horrible, moody man. Why had she ever thought that he had changed?

"This is nothing. Empty sheets." She flicked through the pages to show him. "I wanted a reason to come and see you." Her voice sounded hollow, like it belonged to a victim.

But she wasn't a victim.

She wasn't hurting because of the sex. He hadn't used her. She'd used him, she'd wanted the fantasy, had wanted to believe that there could be something between them. Had wanted to know that he wanted her as much as he'd wanted Helen or Demi, or the other socialites.

She wanted to know that he desired her.

And he had, for that one night. But now, he was filled with contempt. If she didn't understand that he had dismissed her, that she didn't count, and didn't matter, she was just plain stupid.

"Why?"

Why?

"I missed you." There. She had said it, because she could no longer keep it to herself. "I thought ... I thought it meant something ... what happened between us."

His lips were firmly pressed together. She searched desperately for some emotion in that cruel hard face of it, but found none. He simply stared at her as if she were a statue.

Her heart lurched violently inside her ribcage. Everything she'd wanted to believe, was not how it actually was. She'd made a terrible mistake.

Dominic didn't even bat an eyelid. In the stretched out silence, the way he looked at her, made her feel like one of those desperate women who probably threw themselves at him, while he gazed at them with pity.

Well, she was not one of those women. She had no interest in his money, or his status, and she didn't care for his wealth.

She'd found a connection, a heart that fit with hers, and while she might have backed away too soon, she'd come to him now to say she was sorry.

Only, she'd seen his true colors.

"I made a mistake."

She needed to run as far away from him as possible.

CHAPTER FORTY-FIVE

ELENI

Eleni rushed out of the office, past Miranda's desk and rushed straight into the restroom. Miranda cried out after her, but Eleni ignored her.

In the safe space of the toilet, she locked herself in a cubicle, put the seat down and sat on it. Covering her face with her hands, she closed her eyes and wished she could disappear.

Dominic hadn't wanted anything to do with her.

He'd looked at her like she was filth. Discarded her like a dirty rag. For the first time ever, she profoundly understood what her mother must have suffered at the hands of her first love, when he'd ditched her.

Tears streamed down Eleni's cheeks, and she quickly wiped them away with the back of her hand.

She wasn't in as bad a situation as her mother had been. She was not pregnant. She wasn't in love. It had been lust.

One hot, smoldering, reckless night. She would, in time, get over it. She had a mountain to climb. New brighter horizons to reach for.

She had a month left of her contract. Alternatively, she could hand in her notice and leave now, but that would be running away and she wasn't one to run. Despite having saved up enough money for her trip, she would see her time out with dignity.

The sound of a door opening made her sit upright. "Eleni? Are you in here?"

A knock sounded on her door.

"Eleni?"

Miranda.

She wasn't ready to face Miranda. Not now. Not like this. "Yes." She forced herself to sound cheerful but failed miserably.

"What happened? Why are you in here? Are you *crying?*"

"No!"

"Then come out. Let me see."

Eleni snorted. "Shouldn't you be back at your desk in case your lord and master comes back?"

"The lord and master in my dreams, you mean." Miranda's attempt at a seductive voice was the last thing Eleni wanted to hear. She dabbed at her eyes, smoothed down her hair, pinched her cheeks to add some color, then rubbed her lips together.

But what for? She wasn't thinking properly. It was Miranda on the other side of that door, not Dominic.

The less she thought about Dominic the better it would be for her mental health. She was done with him and his moods and his grumpiness.

Forcing a huge smile, she opened the door.

"We should go out tonight, after work," she suggested. Miranda looked at her suspiciously.

"What happened?"

Eleni washed her hands, caught a glimpse of herself in the mirror. She didn't look too bad. "Nothing. You know how grumpy Dominic can be."

"I did warn you."

"I should have listened. Dinner and drinks, you and me, tonight?"

Miranda's face lit up like a firework. "Can we?"

"We can do anything we want. I'm thinking of going home this weekend."

"Again?"

"What?"

"You're going home again?"

Because you were in Santorini last weekend, remember?

Eleni stared at her friend.

"Did you go home or not?" Miranda asked, "because you keep forgetting."

She didn't want to talk about it. "It wasn't such a great weekend. But I'm going back. Why don't you come with me?"

"Can I?"

Eleni nodded. For the first time in a long time, the idea of returning home felt good. She longed to see Spetses and to connect with Stefanos, to get back to the familiar, a place where she belonged.

DOMINIC

W hat the hell was he supposed to tell Eleni?
How the hell was he supposed to tell her?
Hector Galatis, the crazy old Greek, is your father.

Dominic was a mess. The hurt in Eleni's eyes had wrecked him. She'd looked excited to see him, for about two seconds, until he'd gone all cold on her.

How could he not have?

She'd told him she'd missed him.

She'd said that she thought them being together meant something.

But he couldn't let her see how he really felt. He couldn't react. He hadn't been able to think properly ever since he had understood the weight of what Hector Galatis' had unwittingly revealed.

And now he was conflicted.

When Eleni had come bounding into his office, looking like the picture of happiness, he hadn't known what to do, so he'd done the only thing Dominic Steele knew how to do.

He'd behaved like an ass. He'd pushed her away.

Because the deal was paramount. Nothing mattered more than the deal.

Right?

The deal his father and brother were waiting with bated breath for him to complete successfully, and it sounded to him as if Galatis was coming around to forming an alliance. He wasn't happy with the profit split, but that was something they could work on later.

Galatis coming to see him in his office had been a move that was unheard of, but now Dominic understood. One look at Eleni's hair slide had triggered Galatis' suspicions. That's why the man had been so impatient to see him. That's why he turned up here, at his office.

Dominic hoped he'd thrown him off the trail by telling him that Eleni's aunt had given her the accessory.

He'd done what he could to protect her. Galatis was coming back with a response to Dominic's proposal and if it looked good, his work here was done.

That's all he needed to focus on.

Enough of Eleni. He couldn't afford to get constantly wrapped up in emotions that didn't serve him. She was still heartbroken over a dead man.

And she still didn't even know the half of it.

CHAPTER FORTY-SIX

ELENI

"Your mother is really sweet." Miranda picked up a tequila shot from the neat little row that Stefanos had lined up, examined it, then set it back down again.

"She likes you." Her mother was a judgmental person, but something seemed to have softened her lately.

When it had happened Eleni couldn't tell for certain—it might have been that time on her birthday when her mother had told her about her father, or it might have been when Eleni had moved away to Athens, giving them both the space they needed.

Last night, soon after arriving back at the island, her mother had cooked a nice dinner for the three of them and had insisted they sit around the table and eat and talk. She wanted to know more about Eleni's job and how she was finding her new life, and she was also interested in hearing about Miranda's life in the city.

Coming home had been the break Eleni needed and Miranda coming with her was a bonus. Miranda had become her go-to person in Athens, and Eleni now wanted the chance to repay her for her kindness.

Music thumped inside the rowdy bar and it was so loud it could be heard outside where the three of them now sat on benches under a canopy umbrella. Phoebe couldn't get anyone to look after her baby, and Angeliki was on a date.

"Are we ready?" Stefanos sat down next to her, facing Miranda. They all picked up a tequila shot—omitting the hand licking and salt sprinkling altogether. He counted to three. They downed it on three. Eyes narrowed, mouths crinkling as they sucked on lime wedges.

"Ewwww." She shook her head, disgusted by the tartness. Miranda's face scrunched up, and then her eyes widened. "Another one?" They each had two more shot glasses left on the table, but they'd already gone through a pitcher of Sangria.

Stefanos clapped his hands together. "My kind of girl." Miranda beamed at him, but at least she knew that it was no use trying to attract his attention. Eleni had made sure to let her know Stefanos wasn't interested in women. Just like she'd let it slip to Stefanos that Miranda had a crush on Dominic.

"Ready?" Stefanos counted to three again, and they all had another shot.

Then another one.

"Shouldn't we slow down?" Eleni gave Stefanos a dirty stare. She didn't want Miranda throwing up at the table, or at home.

"Another one! Let's do it!" Miranda cried. "I'm having so much fun."

They'd also been out last night after dinner, doing more of the same. Eleni felt compelled to go wild, in order to forget recent events. Alcohol and dancing were a sure fire way to do this.

She'd laid low at work after that interaction with Dominic, and stayed out of his way.

Two days of late nights, partying and drinking and dancing, and Eleni knew she had to slow things down before returning to Athens tomorrow. She had planned something sensible, a long and lazy brunch by the sea in the afternoon. The weekend had given her time to clear her head.

"I'll get another round," suggested Stefanos, getting up to go to the bar.

"No, don't. I think we've had enough." She flicked her gaze at Miranda who had stood up and was dancing away. She had never seen Miranda like this. Uninhibited and free.

Stefanos made a clicking sound with his teeth. "She's having a good time. Why don't you let her have some fun?"

"Please can we have another shot?" Miranda pleaded.

"You've had three!" Eleni cried.

"Are you policing me? I'm having fun. I *never* have fun."

Stefanos gave Eleni a told-you-look. "Let the poor girl have some fun."

"Yes, let me." Miranda pouted. "I never have any fun at work."

"Talking of work, tell me more about Dominic Steele," said Stefanos, shimmying up the bench to move closer to the dancing Miranda.

Eleni shook her head. "No work talk," she cautioned, suddenly developing an urge for another shot of tequila.

"Dominic is rude and ungrateful and it's no fun working for him. No fun at all. None," Miranda continued. She started to sway erratically to the music. Eleni couldn't work out if she was drunk and having trouble with her moves, or whether that was how she really danced.

Stefanos folded his arms, jerked back his head, and stared at them both in turn. "You're working in close proximity to one of the hottest men on the planet and you're complaining?"

Miranda moved her arms and hips in tune to the music, closing her eyes and losing herself. "Dominic doesn't even know I exist," she shouted, over the music.

Eleni didn't want to hear that name.

"One more shot, pleeeaase!" Miranda begged.

"I should put her out of her misery," suggested Stefanos.

Eleni shrugged. "Okay, get one more round of drinks. Just one." She opened up her bag to take out some notes, but Stefanos waved her hand away, refusing it.

"You pay when I come to Athens," he said, and disappeared into the dark pit of people gathered at the front of the bar.

"I'm not going to be in Athens for too long," she said to herself, sitting down again.

"Come and dance with me," Miranda shouted, her hips swaying even more vigorously to the music.

"I'm having more fun watching you," Eleni shouted back.

Sitting in a busy place, surrounded by people on a hot summer night, she should have been happy. She should have been carefree.

She had been, this time last weekend. The difference between what had happened last weekend and this one was so monumental, it was as opposite as day and night.

She lowered her head, clasping the back of her neck with her hands. She'd never felt lonelier.

If only she could erase everything that had happened between her and Dominic. There were so many memorable moments between them. From the first time she'd taken his order for espresso, to the party on the yacht, the time when he'd come to the taverna to give her his business card, when he'd unstuck her heel from the pavement, when she'd accompanied him to the meetings with Galatis, when he'd insisted she stay at his house to recover from her ankle.

There were so many.

And of course, the weekend in Santorini.

She couldn't erase Dominic from her mind if she tried.

But maybe like it was with Jonas, she would in time. It would happen gradually.

Their night together had been too potent, too intense. He'd taken her mind, body and soul, taken her heart and ruined her for other men.

"Here we go!" Stefanos returned with a tray of six tequila shots.

Eleni looked horrified. "I said one each!" At this rate, Miranda was going to throw up and then fall asleep.

Miranda clapped her hands together with glee.

"It was buy-one-get-one-free offer." Stefanos pouted as if he were a naughty child who'd taken too many sweets. "Relax. You've been so uptight, Leni. Should I even ask why?"

As always Stefanos could read her like a book, but thankfully, with Miranda around, he hadn't been able to catch her alone to interrogate her.

"I'm just tired, that's all," she lied.

"Okay, let's go then," Stefanos lifted his shot glass. "Ready!" They lifted their glasses and downed them in one. Miranda shivered, and Stefanos grinned, Eleni felt even more lightheaded. She pushed her glass away. "I'm done. I can't have anymore."

"Lightweight," Miranda poked her in jest.

"Oh, I'm a lightweight, am I?" Eleni side-eyed her friend. It was good to see her friend letting her hair down and Eleni wished she could feel the same, but she wasn't going to feel that trouble free for a while.

Getting over Dominic would take time.

Stefanos sat down, and Miranda did too. "Are you going to tell me what's the matter?" He pushed another shot glass towards her.

Eleni pushed it away from her again. "Not now. I've drunk too much." She didn't feel so great. Fanning her face, she looked around, trying to find an exit in case she needed to throw up. That's when she caught sight of the bodyguard. At six foot something, dressed all in black and looking as out of place as an iceberg in the desert, Sven was impossible to miss.

But if Sven was here it meant …

Immediately she looked around, her heart pulsating at a memory recalled. On a hot summer's evening, filled with people and laughter, a shiver passed over her.

Dominic would not be far away.

"What's the matter now?" Stefanos asked.

"I thought … I … saw someone." She turned towards the bodyguard again, but he had disappeared. She was seeing things. Holding her head in her hands she took a deep breath. She was a hot mess.

"Eleni?"

She felt him long before she heard him. Goose bumps scampered across her skin. A tingling started in her belly. Her sixth sense alerting her. She didn't need to lift her head or look up.

Dominic's hand touched her arm gently, sending a ripple of charge through her skin, enough to make her heart jolt, even as her mind filled with all manner of thoughts.

"Dominic!" A loud crash followed. Miranda crashed onto the bench alongside her, knocking an empty cocktail pitcher over.

"Miranda." Dominic's voice was level. "This is a surprise."

"What are you doing here?" Stefanos asked him, sounding as shocked as Eleni felt. His questioning gaze burned into her.

"Don't look at me, I don't know what he's doing here." She couldn't bring herself to look at Dominic. She still couldn't believe he was here, turning up most unexpectedly. She'd come here to get away from this man, and this—him being here—was abnormal. Stalker-ish.

"You are the most handsome looking man I have ever worked for," gushed Miranda. "You're so—"

Eleni grabbed Miranda's hand. "Stop talking." Miranda freed her hand away, standing up shakily. Her face was flushed. "But ... I want to tell him. I neeeed to tell him."

"Oh, Jesus." Beside her, Dominic facepalmed.

"Why don't you and Miranda go inside and dance?" Eleni suggested, deciding to have some fun.

"Dom will you come?" Miranda squealed.

Dominic's face twisted. "Don't call me that."

"But will you"

"Yes, Dom, why don't you?" Eleni suggested. Under the veil of darkness illuminated by lights, Dominic's face shimmered.

"I don't dance."

Miranda collapsed onto the bench again in disappointment.

"Miranda will be happy to show you," Eleni insisted, enjoying watching Dominic squirm.

"I so will!" Miranda sprang up like a Jack-in-the-Box. "This is already one of the best nights of my life!"

Eleni winced, feeling uneasy. As much as she enjoyed making Dominic uncomfortable, she didn't want to do it at Miranda's expense. Her friend would be most upset when she sobered up.

"We need to talk," Dominic said, staring at Eleni.

"We can talk any time you want, Dom," Miranda chimed in. "I'm all ears, I always have been. *Always*."

"For the love of God." Dominic wiped his hand over his face, before bending down and putting his face level with Eleni's. He put his hand over hers. "Please. It's important."

Electricity sparked at their touch, and she yanked her hand away. Her head felt light and now that she knew she wasn't seeing things—now that Dominic was here in the flesh, for real. Her mind calculated that he'd sought her out for a reason. She stood up, then wobbled as if her legs were boneless. She'd had too many shots, too quickly, and on top of cocktails. This was the second time she was in such an inebriated state with Dominic around.

Why did this always happen?

She needed to sober up fast, but she immediately fell back down on the bench.

"How much has she had?" she heard Dominic ask the others.

"Not enough!" cried Miranda. "Loosen up, Dom. Have some fun. Have some!" She pushed a shot glass of tequila under his nose. Dominic pushed the glass away and Eleni held her head in her hands, embarrassed for her friend.

"We need more cocktails!" cried the new and extroverted Miranda.

Eleni couldn't let Miranda continue to make such a fool of herself. At this rate Miranda wouldn't have a job left. Dominic would fire her first thing on Monday morning.

"I need some air." With all the strength she could muster, she hauled herself to standing, and forced herself to stay up.

"But we're already outside." Miranda giggled helplessly.

Eleni shivered when Dominic inched closer and placed a hand on the small of her back. With his other hand on her arm, he helped her to stay upright. She did nothing to pull away, needing his support in case she wobbled and fell back down again.

"I'll take care of her," she heard him say.

He ushered her away from the noise of the club, from the crowd of people milling around. She swallowed gulps of air, needing to clear her head, her heart and her dignity.

When they were away from the noise and hubble bubble, she wrested herself away from him.

"Why are you here, *Dom?*" Why now, after the way he'd treated her that last time? Why follow her all the way to Spetses?

"We need to talk, Eleni."

"We're done talking, Dom."

She heard his sharp—and pissed off—intake of breath. "I'm not."

"I am," she announced. It had turned from a hot balmy night to a hot night filled with irritation.

"I'm sorry for the way I behaved when you came into my office."

"I won't be doing that again. You let me know exactly what you think of me."

"That's not what happened. I was rude to you, and I'm sorry, but I had my reasons."

"We all have our reasons for the things we do, Dom. At least now I know how my mother felt when the man she loved spurned her. She warned me about men like you. She told me to be careful of men like my father."

"I am *nothing* like your father."

She scoffed. "I wouldn't know what my father is like."

He looked at her blankly. That seemed about right. He had nothing to say in his defense.

"You hurt me," she said, waving her finger at him, then

blinked, because she was seeing two fingers. Maybe three. She also needed to zip that mouth of hers.

Dominic took a step nearer, and there it was again. He was drowning her in his ocean breeze scent. It took a huge effort for her to not nuzzle up against his neck and take a deep inhale.

"We need to talk, Eleni. It's important."

"I don't want you trying to sweet talk me, Dom. My mother told me that men sweet talk and buy gifts, and shower women with money and jewels. I don't need that from you, or anyone. I never have."

"That's what I love ... that's why you're so different, Eleni. That's why I can't walk away."

She blinked, her knees going weak, her legs in danger of buckling under her. Had he said he loved her? Had he said the 'L' word? Or was she hearing things? Projecting her wishes into the ether?

She swayed again, but he put his arms around her waist and anchored her to him. She was about to push him away, but that scent of his drenched her in memories so intense and so vivid, she didn't want to move away. *Ever.*

"Do you remember what we did last Saturday?" she whispered, giggling at the memory.

"I will never forget it."

"How you made me come..." She threw her arms around him, her lips inches from his. "So many times ..." She moved to press her lips against his, but he ducked his head.

He let out a sigh. "Not like this. Not when you're drunk."

Two gasps followed, shocking her out of her drunken bubble because those noises didn't come from Dominic. Two heads bobbed out from behind a bush near the pathway.

"So, *that's* what happened," Stefanos said slowly, coming into her hazy view. Miranda paced around, waggling a finger in her direction. "I knew it …. I knew something was up. I knew you lied about last weekend."

Before Eleni could answer, Dominic cupped her chin and made her face him. "Please come with me," he begged. "This concerns you."

She was so tired, so lethargic, so drunk, that all she could do was put her arms around him and lean against the wall of his chest.

CHAPTER FORTY-SEVEN

DOMINIC

The past few days has been difficult. The idea of doing business with Galatis—his main purpose for coming to Greece in the first place—no longer mattered.

He was so close to getting what he wanted, but he wasn't happy about it, and he'd been grumpier and meaner than ever.

He hated himself for it and had been wrestling with his decision, but he couldn't in good faith do business with a man like Galatis. Because he was in love with the woman this monster had wished had never been born.

He'd tried, and failed, to forget that she was in love with someone else. He'd tried and failed to forget her.

Maybe his father was right, Alexander was cut out for the ruthless world of business. His brother could disregard emotion in favor of dollar signs.

Dominic thought he could do it, but when his conscience was uneasy, and it was five o'clock in the morning and he hadn't slept, he knew it was time to do something.

Eleni needed to know about Galatis' visit.

There was a chance that the old man wasn't her father, in which case Dominic could go ahead with the deal and not feel guilty about it. But he needed to know the truth—*if* Eleni wanted to know. If she didn't, then he would worry about that when the time came.

But first he had to find her and tell her. When Miranda had let slip that she and Eleni were going to Spetses for the weekend, he'd known where to find her. But he hadn't expected her to be drunk and doing shots in a bar. It made things difficult.

His first concern, when Eleni had collapsed against him, was to make sure she didn't fall and hurt herself. His second concern was to talk to her in private, but now her two friends eyed him like Dobermans waiting to pounce.

They'd heard, and they knew.

Miranda eyed him like a velociraptor, ready to shred him to pieces. "Can you both leave us?" he growled. "I need to talk to Eleni in private."

"I bet you do." Eleni's protective sidekick from the taverna was on him like a hawk. "What do you want from her?"

"You took Eleni to the wedding in Santorini?" The look on Miranda's face made him wince. He didn't need to answer his PA, but he needed to be careful with Stefanos.

"Wedding? What wedding?" Stefanos asked.

Eleni made a moaning noise against him as she snuggled even closer. Her arms tightened around his neck, and down below his cock shot to attention.

For fucks' sake. This woman had only to breathe on him and he was hard.

"I'm so tired, Dominic. Want to sleep," she murmured.

"I'm taking her back to my hotel," he announced.

"You'd like that, wouldn't you?" Stefanos quipped.

"To do what?" Miranda wanted to know.

"To talk," he snapped. "And nothing else. I could take her back to her place." But he knew it wouldn't be ideal, because what he had to tell Eleni he didn't want to do under the same roof as her mother. "Here, take my watch." He scraped his Rolex off his wrist and held it out to Stefanos.

"What am I going to do with that?" Her friend looked at him as if he were an idiot. "What is it? A ransom?"

"That's not how ransoms work, dickhead." He tightened his hold around Eleni's waist. Her face was buried deep in his neck, and his manhood had a mind of its own.

Miranda snatched the watch and pressed it to her chest as if it had more than monetary value for her.

Jesus.

He eyed Stefanos. "Miranda has my number. I'm staying at the Poseidonion."

"Of course you would stay there." Stefanos inched closer to him. "If you hurt her ..."

"He's not going to do anything to her," Miranda cried.

"Trust me." These were his last words to the dynamic duo as he slowly manoeuvred Eleni. "Come on. Come with me. I've got you." With an arm around her waist, and her arm around his shoulder, he lead her back to his hotel which was only a short distance away.

The light of the bedside lamp turned Eleni's skin golden. An hour had passed since Dominic had brought her here, but she'd fallen asleep as they got into the elevator.

He carried her to his room and had slipped off her shoes, then put her into his bed.

Now he sat on the armchair, watching her sleep, waiting for her to awaken. He longed to touch her, to run his fingers gently along the contours of her face, but he held back, and instead turned the lamp off, needing to catch some sleep himself.

He awoke to the sound of birdsong and, judging by the slivers of light filtering through the blinds, he must have been out a good few hours. Eleni stirred, and then sat up in bed, wiping her face with her hands. She looked around the room, confused. "What am I doing in your bed?"

He kept his distance and remained in his chair. "You'd had too much to drink."

She moaned. "That seems to be my default whenever you're around."

He got up and poured her a glass of water. "Take this. You're dehydrated."

She emptied the glass. He walked back to the side table and poured her another glass. By the time he returned, she'd turned the lamp on. "Here."

She sat up and blinked a few times. "Why am I here?" she asked, then took a few gulps of water.

"Because we need to talk."

"Talk away. I'm in your bed ... you have me where you want."

He scowled not liking what she said. "If I remember correctly, the last time you were in bed when I was around, you were the one doing the begging."

She drank the rest of the water and said nothing.

"You were drunk earlier. You were hugging me. You could barely walk. What was I supposed to do?" he asked.

"You could have left me where I was, with my friends. Having fun."

"Were you though? You looked pretty miserable to me. You were holding your head in your hands when I came over."

"How long were you watching me for?"

"Not long."

"Why are you here, *Dom?*"

His mouth set in a hard line and he had to force himself to not react. She knew it pissed him off. He stood up, shoved his hands in his pockets. He was still in his same clothes from yesterday and it was ... he raised his wrist to check but he didn't have his Rolex anymore. Miranda did.

He glanced at the bedside clock. It was almost five in the morning. They had plenty of time. "I wanted you to stay at the villa."

She rolled her eyes. "That, again."

He wanted her to know that him being cold to her the other day wasn't a true reflection of his feelings for her.

"I had to get back," she said, her voice dull and flat, as if she was fed up with him.

"You didn't."

"I don't own the company, Dominic. I had a job to return to."

"But I wanted you to stay." If only he could tell her how he really felt about her.

"What was so important that you came all the way here to tell me?" she asked. "You stalked me at the bar."

"I didn't stalk you." He shrugged. "Well, maybe I did. A little."

"You came out here all the way to speak to me. But when I wanted to see you that day in your office, you couldn't wait to get rid of me. What's so important all of a sudden?"

He braced himself. The news would hit her like a tsunami

and he was going to make sure she didn't get swept away and drown. "That day ... that day in the office, I didn't know what to expect from you. You were the one who left the villa, Eleni. I wanted you to stay with me, but you're still in ... your boyfriend ... I understand your regret."

She shifted forward, her eyes wide with confusion. "My regret?"

What else would it be? She was still pining for the man. "I asked you to stay, and when you didn't, I assumed that ..." He had never been in the position of having to explain himself. He'd never been in the position where he'd had to compete with a dead man, but there was no point in harping on about things he couldn't change. "Hector Galatis came to see me earlier."

She rolled her eyes. "And what? You're blaming your bad mood on Hector? You can't keep blaming others, Dom. You can't keep blaming your father, your brother, your business rivals, the air conditioning units, the sun ... each time something doesn't work out the way you want."

"I'm not blaming anyone."

"Then why are you telling me that Hector came to see you? What do I care? You wanted me out of your office, and all I wanted was to see you again. I missed you."

His breath stilled in his chest and his lungs stopped working. It was possible that he had misheard, that he was about to have a seizure or something.

"You ... *missed me,* did you say?"

"Do you just want me to repeat it again for the sake of it? Yes, I missed you." She reached over and placed her empty glass on the bedside cabinet. "I didn't know how to be around you. I slept with my boss. You might not care about how it looks, but you're my boss, Dominic. I'm on a short term contract. I'm just an employee."

"You're so much more than that."

She stopped and stared at him, her lips twisting, a crease in her brow. She seemed to be having an internal crisis about what to say. She sank back against the headboard, resigned, as if she'd been defeated. "It might have taken me a few days to realize it, but I missed you. I wanted to be with you, Dominic. I loved the night we had."

Holy shit.

She frowned. "When you returned to the office, I wanted to tell you that I regretted not staying with you, and if I could have had that moment again I would have done things differently."

"At the villa?"

"With you, I don't care where it was. I don't need villas and yachts to make me happy."

He flinched and raked a hand through his hair as he paced the room, his insides in turmoil. He had so many things to tell her, and none of them were good. He rewound her words in his mental playlist, needing the reassurance. "You would have stayed with me?"

She nodded, her brows pushing together as if she didn't understand why he was having such difficulty grasping this.

"And ..." He couldn't bring himself to say his name. "What about your ... the ... reason behind your expedition?"

She pulled the duvet off. "It's hot in here." She fanned her face. Her sea-green strappy summer dress had ridden up and revealed legs long and golden. His cock twitched. One of her straps had fallen down, and he longed to run his hand along her soft skin and put the strap back.

But there lay a danger in such thoughts. He was caught in a dilemma. Torn by duty to family and his feelings for Eleni.

She stood up and stretched, causing her strap to fall further down her arm. She was a sultry picture; bedraggled, looking sexy, scantily clad even though she was fully clothed. A bare shoulder, long, long legs. He wanted to wake up to her every morning, like this.

She walked to the windows and opened the blinds. The blue morning light with only a hint of yellow poured into the room.

"Your expedition," he prompted, desperate for an answer.

"I don't know myself if I want to do it. Whenever I think about it, I feel guilty. I feel like I'm cheating on Jonas, but I can't be because ... because he's not here."

"Cheating because?"

"Must you make me say it? Must you be so cruel?" She turned around. "Why do you think, Dominic?"

She was still in love with her boyfriend. "It's not cheating if he still has your heart." It killed him to say it, but she'd only wanted Dominic for the sex. For his cock, not his heart.

"Is that what you think?"

He couldn't answer her.

"What is so important you had to come looking for me?"

He had to tell her. She needed to know.

But he needed to make sure. If he was going to do the right thing he had to be certain, because a hair slide by itself was no guarantee of the fact.

"Hector Galatis came into my office that day, before you did."

"Miranda warned me that you were in a grumpy mood."

"Hector turning up made it worse."

"You didn't get the deal?"

"I'm closer to it. He seems interested, give or take a few minor points but we might potentially have a deal."

"You did it! You got what you wanted."

"Did I?"

"Yes! You just said you did. You've come so far. Galatis sounds like he's giving you what you want."

"I don't know."

"What don't you know?" She squinted. "Why weren't you happy, when he came to see you that day?"

"Because he didn't talk much about the deal. He talked about you."

"Me?" Her eyes turned huge. "Did he figure out that I work for you?" She placed a hand against the wall.

Dominic waved her remark away. It didn't matter. "He was most intrigued about your hair accessory."

"My hair slide?"

He nodded. "He said it was a custom piece, one of a kind, that he'd given to someone once."

The color drained from her face, she leaned against the wall as if she needed something to steady her, then, slowly, she slid down it until she was on the floor.

"Maybe ... maybe he ... maybe there were other pieces made ... and this wasn't..." Her voice was a whisper. He could see the cogs of her brain whirring, could see the shock splintering through her.

She put a hand to her neck. He rushed to her side and crouched on the floor, taking her hand in his. Waiting for her ... A gut-wrenching shock like this took time to sink in and digest.

"You think Hector Galatis is my father?" she whispered.

"I don't know for sure ... but he could be ..."

Her head rolled back and she stared up at the ceiling. "He told my mother to get rid of me. He didn't want me."

"I've never really liked the man, and now I hate him more than ever." He slid her fallen dress strap back into place but couldn't move his hand away. Didn't want to. His fingers closed around her bare arm gently.

"He discarded my mother when she was pregnant. What kind of a man does that? My mother said he had a wife and..." Eleni clapped a hand to her mouth. "I met his wife," she whispered, looking distraught. "She was ... nice."

"We have to be sure, Eleni." He stroked her cheek, unable to help himself.

"You think Hector Galatis could be my father, potentially?" Her voice turned faint. "I think I'm going to be sick." She bent her knees, then hunched over, her face in her hands. He rushed to fetch the wastepaper bin.

"He was a married man, with a family," he heard her say. "I don't know what to do. I don't know how to ask my mother."

He placed the bin near her. "Do you want to get some fresh air?"

"No-I ... this is a shock." She seemed so frail and so broken. "I feel like I've been hit by a yacht, and there is nothing left of me."

He cupped her face, his insides emptying. "Don't say that. I want to take care of you, I ... I don't want you to face this alone." She didn't hear him, or perhaps his words were more white noise in the sea of her misery.

He was going to stay by her side no matter what she had to say about it. "Your mother has the answer, but ..." He stroked the back of her head, worried, because he'd never seen her like this before.

Not even Ioannis had been able to make her feel so low. "Do you want to know, the truth?"

Because if she didn't, there was no need for it. He would have to make his decision blind.

"I don't want anything from Galatis. I don't want him in my life, but I want to know the truth. It's time my mother told me who my father is."

CHAPTER FORTY-EIGHT

ELENI

Dominic wouldn't let her walk back home alone in the early hours.

Eleni couldn't remember if he had always been this protective about her, or if it was something recent, but it made her feel cherished, and that gave her some solace.

Her life had become the stuff of soap operas; the sort of show her mother would watch if it ended up as a show on TV.

But this was her life, and she was suddenly weary of facing more curveballs. What was supposed to have been just a short term job in Athens, had now resulted in something much bigger, with life-changing consequences.

She'd fallen in love with Dominic, had moved on with her life, and now she stood at the precipice of discovering who her father could be. That there a possibility it might be Hector Galatis, one of the richest men in Greece, made her insides hollow out at the thought.

The irony of it, if it were true.

She had despised the rich, until she'd fallen in love with Dominic, and now one of the richest men in all of Greece might turn out to be her father.

"Of all the men, in all of Greece, it had to be him." She turned to Dominic. "Are you... is this...?" She tilted her head, because the coincidences were too many.

"What?"

Involved, somehow, she wanted to say. In the silence that followed, she tried to think it through. How it was all tied together. Dominic and Galatis, and her. It was either a conspiracy, or fated, her and Dominic meeting, but her brain was fogged over and she couldn't quite work it out.

"Why did you give Miranda your watch?"

"I don't honestly know. I wasn't thinking straight. I don't think straight when you're around." His voice was at a lower frequency, one which only her heart could hear and make meaning of.

"But—"

"I guess it was some sort of ransom. I take you and give them my watch. But you're much more precious than the watch, than anything I could ever own." Silence hung in the air while she absorbed his words and let them seep into her.

He'd come all this way to tell her face to face when he could have summoned her to his office instead. That had to mean something. She *wanted* it to mean something. Now she understood why he'd been cold to her that day. She was reeling from the news herself and could see how much of a shock it must have been for Dominic. Maybe he felt torn, about the deal, about Galatis? She hoped not.

They stopped at the door of her apartment building. Dominic's eyes were dark, the shadows under them making him look haggard and suddenly so much older. Her heart softened. She wanted to put her arms around him and forget the mess that was her life, the landscape of ruins she'd been trying to navigate these last few years.

She wanted the bubble that had been Santorini. The magic and music of being adored by Dominic Steele, even if just for a night. He had cherished her like no other and now that she'd had a taste, she wanted it for always.

"I have to do this, alone."

"I know." That muscle flexed along his jawline again. "I'm going back to Athens. You take all the time you need. Paid, of course."

A small fissure formed in her heart. "It's not always about the money, Dominic."

"I know. I just want to make sure that you're okay."

There was so much unsaid between them, and it seemed rude to walk inside and leave him. She didn't know whether to shake his hand or touch his arm. Or ...

"Goodbye, Eleni. Good luck."

She took a deep breath and walked in.

Her mother was up, floating around in her short nightie, a cup of coffee in her hands. "This is late, Eleni. It must have been a good night." She patted the space on the small sofa beside her. Eleni walked over and sat, her heart in her throat.

"Where are your friends, Leni?

Miranda.

She'd forgotten all about Miranda and Stefanos. Stefanos would have taken Miranda back to his place.

"Mama, I want to ask you something. Is Hector Galatis my father?"

DOMINIC

He was back in Athens by noon, minus the Rolex he wasn't sure why he'd given to Miranda.

He'd wanted to stay in Spetses, stick around, be there for Eleni in case she needed him, but he didn't want her to feel pressured. It was best that he left her alone to deal with the juggernaut of shock he'd hit her with. Discovering her father's identity was a minefield of emotions, but knowing he could be Hector Galatis, made things so much more difficult to come to terms with.

He'd walked her back to her home in the early hours of the morning because as soon as he'd told her about Hector, Eleni hadn't wanted to talk more.

The news had crushed her, and he sensed she needed to speak to her mother. For the next few days, he tried to focus on his work as well as shield questions from his father, and Alexander, and Hector, who wanted to know where he and Hector were with the deal.

Eleni had texted him to say she was taking a few days of leave, but he had no idea when she would return, or what the news she had would be.

Patience wasn't his strong suit, and his mood was as crabby as ever.

Seeing Miranda back at work on Monday had made for an awkward moment. But when she'd silently returned his Rolex to him, he got the feeling that she would keep quiet about all she had heard. Though she would probably give Eleni a hard time about it.

While he waited to hear from Eleni, he would arrange to meet with Helen and go through the Galatis' deal, just in case.

ELENI

"Shame you can't host me an engagement party on your yacht."

Dominic leaned in and kissed Helen on the cheek again. "Congratulations. Getting engaged in Venice is about as romantic as it gets."

"Not that you'd know. You're not the marrying type, Dominic. Pity, really." She slowly let go of his hand.

Eleni stared at them both, her fingers on the doorknob. "I'm sorry but I thought ... I thought I heard you say I could come in." She felt like a fool, embarrassed and silly. But, surprisingly, the smile didn't slip from Dominic's face. It widened, his eyes filling with concern as he strode towards her.

"Helen got engaged in Venice," he explained, as the lawyer dutifully showed off her ice cube sized ring.

"Con-congratulations." Eleni's mouth dried up. "I'm ... really happy for you."

"Thank you." Helen picked up her briefcase. "Galatis has agreed to your proposal, and he is happy with the terms. We should sign. Or do you want to run this by your father first?"

Dominic hesitated as he smoothed down his tie. "I've got this. Leave it with me."

Helen flashed Eleni a smile and moved past her with a grace that Eleni could only dream of.

Dominic closed the door behind her and turned to her, his eyes searching her face. He reached out, and for a moment she thought he was about to take her hand, but any happiness she'd felt at wanting to see him had vanished when she'd walked in.

Fresh into work, and late, arriving mid-morning, she'd felt

compelled to share her news with Dominic. But she hadn't been prepared for what she'd heard.

"There is nothing going on between me and Helen," he said, mistaking the reason for her silence.

"I know."

"Are you okay?"

"I was okay."

"Come," he gently took her by the arm towards the seat opposite his desk. "Sit down. I've ..." He stopped abruptly, then perched on the corner of the desk.

"You've?"

"I've missed you. I ... was worried about you." Not only did he look somber, but there were tiny lines at the corners of his eyes that she hadn't noticed before.

She sat, feeling wooden and stiff, trying to reconcile the warm feeling in her stomach before she'd knocked on his door, to how she felt now.

"Hector Galatis is my father."

He let out a sigh. "Jesus. It's true then?" He leaned over and took her hands in his, asked her a million questions about how she was, was she okay, how her mother was, what her mother said. She recounted it all like a robot reading a speech from a teleprompter.

It hadn't taken a lot get the answer. Eleni had simply asked her, "Is Hector Galatis my father?"

When her mother had replied, "How do you know?" She'd gotten her answer. They talked for hours, first her mother, reliving that time in her youth when she had been in love with the monster, and then Eleni had told her mother everything, about Dominic, the son of a billionaire, how they had met, and how good he'd been to her. About how he'd captured her heart, about how she was falling in love with him, and how she was forgetting Jonas. She'd told her about the fake date for the wedding, and how she'd gone away with Dominic to Santorini. It had all come hurtling out, the things she'd kept inside her, the things she'd wanted to tell her friends, but hadn't been able to.

She'd cried in her mother's arms, talking about Dominic, blurting out all the ways in which he made her angry, and irritated, and happy, and all the ways he'd shown her kindness. How he always seemed to want the best for her.

Her mother had listened, stroking her hair and holding her. It seemed at last as if her mother had become the mother Eleni had always wanted.

News of Hector Galatis had fallen to the wayside.

Eleni didn't know the man, except what little she had seen and heard from Dominic, and the little she had seen at the wedding. Now she felt sorry for his wife, the lovely woman he had cheated on.

She also had half-siblings, but she would never know them, had no desire to know them, or be a part of that world.

She didn't tell Dominic about her confession to her mother, only what he wanted to know, the confirmation about Galatis.

And now she was coming to terms with what she'd heard Helen say. It was one shock after another. Galatis being her father meant nothing to her, and she'd been eager to come and tell Dominic, only, now she wasn't sure what to make of this new revelation.

"You're upset, I know this must come as a huge shock to you."

She was barely cognizant of Dominic's hands on hers because her mind was trying to work it all out. She wanted to catch him red-handed. "You said you didn't own a yacht."

His brow creased. "I don't."

"Then why did Helen ask you to throw her an engagement party on your yacht?"

He looked confused. "How many times do I have to tell you that Helen and I don't have anything? We've never had anything." He wiped a hand over his face, understanding dawning in his expression. "That night when I told you I was going to see her, that night you'd sprained your ankle and you stayed at my place—I lied. I went to the office to work, maybe get some sleep. I lied because I didn't want to make you feel uncomfortable, and I sensed you might feel that way spending the night at my house if I stuck around."

He did what? Now she was confused. "You lied about going to her place?"

The skin around his eyes tightened. "Men hit on you, Eleni. They make advances. I've seen it. I didn't want you to feel uncomfortable. You didn't want to stay at my place, but I thought you should, it was the right thing to do given..." he gestured at her foot. "I did it because I didn't want you to be uneasy."

So, he'd lied about going to Helen's. *Okaaaay.* "I asked you once, and you told me you didn't have a yacht." She wasn't going to let this go.

Just when she thought there might be a way for them to be together, he'd gone and messed it up. She hated people who lied even more than she hated billionaires with yachts.

Dominic's gaze shifted to the floor, the surest sign yet of his unease. "She said it was a shame I couldn't host a party for her. Meaning, I don't have a yacht, not now." He gave her a peculiar look and she prepared for it, her muscles hardening, getting ready for the hit.

"My family used to have a yacht. It was called The Dream Princess." His gaze held steady as the name reverberated somewhere deep in the dark basement of her memories.

She knew that name.

The Dream Princess. The mere mention of it made her nauseous. The memories rushed back like a tidal wave and she struggled to breathe, her chest seizing up, her lungs filling with rage.

And then, like a thunderbolt ... she understood.

That was Dominic's family's yacht. "You knew?" Eleni's breathing turned shallow. The Dream Princess had been the yacht where the party had taken place, the one where the drunken guests had gone into the water on jet skis, and crashed into Jonas, killing him.

"Stefanos told me."

"When?"

"That first day we met. I didn't understand why he pleaded with me to not call the manager."

Dominic had known all along. From that moment in the taverna, even before Ioannis assaulted her on the yacht. Dominic had known. He might not have known her, but he knew *who* she was.

"But we sold it. We sold it right after the accident." He paused as if he was waiting for the news to sink in.

There had been compensation for Jonas' family, but his family were broken. They would never be whole again. There were some things which money could not buy, and nothing would bring Jonas back.

Nausea made her gut shrivel, her head dizzy, her breathing hard. He'd held back a huge secret, and she'd gone and fallen in love with him. If she'd known, she would never have gone near him. "Is that why you felt sorry for me? Why you offered me the job?"

He looked away, as if needing time to weigh his response. It was a few moments before he could face her again.

"I felt bad for you. When we met at the taverna, I was on my way out when Stefanos told me. That's when I realized."

"And, what?" This was the worst. Even discovering who her father was, a man who had played no part of her life, a man she'd never known until now, wasn't so bad in comparison to this news.

She had feelings for Dominic, but now she'd discovered that she'd slept with the man who had been indirectly responsible for Jonas' death. If it weren't for him and his wretched family, the billionaires flaunting their wealth in their big fancy yachts, Jonas might still be alive today.

"Were you there?"

"What?"

"Were you there when it happened?"

"Yes."

"And did you stop the party? Or did you and your family finish enjoying your canapes first?"

He clenched his eyes shut, gave a quick nod. "It wasn't like that. We didn't see it happen—"

"Lucky you. You were saved from that trauma, too."

"The area was filled with people getting hysterical and then the police and emergency services arrived—"

"It ruined your party. How upsetting for you all." She got up, her stomach turning queasy, her legs weak. There was only so much devastating news a person could take at any given time.

Dominic stood up, looking wretched. "Don't go. We need to talk about this."

"All this time you knew, and I had no idea. You felt sorry for me. That's why you were so nice to me and you did so many things for me. You were trying to get over your guilt." She waved her hand at him, halting him when he started to speak. "You might not have killed Jonas with your bare hands, but if you Steeles hadn't been here, my boyfriend would still be alive."

"That's not how life works, Eleni. We don't get a chance to rewind and go back and do things differently. I wish we could, and then you'd still have Jonas and we would have never met."

"I wish we could, too, because I would never have let myself fall for you."

His mouth fell open and she rushed away from him, not wanting to hear another word from him. "Don't go. Eleni, *don't*."

"Would you have ever told me?" She stood by the door.

"I've wanted to tell you for a long time."

She shook her head, a disbelieving snort coming from her. He'd had so many chances, so many moments when he could have come clean. It was only because she'd heard Helen that she and Dominic were having this conversation at all.

The man was a liar. She should never have trusted him.

CHAPTER FORTY-NINE

DOMINIC

He was a billionaire's son and heir to a billionaire fortune, along with his brother.

Money *should* have mattered.

And yet, in the scheme of things, nothing mattered except doing the right thing. He knew in his heart what that was. It was to walk away from Galatis, and to throw away the deal he had been working so hard on.

He didn't want to do business with the man. The cheating, lying, so-called family man with a wife and children who had then had an affair—maybe one of many—and who'd told his mistress to abort their baby.

The baby which had grown up to be Eleni.

There would be consequences for him. His father would be disappointed, but perhaps not surprised. Alexander would be rubbing his hands in glee. Dominic wouldn't get the twenty-five percent stake in the business, but he didn't care about that.

He could draw a line under this chapter and put it behind him. Forget about Eleni, the girl who had stolen his heart, without her even knowing about it. He could try to move on.

He picked up the phone, bracing himself for the confrontation that would surely come when he told his father that the deal was off.

ELENI

Eleni didn't want to deal with Miranda, on top of everything that had happened. Having to explain herself, confess that she had lied and gone away with Dominic, and worse, had slept with the man Miranda adored, no. She did not want to face such questions. She already felt guilty, and wretched and a bad friend.

But Miranda had persisted, and off they went to lunch. Her insides churned at the way Miranda stared at her, as if she could X-ray into her brain and see everything that had taken place on that fateful weekend. Eleni blushed just thinking about it. "Why are you looking at me like that?" she asked Miranda.

"Are you going to tell me?"

"Tell you what?"

"Everything."

She couldn't lie or deny it, not to Miranda, and yet, she didn't want anyone to know, not at the workplace. And Miranda was a workplace colleague.

No. Miranda was her friend.

She squeezed her eyes shut. "Hector Galatis is my father,

and I went with Dominic to the wedding, not Helen. I slept with him. I think I'm in love with him."

She didn't dare open her eyes, expecting to hear cutlery dropping, or a glass falling over, or some other manifestation of Miranda's surprise.

But there was only silence, and the sound of cicadas in the midday heat. She opened one eye, then the other. Miranda was still eating. This was a good sign. Her appetite hadn't been affected by this breaking news.

Then, after she had chewed her mouthful thoughtfully and swallowed, "I had a feeling something was going on. It was nothing you both said, but I sensed it. Looking back, it all makes sense, how you both left work early that weekend and came back tanned at the same time. You don't have to be Hercule Poirot to work it out." Miranda waved her hand between them. "It doesn't matter."

"I'm sorry," Eleni said. Her appetite vanished in a flash and she couldn't eat her lunch.

Miranda looked at the untouched fried zucchini balls and salad on Eleni's plate, and Eleni wondered if her friend had even heard her. Maybe Miranda was suffering from acute heartache which had somehow rendered her temporarily deaf. "You have it." She pushed her plate towards her friend.

Miranda gladly accepted it. "That's how you stay so thin and me so—"

"Voluptuous."

They smiled at one another.

"It just happened, I'm not sure how it happened..." Eleni struggled to find a gentle way to make her confession and wondered if she should stop talking altogether.

Miranda's frown deepened. "You don't know how you ended up in bed with Dominic and had sex with him? It just *happened?*"

She replayed it again, the events of that weekend, as she had many times since. The pool, the two of them talking, sipping lemonade, getting in the pool, and ending up in her bed. It had been the best sex of her entire life. She stared at the table, her cheeks heating.

"I'm your friend, Eleni. I'm happy for you. I have fantasized about that man because ... how could anyone not? Have you seen that gorgeous butt of his? But it was all just a fantasy and nothing more. There is no way that Dominic Steele and I would ever be together. Not even in parallel universes."

It was clear to her that Miranda was trying to put on a brave front. But what she'd just said, also rang true for Eleni. Never would she have ever thought of her and Dominic together. And yet when it had happened, it was so natural, like life taking its course. Him coming to Spetses to break the news about Galatis, even after things had turned cold between them, was the kind of thing someone who cared would do.

Maybe it wasn't insane for the two of them to be together. What seemed insane was being apart.

Miranda continued. "I've walked in on him when he's stripped off his shirt. The man can't stand the heat, lucky for us, and if you time it right, about ten minutes after he walks in from a meeting, usually with Galatis—" She stopped. "Did you say...? Did you ... is Galatis your father? Did I make that up?" Her friend's face turned a multitude of expressions. "Am I going mad? I did make that up. The shock of Dom being unfaithful must have mashed up my brain—"

"You heard right."

A zucchini ball fell from Miranda's fork. "Are you sure?"

"My mother is."

Miranda leaned forward and reached for Eleni's hands,

shaking her head as she gazed at her with sorrowful eyes. "My dear Eleni. This is ... a bigger shock than you and Dominic being together."

"We're not together. We just slept together."

Miranda fanned her face. "Do I get any details on that?"

Eleni's insides quivered. She was lost again, her feelings for Dominic constantly flip-flopping between hate and desire.

"Forget I said that." Miranda crunched on another zucchini ball. "Tell me everything else, from the beginning, but slow down. I can only take one piece of drama at a time."

Eleni let out a breath. It was so difficult to say it all out loud and there was so much Miranda didn't know—about Jonas, and the yacht, and her Mount Kilimanjaro climb. Now was the time to tell her.

She did so, slowly, and Miranda listened to it all.

CHAPTER FIFTY

DOMINIC

He dreaded the knock on the door, of Eleni coming in and handing in her resignation.

He'd been waiting for it, his heart jolting each time someone knocked or came into his office.

He'd stayed out of her way. She'd stayed out of his. He'd told Miranda he wanted no interruptions, unless it was Eleni, and he'd stayed in his office working hard on the new deal he was formulating.

Whatever Eleni decided, he would respect her decision. Her contract was up next month, but it could be extended if that's what she wanted. He had a proposal for her in case she was interested.

Just as he'd known, he'd had to hear it all from his father, how disappointed he was. Dominic hadn't fully disclosed the real reasons for not wanting to do business with Galatis. He wasn't sure he'd convinced his father of the dangers of relying on one egotistical man, that he hadn't liked the way Galatis had messed him around, that maybe creating a consortium of a few smaller but likeminded companies might be the better way to go.

His father had listened, and that had been a good sign. "Make it happen," his father had ordered. "And don't come home until it's done."

Dominic worked hard at putting the new deal together and braced himself for the networking and negotiating it would entail. At least it served as a good distraction from the problems in his personal life.

He'd been looking forward to discussing work matters with Nikolaos when the man finally returned to work next month, but that plan had altered too, catching him off guard completely.

When the knock on the door came, he stared at it, immobile, not daring to breathe, dreading Eleni coming in and telling him the bad news.

Last thing on a Friday afternoon would be the perfect time to tell him she was leaving.

But he heard voices, and none of them belonged to Eleni.

Miranda shouted. "Mr. Galatis, Dominic expressly insisted he didn't want—"

"I demand to see that man!" It was a roar.

Galatis.

Oh. Fuck. Now he wished he hadn't sent a confirmation that he was withdrawing his offer to work with the man. He should have waited until Monday.

Dominic marched to the door, frustration battling with rage and unleashing an ugly fury.

Miranda's flushed face greeted him. She was trying, unsuccessfully, to wedge herself between the door and Galatis.

Dominic hated that the man had put her in such an awful position. "It's okay, Miranda. Thank you. I'll deal with this." His eyes fixed on Galatis. "Hector." He opened the door wider, letting the man in.

"You are not happy?" the old man bellowed, settling himself into the chair with remarkable speed. "You haven't changed the seating. This is most uncomfort—"

"There's no need for me to change the seating, Hector. We won't be doing business together."

"You are making a mistake, Dominic. I agreed to all your terms. I gave you what you wanted."

"I can't do a deal with the devil."

The old man glared at him, before he started coughing, and it soon turned into a fit.

Dominic hoped he wouldn't keel over and die. He already had enough shit to deal with.

It took a long, painful minute for the coughing to subside. Dominic poured the old man a glass of water and handed it to him.

"Your brother has been calling me." Hector took a few sips and returned the glass.

"Alexander can be so predictable." Dominic had expected this. Nice to know his assumptions had been proven right.

"But I refused to take his calls."

This was a surprise.

Galatis spluttered into his handkerchief.

Oh, Jesus. Dominic looked at his watch. He had important things to deal with. Galatis was in his past now.

"Your father can't be happy with you," Galatis challenged.

He wasn't. Dominic didn't stand to get his twenty-five per cent stake of the company, because he hadn't proved himself. He wasn't allowed to return to the US because Nikolaos wasn't coming back to the company, and Dominic would have to stay there until a suitable replacement was found.

This wasn't the hardship his father expected it to be. Dominic got to stay in Greece for longer, and while he was here, he planned to get his own deal going with a consortium of smaller companies. "I won't do business with you, Hector. It goes against all of my principles."

"Principles!" The old man barked. His face was unreadable, as if Dominic had compounded his misery and confusion tenfold. He was sure that few men had ever turned down the chance to do business with the so-called great man. "Principles do not matter as much as you think."

"But they do, Hector. They do, to me. You had the audacity to tell me that behind every successful man is a strong woman. You told me you were a family man, that everything you did in your rag-to-riches story, was for them."

"It was!" The old man's eyes glittered with indignation.

"You are the worst example of a family man. You are the worst kind of man."

Galatis's mouth opened, his face turned red, and then, just as Dominic was worried he might erupt and explode, he said, "This is about the girl, isn't it?"

Dominic lifted his chin, wishing this man all kinds of torture.

"It is true, then. She is who I think she is."

Dominic bit down on his teeth, fighting for composure.

"I am a man of principle, Hector, and she is the woman I love."

"You are stupid to stand by your principles." The man slumped back in the chair. "You love ... my daughter?" he asked, apprehensively.

"She's not your daughter. For that to be true would mean that you cherished her, that you wanted her in the first place and that you raised her. Any man can be a father, but it takes someone special to be a dad. You are not that man."

"Don't ever call me your daughter."

Eleni was in the room.

Dominic spun around. He'd had his back to the door, and now he felt the color drain from his face as he turned around. How long had she been here? How much had she heard? He'd been so wrapped up in dealing with the man's coughing fit he hadn't even heard her come in.

Galatis started to cough again, the dry cough quickly turning into a loud, chesty, coughing fit. Staring at Eleni, he handed the man the glass of water again, not taking his eyes off the woman who stood before him, in a smart summer dress.

God, how much he loved her in it. How much he loved her.

When the coughing stopped, he and Eleni were still looking at one another, their gazes locked, a lifetime of words unsaid between them.

Galatis turned his attention to Eleni. "Your mother …how is she?"

"My mother wants nothing to do with you, and you don't deserve to even say her name."

"But—"

"Stop. No more." Dominic edged towards Eleni, as if he somehow needed to protect her from this man even now. "You should go, Hector. This is obviously taking a toll on your health."

"The deal, Dominic. Don't make a foolish mistake. We can do great things together."

"I'm not, and we won't. I'll make sure The Steele Corporation never does business with you again.

"How will you? You have disappointed your father and your brother—"

"I wouldn't trust too much what Alexander tells you."

"You are making a mistake. The Galatis name means something here in this country."

"People don't know what I know."

"Business is always without principles, Dominic. Men don't get to where I am by being pure and good." He stood up slowly, staring at Eleni as if he needed to imprint her face in his memory. Dominic wanted nothing more than to put his arm around her protectively, hug her close to him.

But he couldn't. He had no claim on her. She hated him.

But still, he worried about her.

"Leave, Hector. Do the decent thing by Eleni now."

Galatis looked at Eleni for a long time, something sad unfurling in those puffy eyes. "I was happy with your mother ... I just couldn't..."

Dominic resisted the urge to stuff his fist down the man's mouth. To shut him up. To stop him. But this was likely the last time Eleni would ever see him, and she seemed to want to listen to what he had to say.

"My mother is very happy, and in love. She has never talked about you, until recently, and even then it was to give me that gift you gave her. You occupy no space in my mother's mind or heart. She doesn't think of you."

Galatis shuffled slowly towards the door looking like a man burdened. Whether it was by regret, or because of the choices he'd made, Dominic doubted that Eleni even cared to know.

"You are young and consumed by emotion, Dominic. My door is open to you. Come and see me when you are calmer."

ELENI

B reath charged up her throat. Her heart thundered.
Lately, every visit to Dominic's office was filled with
so many life-changing moments.

He loved her.

That's what he'd said.

Dominic, the man she was in love with had uttered the
words she'd only dreamed of hearing.

"Why aren't you doing the deal with Hector?" *With my
father*.

The words didn't feel right. Because they weren't right.
Hector Galatis would never be her father. He'd done the deed
to help conceive her, but he had no more claim to her than
any other random stranger.

If there was a love that lifted, a love that was bottomless
and deep, a love that had the power to transform, it came from
this man who stood before her, his eyes filled a steely
determination as if he wanted to put things right.

"I can't." Dominic closed the door, and it was just the two
of them now.

"Because of me?"

"Yes."

She wouldn't let him throw it all away just because of
what Galatis had done. Dominic had worked for this. It had
been painful watching him run around after the old man, and
now Galatis sounded eager to sign off on the deal. She
stepped towards Dominic. "You can't let this go," she pleaded.
"Not now, not because of me."

His eyes softened when he looked at her. He wasn't as
good at hiding his emotions. Not anymore. Or perhaps she
was just better at reading him.

"It's my choice. You don't get a say in this, Eleni."

"But I don't care what he did. That's in the past. That man will never be a part of my life, so why does it matter?"

"It matters to me."

Her stomach twisted into knots. It mattered to her that he didn't lose the deal on account of her. His family was waiting for him to fail and she would not let him. After everything he had done for her, she would not let him fail on the matter of principle and high morals for something that she didn't care about.

Galatis was a nobody in her life.

She moved towards Dominic, swallowing the space between them, and yet, stopped herself short. Even now, being around him was potent. Electric. Her body was already reacting.

Damn this man.

"What did your father say?" *And Alexander.* Eleni didn't want to think about what his brother would have made of this.

"It doesn't matter," Dominic replied, his voice monotone.

"It matters to you, Dominic. Does your father know the truth? That you are putting emotions before logical reasoning?" She was worried that he was making a bad mistake.

"My family isn't happy with me. I didn't give the real reason for calling the deal off. Not yet. I don't want to drag you into it. But I plan to work on something that could be a better solution."

"What solution?" She hadn't planned to face Dominic just yet. She was going to go home for the weekend again, to clear her thoughts when Miranda had told her that Galatis had come to see Dominic again.

Her contract ended next month and she had saved up more than enough to climb the mountain.

For her, for Jonas, and to put the past behind her.

"Are you okay?" he asked, tipping his head back and looking at her through his lashes, making her stare up at him. Her heart began to plummet again. Being around Dominic had the same effect as being on a rollercoaster and freefalling from a great height. Her insides churned and twisted and then became light and lithe again.

With one word or one look he could make her feel so many things. This man possessed her body and soul, and had the ability to change her moods and thoughts without even knowing.

"Why did you come in here? I didn't want you to ever have to face Galatis again." Then his eyes widened. "Or did you come to see me?"

There was hope in his voice.

"Deflection is your superpower, Dominic. You haven't answered my question." She'd picked through fragments over their conversations, and had seen how deftly he avoided answering the important questions. "What solution were you talking about? For the deal?"

He didn't have long left here. He'd told her he was only here for the summer. What could he fix in such a short time?

He started to roll up his sleeves and her insides bottomed out. She could not lose her head now even as images of the pool and Dominic in it flashed past her.

"I'm working on another deal, involving more companies. It's better to have more and to spread the risk rather than to rely on the main man at the top. A wise woman gave me that piece of advice once." The corners of his lips twitched, as if he was trying his best to stop himself from smiling.

But she couldn't help it. She smiled, and once more her gaze went to his lean and muscly forearms. They'd held her once. How could she ever forget lying in bed with his arms wrapped around her?

He looked at her as if she were the only thing that mattered, as if he needed her as much as air itself. She dragged her gaze up to his eyes. His brows pushed together.

He knew.

She had a thing about his forearms and he *knew.* Mercifully, she had the presence of mind, just about, to stop herself from chewing her lower lip.

Because that would really give the game away.

And because he knew, he stepped closer to her and started to slowly roll up the cuff of his other sleeve.

Her gaze lingered over the bare skin. She almost let out a sigh.

"I'm sorry you had to see Galatis again," he murmured.

"I don't feel anything for him," she managed to say, forcing her eyes level with his face. "Which is why I don't want you to give up the deal with him."

"I won't work with him, Eleni. This is my deal, and I have time to fix it."

Time?

She inched closer, because she was most interested, because she wasn't sure she'd heard right. And because his cologne was so utterly familiar and intoxicating. He slowly, deliberately, annoyingly rolled his sleeve up revealing his other forearm. She was consumed by the urge to smack her lips and kiss it all over, like the uninhibited creature she suddenly became whenever he was around.

"You said this was for the summer," she whispered. Suddenly, she was back in that bed lying flush against his chest. His arms like a protective band around her.

She wanted that again.

"Nikolaos isn't coming back. He helped his wife recover from breast cancer. She's doing well, but he doesn't want to return to work. He said something that stuck with me. He said you can't buy time, and that he wanted to make the most of every moment he had with his wife. "

"She's going to be okay, isn't she?"

"She's going to be okay," he assured her.

"He's a wise man," she said, then, "What does this mean?"

"I have to stay here."

"In Athens?"

He nodded. "Unless you think Linus should take over?"

She didn't realize he'd moved closer until she was in a bubble of ocean breeze. So she did what any hot-blooded female standing next to Dominic Steele's forearms would do. She grabbed them and placed her hands over the veiny smooth surface.

He took a shuddering breath, unusual for a man of his poise. "Did you ... were you here to see me ... for something?" He was faltering. She loved that she had the power to make this man do that.

"Miranda told me Galatis was here. I had to come."

"Oh." He looked down, his stoic mask slipping.

"But I wanted to see you at some point, before the weekend."

He looked at her intently, his gaze bouncing from one eye to the other. "Why before the weekend?"

Her thumbs moved over his smooth skin, as if rubbing them would bring the genie out of the lamp and grant her wish to return to Santorini again. Dominic didn't make a move, didn't take charge, didn't reciprocate. He seemed to be battling with something inside of him, an intense look in his eyes.

"I'm sorry." He didn't wait for her to answer his question. "I'm sorry you found out the way you did, about my family's yacht."

"That's not why I came ..." That electric hum between

their bodies was back again, the zinging and zapping energy bouncing off their bodies.

"I have to explain."

"You don't, not right now."

"It's important. Don't you want to know why I lied?"

She'd done nothing but try to work out why he'd lied. Why he'd done what he did. And today, she wanted to tell him that she was ready to leave, sooner than her contract ended.

She'd planned to go home to work things out because she couldn't move forward in her life until she'd climbed the mountain. There was an expedition at the end of September she was considering going on.

Ending her contract early, next week, if he would let her, meant she could leave work and have time to get herself together, and prepare mentally and physically for the trip because once that was done, she could heal from whatever this had been between her and Dominic.

And in time, she would forget him, too.

That had been her aim when she had believed he would soon be returning to the US. But it sounded like his plans had also changed.

"Dominic, it's not important. I'm sure you had your reasons. I know whatever they were, they were good reasons, but you don't need to tell me." She didn't want to know why Dominic had lied to her because it didn't matter anymore. He was a good man, she knew that much, but him telling her anything more would make it that much harder for her to forget him.

He was breaking her heart, looking at her like that. As if he couldn't bear for her to leave this room without hearing him out.

"It's important for me to tell you. Please hear me out. Please."

"We're going our separate ways, Dominic." Her voice was a whisper. *Please let me treasure the memories we made.*

"Which makes it even more important." There was a pleading in his eyes. She relented with a shrug.

"Everything changed when your friend told me you were the girlfriend of the man who had been killed in that fatal accident. Your boyfriend's death didn't impact my family directly, yes, it was our yacht and those were our guests and they deserved to be punished but—"

"Punished," she scoffed bitterly. "People like you don't ever get punished." Those people hadn't done any time in jail —they had the money to buy themselves that outcome—but they'd paid a huge sum to Jonas' family.

Dominic lifted his hands to her face, framing it tenderly, as if she were a priceless painting. "It shook my family to the core. I know that means nothing. Who are we, after all? We weren't affected. We were able to move on."

She tried to look away, away from his intense gaze, and couldn't.

"I'm sorry. I'm *so* sorry for your loss, for what you had, for what you might have had, for the future that was stolen from you. I read about your boyfriend. I saw his picture, I could put a face to *his* name, but everyone else was forgotten, as if they're not important. But the truth is, the pain for the families and friends and loved ones is unbearable. It's unsurmountable. These people, people like you, they suffer the most." His voice wavered. "You don't get to see the damage done to the lives of the people left behind, of the broken and shattered remnants of what might have been, but when Stefanos told me, I realized who you were. I knew I could do something to make things as right as was possible. I wanted to do something. I couldn't bring your boyfriend back, but I was determined to do everything in my power to make things better for you."

A tear rolled down her cheek, and he wiped it away with his thumb. "I have spent the last few months trying to do just that." He leaned down and pressed his forehead against hers. His warm skin, his scent, his hold on her reassuring. Something she could get used to. "I wanted to make things right." His sweet breath kissed her ear and she fell into him, then. Buried her face in his chest, pressed against that wall of steel and heard his heartbeat.

They stayed like that, connecting, reclaiming, getting back together, until she pulled back a little, as much as his arms around her waist would let her, and looked up into his eyes. "That's all I wanted to do. To make your life better in every way I could. I just didn't expect to fall in love with you in the process. And yet, how could I not? I've never met anyone like you before. Funny, and brave, and smart, and ... there aren't enough words to describe how I see you."

Her heart swelled because this man had taken all her bitterness and erased it with his love.

She hadn't known it then, she'd just taken it all for granted, often feeling surprised that this man of steel who had been so hard on everyone else, had been so good to her.

It was as clear as dew on a fresh spring morning; how he had made it his mission, almost, to put things right.

Somehow he'd swallowed up the empty space between them, and now was a few inches from her, close enough that she could feel his skin, could sense that low thrum of electricity passing between them. His hands slid around her waist, his eyes boring into hers, daring her to tell him to stop.

Which she would never do.

Because the lies he'd told had been white lies; because

he'd wanted to help her. If she'd known who he was, she would never have allowed herself to go near him. She hadn't meant to fall in love with him but there was no way on earth she could have avoided it.

They had crash landed together.

Two continents apart.

Two different worlds.

And yet, they weren't so different, after all.

Fated.

As if it was meant to be.

She could not imagine her life without Dominic, not now that he had gone and told her all of this. She who had been prepared to walk away, could no longer do that because a love like his was as rare as it was priceless. In a life where she had hungered to feel loved and to belong, she'd found her knight in shiny aviators, even though she had despised him on first sight. Even though she hadn't been looking for him.

"Jonas was the first man to love me, to really love me. He made up for the love I hadn't really gotten from my mother. I've never known my father. But Jonas filled all my emptiness. When he died, a part of me died. I have the most beautiful memories of us, but I couldn't find it in me to love again. I never thought I would. My mother said I was silly, crying all the time. 'Stupid young love,' she called it. 'A love that ruins you.' But she's a bitter woman, she *was* a bitter woman and it's only now that I understand why. She said I couldn't grieve for him forever, and I don't now, not anymore. My heart was still in lockdown, until you came along."

He looked at her with eyes bright and shiny, and full of hope. "Me?"

"Yes. You." She paused, examining the starbursts in his eyes as if they were a new wonder of the world. Dominic was such a wonderful man, and he loved her. She'd heard it with her own ears. "I'm in love with you, Dominic."

"Yeah?" he asked, all playful, displaying his rare side. He nuzzled her lips as if he were too scared to do anything more, but then his tongue rolled over her lower lip, teasing, playing, slowly starting to drive her insane. He deepened the kiss, gently angling her face just so, his tongue sweeping her mouth and making her forget everything but this. He was demanding, controlling, urgent with need, and his tell-tale hardness a reminder of what was to come.

All he had to do was kiss her and she was gone. Her body turned into an inferno, a raging heat consuming her. She was deluding herself if she thought she could walk away from him, from this.

To what? An empty life, bereft of the passion he'd made her feel?

No.

She did not want to go back to that again.

She raked her hand through his hair, tugged it brazenly, not caring to tone down her desire. The warm familiarity of his scent, his skin, his breath, carried a reassurance that he was hers, he belonged to her, and that, maybe, they belonged together. That she would be okay, and he would be, too, and that whatever life threw at them, they could handle.

His mouth exploring hers turned her brain to jelly. His hardness poking her reminded her of that night, the one she wanted more of. She sighed against his lips and pressed her body to him, acknowledging, agreeing, giving in.

But ... she'd come in here for a reason.

The reason.

She pulled back. "You said you're not going back to the US yet?"

"Not for a while. My father believes he's punishing me by

keeping me here, but this is the best outcome I could have hoped for."

"But ..." But what? It didn't matter. Everything changed in the face of his revelations.

"You can stay here," he told her, his hands palming her bottom. Did he even know what he was doing? "We can be together if that's what you want—"

"What I want? What do you want?" She needed to hear it from his lips.

"I have my hands on your butt, what do you think I want?" He blinked. "It's...it's not that ... not the sex. Not *just* the sex, that's not it. That's not—"

She tiptoed up and kissed him.

"I want to be with you, Eleni. But if you want to leave here, we can still see each other. Spetses isn't that far." His hands stilled, as if their future together was a decision only she could make.

"I was going to climb Kili," she blurted out. Her goal stood before her, huge and unmoving, like the mountain itself, something she needed to do before she could let the past rest in peace.

Dominic pressed his forehead to her. "I understand. And you must. I'll still be here. Trying to create a consortium that holds bigger potential than Galatis, will take time."

"But you'll do it," she said, mumbling against his lips, the urge between her legs, heating and growing.

He laughed. "With no Galatis making me angry, I will."

They pulled back.

There was hope. A chance for something.

He seemed to hesitate. "And you ... depending on what you decide to do, I want you to know that your contract here can be made permanent. We have several positions open in the company and—you wanted to talk to me before the weekend," he stated, suddenly. "What happens at the weekend?"

"I was going to go home again." She searched his face. "But now, I'm not sure I want to ... leave..."

Their eyes locked. An understanding growing between them; one their bodies seemed aware of.

"You were going home because?"

"I needed time alone, to think. About Galatis, and you and everything else."

He frowned. "Sounds deep. You could do your thinking in Santorini. There is a villa with plenty of rooms, where you could be alone and do your thinking all day long, if you so needed. By the pool, even." His need for her glinted mischievously in his eyes.

Her carefully considered plans fell to the wayside. She'd once told him that if she'd had the chance to do it again, she would have stayed with him after the wedding. Dominic was offering her a chance now.

She had the opportunity to make things right with him. To show him how grateful she was for everything. To discuss the reality of what these changing circumstances meant for both of them.

"I would like that," she murmured. He claimed her mouth and sealed it with a passionate kiss that made her shudder. Desire coiled in her belly.

"I'll get Miranda to book the plane tickets." He winced. "Or maybe ... not."

"She's fine, with you and me, with *this*. She'll go to Spetses, without me. My friend Angeliki has threatened to set her up on a date."

"Wonderful." He kissed her again. "I have a better idea. Let's leave now."

"What?"

"Now. I have a meeting with Linus next, and I prefer to miss it. We can leave now. I'll get the tickets at the airport."

Of course he could. "Now?" she cried, incredulously. "What will people say?"

"I don't care, and neither should you." His palms rested along the sides of her face, warming her already heated skin. "Sometimes, Eleni, you have to decide what you want, and go for it."

That's what she had done, taking up his job offer, for different reasons back then, but it had led her to an unexpected outcome. A new direction for her life.

No more being stuck in limbo.

"I do know what I want." Her heart missed a beat again, because of the way he looked at her. "And I want you, Dominic."

EPILOGUE

Four months later ...

ELENI

F lames danced in the open fireplace as the housekeeper opened the door wide and welcomed them in. Dominic greeted her as if she were an old friend.

Eleni's nerves fluttered in her belly and apprehension steeled her gut. In an attempt to calm herself down, she focused on the rustic splendor of Dominic's parents' home in a place called Aspen.

Outside, everything was carpeted in a thick layer of lush snow. Even the trees were white, and as they passed huge mansions and hotels, from their log cabin not far from here, all she'd seen was white snow and fairy lights.

She felt like a child seeing a miracle for the first time.

She'd never seen snow before and her insides squealed like a class full of excited children.

It was all so new to her. She'd never been to the US before, and she'd just about recovered from spending a few days in New York in Dominic's penthouse there.

She looked around at the jeweled opaque chandeliers which were suspended from the high ceilings and gave a charming ambiance to the place. Family photos adorned the walls, and she squinted at what looked like pictures of the boys when they were young, eager to see them up close and properly later.

Dominic squeezed her hand again, reassuring her.

"Eleni," an older woman, striking, gorgeous, poised—everything she expected Dominic's mother to be—came towards her with outstretched arms and hugged and kissed her. "We meet at last. We have heard so much about you, dear."

"Hey, mom," Dominic went to kiss and hug his mother, but his mother came straight for Eleni.

"Nice to meet you, Mrs. Steele," Eleni said.

"We'll have no formality here. Please call me Susan."

"I have a little gift for you from Greece." Eleni held out a boxed gift set. She'd bought the finest honey, olives and olive oil from a quaint little shop in Athens. Dominic's mother gushed and told her she shouldn't have, then thanked her, and kissed her on the cheek again.

Next to her stood a man who looked much like she imagined Dominic might decades from now. He stretched out his hand. "Wonderful to meet you."

Knowing Dominic's history with his father, Eleni tried not to be too judgmental. Mr. Steele eyed her with what looked like trepidation. She wanted him to like her. She wanted to be accepted; for her sake, for Dominic's sake. Her heart stilled as he remained quiet, and then he took her hand in both of his. "I'm sorry, for your loss, Eleni."

"Dad," Dominic groaned in a strained voice.

"Honey." Susan nudged her husband lightly; a move which didn't go unnoticed by Eleni.

"It's ... it's okay," Eleni said, remembering the conversation she'd overheard a few days before, when she'd been looking for her panties which Dominic had ripped off the moment they'd walked in from dinner. Earlier, at a fancy restaurant near the Empire State Building, Dominic had been unable to keep his eyes off her cleavage. She'd deliberately worn a dress that showed off more than she usually would. She liked that Dominic wanted her. She loved the way he looked at her, and she lusted for the things he did to her.

They hadn't been able to keep their hands off one another once they returned home. A fast and frenzied bout of lovemaking followed, with Dominic holding her up against the wall, her legs wrapped around him as he slammed into her.

She'd later found her panties thrown carelessly over a lampshade and slipped them back on, not intending to eavesdrop, but unable to stop when Dominic's father had called, wanting to know about their travel plans to Colorado. Dominic had urged his father to not talk about the accident because he didn't want to upset Eleni.

"I'm sorry," Dominic's father repeated. "But I can't welcome you to my home, and not make any reference to what happened. My family is profoundly sorry for your terrible loss." His hands remained over hers, as if he needed her to hear his apology. In that instant, he didn't seem so scary.

"I appreciate that, Mr. Steele. Thank you, for saying that."

"Call him Robert, dear. He's not as important as he thinks

he is. Shall we have drinks?" Susan asked, gently pulling her husband away with a smile.

"Come and sit," Dominic suggested, keeping her firmly by his side. "You okay?" His eyes pierced into hers as they sat down on huge soft sofas in front of the roaring fire. Once more it felt as if there was just the two of them here. The fire, his parents, the sound of the champagne cork popping, all slipped into the background.

"Yes." She prayed he wouldn't kiss her. The man sometimes, but never in the office, mercifully, went into PDA mode, not caring who witnessed their public displays of affection.

Everything Dominic did was to protect her and to keep her safe. He hadn't offered to come on the climb with her, somehow understanding that she needed to do this alone.

But even when she'd climbed Mount Kilimanjaro a couple of months ago, she hadn't known his reach, his need to keep her safe.

It had taken her seven days to do it. The trekking agency she'd gone with was brilliant, and she hadn't needed to worry about food, water and camping equipment. She just had to cover enough ground every day, and she'd gone slowly, at a pace which suited her.

She'd become good friends with people she'd met there and whom she still kept in touch with because climbing Africa's tallest peak was an experience that had that kind of life-altering effect.

There were many times she thought of Jonas on that trip, of how different things would have been if he'd been here. Of how her life would have been if they had climbed the mountain together.

Living proof of how lives were so radically altered by a moment's recklessness, she had cried many tears when she reached the summit. Tears for Jonas, for a second burial of sorts, of putting him to rest but not forgetting him. Of not feeling guilty that she was here alone.

Her friends had comforted her, and some, like Tane, the huge, tatted, Samoan guy she'd met at the Londorossi Gate where they'd started the trek, had become a pillar of support.

When the group finally made their way back down again, she was so bone tired and exhausted, that she had to sit down and rest, in an attempt to catch her breath. A few yards away Tane was talking to someone who looked so much like Dominic, she'd wiped her eyes, wondering if she was seeing things.

But it really was Dominic in the flesh, talking to the guy she'd recently befriended. Dominic, who was supposed to be all the way back in Greece, was here, in Tanzania.

It wasn't until later that she discovered Dominic had flown here, unbeknownst to her, that he'd hired Tane to keep her safe. Some women would have found this behavior controlling, or suffocating, but she understood Dominic and his need to look after her. The man had taken it upon himself to make her feel more loved and cherished than she'd ever believed was possible.

That's what this man did. He was protective, and caring, and he was always there for her. Making up, it seemed, for all the times in her life she had felt alone.

Recently, he had returned to the US to spend Thanksgiving with his family, and that was when he'd announced that he was dating Eleni. That was also when he told them who she was.

So much had changed since then that she barely recognized the person she was anymore.

She had stayed on at Steele Shipping, but had moved to a different department, though she and Miranda still saw each other almost daily. Eleni refused to move in with Dominic, but she had moved to a small apartment that felt more like home than her room in the hotel had.

As for her mother, she doted on Dominic. He'd spent Christmas with them in Spetses, and for the New Year, Eleni and Dominic had come to New York and spent a glorious week there.

But she'd been nervous about this visit to see his parents. Dominic had assured her that they wouldn't be staying at the family chalet. This man and his family seemed to own a home in every city, and Eleni had come to take things in her stride, never knowing what any moment with Dominic might bring.

She, who had hated people like him alighting on her tiny island, now had a front row seat in his life. But deep down, she knew that Dominic was a good man, and as they sat in front of the roaring fire together, in a country she'd never been to, meeting his parents, going skiing tomorrow, with this billionaire grumpy boss who loved her so completely, she was filled with deep gratitude for the blessings in her life.

"Isn't Alexander coming?" Dominic asked, looking around at his parents.

"He's on his way," Robert handed out champagne glasses to everyone and proposed a toast.

"To Eleni, welcome to the family." His father turned to Dominic and gazed at him proudly. "To Dominic and the new consortium."

"The deal isn't done yet, Dad." A flush crept along Dominic's cheeks.

"But you're working on it."

Susan looked at her son, her eyes full of pride.

"You started without me?" Alexander strode through the door, a whirlwind breaking up their cozy little soiree.

"You're late," his mother remarked. But Alexander was too

busy grinning, his gaze bouncing between Eleni and Dominic. He poured himself a glass of champagne. "Since we're toasting, to Eleni and Dom, but especially to Dom. Looks like you might pull it off, bro. A deal without Galatis. Who would have thought?"

"You jealous?" Dominic growled.

"It's a great deal..." Robert interjected. "*If* it works out."

"No reason why it shouldn't," said Dominic.

"You've got a real fire lit under your butt, Dom. I didn't think you had it in you to ditch Galatis, and move on. To say I am impressed would be an understatement. But I still don't understand what Galatis did to make you back off."

Eleni braced herself. She'd spoken to Alexander a few times on the phone and had suffered the jokes and jibes, all lighthearted, about her pretending to be a maid the last time they met. She was waiting for him to say something now.

No one in Dominic's family knew that Galatis was her father, and that this was the reason why Dominic refused to have anything to do with him. She'd urged him to tell them, because she didn't want secrets, and there was nothing to hide, but Dominic was obsessed with getting the deal finalized first.

"Have you met Hector Galatis?" Eleni asked him, forcing a smile. "The man had Dominic running all over the place. He was a joke. He's not someone you can take seriously."

Alexander's jaw dropped. "Do know who you're talking about? The richest man in all—"

"It doesn't matter who he is. It's what a man does that matters." Even she was surprised when those words flew out of her mouth.

"Will you boys stop with the business talk?" Susan got up. "Let me see how the dinner's coming along, excuse me." Eleni got up too, ready to follow her, to help. She wasn't used to sitting around doing nothing.

"No dear, you stay. Dinner's almost ready to be served." Her husband followed her.

Alexander came over to them and sat beside Eleni. "How about you tell me how you and my brother *really* met?"

She glanced over at Dominic, saw the gnarly knot form between his brows. She wanted to get on with Alexander, didn't want any rivalry or bad blood between them. She didn't have any siblings, and it had been only her and her mother for the longest time, until Jonas had come along. Now she had the chance to belong again, to be a part of something, and she didn't want things to start off badly. "We met in a taverna."

Alexander raised an eyebrow. "Sounds groovy. Care to embellish?"

"Dinner is ready," Susan announced, and in the next few seconds, Dominic was tugging her to standing, his arm in hers.

Alexander got up. "Feeling possessive, Dom?"

"You came alone?" Dominic threw back, his eyes twinkling with mischief as they walked over to the table. "What happened?"

"You didn't hear?" His father sat at the head of the table. His mother at the other end.

"Robert, not now. Alexander doesn't want to talk about it."

Alexander sat down, facing Eleni and Dominic. "I don't care. Talk about it, but there's not much to say. We split. Me and Mia are no more."

"Huh," said Dominic. "I didn't even know. When *were* you and Mia a thing?"

"Zanzibar. Summer. Not that you would know, seeing that you were busy with your .. ahem...housekeeping."

"Now, *that* was fun," Eleni said, remembering that time.

"But you must have been in pain, pretending to walk around even though you'd just sprained your ankle." Dominic's thumb rubbed the side of her hand. She loved his little touches, his endearments, the way he looked at her.

"I tried to get out of there as fast as I could," she said.

Alexander shook his head, then sipped from his champagne glass. "I knew something wasn't quite right. I couldn't put my finger on what it was."

"And here we all are," Susan said, looking around the table with a huge smile on her face. "My boys have come home."

"Not for long, Mom." Dominic put some food on his plate and passed the serving plate to Eleni. "We're back in Greece next week."

"But this is nice." Alexander took the plate from Eleni.

"Why don't you come skiing with us?" Eleni asked Alexander.

Dominic groaned loudly. "I'm sure he has better things to do."

"I would love to, but I'm busy." Alexander eyed Eleni with surprise. "But thank you for asking me. Do you ski?"

"No. This is the first time I've seen snow."

A chorus of shock went around the table.

"Then you're going to have a lot of fun, even if it's with Dom." Alexander lifted his glass to his lips.

"I always have fun with Dom*inic*." She stressed the rest of his name on purpose.

"Let's eat." Robert ordered.

The rest of the dinner went surprisingly well. The boys talked, and when it wasn't business related, they got on. It was a competitive rivalry between them, the need to outdo one another in their father's eyes, as far as she could tell, but one she wanted to put an end to if she could.

Soon, the atmosphere relaxed as the champagne and wine flowed, and their bellies filled.

Eleni sat back and looked around the table, her heart as full as her stomach. The last few months had been a whirlwind, and the start of a brand new year held so much promise. She couldn't imagine what this year would bring.

A few hours later, they bade their goodbyes, promising to come back after they had been skiing.

The snow crunched beneath her boots as they left Dominic's parents' place and walked to the car. Their bodyguard lurked in the shadows. She'd become so used to him that he might as well have been invisible.

"Where are you going?" Dominic called out. He stood by the Jeep, the dark night hiding his features.

"Snow!" she shouted. Arriving only a short time earlier, they'd only had time to dump their luggage at the cabin and get changed before coming to meet his parents. She hadn't had a chance to fully appreciate the snow yet. Under the cover of darkness wasn't the right time either, but the dull crunch of soft, powdery snow enchanted her. She bent down and touched it gingerly, rubbing her fingers around the flakes and watching them disappear. Dominic crouched down beside her.

"Look," she said, grabbing a handful of snow. "It's so soft."

He laughed.

"Don't laugh at me! I've never seen it before."

"Enjoy."

She scooped up a handful and got up slowly.

"Don't," he cautioned as if he could read her mind.

She wasn't going to, hadn't planned to, but he'd planted an idea. She threw it at him.

"Huh." He stood up slowly, hands on his hips. She scooted away, looking over her shoulder to see him scooping snow in his hands. He raced up to her and threw it. The spray of feathery snow landed on her arm.

And inflamed her senses.

If that's what he wanted ...

She grabbed armfuls of more snow, made it into a ball, but before she could throw it at him, a lump of snow landed on her other arm. Then another ball landed on her hair, then another one on her leg.

They came quickly, like balls from a tennis ball machine.

She squealed.

And just like that, her first snowball fight began. She and Dominic raced around the grounds outside his parents' chalet, like giddy teenagers.

Until she suddenly felt very cold.

And started to shiver.

"What is it?" Dominic rushed to her side.

"C-c-c-cold."

Her new suede boots were wet and her feet were starting to get cold. She rubbed her arms.

"Come on."

They rushed into the car, and he turned on the heater at full blast. Her teeth chattered all the way home. She could not get warm. It probably didn't help that she only had on a dress underneath with a ridiculously thin, long cardigan over it. She hadn't come prepared for a full-blown snow assault.

When they reached their log cabin, Dominic helped her out of the car and they rushed inside. She rubbed her hands together in vain trying to get warm and desperately failing.

He looked worried. "You're not used to it. I should have told you to layer up. I should have insisted on a hat, gloves and scarf at least."

"I'm n-n-not a ...ch-ch-child, and we h-h-had f-f-fun..." she stammered, her teeth chattering uncontrollably.

Inside she rushed to their bedroom, Dominic helped her to unzip her suede boots, before she quickly got out of her wet dress and into her warm pajamas.

"Come here," Dominic hugged her close to him. She had envisaged stripping naked and getting into the bed, where she was sure they would have found a better way to keep warm, under the covers, his skin on hers.

But this, with his arms around her, his body warm, his chest hard and unyielding, this was just as good.

"Better?" he asked, rubbing noses with her. Her teeth had stopped chattering, and she could feel her fingers again.

"Always better with you around."

He kissed her. His warm mouth on hers, soft at first before turning greedy. Sparks scampered down her spine, and his hands, big and warm, skimmed under her top and rubbed her bare skin.

There would be fire and heat, soon enough. With this man, there was always the certainty of that.

Thank you for reading LOVE AMONG THE RUINS! I hope you enjoyed Eleni and Dominic's story which I loved writing!

I have an EXTENDED EPILOGUE that you can get by SIGNING UP FOR MY NEWSLETTER!
http://www.lilyzante.com/newsletter

Existing subscribers will automatically receive this. There is no need to sign up again.

If you loved Dominic, you might like Tobias, a tormented billionaire who meets a debt-ridden single mom:

"Anything can be bought, Savannah, and everything has a price."
"Only in your universe, Tobias."

THE GIFT, BOOKS 1-3 is an opposites attract billionaire romance featuring a ruthless businessman with a heart of stone and the struggling single mom determined to make a new start. This is a rags-to-riches feel-good Cinderella story set in New York.
Read an excerpt at the back of this book

I appreciate your help in spreading the word, including telling a friend, and I would be grateful if you could leave a review on your favorite book site.

Thank you and happy reading!
Lily

EXCERPT FROM THE GIFT, BOOKS 1 -3

Screaming children wreaked havoc in the toy store, and their cries of laughter rang straight through Tobias Stone's ears.

Not much excited him these days but it was hard not to get caught up in their excitement, hard not to feel their joy, hard not to hear their high-pitched shrieks. Hard to dismiss the wonder on their faces as they played with the display toys and stared wide eyed at the shiny new boxes that were displayed so enticingly on the shelves.

It made him feel better about himself and made Christmas more bearable to know that he was spreading a little happiness. Or rather, his foundation was. The huge toy store had been closed to the public for the evening while the Tobias Stone Foundation invited children from the city's adoption centers to visit the store and select a toy of their choice.

But he was also aware that he'd had to miss an important meeting that had suddenly come up. Luckily Matthias was standing in for him but he would need to return to the office soon. His multi-million dollar hedge fund didn't stop running just because Christmas was coming.

His eyes darted around the place, and he glanced at his watch again, getting anxious and needing to leave. Contemplating his escape he looked towards the exit and saw a child peering through the glass doors.

"I'm going," he told Candace, his hard-as-nails assistant.

"Not yet, Tobias. It's barely been an hour. Smile." She flashed him her false one. "At least make it look as if you're having a good time."

"I *am* having a good time but I'm in the middle of important negotiations, in case you'd forgotten."

It was all very well hosting an evening for children from the city's adoption centers—and it made him feel good about himself for a change—he still had a business to run.

"People need to see your face, Tobias. It's good publicity for you to be seen mixing with all sorts of people—especially these poor kids at a time like Christmas. It adds credibility to your philanthropy."

He didn't mind giving his wealth away. If anything, he thrived on it and there was no way that he was going to get through his millions in his lifetime. He liked to think that he didn't spend too extravagantly, but he had the usual billionaire playthings—luxurious properties around the world, a private jet and a private island, to mention a few.

Even though he enjoyed the finer things in life he worked damn hard and preferred to remain low-key, as much as was possible for a man with his wealth and history.

While giving away his wealth made him happy, making money did too.

"If we could just have a few shots of you with the children, sir," said the photographer herding a group of children together and leading them towards him.

"What a brilliant idea," agreed Candace and took his arm.

"How about near the tree?" She led him over to a beautifully decorated Christmas tree lit up with warm, golden colored lights.

"Smile, everyone," the photographer ordered.

"Is this necessary?" Tobias asked, giving the man a tight-lipped smile.

"Smile," said Candace smiling through her gritted teeth. Tobias obliged as a group of young children, barely reaching his waist, gathered around him as though he was Santa Claus.

"You are so kind, Mr. Stone," gushed one of the women from the adoption centers as she gave him a dazzling smile. "This is so very generous of you, taking the time to give these children a Christmas present." He nodded at her, barely hiding his look of unease. While he liked giving his wealth away, being thanked for it made him uncomfortable.

"Would you mind if we had a photograph taken together? People will be so much more interested to read it if they see your picture." She smiled at him sweetly.

"Vanessa? Hurry up!" She called out to her colleague, another matronly woman who looked as though she'd be more at home baking pies.

Tobias returned a fast smile, conscious of time slipping away. It would be the morning of the next day in Hong Kong and he was anxious to sit in on the negotiations.

"Thank you, ladies, but I must leave." He broke away from the group, determined to disappear before Candace asked him to do something else. She was like a fiery Doberman, silky, fast, super alert and she made sure he was seen in the right places with the right people at the right time.

"You're still making the most eligible bachelor lists," she told him. But he had no interest in these things. He preferred to pay for sex, seeing it as nothing more than a transaction which required payment. There was no emotional attachment that way.

"I'm leaving," he growled; he'd been here an hour already but as he turned around and headed towards the exit, he saw the same child still peering in. "Has nobody let him in?" he muttered and strode up to the large glass doors of the store.

"It's a win-win deal, Tobias," Candace had told him. "You buy those poor kids a toy and come out looking like a saint." Tobias grimaced at the thought. He wasn't a saint. Not by a long shot.

But that wasn't the reason he'd gone along with her idea of giving Christmas gifts to children less fortunate. He'd done it because for the longest time he'd hated Christmas and had avoided the festivities. Christmas was about being with loved ones and Tobias was alone.

It could have all been so different.

This had been the second year they had run this event, and this year he'd even been looking forward to it. But he was now anxious to return to the office even though it was past eight o'clock. Apart from work, Tobias didn't have much else to occupy him. His millions couldn't buy him peace, love or happiness, though whiskey and Naomi made the world tolerable.

He walked up to the door and the sight of the child looking through the glass, wide-eyed with wonder, reminded him of himself; of how he'd been at that age. He had been dirt poor once and remembered the time when he used to stare at other kids who had the things he never had.

"Where are you going?" Candace tottered up on her heels behind him.

"I'm letting him in."

"But we're closed to the public this—"

"Where the fuck is his mother?" Tobias snarled. The

security guard nodded at him, as Tobias flung the door wide open and peered at the child who stared back at him with fear in his eyes.

Immediately his hardness melted. "Do you want to come inside?"

The child's body language perfectly illustrated his dilemma. One foot was poised as if he was ready to enter but his solemn face indicated no immediate desire to make a move.

"Don't just stand there," Tobias said. "If you want to come in, then come in." He looked around for signs of the boy's parents and saw a woman with her back to the child, talking on her cellphone. She turned around just at that moment, her gaze landing on the child, before moving to him. She rushed towards them and stopped at the door, just behind the boy. The child stared at his mother but said nothing.

"Jacob, we can't go inside," the woman said.

"Can I have just one look? Please, Mommy?"

Tobias watched the exchange; the woman appeared to waver and then stared at Tobias.

"Are you open?" she asked him.

"Yes." He pulled the door wide open and moved away.

"Pleeeease, Mommy? Just a look?"

The woman appeared to consider it. And the longer she took, the more the child's anticipation grew. It annoyed the heck out of Tobias.

"Why don't you let him in and put the kid out of his misery?" He gave her the once over, taking in her scuffed shoes and the huge tear in her tights.

"He's not miserable," she retorted, fast as lightning.

"He doesn't look too happy to me."

She narrowed her eyes at him. "Ten minutes, Jacob. No

more." The boy smiled so brightly that it brought a smile to Tobias's tight expression.

He remembered that look and wished he still could feel that level of excitement about anything. Even winning new deals and reaching the next milestone in his business had lost its sparkle.

Nothing mattered much, anymore.

Christmas, with its gaudy commercialism, packaged and dressed up in dazzling bright baubles and sparkling lights, had lost its allure for him years ago because now it reminded him of the life he could have had. He would still have been insanely successfully, disgustingly rich, but he'd have had someone to share his wealth with.

Now he carried too many memories of the wrong kind.

He watched as the woman—the boy's mother, he presumed—stepped aside warily and looked around the store. Candace sidled up to him. "We're *not* open to the public, Tobias," she seethed. "You can't just let any strays in. This is specifically for kids from adoption centers."

"It doesn't matter," he replied, noting that the boy wore a coat that was obviously one size too small for him.

The boy's mother walked up to them. "Is something going on in the store?"

"We're not open to the public," Candace replied.

"You're not? I'm sorry, we'll leave."

Tobias walked over to the boy who was happily sitting on the floor playing with Iron man and a fighter jet.

"So you like Iron Man, huh?" Tobias asked, crouching down.

The boy nodded. He held the fighter jet in one hand and the figurine in the other.

"Did you write your letter to Santa?"

"Yes."

"What did you ask for?"

"Coloring books."

"Coloring books?" asked Tobias in surprise. "So you must already have an Iron Man?"

The boy shook his head.

"Would you like to have Iron Man?"

The boy stared down silently and shrugged.

"Did you know that tonight is a very special night?" Tobias asked, eager to get the boy talking. "You can pick anything you want from here and it will appear under your tree on Christmas Day."

The boy frowned as he stared back at Tobias. "You're not Santa."

"No. I'm not, and I'm sure you'll get your coloring books from him. But, see all of these children here?" Tobias waved his hand around. "They're all going to pick a toy and they get to open it on Christmas Day. You can, too."

The boy looked at the floor again, as if he didn't trust him. Just then Tobias's cell phone rang and he answered it, standing up slowly.

It was Matthias. "It's not going too well. You should get back to the office. There are a few things we need to discuss."

"I'm coming," replied Tobias and watched as the woman rushed over to her son and told him they had to go. He hung up and walked back to Candace. "Why did you do that?" he growled at her. "How much trouble is one extra child going to be?"

"Why did you do that?" He growled at her. "How much trouble is one extra child going to be?"

"If you let one in, you won't be able to stop the rest."

Tobias didn't care too much for Candace's opinion. He was too busy staring at the child. He saw the boy's face drop, saw him leave the toys he'd been playing with and get up slowly.

"Fucking ridiculous," he hissed under his breath, then walked over to the mother and son. "You should let the poor kid stay," he told the boy's mother.

"He's not a *poor* kid," the woman threw back.

"Well, it certainly looks to me as if he doesn't want to leave just yet."

"That other woman told us we had to—"

Fucking Candace. "I don't care what she said," Tobias snapped, a little too angrily.

"Tobias, let me handle this." He felt a tightness in his chest as Candace suddenly appeared by his side again.

She put on what he now knew to be her best and most false, over the top persona and explained. "Tonight is a charity event hosted by the Tobias Stone Foundation for a few of the city's adoption centers. This store is closed to the public for a few hours. Why don't you come back tomorrow? You can shop all you want then."

Tobias ground down on his teeth. If he lost his temper now, it would give the wrong type of publicity for the Stone Empire. Before he had a chance to say anything to his PA, the boy suddenly spoke up. "I saw you on TV," he said, shyly.

"I don't think you did, honey." The boy's mother gave Tobias an apologetic look.

"I did, Mom. He *was* on TV." For the first time Tobias tried to hold back a smile. The woman slipped her hand through the boy's. "Come on," she said, obviously not believing a word. "Let's go."

"I did, Mom." The boy turned to him. "You were on TV, weren't you?"

But the woman appeared to be in a hurry. "I'm sure you saw him, honey. Come on. We need to get back."

Tobias watched as they walked away and then the woman bent down and pulled something out of her bag then handed it to the boy. When the boy put it to his mouth Tobias realized it was an inhaler.

He glared at his assistant. "Was that really necessary?"

BOOKLIST

The Seven Sins:(New Series) A series of seven standalone romances based on the seven sins. Steamy, emotional, and angsty romances which are loosely connected.

Underdog (FREE prequel)
The Wrath of Eli
The Problem with Lust
The Lies of Pride
The Price of Inertia
The Other Side of Greed

The Billionaire's Love Story: This is a Cinderella story with a touch of Jerry Maguire. What happens when the billionaire with too much money meets the single mom with too much heart?

The Promise (FREE)
The Gift, Book 1
The Gift, Book 2
The Gift, Book 3

The Gift, Boxed Set (Books 1, 2 & 3)
The Offer, Book 1
The Offer, Book 2
The Offer, Book 3
The Offer, Boxed Set (Books 1, 2 & 3)
The Vow, Book 1
The Vow, Book 2
The Vow, Book 3
The Vow, Boxed Set (Books 1, 2 & 3)

Indecent Intentions: This is a spin-off from The Billionaire's Love story. This two-book set consists of two standalone stories about the billionaire's playboy brother. The second story is about a wealthy nightclub owner who shuns relationships.

The Bet
The Hookup
Indecent Intentions 2-Book Set

Honeymoon Series: Take a roller-coaster journey of emotional highs and lows in this story of love and loss, family and relationships. When Ava is dumped six weeks before her Valentine's Day wedding, she has no idea of the life that awaits her in Italy.

Honeymoon for One
Honeymoon for Three
Honeymoon Blues
Honeymoon Bliss
Baby Steps
Honeymoon Series Boxed Set (Books 1-4)

Italian Summer Series: This is a spin-off from the Honeymoon Series. These books tell the stories of the secondary characters who first appeared in the Honeymoon Series. Nico and Ava also appear in these books.

It Takes Two
All That Glitters
Fool's Gold
Roman Encounter
November Sun
New Beginnings
Italian Summer Series Boxed Set (Books 1- 4)

A Perfect Match Series: This is a seven book series in which the first four books feature the same couple. High-flying corporate executive Nadine has no time for romance but her life takes a turn for the better when she meets Ethan, a sexy and struggling metal sculptor five years younger. He works as an escort in order to make the rent. Books 4-6 are standalone romances based on characters from the earlier books. The main couple, Ethan and Nadine, appear in all books:

Lost in Solo (prequel)
The Proposal
Heart Sync
A Leap of Faith
A Perfect Match Series Books 1-3
Misplaced Love
Reclaiming Love
Embracing Love
A Perfect Match Series (Books 4-6)

Standalone Books:

Love Among the Ruins
Love Inc
An Unexpected Gift

Sign up for my newsletter and get a FREE book

https://www.lilyzante.com/newsletter

ACKNOWLEDGMENTS

I owe a big 'Thank you' to the wonderful ladies in my proofreading group for their patience and support, as well as their tolerance for my ever-changing deadlines. They check my manuscript for errors, typos, inconsistencies and the many strange words and phrases which often find their way into my stories.

They give me the confidence to release each book and I am eternally grateful for their help and support:

Marcia Chamberlain
Nancy Dormanski
April Lowe
Dena Pugh
Charlotte Rebelein
Carole Tunstall

I would also like to thank Tatiana Vila of Vila Design for creating this awesome cover.

ABOUT THE AUTHOR

Lily Zante lives with her husband and three children somewhere near London, UK.

Connect with Me

I love hearing from you – so please don't be shy! You can email me, message me on Facebook or connect with me on Twitter:

TikTok |Instagram | Website | Facebook | Twitter | Email

tiktok.com/@lilyzantebooks

instagram.com/authorlilyzante

facebook.com/LilyZanteRomanceAuthor

twitter.com/lilyzantebooks

goodreads.com/authorlilyzante

bookbub.com/authors/lily-zante

amazon.com/author/lilyzante

Printed in Great Britain
by Amazon

11752039R00287